DATE DUE			

A Confusion of Princes

ALSO BY GARTH NIX

THE ABHORSEN TRILOGY:
SABRIEL
LIRAEL
ABHORSEN

ACROSS THE WALL:
A Tale of the Abhorsen and Other Stories

THE RAGWITCH

ONE BEASTLY BEAST:
Two Aliens, Three Inventors, Four Fantastic Tales

SHADE'S CHILDREN

GARTH NIX

A CONFUSION OF PRINCES

HARPER
An Imprint of HarperCollins*Publishers*

 For information address HarperCollins Children's Books, a division of HarperCollins Publishers, 10 East 53rd Street, New York, NY 10022.
www epicreads.com

Library of Congress Cataloging-in-Publication Data
Nix, Garth.
A confusion of princes / by Garth Nix. — 1st ed.
p. cm.
Summary: "Battling aliens, space pirates, and competitors, Prince Khemri meets a young woman, named Raine, and learns more than he expected about the hidden workings of a vast, intergalactic Empire, and about himself"— Provided by publisher.
ISBN 978-0-06-009694-6 (trade bdg.)
ISBN 978-0-06-009695-3 (lib. bdg.)
[1. Science fiction. 2. Princes—Fiction. 3. Adventure and adventurers—Fiction. 4. Inheritance and succession—Fiction.] I. Title.
PZ7.N647Con 2012 2011042308
[Fic]—dc23 CIP
AC

Typography by
12 13 14 15 16 LP/RRDH 10 9 8 7 6 5 4 3 2 1

First Edition

To ANNA, THOMAS, *and* EDWARD,
and all my family and friends

and to

PHIL WALLACH, *game designer and software engineer,*
and LES PETERSEN, *illustrator and graphic designer,*
who with me worked on the online game Imperial Galaxy,
which was based on this book well before
I finished writing it

and also to

ROBERT A. HEINLEIN *and* ANDRE NORTON

A Confusion of Princes

1

I HAVE DIED THREE times, and three times been reborn, though I am not yet twenty in the old Earth years by which it is still the fashion to measure time.

This is the story of my three deaths, and my life between.

My name is Khemri, though this is not the name my parents gave me. I do not know who my parents are, and never will, for I was taken from them as a baby.

This is one of the secrets the Empire keeps well. No Prince may ever know his or her parents, or the world of their birth. Even trying to find out is forbidden, which just about sums up the paradox of being a Prince. We have vast power and seemingly limitless authority, except when we try to exercise that power or authority beyond the bounds that have been set for us.

It's still about a million times better than being an ordinary

Imperial subject, mind you. It just isn't everything that I thought it was going to be when I was a child, a Prince candidate being carefully raised in considerable ignorance in my remote temple.

So I'm one of the ten million Princes who rule the Empire, the largest political entity in recorded history or current knowledge. The Empire extends across a vast swath of the galaxy, encompassing more than seventeen million systems, tens of millions of inhabited worlds, and trillions of sentient subjects, most of them humans of old Earth stock.

It is Imperial policy that all these mostly planet-bound yokel types know as little as possible about the apparently godlike beings who rule them. Even our enemies—the alien Sad-Eyes, the enigmatic Deaders, and the Naknuk rebels—know more of us than our own people.

The ordinary folk think we're immortal. Which is natural enough when they typically have something like their grandfather's grandfather's grandmother's nice commemorative stereosculpture of a good-looking young Prince on the family mantelpiece and then they see the same Prince handing out Grower of the Month awards at the annual harvest festival or whatever.

It would be the same Prince too, because while we're not actually immortal, if we get killed we do mostly get reborn into an identical adult body. It's a technical difference, I guess.

And it's only *mostly* reborn. Our enemies know that we do not *always* come back from the dead. To have died three times like me is no big deal for a Prince of the Empire. There are others who have died nine, twelve, twenty times and still walk among our ranks. There are even Princely societies where you have to have died a certain number of times to join. Like the Nine

Death Lifers. Bunch of idiots if you ask me. All suicidal for eight deaths and then supercautious afterward? Who'd want to join that society?

Particularly since you never know if you *are* going to be reborn. It's up to the Emperor, and every now and then a dead Prince's name just vanishes from the lists without explanation, and if you're dumb enough to make inquiries, you meet a lot of blank-eyed priests who don't know anything and a weird kind of absence of anything about that dead Prince if you directly ask the Imperial Mind.

But before I get into my whole life story and all, let me take you through the bare facts of my childhood. I am presuming you're not an Imperial Prince, which you'd better not be or I'll have wasted all the careful preparations that are supposed to make this record detonate with a ridiculously large antimatter explosion if it is accessed by any kind of Princely sensory augmentation.

I guess not recording it in the first place would be more secure. But I have my reasons.

So. I would have been close to a year old when I was taken from my parents. Though I have no recollection of my early life, it is likely that I was born on a typical Imperial world of the outer quadrants, a planet once marginal for human life but long since remade by the trinity of Imperial technology: the machines of Mektek, the biological agents and life-forms of Bitek, and the wide-ranging and powerful mental forces of Psitek.

This is important, because if there's anything that makes the Empire what it has become, it is these three teks. Sure, the Sad-Eyes have better Psitek, but then we kick their parasitical little guts in with Mektek and Bitek. The Naknuks have taken Bitek further than we have, so we do them in with Psitek and Mektek.

The Deaders . . . it's a bit hard to know exactly what their primary tek is since they always blow themselves up when they're beaten, but certainly the trinity of teks works against them as well.

All Imperial tek is managed and controlled by priests, who are divided into orders that worship different Aspects of the Emperor. They serve Princes in all technical roles, but it's worth remembering that they also get orders directly from the Imperial Mind. Princes forget that sometimes, usually to their cost.

Okay, where was I? Getting taken from my parents. Here we go.

On a day like any other day, my parents would have had no knowledge that by nightfall their infant son would be gone forever.

The first sign would have been a gathering darkness, a vast shadow too sharp edged to be a cloud. Looking up, they would have seen an Imperial battleship glide across their sky, an enormous, jagged flying mountain of rock dotted with structures built to the fashions and whims of the Prince in command.

Under the shadow of the ship, bright spots of light would suddenly spark, thousands and thousands of them, that a moment later would fall like brilliant rain.

They would know then, I suppose, my parents of long ago. Imperial battleships do not drop thousands of mekbi troopers on rural villages without reason.

Sometimes I wonder what my parents did as the first wave of troopers descended, and the wasp-ships launched as well, spiraling down to establish a perimeter to make sure no one tried to evade the opportunity of giving their children to the Empire.

I suppose they did nothing, for nothing could be done. But unlike most other Princes, I know something about ordinary children. I have seen parents and their children together when they are not awed or terrified by the presence of a Prince. So I know that the bond between them is stronger than Princes—who have no parents and are not allowed to have children—can imagine. So perhaps they tried to escape, desperation driving them to flee or hide.

But with a perimeter established and search squads armed with advanced scanning tek, there could be no hope of evasion. My parents must have eventually joined the lines of people waiting for the troopers to check everyone against the census while the Priests of the Aspect of the Inquiring Intelligence mentally investigated any anomalies. Maybe there was a Sad-Eye infiltrator lurking inside a host body, or a Naknuk spy, or some small domestic criminal or terrorist, but these would be rare excitements. Mostly it would be routine.

Then, finally, at the head of the line, my parents would have met the Priests of the Aspect of the Weighty Decision Maker, priests with glittering eyes, blue fluid swirling behind the transparent panels in their shaven skulls, all attention focused on the approaching couple and their child.

The genetic testing would have taken only a few minutes, using Bitek viral assays and ultrascopic Psitek scan. Then the terrible news, presented as an opportunity for joy and delight in being able to serve the Empire.

"Your child is accepted as a Prince candidate."

Sometimes I think about what it must have been like for my parents to hear those words. I also wonder what choice they made next, for the Empire in its great compassion does allow such parents one choice.

Not to keep the child, of course. The Empire needs Princes

and so must take the candidates. But it does allow the parents some small mercy. They can be made to forget they ever had that child, their memories thoughtfully rearranged by the Priests of the Aspect of the Emperor's Loving Heart, before they are physically relocated to another world to begin anew.

Or they can choose death. As with all Imperial justice, this is done on the spot. It would be fast, faster than they might expect. Mekbi troopers stand behind the parents when they state their choice. Accelerated muscles and monofilament blades act upon the mental command of the presiding Prince, and it is all over in a moment.

I do not think of my parents often, for there is no point. But I do have some reason to hope that they chose memory erasure and a new start, and that somewhere out among the far-flung stars they live still and have new children. Children who were not taken away to be made into Princes.

That is how I became a Prince candidate of the Empire and embarked on my candidacy, being shipped from temple to temple as each stage of my remaking was successfully completed.

For Princes are made, not born. The genetic testing is merely to see if we have the potential for all the meddling that is to come, and a reasonable probability of surviving it.

I don't really remember the first decade of my candidacy. I only know what I was told about it later. For many years I was kept in a dream state, in a bath of Bitek gloop, my mind directly stimulated with educational and developmental programming, while viruses rewrote my DNA and changed and improved every part of my body.

Even after I was brought up into consciousness, I was often returned to the dream state in order to aid recovery from the surgeries that bonded Mektek enhancements to my bone and flesh.

Once my organic body met the requirements and the Mektek enhancement was done, I spent most of my time in the sometimes nightmarish mental space where I learned the particular Psitek capabilities reserved for Princes, the arts of domination and command, and the more ordinary techniques of mental communication, shielding, and so forth.

I'm not sure if you can call this a childhood, now that I think about it.

From the age of ten to seventeen, I was fully conscious, being taught more mundane things by various priests, and I played with holographic friends and the mind-programmed children of servants. It was always my games we played. From very early on, I knew I was a Prince, and very special, and in my own mind absolutely certain to rise even higher and become Emperor in time. Everything reinforced this, and in fact for some time I thought I was the only Prince in the whole galaxy, a willful misapprehension that persisted to some degree even after I had been taught that I was one of millions.

This was because even though I had been told of the existence of other Princes, I had not yet met any. Nor did I know when I was going to, until one day I awoke with the familiar mental voice of my tutor, Uncle Coleport, whispering in the back of my mind. (I called him "Uncle" because that is the mode of address for male priests. Female ones are called "Aunt," but of course there is no familial relationship.)

:Prince Khemri. This is the day of your investiture, the sixteenth anniversary of your selection. Your Master of Assassins awaits an audience:

I opened my eyes and smiled. It was the first time in my life that I had been addressed not as "Prince Candidate," but "Prince." My remaking and training was complete. I would commandeer a sleek, deadly warship, probably a Verrent corvette or something similar, and go out into the Empire and immediately make my mark.

Or so I thought.

As I was dressed by my valet, a mind-programmed thrall, I reviewed what I knew about the investiture of a Prince, which was surprisingly little. The first step was to be assigned a personal court, and the most important member of that court was the Master of Assassins. He or she was directly assigned by the Imperial Mind and so could be entirely trusted. My Master of Assassins would help me select my other staff and vet them, an essential process. If a Prince could not depend upon their court, they would not long survive.

I met my Master of Assassins in one of the temple's reception rooms, a chamber of pleasant waterfalls paying homage to a past Emperor's love of water features. It was a favored spot for punishment details, and as was often the case, the sound of the falling water was being suppressed by the work of novices who stood in the pools up to their waists, blue pulsing in their temples as they flexed their Psitek strength. I had been there once when the rumble of a waterfall suddenly cut in, and I saw an unconscious novice float by and be sucked under where the flowing river met a bulkhead. The priests also undergo harsh training, sometimes with fatal results.

:My name is Haddad <<identifier>>. I am sent by the <<Sigil of the Imperial Mind>> to serve you, Prince Khemri:

Haddad was also a priest. All the assassins are priests of the Emperor in Hier Aspect of the Shadowed Blade. Unlike most of the other Aspects, assassins do not specialize in any one of the trinity of Imperial techs; they are generalists who use all techs in the service of their Prince.

:Greetings, Uncle Haddad. I accept you, and bind you
to my service:

"Good, Highness," said Haddad. "Speak aloud. What weapons are you carrying?"

"None," I replied. I was surprised. "We are in a temple—"

"We are in a *reception room* of a temple, Highness," said Haddad. "It is not covered by the general truce. Have the priests here trained you with Bitek weapons?"

"No. . . ."

"Any weapons?"

"Sword and dagger, hand blaster, nerve-lash, the basics for dueling," I said. Haddad was looking around, moving about me, an ovoid instrument that I did not recognize in his hand. I presumed it was some kind of weapon.

For the first time in my life, I was becoming nervous, and already the euphoria of becoming a Prince was fading, to be replaced by an emotion that I had never really felt before and was slow to understand.

Fear.

"Slowly back away toward the inner door, Highness," said Haddad. He had stopped circling and was now intent on one of the waterfalls, watching the novice who stood there, supposedly shielding us from the noise of falling water.

I hesitated for a moment. Now that I was finally a Prince, I was reluctant to take any more orders from a priest. But there was something in Haddad's voice, and after all, he was my Master of Assassins. . . . I started to retreat toward the inner door that led into the temple proper.

The novice in the closest waterfall moved. His hand came out from under a sodden robe, ready to throw a small silver box. But before it left his hand, Haddad fired his weapon. A blindingly bright bolt of energy shot across the chamber, shearing the novice in half.

"Back!" shouted Haddad as I stood watching in disbelief, still several feet from the door. His voice cut through even the sudden roar of the waterfall. "Back!"

The small silver box rose from the bloodied water to hang in the air, and it opened like a flower to reveal a central stamen of pulsing red that was pointed directly at me. Haddad fired again, but the box jinked away, and the energy bolt missed it by a hair.

I turned and dived for the door, a door that exploded in front of me as the silver box delivered its payload directly above my head. I rolled away from the smoking, molten remains of the doorway and twisted around, thinking that I would see the silver box reorienting itself for another attack.

Instead I saw it struck by Haddad's third shot, my additional eyelids and visual filtering automatically adjusting so that I was not blinded forever by the brilliance of the nanofusion implosion as the box's power plant overloaded.

Haddad picked me up, and together we ran to one of the other doors and entered the temple. A Priest of the Aspect of the Mending Hand coming the other way bent his head to me before leading his gang of acolytes onward to repair the damage caused by the would-be assassin.

"How did . . . who would . . ." I started to say, the words

I wanted not coming readily to my tongue despite the efforts of internal autonomous systems that were trying to steady my heartbeat and restore calm.

"We will talk in your quarters, Highness," replied Haddad. "They are safe. For now."

My chambers in the temple were one of the things I was looking forward to leaving behind. Already in my imagination I had planned far more extensive and luxurious accommodations. I knew as a Prince I could commandeer such things, provided they were not already the property of another Prince or protected under the authority of a Prince, a temple, or the Emperor Hierself.

But I was glad to enter the simple living chamber that day. I sat down in the single chair as Haddad stood before me, and we both looked at each other, though of course Haddad kept his eyes down, as was only proper.

I had not seen an assassin before, or at least had not recognized any, for Haddad looked no different from any other priest. The priests of each Aspect had their own distinctive formal robes, but they rarely dressed in them, usually adopting simple tan-colored robes or shipsuits, one-piece coveralls like the one Haddad wore now.

He was tall and spare of frame, and looked to be around forty or fifty years old. His skin was lighter than my own, and more yellow than brown. His head was shaved, to reveal the transparent panels that ran from his temple to the back of his ear, the mark of a full priest. I could see the sheen of blue cooling liquid pumping around his brain, indicating that he had some Psitek activity running, though I could detect nothing with my own Psitek abilities. He had one natural eye, the iris a deep brown color, and one Bitek replacement, which was entirely green, without a pupil, and obviously specialized, but I did not know its type or purpose.

I wondered what he thought of me and how I measured up. He would have served Princes before me, as assassins were transferred by the Emperor every ten years. Haddad might well have been Master to other newly hatched Princes about to embark on their careers.

I was taller, faster, and stronger than the priests, the novices, and the mind-programmed servants I had lived among, but now a faint shadow of doubt crept in as Haddad stood before me. Perhaps I was not much of a Prince. Maybe I would be not quite as fast, or strong, or tall as the others. I might even be ugly, for I had the face I was born to have, Princes being forbidden to change their appearance, apart from enhancements or necessary repair. I had never thought of this, because I had never shared the company of equals, or even those who might venture an unbiased opinion.

:What was that silver box . . .:

I began to send, but Haddad interrupted.

:Mindspeech not recommended:

"There are too many people within the temple and the outer grounds who can eavesdrop on mindspeech in close proximity," said Haddad. "I am blanking the aural receptors and other devices in the room, so it is best to speak aloud."

"Good," I said, trying to act as if I was in command and Haddad was acting on my instructions. But it did not sound like that, even to me.

"You did well to evade the flower-trap's firebeam, Highness," said Haddad. "However, you must take it as a warning of things to come. A Prince or number of Princes are aware that you have ascended, and they seek to remove you before you become even a potential threat."

"What? Already?" I asked. While I knew about competition between Princes, at this stage I thought it was more chivalrous and I had no idea it was so . . . well . . . lethal. "I haven't done anything yet! I haven't even connected to the Imperial Mind!"

"It is because you have not yet connected to the Mind," said Haddad. "If successfully killed now, you are permanently removed, with no chance of rebirth. One fewer Prince to contend with, and the Emperor's abdication is only two years away."

"That makes it even more foolish of them," I said. "When I become Emperor, I certainly won't forget or forgive these attempts on my life!"

Haddad didn't even blink at this remarkably naive assertion.

"I suspect they do not recognize your true potential at this stage, Highness," said Haddad. "It is simply a common and accepted strategy to remove any newly ascended Prince candidates as an opportunity kill."

"It's a pathetic strategy," I muttered. "I wouldn't do it. Where's the honor in taking out a new Prince?"

Haddad was silent, no doubt thinking that either I was a soft idiot or I would soon change my tune.

For my part, I was bottling up a sudden rage at the priests who hadn't told me that I might be assassinated straightaway and had neglected to inform me that the Emperor's abdication was so close. I was aware that the Emperor abdicated every twenty years, and one of the ten million Princes of the Empire would ascend the throne. But I did not know how this came about, though I presumed the existing Emperor chose their heir, and I had not known the next such abdication and ascension was only two years away. I would have to work fast to do some glorious deeds and make myself known so the Emperor would choose me to be hier successor. Which was annoying, since I wanted to just look around the Empire a bit first, in my own ship. Though I supposed some adventures might come my way in any case.

"The priests should have told me about all this," I said after a few moments of silence.

"It is an intentional part of your education, or lack of education, Highness," said Haddad. "The winnowing begins as soon as you are made a Prince. Approximately thirty-two percent of all ascending Prince candidates do not last past the first hour out of their childhood temple."

My internal chronometer said I had been a Prince for all of thirty-five minutes. If I made it through another twenty-five minutes, I'd be ahead of the statistical curve. . . .

"Our first priority must be for you to connect to the Imperial Mind," said Haddad. "This will have three positive results. Firstly, it will remove the possibility of permanent death, and so the benefit of assassinating you will reduce, possibly enough that any plans already laid will be postponed. Secondly, it will allow you to access resources and information necessary for your protection and future plans. And thirdly, you will be able to call upon the Mind to witness, and this will make blatant breaches of the law against you more unlikely."

"What?" I exploded. This was getting worse and worse. "Blatant breaches? You mean a Prince could act against the Imperial Law?"

"It is a question of the potential benefit versus the potential punishment," replied Haddad. "There are also ways and means of obscuring the Mind's viewpoints and capture of information so that it is not entirely clear whether a breach has been committed or not—"

"I'm going to go and ask Uncle Coleport some serious questions," I interrupted. "With a knife."

"There's no time for that, Highness," continued Haddad, as unruffled as ever. "Do you have any possessions you need to pack?"

"What?"

I was stuck thinking about what Haddad had just told me. I had been taught that the Imperial Mind watched over everything, that it knew everything, and that Imperial Law was always followed to the letter. Though of course Imperial Law was not for the ordinary citizens of the Empire. They had to do whatever their ruling Prince decreed. Imperial Law was for Princes, setting down how the authority of a Prince worked with other Princes, the precedence of Princely commands, and so on.

"Possessions . . ." I repeated slowly. Though my mind was supposedly as accelerated as my body, I did not find my thoughts coming quickly.

I looked around my living chamber and through the doorway to my bedroom. All my clothes were brought to me, fresh and new, each morning. Information flowed to my mind directly, or sometimes via secure pods that were also brought to my rooms. Practice weapons came from the armory and went back there at the end of a session.

"No. I have nothing. Uh . . . where are we going and . . . why are we going anyway? Surely it would be better to stay here and . . . um . . . plan . . ."

My voice trailed off. Though I had long imagined the day when I would become a full Prince, none of my daydreaming had included being almost killed and then having to flee. Mostly it had consisted of looking at the specifications of various extremely fast and deadly starships.

"We can't remain here," explained Haddad. "This temple will not allow you to stay beyond the first hour, Highness, and we must reach a place of relative safety, somewhere where you can access the Imperial Mind. Had you planned which service to join for your initial career?"

Princes supplied the officers of all the key services of the Empire: Navy, Marines, the Diplomatic Corps, Survey, Imperial Government, Colonial Government . . . but they all sounded like hard work, and though I had expected I would join one of them at some stage, the thought of yet more training did not appeal to me. Also, it would mean putting myself into a hierarchy of Princes where I would be the lowest of the low. It would be much more fun to simply go somewhere interesting and be a Prince at large, preferably the only one around. Then I could do whatever I wanted.

"Uh, I don't want to commit to any service and all that training malarkey," I said. "I want to enjoy myself first. Get a ship—you know, a corvette or maybe something smaller, of course with high automation, head out for some distant stars, see something beyond this moldy old temple, smoke a few Naknuk ships or the like. . . ."

I looked at my Master of Assassins.

"That's not going to happen, is it?"

"Not advisable," said Haddad tersely. "The nearest shipyard that might have a vessel not already earmarked for a Prince or under the aegis of a Prince would be . . . Jearan Six. We'd have to go commercial from here, several changes, several lines—the risk would be extremely high. Also, it would mean delaying your connection to the Mind."

"Can't I connect here, before we leave?" I asked. I knew the procedure. Though I would later be able to communicate with the Imperial Mind wherever there were available priests to relay, my first connection needed to be from within the inner sanctum of a temple.

"It is forbidden for Princes to enter the sanctums of temples other than temples of their own service when on duty, or on direct Imperial orders," said Haddad.

"But I go to the sanctum here often . . . ah . . . when I was a Prince candidate I went there . . ."

"Exactly, Highness. The optimum possible node now is the Temple of the Aspect of the Noble Warrior on Kwanantil Nine, which serves the Kwanantil Domain Naval Academy of the Imperial Navy."

"But you said a Prince can only enter the sanctum of a temple of their own service, or with direct orders," I said. My augmented and accelerated brain clearly wasn't working as it should.

"Yes, Highness," said Haddad.

"You mean I'll have to join the Navy."

"Yes, Highness."

My dream of a slender space yacht, lavishly appointed and crewed by suitably attractive mind-programmed servants, disappeared, driven away by the fresh, sharp memory of the flower-trap's sunbeam going over my head. Next time, there might be more than one assassin, more than one sunbeam. . . .

"In addition to connecting to the Imperial Mind, the Navy would also offer you a high level of protection, Highness. Apart from the vacation period, cadets at a Naval Academy or officers on active service may not be assassinated. Not legally, though accidents do happen. You must always be vigilant."

"It just gets better and better, doesn't it?"

Haddad nodded. I wasn't sure if this was in agreement or just some kind of punctuation.

"What are the alternatives and the probability of success?" I asked as crisply as I could. This line was straight out of one of my favorite Princely biographies, a Psitek experience of thirty-nine episodes entitled *The Achievements of Prince Garikm* that I had lived through numerous times. Garikm was always snapping it out, or some variation, like the immortal short form "Alternatives! Probabilities!"

"Without a priest to calculate the probabilities I cannot say exactly, Highness."

Oh yeah. I'd forgotten that when Garikm said the line, he had about fifty fawning priests standing by to figure out probabilities. All I had was one Master of Assassins and a lot of problems. I had also just begun to realize that the "biographical" Psitek experiences were probably a load of crap. At least none of them ever showed Princes just killing each other or organizing assassinations. It was all formal duels and clever outmaneuvering that left one Prince looking stupid. Not lying headless on the ground with a burning wound where their neck used to be.

"Despite the lack of probability analysis, I believe a fast transit to Kwanantil Domain Naval Academy and entry into the Navy provides the optimal path for your survival."

"Right," I said. For a moment I adopted my "Prince Garikm thinking" pose, but unlike when I'd posed in a Psitek simulation, it just felt silly now. Resting your chin on two bunched fists is pretty unnatural. Instead I paced around my room. I didn't even notice I was flicking my fingers nervously until I hit my own leg and flinched.

What the hell was I going to do? Haddad knew far more about my situation than I did, and obviously had a much better grasp of what could be done. But could I trust him? Maybe there were some other alternatives, but how could I find out what they were in the twenty-odd minutes before we got kicked out of the temple? The temple that was the only place I really knew, though I would never call it home . . .

"We must move soon, Highness," said Haddad as I continued my pacing.

I stopped and looked at him. He'd saved me once already, maybe twice.

"Okay, damn it," I said. "I'll join the Navy. So let's go to Kwanantil Nine."

I paused, then added, "Uh, how do we get there?"

"I have an idea, Highness," replied Haddad. "But I am afraid it will not be a comfortable journey."

He quickly outlined his plan, which of course I approved, given that I had no other ideas. Then he gave me two of his many weapons: a three-shot deintegration wand that went into two loops on my inside left sleeve, and an egg-shaped phage emitter that I had to initialize with a lick of my tongue so the Bitek agents inside would not act against me. That sat in the top of my boot, in a pocket that had always seemed extraneous frippery. My clothes had many such loops, pockets, and pouches. I had never wondered why they were there before.

"I am ready," I pronounced.

But I wasn't, not at all.

2

WE TRAVELED TO Kwanantil Nine aboard the largely automated museum ship *Beyond the Veil of Time,* positioned within a diorama depicting a scene from ancient Earth, a sporting contest of two pugilists surrounded by a crowd. Apart from Haddad and myself, the actors were all mind-programmed lackeys who, even while in the vast hold of the ship without an audience, performed their parts on the hour, every hour. Without alteration, save for the occasional replacement of one or both of the pugilists when they became too damaged, new ones being brought out of the exhibit's internal cold store.

The diorama was contained within a crystal hemisphere some hundred meters in diameter. In addition to the arena where the pugilists fought, there was a tavern, where Haddad and I remained, disguised as drunken patrons. Should anyone enter the diorama, we needed merely to slump in our corners.

I was impressed that Haddad got us aboard without anybody noticing. The hour we spent sneaking through the temple, with Haddad circumventing various monitors, dodging guards, and then boarding the ship through a supposedly one-way waste umbilical, was very educational. At least after I got cleaned up I appreciated the educational aspects.

Perhaps the most important lesson for me was not to accept what I saw or heard at face value and to look beyond the official description or information to see if there was something I could use.

I had been a bit concerned that someone would come and look at the diorama. After all, you'd think if the show was constantly on, it was because some Prince wanted to come and see it.

But again, Haddad had chosen well. There was no Prince aboard, and the only crew were a bunch of priests who never strayed from their command or engine-room shrines. The exhibit was just being kept in tune for delivery to its intended owner. It was the property of a most senior Prince, Governor Prince Achmir XII (the numeral referring to his eleven deaths). Achmir was the governor of the Kwanantil system, which I learned was an important fief of fourteen tech-shaped worlds and large moons.

So the ship was going to the Kwanantil system, and since there was a Naval Academy there, that's where I was headed too. To sign up and wave good-bye to my long-held plans for frolicking about the galaxy without a care in the world.

Unfortunately the diorama was destined for Kwanantil *Four,* the capital world of the system, and the Naval Academy was located on a planet in the ninth orbit. Haddad said we could not risk a transit through Kwanantil Four, so we had to get off the ship before it arrived there.

But just as he had chosen the ship well, Haddad had also planned for this eventuality. He set it all out for me, just like Garikm's own Master of Assassins did in the beginning of each episode of *The Achievements*.

The wormhole exit for the Kwanantil system lay beyond the eleventh orbit. Exiting it, the museum ship would slow for boarding and inspection, purely a matter of form given that it was operating under the aegis of Prince Achmir. Following that administrative check, it would begin to accelerate toward the inner worlds, but on a spiraling path that would take us close to Kwanantil Nine.

At the point of closest approach to the ninth planet, we would leave the ship.

I had approved of this plan in general, until the detail emerged that we would not be leaving in a lifeboat or smaller vessel, for any such craft would be fired upon by the guardships of the Naval Academy unless we could get prior authorization. But I could not seek that authorization as I had not yet connected to the Imperial Mind, and in any case, I had no household priests to relay my communications.

Instead of safe passage in a lifeboat, we would equip ourselves with protective suits and stealth mantas that would not be picked up by scanners until we were very close. The mantas were Bitek personal vehicular and reentry organisms that Haddad had been growing in the cellar of the tavern from molecular templates, feeding them with the biological material of the dead pugilists and sand from the arena. Shaped like the marine rays of Earth, they were some five meters long and four meters wide when fully deployed, containing pressurized gases in directional glands for maneuvering in space, and their undersides were a heat-resistant ablative material to allow a gliding reentry into atmosphere.

But even equipped with the mantas, we could not successfully land, at least not alive. While the ninth planet had been partially shaped to support life, it still didn't have much of an atmosphere, and our glide path would slow our approach speed to only four or five hundred kilometers an hour.

For the final descent, Haddad had also equipped us with contragravity harnesses, military-issue ones as worn by mekbi troopers rather than the superior variety used by Princes. Unfortunately, without the additional internal power supplies of these troopers, our contragravity harnesses would operate for only three minutes.

In the airlock, Haddad assured me this would be plenty of time and everything would work out. I was a bit annoyed again that he couldn't tell me the probability of success, even though I knew we needed a priest from the Aspect of the Cold Calculator, who specializes in working out the odds. Because in the biosim Prince Garikm would be given at least a dozen Cold Calculators, I presumed every Prince would be given a whole stable of probability advisers. Of course, I was wrong about that, as I was about so many other things.

"Have you used a manta before?" I asked. We had talked at length about the Princes Haddad had served in the past. He told me all of them still lived, and the most recent hadn't even died once, a most remarkable statistic. Though Haddad did not say so, I was beginning to understand that I had been assigned a very experienced and senior Master of Assassins, who was far more capable than I could have expected so newly emerged from my candidacy. As I would later learn, most new Princes were assigned apprentice assassins who were promoted to Master when they joined their Prince, a fact unsurprisingly linked to the high mortality rate of neophyte Princes. Most of whom, like me, would have begun their short Princely careers thinking that competition between Princes was like an ordered game, when in fact, as Haddad explained, it was a brutal struggle in which Princes did whatever they could get away with.

"Once in training, three times operationally," replied Haddad. "The manta is a well-proven piece of equipment, and the environment of Kwanantil Nine is within deployable parameters. I would prefer better suits, as the atmosphere recycling in these is inferior and there is small margin for delay. However, it could be worse. Follow my lead, Highness, and we will soon see you connected to the Imperial Mind and established as a cadet of the Naval Academy."

I nodded, stiff necked, and thrust my hands into the manta's nerve sockets behind its head, establishing contact, as they had no Psitek controls. It rippled under my fingers, eager to launch into space and extend its body. I held it back using the slight variations in finger pressure that Haddad had mentally transmitted to me earlier as a tactile memory.

To aid our departure, Haddad had bypassed the safety devices to allow us to use the emergency jettison feature of the large airlock, blowing off the outer door and using the air contained within to shape our initial vector.

:Prepare for ejection: sent Haddad.

:Ready:

The outer door blew off, and out we went in a cloud of air and water vapor. The starfield spun around me, and for a moment I lost my bearings. Then I saw Haddad, his manta already rippling out like a dark shadow all around him. I lost him again for a moment as my own manta righted itself, but a minute later my internal guidance kicked in, my fingers pulsed at the manta's nerve controls, and I was lying on the back of a fully extended manta that was gently pulsing its gas glands to match Haddad's course and velocity.

I glanced over my shoulder and saw *Beyond the Veil of Time* receding on a tangential course as its slow but inexorable thrusters built its speed back up. It was still recognizable as a dull nickel-iron asteroid, which it mostly was, the ship parts being tunneled inside, but soon it would be no more than another fading star in the great swath of light and dark all around me.

We were twenty-eight hours in transit to Kwanantil Nine. This turned out to be a long time to spend in a vacuum suit on the back of a manta, cut off from all communication. Haddad had insisted that we should use neither mindspeech nor Mektek commpulse unless absolutely necessary.

I had never been left alone for so long in the company of nothing but my own thoughts, such as they were. I was still too newly hatched as a Prince, and devoid of experience, to think deeply on any matters save my own immediate concerns. Even there, I lacked the knowledge to properly evaluate my position and prospects. Perhaps it was just as well.

Instead, I dreamed, fantasizing about my future life, setting my own no doubt glorious exploits against a background of how I imagined the galaxy was, rather than on its actuality. The next year that I would necessarily spend as an officer cadet in the Navy occupied only a few minutes of my imagining, because I knew nothing at all about that life. Instead, I skipped over this immediate future and dreamed of something very like the first episode of Prince Garikm's *Achievements*, with me being the heroic singleship pilot, intervening at just the right moment to win a titanic battle against the Naknuk, leading to honors, the adulation of my peers, and in Garikm's case (in episode 39) becoming the youngest ever grand admiral of the Imperial Fleet. Naturally, this would then lead to the Imperial throne. I would be Emperor, master of the greatest interstellar Empire of all time!

As with so much else, my fantasies were built on ignorance. It took me some time to learn that the ranks and honors so eagerly sought by Princes often did not bring the adulation of peers, but instead jealousy, resentment, and a great increase in backstabbing.

Wrapped in dreams, I found the time passed slowly. Every now and then I had to correct the manta's course and velocity, with suitable bursts of gas from its glands and vents, keeping station behind Haddad, who led the way.

Then, almost as if the twenty-eight hours had been but a blink of the eye, we were entering the thin and gloomy atmosphere of the planet. The mantas went into automatic reentry mode, and as instructed, I drew in my arms and legs to huddle in the most thermally protected portion of the manta, in the center of its back.

The ride down was faster and much more difficult than I had expected. The manta bucked and spun, and several times I was almost thrown off as a sudden tilt threatened to upset the manta and make *me* the recipient of white-hot lances of superheated air rather than its ablative silicon underbelly.

But the manta's design was good, Haddad had grown it well, and my balance and strength were of course far better than any normal human's. I held on, kept the trim, and like a falling star I shot through the heavens, until at ten thousand meters the manta and I parted company, me into free fall and it into a long glide that would end in a not very spectacular explosion somewhere on the horizon.

Haddad had separated some distance away. Though I had never skydived, my body knew how to do it, one of the many basic skills programmed into mind and muscle memory. As with all such programmed skills, while I possessed the basics, I had neither style nor noticeable flair. Nevertheless, I starfished to correct my spin and put my contragrav harness on standby as Haddad speared toward me, matching my descent rate with real skill and experience.

:Activate harness:

My harness suddenly bit into my flesh as the antigravity coils warmed up. But still I plummeted down, the thin air hardly slowing my fall, the antigrav slow to build. The dark ground beneath grew closer and closer . . . a lot closer a lot faster than I thought it should be. I was just about to scream out something both verbally and in mindspeech when Haddad's mental voice sounded calmly inside my head.

:Emergency full reversal on my mark: sent Haddad, and then a moment later :Mark:

My harness whined, the straps cut deeper still, and suddenly I felt as if I were no longer falling, though my internal instrumentation recorded that I was in fact still descending, albeit slowly. The ground was close enough to discern some details, though only through augmented eyes. Kwanantil Nine was a long way from its star, and neither of its two moons had yet been turned into an auxiliary sun, so the light was akin to a dim twilight on a world shaped to the standard of old Earth.

:We are being tracked: sent Haddad, a focused mind-send to me, which he immediately followed by a wider, more powerful cast.

:Prince Khemri <<identifier>> and Master of Assassins Haddad <<identifier>> landing by manta do not fire code Gorgon Head Five Six <<code>> relay to Imperial Mind:

That was directed at the installation I could now see clearly below, a typical Imperial surface cube some two hundred meters a side, made of local dirt bonded together by Bitek agents, internally reinforced with Mektek armor and Psitek force shields. It would just be an entry building, with the Naval Academy proper located many hundreds of meters below. Sometimes a thick layer of earth and stone could prevail as a defense, even when Imperial tek failed.

The top of the cube bristled with various autoguns and launchers, many of which were now pointing at me. Faint orange flashes were cycling in the corner of my eyes, warning me of targeting lock-ons, till I noticed the warnings and turned them off. We were so close at that point that my internal systems would only be able to provide enough warning time for me to know I was going to be vaporized a microsecond before it happened.

Fortunately, Haddad's mind-send worked, though the last part about relaying to the Imperial Mind wasn't true, unless the priests in the academy did it for us. I had no household priests to relay. I guessed Haddad had sent that so that any Prince who did think I was an easy target would have second thoughts, just in case I had an unseen vessel somewhere nearby loaded with priests relaying everything.

We landed a kilometer from the cube, my contragrav harness

losing power in the last five meters so that my planned perfect landing ended up being rather less dignified as I sprawled in the dark-blue earth. I barely had time to stand up before we were ringed by mekbi troopers, the Bitek human-insect hybrid grunt infantry of the Empire, clad in their dark Mektek armor. I could sense their internal systems and active weapons, and could almost, but not quite, make out the mental chatter between them. But it was all a distant whisper, and I couldn't hear their command channel, either, as that was locked into Naval service only and their immediate commander.

Who, as it turned out, was a senior cadet annoyed at having an unscheduled arrival during her final watch. She landed in front of me as if she had come down a single step, and her elegance wasn't solely due to her vastly superior zero-G equipment. Her Master of Assassins, I noted, stayed above, and there were several other blips showing up in my Mektek and Psitek scans that suggested assassin apprentices in a standard formation above and behind the mekbi troopers.

"Prince Khemri," she said with distaste, not even bothering to raise her gold-mirrored visor, as would have been polite. "State your business."

"Joining the Navy," I replied. I didn't raise my visor either. "Who are you?"

I was just answering rudeness with rudeness, since I already knew who she was. Princes radiate their identity to Imperial friendlies through Psitek, via numerous wide and narrow Mektek comm bands and also, when in the appropriate atmosphere, via coded pheromones.

So I knew she was Prince Atalin, that she was three years older than me, an advanced cadet. Not only was she a cadet officer of this Naval Academy, but she was in fact the Senior Cadet Officer, winner of the Sword of Honor in her first year and holder of numerous prizes for coming in top in various subjects, all of this pretty much adding up to her being the best thing to deign to attend this academy since the foundation of the Empire.

And she was a member of House Jerrazis, a group of Princes led by Vice Admiral Prince Jerrazis the Fifth, who I could look up if I chose to but didn't right at that moment. Which was, of course, a mistake.

"You know who I am," she said, and raised her visor, though it wasn't out of politeness. It was so she could wrinkle her nose to indicate her distaste for such a lowly creature as myself.

I didn't raise my own visor. It seemed a better snub than wrinkling my own nose back at her.

Even though I could see only the narrow band of her face from halfway up the nose to just above her sharp brown eyes, I was immediately struck with a sense of familiarity. But I knew I couldn't have met her before. I'd never met any other Princes.

So why did she look so familiar?

"You are logged as a visitor," she said. "If you depart from the authorized route to the temple, you will be in breach of Naval regulations and may be detained."

She sent something to someone else by mindspeech at the end of that, but I couldn't pick it up. I presumed it was a communication to the Imperial Mind. Soon I would be connected too, and would not be so much in the dark.

"Uh, what is the authorized route?" I asked.

Atalin didn't bother to reply. She just sniffed, her visor slid down, and she waved the mekbi troopers away before suddenly taking off to jet back to the cube. Her Master of Assassins lingered for a minute or so, looking down at Haddad, and again I caught the edge of a whisper of mental communication. It must be odd, I thought, for assassins to work against each other when they were also all priests of the same Aspect, but I suppose it was no more strange than the competition of Princes. The whole Empire was based on this competition, after all.

"I have the route. We must get inside before our oxygen reserves fail," said Haddad when we were alone. "The atmosphere here is not sufficient to sustain even augmented life."

I hadn't noticed that my suit was indicating it could no longer refresh my air and that it was drawing on the small reserve supply of oxygen.

"How dare they just leave us here!" I spluttered, wasting some of that precious oxygen. "I will protest!"

"Not recommended, Highness," said Haddad briefly. He was already pulling at my elbow, urging me forward.

"But I am a Prince of the Empire!"

That cry sounded like a pathetic bleat, even to my own ears. Haddad did not reply, so I stopped the bleating and increased my pace.

We entered a pedestrian airlock of the cube two minutes before my emergency oxygen reserve ran out, even though I had tuned my metabolism to operate on a very low pressure indeed. It was pleasant to reoxygenate, but as I was learning could be expected, Haddad did not let me dwell on it. He hustled me through the airlock, past a guard of mekbi troopers who slammed satisfactorily to attention as I passed, and straight to a drop shaft. There he paused to test that it was in fact operating—the fail-safes had not been subverted—and that it would provide a suitably sedate descent some twenty floors down to the reception rooms of the Temple of the Emperor in Hier Aspect of the Noble Warrior.

I felt some slight relief as we entered the main reception hall, though I did not relax my guard. I had learned that lesson already. Here, instead of waterfalls to be silenced, groups of acolytes struggled to keep dozens of crystal chandeliers in place by Psitek energy alone, in yet another test of their suitability to become full priests. As they stood directly under each huge, spiky array of lights, there was considerable incentive for the acolytes in each group to work together.

We passed through without incident into the next chamber. This vast room resembled a junkyard, save for a central avenue that was kept clear. Everywhere else, acolytes labored over complex Mektek devices, though it was not clear to me what was being tested, for the acolytes did not seem to be in any danger, unlike those in the outer room.

I breathed easier as we reached the end of the chamber, presuming that we would now enter the temple proper and I would be safe, at least momentarily, from assassination.

But passing through the next gateway hub, we did not enter another reception room. Instead, what lay ahead was one of the temple's utility chambers, part of its Bitek support systems, a vast organic-waste recycling hall that mimicked the ecology of some fecund planet, presenting us with a bubbling swamp of rotten organic matter and decomposition jelly, to be crossed via a very narrow transparent bridge that was several hundred meters long.

Haddad paused as we entered this chamber.

:Maximum Alert, Highness. There will be assassins here:

I looked around, noting the closer acolytes in their hooded Bitek-repellent robes, who were raking the muck with gene-sorting staves that resembled living tree branches crossed with crocodile tails.

Some of those acolytes were almost certainly not from the Aspect of the Noble Warrior. They would be apprentice assassins, or even Masters, since I couldn't see the size of the transparent panels in their heads under their hoods.

The deintegration wand slipped into my hand and I drew the phage emitter from my boot. Haddad set off ahead of me, and I stepped onto the bridge.

THE ATTACK CAME when we were almost exactly halfway across the bridge, but not from any of the acolytes I had been carefully watching. I got the barest time sliver of warning from having my senses ramped up to maximum (a level that could not be sustained for very long) and so was able to dive into the swamp a fraction of a second before the bridge was smashed into pieces by the sudden eruption of a Bitek penetrator beneath it, a five-meter-long diamond-hard spike normally to be found as a ship weapon mounted on the front of a Mektek missile.

I saw the penetrator through a meter or more of Bitek gloop, my arms flailing as I tried to regain the surface. The stuff was sticky, and denser than water. I was still in my suit, but the visor was open, so defensive membranes had automatically slid across my eyes and ears. I could feel the pressure of the slime. Even if it was only the regular environmental gel that was designed to break down organics. There was also a good chance that this was some restructured assassination variety. I kicked harder and broke free.

Unlike back in my candidate temple, this time I was armed and ready and looking for further assailants. I took in Haddad nearby, skating on the gloop, so clearly his contragrav array had some power left or he had managed to partially recharge it en route via the base's energy web, something I should have thought to do. He slid to the nearer novice and a loop of scarlet energy took off the priest's head, even as the assassin raised his sorting staff, the barrel of an energy gun protruding from the crocodilian tail.

A second novice was only a few meters away from me. He looked straight at me, his face vacant under the hood of his protective garment. He was about my own age, I thought, himself plucked from his family to join the priesthood, just as I had been taken from mine to become a Prince.

I saw no menace in him, and he did not move.

But I shot him anyway, because I could take no chances. A pulse from the deintegration wand struck him high on the chest. His headless torso stood straight for a moment, then toppled into the muck. A few seconds later, blood swirled to the surface.

I stared at the pattern it made, my internal Bitek systems going into overdrive, trying to calm the human response inside me. I felt sick and triumphant and overexcited all at the same time. I had read and watched so much about Princes destroying their enemies in combat, but the reality was different, even from the Psitek simulations I had experienced in some of my combat training, which were supposed to feel just like the real thing.

They didn't. Nothing did. Nothing was as horrible, or as compelling, as watching that swirl of blood and knowing that I had killed a human being. Though all my training said it was entirely right to do so, that a Prince of the Empire can and must kill, somehow it did not *feel* right.

Haddad broke me out of my reverie.

:Highness! To the northeast door, fast!:

I ran, waist-deep in the muck, lunging forward to increase my speed. I made it to the door, with Haddad circling behind me, and sent a Psitek opening order. The door slid up, and I jumped through, my weapons ready.

But the corridor beyond was empty. Haddad sealed the door behind us and bent close to my face, his eerie Bitek eye glinting as he examined the goop that my helmet was trying to flush away from my face without notable success.

"Normal digestive gel," he pronounced. "You can just wipe it off for now, Highness."

I wiped, but the stuff was very sticky and wouldn't come off, which was disturbing, even if Haddad had declared the material to be innocuous.

"So I'm safe?" I asked. "We are in the temple proper, aren't we?"

"We are. But never presume complete safety, Highness," said Haddad. He was looking all around us, the blue fluid in his temples pulsing with Psitek activity. "However, the probability of hostile action has greatly decreased, and will decrease further as soon as you are linked to the Imperial Core. The sanctum is that way."

He pointed to the left. The corridor was a simple bored tunnel and had no markings of any kind, either physical or any kind of tek overlay. Nor did I have a map. When I was formally inducted into the Navy, I would receive both a Mektek virtual reproduction and a Psitek experiential grid of the base, but right then it was just a featureless maze, and I recognized again that without Haddad I would be lost, in more ways than one.

"So who set me up for that assassination attempt?" I asked as we walked along the tunnel.

"It is impossible to determine at this point," replied Haddad. "As you are not connected to the Imperial Mind and not yet enlisted in the Navy, you are essentially fair game to any Prince of sufficient cold-blooded determination. But it had to be a Prince with some authority over the utility spaces between the academy and the temple, and over Naval armaments."

"The directions you got," I said a few meters farther along. "They were from Prince Atalin's Master of Assassins?"

"Yes," said Haddad. "However, it would not be the cadet herself who arranged the attempt. That Bitek penetrator must have been in place for a long time, a trap set for just such an opportunity. A cadet, even a cadet officer, could not have obtained it, nor would they have sufficient authority to replace the usual priests of the gunge room with their assassins. Atalin's Master of Assassins was simply being used as a conduit to direct us to the assassination venue."

"So why *did* we follow those directions?" I asked.

"Because I knew there would be an attempt if we did, Highness," replied Haddad. "And as soon as we entered the recycling swamp, I knew it would be there. Better that than a total surprise."

I frowned. This didn't sound right to me.

"Couldn't we just have gone a different way?"

"Yes, Highness," said Haddad. "But by confronting the ambush site, we have now taken out two assassins of the Prince who plots against you rather than leaving them in place for potential later action."

"Right," I said. "Strategy. Good. Uh, just let me know next time, okay?"

"I will endeavor to do so, Highness," replied Haddad.

Even back then I knew Haddad wasn't actually agreeing that he would tell me next time. But before I could take him to task, we arrived at a much more ornate door than the previous examples. This one had gold trim around it and looked as if it might be made of some ancient, precious timber.

"We are here."

There were no novices beyond this door, for we had reached the sanctum of the temple. Sanctums differed according to the traditions and choices of the upper priesthood of each Aspect. This one was a cavernous room that had been made to mimic a forest glade on long-ago Earth. It had a blue sky and an artificial sun that sent warm beams of light down between tall stands of bamboo, flickering across the clear, rushing water of a stream that flowed in from an unseen bulkhead behind an illusory hill to our left and into the bamboo forest.

"Go on," said Haddad. "I will await you here, Highness."

"Uh, this is just like the sanctum back at my candidate temple, right?" I asked. "I mean, it looks different, but there'll be a senior priest somewhere in the middle of all this . . . won't there?"

Haddad nodded and pointed to the beginning of a rough path that led into the bamboo forest alongside the stream.

"Imperial Mind," I muttered. "Connection time. Here goes . . ."

I walked into the bamboo, following the path. After a dozen meters or so, the stream curved to the right and spread more widely, as the bamboo grew more sparse, to make a forest clearing.

A small stone bridge spanned the stream, and sitting in the middle of the bridge was an arch-priest with a fishing pole. I knew she was an arch-priest, for she had a band of clear crystal set into her skull all the way around, not just the two panels at the temple of an ordinary priest. Blue fluid boiled and pulsed inside, giving momentary glimpses of the woman's brain.

I had not been expecting an arch-priest. As far as I knew, they were normally found only at the Imperial Core, and certainly not at small temples in secondary Naval academies out on the fringes of the Empire. But I quickly rationalized it as being obvious in retrospect. I wasn't just any old Prince, so naturally there was an arch-priest waiting for me.

I stepped forward proudly, my footsteps loud on the timber slats of the pathway that led to the bridge.

At the bridge, I stopped. The arch-priest sat where she was, eyes following her line down into the water. She was utterly still, the only movement I could see the flash and roil of the fluid in her head.

"Uh, Great-Aunt," I said, lifting my chin and attempting to sound commanding. After all, even arch-priests were at least technically subservient to Princes of the Empire. "I am Prince Khemri. I desire . . . I wish to connect to the Imperial Mind."

The arch-priest turned her head. She looked no older than Haddad, perhaps forty or fifty Earth years, but was undoubtedly far older. Her eyes were Bitek replacements, each with three pupils like shriveled black currants arrayed in a triangle within an orb of yellow gel.

:Remove all your clothing and enter the stream, Prince Khemri: she sent, and turned back to look down her fishing line to the water below.

I turned around, not from modesty, but to look back along the path through the bamboo for Haddad, seeking reassurance. But he was nowhere to be seen, and the boundaries of the glade appeared to have extended. I could see more stands of bamboo, and larger trees, in all directions, and my observational tek told me they were not some sort of projection but real. Either the chamber was getting bigger—which was certainly possible—or my systems and mind had been subverted.

"If you wish to join the Imperial Mind, enter the stream," said the arch-priest aloud.

Her voice was quiet, but redolent with authority. She spoke without any indication of impatience, but I suddenly felt that there was no time to be wasted. At a command, the suit fell away from me; I quickly removed my undergarments and, without further hesitation, strode into the river.

Almost immediately, I realized it was not water that I was entering but some kind of clear Bitek fluid. A moment later this realization turned into fear, as I lost control over my limbs. There was no warning; none of the defensive measures that had been grown, implaced, or inculcated within me were activated. I was simply paralyzed and fell face forward into the swiftly flowing stream of liquid.

As my head submerged, all my awareness of the physical world of the temple vanished. Instead I found myself suddenly transported to a void where I was shooting through empty space like a projectile, twisting and dodging to avoid intense energy beams of different colors that were coming toward me. It was all happening incredibly fast, and it got faster still. I accelerated, and more and more energy beams shot at me, now coming from all directions, and I twisted and flipped and turned—all without any conscious direction on my part—as I dodged them and continued on to whatever might be my final destination.

Then I saw it—or sensed it, as I wasn't entirely sure how I was experiencing this whole thing. I was traveling at some phase-shifted speed toward a vast ball of blue-white incandescent gas, which was also the source and somehow the target of the energy beams.

The next second, I smashed into the surface of this object and everything went black, just for a second, accompanied by the most intense pain I had ever felt, pain that exploded out from the very center of my brain.

:Welcome to the Imperial Mind, Prince Khemri:

The voice was soft but penetrating. It cut through what I realized were my own mental moans and whimperings. As it continued to speak inside my head, the pain diminished.

:Connection established Prince Khemri <<identifier>> and running nil interruption to date. Check. Check. Return to physicality:

Suddenly I was back in my own body, choking, my nose and mouth full of fluid as I flailed about in the strange stream. Something touched my chest; I grabbed it and hung on.

It was the arch-priest's fishing pole. I held it in a death grip as she effortlessly hauled me out of the fluid. I could still feel the presence of the Imperial Mind in the back of my head. It was like sitting close to someone, feeling the occasional shift of their body, hearing the soft repetition of their breath. I knew that with this connection, sustained by my own or other priests, I could call upon the Imperial Mind to bear witness, to look out my eyes, to use my ears, to feel what I touched, to experience what I experienced. I could communicate with the Mind and, via it, with other Princes, no matter how distant, provided there were sufficient relays between.

Information flowed to, through, and from me. I was a node in an information network of unrivaled capacity and sophistication. I could query the Imperial Mind on any subject, could retrieve data on anything the Empire knew, or at least would allow me to know.

I was now truly a Prince of the Empire.

"Yes," said the arch-priest. "You are indeed."

I looked at her suspiciously.

"I don't think you're meant to monitor my thoughts, Great-Aunt," I said stiffly. "Nor is it supposed to be possible."

"A great many things are not as you have previously thought, Highness," said the arch-priest. "We have very little time before you must report to the Commandant of the Academy; let us not waste it. First of all—"

"I'm sure I can report whenever I choose," I interrupted. I was flush with the confidence of being connected to the Mind, and I wanted to show my superiority.

"I said we cannot waste time," repeated the arch-priest. Blue fluid flashed in her head, and I was suddenly struck down, to lie panting on the bank of the stream near my abandoned clothing.

"But . . . but I am a Prince," I protested. "You can't—"

"I can," said the woman. "I am your sponsor before the Imperial Mind. I hold the keys to your augmentation, across all teks. I am a surety for the Emperor, one additional safeguard for your loyalty."

"No one told me," I grumbled. I wished I did not sound so pathetic, but it is difficult to be dignified when you are naked and have been struck down from inside your own head. "Who are you, anyway?"

"My name is Morojal, and I am Arch-Priest of the Emperor in Hier Aspect of the Emperor's Discerning Hand. Listen carefully."

"I'm . . . listening," I muttered. Inwardly I was wondering what was the sphere of responsibility of the Aspect of the Emperor's Discerning Hand. At that time, I'd never even heard of it, and I thought I knew all the Aspects. Later on, I would find out that this Aspect was, as far as most Princes knew, concerned only with the death and rebirth of Princes. But its priests also pursued more shadowed activities.

"First of all, you will never mention that your connection to the Imperial Mind was facilitated by an arch-priest to anyone save your Master of Assassins. I was not here, you did not meet me, you will never mention my name. This applies particularly to the Commandant. You are permitted to disobey orders of your Naval superiors in this particular matter by command of the Emperor."

"It's all very well to say that—" I started to complain, only to be struck down again. This time my paralysis was accompanied by a direct communication from the Imperial Mind.

:Obey Arch-Priest Morojal <<identifier>> she passes on direct Imperial instructions <<Sigil of the Imperial Mind>>:

"You understand?" asked Morojal.

"No," I said.

"But you will obey," said Morojal.

I didn't answer for a moment. But I didn't need a Priest of the Aspect of the Cold Calculator to work out the odds here. I didn't really have a choice. Besides, I figured I could tell her I was going to obey and then work out what to do about that later. First of all, I was going to ask Haddad, most particularly about why he was excepted from this command about not mentioning the arch-priest.

"Yes," I said. "You weren't here, I never heard of you, I don't talk to any Navy types about it."

"The Commandant, Prince Huzand, will expect that your connection will be as swift and commonplace as it usually is and that you will report immediately afterward. As you are not aligned with any senior Prince, and as he is actively recruiting, he will with a 0.98 percent certainty offer you attachment to his own House, that led by Vice Admiral Prince Jerrazis the Fifth. You will refuse politely and inform him that you do not want to make a decision of this kind yet."

"Why should I refuse such an offer?" I asked. Though I knew very little about the real politics of the Empire, I knew that young Princes invariably attached themselves to more senior ones, at least at the start of their careers, and that over time these mutual cooperation pacts had become formal organizations known as Houses. Since I had to join the Navy, I might as well join a House led by a senior Naval officer.

"Because the Emperor has other plans for you," said Morojal. "Which require you to not be associated with any House."

"What plans?" I asked. I wasn't surprised the Emperor had special plans for me. But with only two years to go until the abdication, there didn't seem to be any time to waste in getting me ready to ascend the throne. Hanging around the Naval Academy for a year definitely sounded like a waste of time. "Are you giving me a ship and sending me out?"

The three pupils of the arch-priest's eyes rotated in place, like a triple gun selecting a different barrel.

"No," she said coldly. "You will be informed of the plans when you need to know them. For now, you will join the Navy, and study to the best of your ability at the Naval Academy, and await instruction."

:Join Navy. Study hard. Await direct instruction <<Sigil of the Imperial Mind>>: echoed the voice inside my head, leaving no doubt and no room for other interpretation.

"But I thought being a Prince meant I could make my own decisions!" I blurted out. I thought, but did not add, *instead of having my life constrained by priests.*

"You thought wrong," said Morojal tersely. "And you are not having your life constrained by priests. You are serving the Empire. Now go!"

My fingers and toes flexed as I regained control over my limbs. I slowly reached over for my rather crusty undergarments and Bitek-slimed vacuum suit, which were very unattractive but better than nothing. As my reluctant fingers pinched one corner of my underpants to pick them up, Haddad appeared at my elbow, offering clean clothing, including what would be my first Imperial uniform: the very dark blue tunic with purple piping of an officer cadet of the Imperial Navy.

I dropped the underwear and looked around. Morojal the arch-priest had disappeared as if she had never existed, and a much older male priest was standing on the bridge, his eyes downcast. The fishing pole had vanished with the arch-priest.

"The Commandant, Prince Huzand, is waiting for you, Highness," said Haddad. He didn't need to ask me about my connection to the Imperial Mind. I could feel his mental presence as part of a connective web that included an outward link to the Mind, though beyond Haddad all the relaying was opaque to me. Presumably it was being done temporarily by the priests of the academy, a task that in time would be taken over by priests of my own household.

"I'd better go and see him then," I said as I got dressed, transferred my weapons to the new uniform, and sealed it up. "Um, what happens after that?"

"Usually you would be given a week's leave or more in order to establish your household, Highness, before commencing the Academy's training program."

"Usually? What do you know, Haddad?"

"I have no definite information, Highness," replied Haddad. "However, I have seen that this academy is not entirely run on orthodox lines. Any commanding Prince in such a situation has considerable latitude in how they apply Navy regulations. Prince Huzand appears to have taken that latitude further than most, probably because he is well protected higher up the chain of command by other members of House Jerrazis."

"He can't assassinate me, though, can he?" I asked, trying hard to disguise my anxiety. The misplaced confidence I had built up over the years had been dissipating rapidly ever since my ascension and had taken some particularly hard knocks in the last little while. "Or kill me in a duel or something?"

Haddad didn't answer immediately, which did nothing to reassure me.

"A Prince cannot challenge a junior or senior officer of any service while on active duty. Nor would it be legal for a senior Prince to assassinate you. But they can influence more junior Princes in indirect ways. It would be best to presume that this academy is not as secure a territory as I had predicted and wise to keep up a connection to the Imperial Mind at all times."

"I'm doing that now," I said. "I think . . . but I can feel the connection go through you and then priests here in the temple. What if they stop relaying?"

"The relay is now being undertaken by your own household priests, Highness," said Haddad. "They were assigned to you several minutes ago, but they will not appear as unique individuals in the relay chain until you have met them. At that point, you will be able to relay to any of them even without me being part of the chain."

"I've already got some priests? That's good. Uh, how many of them are there?"

"You have been assigned twelve, which is more than usual, Highness," said Haddad. "The number is supposed to be random, as modified by the availability of priests, number of new Princes in the area, and so forth. However, most new Princes would be fortunate to be granted more than a single priest in their first year."

"And I've got twelve?"

Haddad's face did not show any surprise, but it sounded like a big deal to me. I'd been given twelve times as many priests as a normal Prince starting out? Maybe I was even more special than I'd thought. My confidence and natural sense of superiority, nurtured for so long in my candidate temple, began to return in full force.

Unfortunately, massive overconfidence is not a survival trait.

"It is also . . . unusual . . . that all of Your Highness's priests serve one Aspect, in this case that of the Inward Traveler."

"You mean they're not from the Aspect of the Noble Warrior?

I thought this was their temple."

I didn't add that the arch-priest I had met was the head of the Aspect of the Emperor's Discerning Hand. There would be time enough for that later, in more private circumstances. I was very curious that the arch-priest had said I could tell Haddad, and I wanted to know what he thought about it, for I felt he was the one person I could trust, based on what he had already done to keep me alive.

Also, like all Masters of Assassins, he had been directly assigned to me by the Imperial Mind, which meant by the Emperor Hierself, so surely he was completely trustworthy? Though I was a bit confused about that now that I was connected to the Imperial Mind myself. Was it actually the Emperor talking to me when the Imperial Mind spoke in my head? It didn't feel like an individual, like when a priest was mentally communicating with me. In some ways it was almost like hearing myself think.

"There are always priests of other Aspects in any temple," explained Haddad. "However, each temple is consecrated to a particular Aspect and managed by priests of that Aspect."

"So I've got a dozen Inward Traveler priests. They're Psitek specialists, right? Navy communication and control? That kind of makes sense."

"It leaves your household very weak in Bitek and Mektek, Highness," said Haddad. "Though perhaps this weakness is counterbalanced by a strong and highly redundant connection to the Imperial Mind. In any case, as soon as Your Highness has been assigned quarters, you will meet your priests. In time I hope we will be assigned more, from other Aspects, and I will also be able to recruit apprentices from the nearest Temple of the Aspect of the Shadowed Blade."

"Good," I muttered. "Uh, how do I get more priests? And how many am I allowed to have, like in total?"

"The basic allotment is, as we have discussed, somewhat random," replied Haddad. "More can be granted to you by your superiors in whatever service you join, in this case the Navy, for particular tasks; or by the Imperial Mind, as rewards and acknowledgments of particular services. Certain Imperial honors also come with assignments of priests or other additions to your household. It is worth noting that priests can also be taken away by the same process. As for apprentice assassins, the number depends upon the rank of the Master."

"How many apprentices can you have?" I asked.

"Between four and forty-eight apprentices, graduated in fours, Highness," answered Haddad.

"So how many can *you* have?" I repeated.

Haddad hesitated, which was interesting. I thought a Master of Assassins had to answer their Prince's questions without hesitation. And also act on their orders without delay.

"Thirty-six, Highness," he said, very softly so the priest on the bridge couldn't hear. "But it would be best to keep that to yourself."

So Haddad was a very senior Master of Assassins indeed. Why had he been assigned to me? And why had I been sponsored to join the Imperial Mind by an arch-priest, the head of an Aspect I'd never even heard about, read about, or suspected existed?

It was all very puzzling, and slowly—much more slowly than I should have—I was beginning to realize that I needed to know a lot more about what being a Prince of the Empire actually meant. In fact, I needed to know a lot more about the Empire.

The naïveté of my youth and the arrogance that had been

built up in the process of making me a Prince had combined to make an impressive barrier of ignorance. But that barrier now had the slightest crack in it. At least now I knew that I might not be the best thing the galaxy had ever had the fortune to see, and that I was about as uninformed as a cockroach. Hopefully, despite this lack of information, I would prove to be as impossible to eradicate as those dull, black-carapaced beetles that had accompanied humanity everywhere across the stars.

If I was to prosper, or even survive, I had to become a lot smarter.

Unfortunately, becoming smarter isn't something that happens immediately. I could have done with being very much more intelligent and knowledgeable before my next encounter with the forces that would shape my life, in this case in the person of Prince Huzand, Captain of the Imperial Navy and Commandant of the Kwanantil Domain Naval Academy.

THE TRANSITION FROM the temple to the Naval Academy itself was quickly achieved. We simply followed another plain tunnel drilled through the rock till it ended in a massive armored door. Two mekbi troopers outside the door came to attention as I approached, and the great slab of metal and Bitek armor cycled open. The corridor on the other side was brilliantly lit and perfectly rectangular, and the bare rock sides were now clad in smooth Bitek panels interspersed with occasional metal plates indicating various access points or emergency equipment storage.

There were four mekbi troopers on this side, who snapped to attention as a bored-looking Prince in cadet uniform with silver epaulettes rose from behind a Bitek desk that had been extruded from the floor. He sketched something in the air that was presumably a salute. I knew from his broadcast that this was

Prince Janokh, who was a senior cadet officer, hence the silver epaulettes.

"You're six and a half minutes late, Cadet Khemri," he said sourly. He looked more closely at me and added, "What is that on your face?"

Though I'd wiped it off, the goop had left a bright green stain across half my face, a stain that would need attention from some sort of nanocleanser to remove.

"Bitek digestive gel," I answered. "Someone tried to assassinate me on the other side of the temple. I'll get it cleaned off before I—"

"Too late for that," said Prince Janokh. "The Commandant already ordered you to report at once. Assassination, huh? It looks to me like you just fell in the base recycling swamp."

"No, the bridge I was on was destroy—"

"Save it for your biography," interrupted Janokh. "And get a move on."

At the same time, he sent me directions, providing the required path as an illuminated overlay I could call up over my normal vision.

"Thank you," I said.

He didn't respond, turning back to his desk with studied indifference.

As I hurried along the white corridor, I thought about my first two meetings with other Princes. Both had been surprising, in their own ways. I had not expected to see Princes in such menial tasks as commanding a patrol of mekbi troopers, at least not in person. And I certainly didn't expect to see a Prince sitting at a desk as a not at all glorified doorkeeper.

Everything I had read or seen about Imperial Princes to date always had them on the bridges of mighty warships, or directing vast enterprises from the center of a glittering headquarters, surrounded by attentive priests. It hadn't occurred to me that there might be some intervening stage before even a Prince of the Empire could reach those heights of power.

Perhaps you could call it an awakening of sorts. I was busy thinking about all this as I turned down another equally featureless corridor of white, descended a riser (checking it myself before Haddad could do so), passed another pair of mekbi troopers and another great armored door, and entered the outer office of the Commandant.

My third encounter with a Prince didn't make my thoughts about my own future more positive. Another third-year cadet with silver epaulettes, she sat at attention behind an antique (or Bitek reproduction) desk of very shiny mahogany at the far end of the Commandant's outer office. There was a very long honor board on the wall to the left of her desk, an antique possibly made out of real polished timber rather than a Bitek extrusion. It was headed OUTSTANDING THIRD YEAR CADET and had names on it going back about a hundred years. A priest was carefully painting on the latest name in gold.

It was ATALIN again.

I sniffed and resolved that I would never be that much of a suck-up. Who wanted to have their name on a piece of ancient wood anyway?

There were numerous other priests here as well, a score or more of them all along one wall, interacting with Psitek visualizations or Mektek projections, presumably to do with the operation of various systems in and around the Academy.

As I got closer to the desk, I picked up the Prince's identity.

Prince Lucisk. Like Prince Atalin, she was a senior cadet, returned from a year-long operational Navy tour for advanced studies at the Academy and to act as a cadet officer.

"Prince Khemri," she said, standing as I approached. "The Commandant will see you now. Master Haddad, would you care for refreshment?"

"No thank you, Highness," replied Haddad. He stepped aside and, when I arched an eyebrow at him, gave a slight affirmative nod. Clearly a new Prince and officer cadet did not take his Master of Assassins with him into an interview with the Commandant of the Academy. Come to think of it, I hadn't seen any masters or even apprentices around Prince Janokh, and none of the priests in the outer office looked like assassins to me. This sent a small shiver of apprehension through me. I had already come to heavily depend upon Haddad, and if he couldn't be with me in the Academy . . . that would not be good.

I made sure that I could feel the connection with the Imperial Mind, the slight buzz at the backs of my eyeballs and the base of my skull, which meant it was bearing witness. Whatever I experienced would be recorded far away at the Imperial Core and could be replayed if necessary. If something terrible happened to me, justice would be done.

Also, if I got killed, it should not be a final death. Again, I wasn't sure of the details, but I knew that if I stayed in contact, I would be resurrected. Or at least my life would be weighed up by the Priests of the Aspect of the Discerning Hand and, presuming I wasn't found wanting, I would be reborn. And since I hadn't had the chance to do anything bad yet, I was pretty sure I'd be approved for another go at the Prince business.

Pretty sure . . .

On an even less comforting note, I didn't know what would happen if I just got really badly injured but was still alive. While I had a redesigned nervous system that included a very high pain threshold, I still felt pain. Pain was a necessary warning system and couldn't be done away with altogether.

Thinking cheery thoughts like this almost made me fall over the Bitek-cloned hound that was lying near the door. A long, six-legged beast with jaws the size of my torso, it growled angrily and began to get up as I lurched around its chosen place of repose.

"Down, Troubadour," called out the Commandant. He was at the far end of the office, a ridiculously large, bare chamber almost devoid of furnishings and fittings. The floor, ceiling, and walls were all wooden paneling, some of the boards treated with a Bitek luminescence, so the light was soft and diffuse. There was a Mektek command chair in one corner, with two priests standing on either side of it, but that was it for furniture.

The Commandant was standing in the middle of the room, looking imposing and much taller than any of the other Princes I'd met. It took me a second to work out that he was actually on a kind of ramp that slowly sloped up from where I was, making him a good ten centimeters taller—provided I advanced no farther. Which I wasn't going to do, because there was a visual schematic coming up in my left eye, sent from one of the priests, and it showed a line a few steps ahead of me, and along the line, in flashing letters, CADETS DO NOT CROSS THIS LINE.

"I am Prince Khemri," I said, unnecessarily. He knew who I was, just as I'd got the broadcast from him telling me he was Prince Huzand, Captain of the Imperial Navy, Hero of the Empire Third Class, Initiate of War (Gunnery), Vermilion Wound Badge, Companion of House Jerrazis, and so forth.

"You mean, 'Cadet Khemri reporting, sir,'" said Huzand. "You're late. And what's that filth on your face!"

"It's a Bitek digestive agent," I said. "Someone tried to drown me in the stuff on the way to the temple."

Huzand glared down at me. I'd been worried that I might not be very handsome among Princes, but looking back at him, I knew I'd done all right in the looks department, comparatively speaking. He wasn't ugly—no Prince is ever actually ugly, unless it's by choice, like not having a wound fixed properly—but he had a very round head and sticking-out ears. He looked a bit like the Karruskan cabbage that Uncle Coleport, my last teacher priest when I was only a Prince candidate, had been so fond of. A Karruskan cabbage sitting on top of a very smart tailor's dummy, since Huzand was wearing full dress uniform, complete with illuminated medals and a blindingly white holster at his side that contained a millennia-obsolete gunpowder revolver with an ivory grip, prominently tagged in my visual overlay as GIFT OF THE EMPEROR TO THE TALENTED DUELIST PRINCE HUZAND, PRESENTED ON THE OCCASION OF HIS FIFTEENTH VICTORY.

"The Imperial Mind has no record of any such attempted assassination," he said. "In any case, it—"

"I hadn't connected to the Mind when it happened—" I started to say.

"Silence!" shouted Huzand. Now he looked like a *red* Karruskan cabbage. I wondered why he let his face change like that. He must like it that way, because he could easily dial down the capillary response. "You still haven't introduced yourself properly. Take one demerit, and another for your improper turnout."

I felt the transition of data concerning me from Huzand to one of his attendant priests nearby, and then to the Imperial Mind, and checked it out. It was not good, as it turned out. Apparently I'd been formally in the Navy only since walking into Huzand's office, and I was already in trouble. The actual record went like this:

> Enlistment recorded Imperial Navy Prince Khemri <<identifier>> Cadet Ordinary Commence Naval Record 10:47:05 IST
> Naval Record Demerit Applied Authority Huzand <<identifier>> 10:47:50 IST
> Naval Record Demerit Applied Authority Huzand <<identifier>> 10:48:05 IST

I queried the Mind to see what a "demerit" actually was and came up with the fact that it was a negative value in a score that was used to determine my eventual success at the Academy and graduate outcome in terms of rewards and appointments, but also—more important to me at that exact moment—every demerit meant a week confined to the cadet barracks.

I mean, what is the point of being a Prince of the Empire, one of the masters of the whole damned galaxy, and then you get stuck with stupid stuff like this?

"I never wanted to join the Navy anyway," I said. "How do I get out?"

I said this aloud, but I also sent it as a question to the Imperial Mind. Naturally, I didn't like the answer.

:Initial Service must be completed by order of Hier Majesty:

"I can well believe that you didn't want to join the Navy, Cadet Khemri," said Huzand. "I'm sure the Navy does not want you. I suspect you would do far better in something like *Colonial*

Government. However, you have chosen the Navy, and the Emperor has accepted you. Now we must try to make you into an officer. You will begin by reporting correctly."

I didn't answer for a few seconds. I was still fuming inside, partly at myself. I was going to be stuck in this place, answerable to Huzand and every single Prince downward from him, for a whole year!

But a Prince can do a lot of thinking in a few seconds. I went from anger to consideration to something like acceptance. I was only going to make things worse if I didn't obey Huzand. I had two demerits already, and a quick scan of how they worked showed up worse things than not getting leave from the Academy.

"Cadet Khemri reporting, sir!" I snapped out.

"Better," said Huzand. "I see that you have a particularly capable Master of Assassins . . . have you already been offered sponsorship by a House?"

The mutual cooperation societies commonly were called Houses, the only kind of family that a Prince could have. But I didn't know how these Houses worked, how you joined them, or how many there were, or anything useful like that. I could have queried the Imperial Mind on the spot, but trying to sort through a mass of data while also talking to someone is difficult, and I had not yet learned how to manage it effectively.

Later on, I did ask the Mind, and I discovered that there were more than a thousand Houses. Some were no more than mutual assistance pacts between only a dozen or so Princes, but the most important ones had tens of thousands of members and often quite rigidly defined hierarchies, customs, and duties. House Jerrazis was somewhere in the middle, with fifteen thousand members and a four-tier membership hierarchy. Huzand was effectively the second-in-command, after Prince Jerrazis himself, who was a rear admiral and commander of the Nazhiz Quadrant Fleet.

"No, sir."

"Curious," said Huzand. "You have no special sponsor at the Imperial Core? Some senior Prince who has taken you under their wing? I see it is several days since your ascension, but you have only just connected to the Mind."

"No, sir."

"Very well. Despite your slovenliness and initial foolishness, I am prepared to assist you in your career, and accordingly, you are invited to join—as a probationary member, of course—House Jerrazis. Just confirm your acceptance for the Imperial Mind to record."

"I decline, sir," I answered, rather too readily. If I had managed to get even a bit smarter, I would have taken my time.

"You decline?" asked Huzand. The red tide was rising up the cabbage head. "Are you sure?"

"Uh, I don't want to join a House immediately," I said, exercising some belated damage control. "I want to think about it. Sir."

"Almost all the cadets here at the Kwanantil Domain Naval Academy are proud members of House Jerrazis," said Huzand. "As are many of the officers of the academic staff."

Great. So by refusing the invitation, I'd made myself an outsider. But even so, the arch-priest was a lot scarier than Commandant Huzand, and she'd told me not to accept his invitation.

"I still need to think about it, sir."

"As you wish. The invitation will almost certainly not be repeated."

He looked away from me for a moment, and I caught the edge of some mental communication. Asking about me, obviously, since he looked back and said, "I am informed that you traveled to the Kwanantil system aboard a ship belonging to the Kwanantil system governor, Prince Achmir. Is that correct?"

"Yes, sir," I replied. We had indeed been on a ship belonging to Prince Achmir, but I very much doubted that he knew we were on board.

I also took a microsecond to query the Imperial Mind about Prince Achmir's House allegiance.

:Prince Achmir <<identifier>>. Ordinary member House Vethethezk <<identifier>>:

So Achmir wasn't all cozied up with Huzand and House Jerrazis, which probably meant something. I inquired further. House Vethethezk had more members than House Jerrazis and was older, headed up by Prince Vethethezk XXII, who was Governor of a whole Reach and more than four hundred years old. From my brief glimpse at the data on it, nearly all its members were Imperial Governors, so it seemed unlikely that they would be enemies of a House that was concentrated in the Navy. But I didn't know enough to be sure about this. It was bound to be more complicated.

"Transported here by Achmir and assigned the legendary Master Haddad," muttered Huzand.

I kept my face wooden. The legendary Master Haddad? I knew he was a senior assassin, and very good at his craft. But for Huzand to call him legendary . . . that was something else.

The Commandant fixed me with what was obviously meant to be a penetrating gaze. I guess I was supposed to crack at this point and confess everything he wanted to know, like for example that I was secretly being sponsored by Prince Achmir and House Vethethezk, they'd set me up with Haddad, and that was why I wouldn't join House Jerrazis.

He took a couple of steps toward me—not too many, because that would mean leaving his nifty ramp and standing on the same level—and intensified his stare at my ooze-stained face.

"You resemble someone," he said. "I can't quite place it. . . ."

I felt him query the Imperial Mind, I guess doing a visual match. I caught my identifier in the transmission but nothing else. This was interesting on its own account, as it was the first indication I had (other than Haddad telling me it was possible) that mindspeech could be overheard or listened in to.

Huzand frowned a moment later, but I couldn't tell whether it was a frown of annoyance at not finding out what he wanted or a frown because he'd found out something he didn't like.

"You are aware that body sculpting is forbidden to Princes?"

"Yes, sir," I replied. I didn't know much about body sculpting, apart from the fact that it was forbidden to Princes and that it typically took at least a few weeks, depending on what was being done. "Uh, I've only just come out of my candidate temple, sir."

"Yes, you wouldn't have had time. Nor opportunity, if you did indeed take ship from Thorongir Three straight here. I wonder . . ."

"What do you wonder, sir?" I asked, trying to be pleasant. For some reason, Huzand didn't appear to realize that I was being nice to him.

"None of your insolence, Cadet! You are to join Class 2645, Section Seven, immediately. My aide will give you all the details. Dismissed."

He waved his hand at me. Since I didn't know any drill at that point, I waved my hand back at him. As it turned out, he wasn't saluting; it was more of a "get out of my sight" dismissal, and he didn't appreciate me returning the gesture.

"Go!" bellowed Huzand, pointing at the door.

I got the message and left. The Bitek hound followed me till I half turned and sent a focused Psitek domination command that made it sit back on its haunches as if pulled by a spring, confirming that my earlier education hadn't been a *total* waste of time. I might be ignorant about many things, but at least I could stop an engineered dog-beast in its tracks.

Prince Lucisk was waiting in the outer office. As soon as I saw her, she mind-sent a mass of detail about this Class 2645, Section Seven I was joining, including the unwelcome fact that I was to immediately report to Cadet Duty Barracks Thanruz and would not have time to set up my own accommodations in the off-duty section of the base.

Lucisk had also sent my initial schedule. I had one hour to settle into my barracks, then my first lesson was Naval Drill and Etiquette. There were many lessons on that topic in the schedule ahead, mixed in with a few more interesting subjects like Basic Singleship Operation and Introductory Insystem Tactics, but the first month or so was clearly mostly about ritual, ceremony, and drill. Even worse, most of the drill and the boring stuff wasn't even rapid-learning downloads but actual practice. I cursed when I saw that, though it is true that you never learn anything quite as well from the downloads as when you actually do it.

"You have your schedule, Cadet. Welcome to the Academy," said Lucisk. "Master Haddad, you will need to see Uncle Gerekuz to have Prince Khemri's off-duty accommodations assigned."

"I have already communicated with Gerekuz and have

obtained suitable accommodations, thank you, Highness," replied Haddad. "Though I believe that as my Prince has incurred two demerits, he will not be off duty for several weeks."

"Yes," said Lucisk without inflection. "You had best get moving, Cadet Khemri, if you don't want to incur more demerits."

"Yeah, I guess so," I replied. "Thanks."

Out in the corridor, Haddad leaned in close.

"You need to meet your priests, Highness. I recommend a fast detour to your off-duty accommodations. It will reduce your settling-in time in the barracks, but I think meeting your priests is of more importance in order to establish more relay points to the Imperial Mind."

"Sure," I replied, once again channeling the insouciance of my favorite Prince from history, or perhaps legend, Garikm XXXII. "What can they do to me, anyway?"

Quite a lot, as it happened.

5

CADET DUTY BARRACKS Thanruz, unlike the opulent suite of rooms I had just seen that would be my off-duty residence, was a bare cavern hewn from the rock. Basic beds were lined up in a row, separated by extruded Bitek storage pods. Water was dripping from the ceiling in one corner, and the whole place was very harshly illuminated by Mektek incandescent arrays that had been fixed to the rock above each bed.

When I arrived, some species of lower cadet officer with bronze epaulettes, rather than the silver of Lucisk or Janokh, was haranguing the eight other cadets who would be my classmates for the next year. The cadets were standing in various poses of disinterest, annoyance, and anger at the feet of their beds, obviously experiencing the same disillusionment that I had gone through: the discovery that being a cadet in the Navy pretty much canceled out all the benefits of being a Prince, at least when we were on duty.

I picked up their projections as I walked in. My face was clear now, thanks to Uncle Krughal, one of my new household priests who had some experience in hazardous material cleanup, though as Haddad had foreseen, it was really a job for a Bitek specialist priest—which we didn't have. Krughal's Psitek nanobrushing had removed all the stain, so I knew that it wasn't my dirty face that was making the cadet officer, one Prince Jesmur, snarl as she caught sight of me.

"Cadet Khemri! You're five minutes late. Take your station by your bed."

"Only five minutes!" I exclaimed. "I'm improving. Uh, which one is my bed?"

I asked because there was no overlay to show me, but of course there was only one bed that didn't have a Prince standing in front of it. Call it an early lesson that overreliance on tek overlays is dangerous and thinking is to be preferred.

:Khemri <<identifier>>Naval Record Demerit Applied
Authority Jesmur <<identifier>>:

"What was that for?" I protested as I strolled over to my bed.

"Insolence to a superior officer," said Jesmur. "If you keep at it, I'll assign a group demerit to this class."

All the other Princes looked at me, none of them happily. There were five female and three male Princes, and we all looked quite different. There was a lot of variation in skin, hair, and eye color, ranging from the darkest black skin, dark hair, and purple eyes of Prince Aliadh to the orange-tinted skin and yellow eyes of Prince Fyrmis, who—as was not unusual for some planets—had no hair at all. My own brown skin and black eyes were pretty much in the middle of the pack. My hair at that time was long and tied back in a queue, though later when I became more aware of Imperial fashions, which primarily consisted of the aping of old Earth customs, I had it shaved save for a strip in the middle, a hairstyle called a mohuck for reasons that had not survived the march of history.

It did not take long to learn that in addition to looking different, we also had different abilities, and that even among Princes, no one was created equal. Though we had all been augmented in the same way, that augmentation had built on different genetic potentials. Some of the Princes in my class group were faster than me, stronger than me, and possibly smarter than me. Three were taller, two were shorter, and I guess four of them were better-looking, if you assume a classical approach to beauty, in terms of symmetry of features and so on.

Our seniority within the class group was based on our ascension dates. Much to the annoyance of most of the others, who had come to the Academy more swiftly from their candidate temples, I was the second-most senior. A rather pig-faced Prince called Charoz was the only one senior to me, and then only by a few hours.

Charoz had a nasty glint in his eye, and I could tell he hated my guts from the get-go, possibly because I inadvertently made a kind of snorting noise when he introduced himself, and like I said, he did somewhat resemble a pig.

Apart from Charoz, almost all the other Princes were pretty much interchangeable, at least as far as I was concerned. For starters, with the single exception of a Prince Tyrtho, they were all members of House Jerrazis. Judging from their joining dates, they had received the same offer that Commandant Huzand had extended to me, and they had accepted.

Tyrtho, for some reason, belonged to House Tivand. I guessed that she must have been offered the opportunity while en route to the Academy and had accepted, not knowing that this would put her at a disadvantage. Later I confirmed part of this was true; she had joined Tivand from her candidate temple. But Tyrtho had known that the Academy was dominated by the Jerrazis and had chosen Tivand anyway, because of that House's strength in the higher ranks of the Navy. She planned a long way ahead and had started off much better informed than I was, for the simple reason that she had always asked lots of questions, something she continued to do throughout her Naval cadetship, no matter how unwelcome the questions were.

Tyrtho was the only one who stayed out of what happened next.

"You have about twenty minutes," said Jesmur. "Check the requirement for full ceremonial uniform and report in that uniform to drill hall twelve at eleven forty-five. I have to attend to some other matters; I will see you there."

She looked at me as she left, quite a fierce glare, and made a kind of signal with her eyebrows at the others. It didn't take an accelerated Prince brain to work out that she was suggesting that they teach me the importance of fitting into the unit and all that kind of stuff.

As soon as Jesmur went out the door, the whole bunch (except Tyrtho) moved toward me, their hostility evident. But they had only taken a step forward when a wide-shouldered Prince with a low forehead called Marmro said, "He's connected, witnessing."

"You and Jipru block him," ordered Charoz. He was taking the seniority thing seriously; the order snapped out as if it was some brilliant fleet command.

I felt a slight pain inside my head, and for a millisecond, my connection to the Imperial Mind was lost as my relaying priest, Uncle Frekwo, was blocked. I felt Uncle Aleakh join in and also immediately get blocked, but then two of my aunts joined in and connection was reestablished. All of this happened in the time that my classmates took only one more step toward me. I knew their intentions, for at that point we'd all had the same basic unarmed combat training in our candidate temples. They were moving in the posture called Cranes Advance on Single Fish, which was for advancing on a lone enemy when supported by numerous allies.

"He's still witnessing!" burst out Marmro.

"What?" asked Charoz. He hesitated, his brilliant command mind not quite up to unexpected situations. "Uh, Aliadh and Fyrmis, you block as well."

But I'd already messaged Haddad about the situation and he was relaying too, with first nine and then all twelve of my priests online. I backed up to the door as the other seven Princes continued to move toward me. Tyrtho sat on her bed, watching.

"He's *still* witnessing!" protested Marmro.

"Everyone block!" snapped Charoz.

They all took another step and stopped.

"Still witnessing," said Marmro. He turned around and glared at Tyrtho, which wasn't a good look for him, considering the previously mentioned low forehead. "You'd better not be helping him."

"Doesn't look like he needs my help," drawled Tyrtho. "By the way, Marmro, I think in Cranes Advance on Single Fish you're supposed to be farther around to the left."

"Shut up!" ordered Charoz, just as I sent a command to Haddad to block everyone else and dropped my relay to the Imperial Mind. At the same time, I drew the phage emitter from my boot.

"He's disconnected—" crowed Marmro.

"Maximum dispersal," I said to the emitter, and smiled at my new enemies. "Who would have thought such a nasty Bitek accident could happen to such nice people?"

I felt all of them stop blocking and reach desperately for the Imperial Mind. But they had only one priest each, and junior Masters of Assassins. Haddad and my twelve priests blocked their efforts without too much difficulty, though I was relieved Tyrtho had not joined in on their side. I had a feeling maybe she had more than a single priest.

There were muttered cries of confusion and alarm. Two of the Princes who had been sensibly hanging back now ostentatiously separated themselves from the pack. I marked their names. Aliadh and Calzik. This swift behavior was typical of them both, I would learn. They were very quick to assess who would be on the winning side in any situation.

"We've wasted some of our precious time," I said. "I suggest we do as we're told, get dressed, and go to our lesson. Bear in mind that I'll be keeping up my connection to the Mind at all times, or blocking yours if I need us to have some quiet time all to ourselves. But I'm a friendly soul, and disposed to think the better of all you easily led types. Remember that."

"We'll remember, all right," said Charoz. "You can't stay connected all the time."

"Really?" I asked. "How would you know?"

Charoz glowered at me but didn't answer. Like me, he was

too newly ascended, and he didn't know all the ins and outs of relays to the Mind, or how many priests I had or who might be supporting me, legally or not.

"You'd better not get us any group demerits," he said finally, and turned back toward the beds. The others slowly followed. I waited till they had started getting their ceremonial uniforms out of their lockers, then stowed the phage emitter and went toward my own small patch of ground with its bed and locker.

:Haddad. Stop blocking. Bring up relay to Imperial Mind. Witness. Continue witness unless ordered otherwise, at all times, awake or asleep:

:Confirmed Highness. Well done:

Haddad was being kind. I had only delayed the problem. I knew that the Commandant and the hierarchy of the Academy would look the other way whenever possible, and that my classmates or other members of House Jerrazis would do everything in their power to make my life a misery.

As I put on the ridiculous high Bitek fur busby that completed my ceremonial uniform, I sent a query to the Imperial Mind. The arch-priest had said that I wasn't to join a House because the Emperor had other plans for me. Naturally, being totally wet behind the ears, I had understood this to mean that just like Prince Garikm, any moment now I would receive a special mission from the Imperial Mind and would hurtle off into a troubled galaxy to take charge of something important—and the sooner that happened, the better.

But I didn't get a special mission. All I got back was a truncated version of what I'd heard before.

:Study hard. Await direct instruction <<Sigil of the Imperial Mind>>:

The next three months were not a lot of fun. Even though the priests do most of the work, it is very wearying to keep up a constant connection to the Imperial Mind. I was tired anyway, for the work at the Academy was designed to test us to the limits of even our engineered capabilities. The extra effort of keeping up that connection meant that I was permanently exhausted and nearly always hovering on the fringe of sleep.

My classmates didn't try to physically assault me again, at least not all of them at once. Charoz did attack me a few days after the first assault, when I was asleep, but Uncle Krimhiz was listening through my ears and woke me up, so the Imperial Mind saw as well as heard Charoz hit me on the head with a boot, earning himself four demerits and me a nasty bruise.

After that, Charoz changed tactics. Or probably it would be more accurate to say that Jipru suggested a change of tactics. Jipru was very smart, and Charoz wasn't, so it's unlikely our brave section leader thought of it himself.

Instead of physical assaults, they turned to small, sneaky means of making things troublesome for me. Like taping my locker shut with an industrial Bitek bond just before the Commandant's Parade. This tremendous waste of our time took place every week, when we had to march about in ceremonial uniforms, circling the vast subterranean parade ground in front of Huzand, who of course stood on yet another platform and looked down at us. Missing the parade or being in incorrect or incomplete uniform would have earned me at least two demerits. I got around that by cutting the door open with my deintegration wand, but I still received a demerit for damaging equipment, as Charoz reported the damage before I could get it fixed.

They also sabotaged my bed, sawing through its legs so it collapsed when I got in; drew graffiti on the floor next to my locker, which I would be blamed for; and generally tried to get me into trouble.

Though I typically didn't know who had done these things, my official policy was always to take out my retribution on Charoz. He was the leader, after all. So when they glued my locker shut, I glued his shut. When they sawed through my bed legs, I took off the heels of every pair of his boots, and so on.

It became quite complicated, because naturally they didn't want to be caught doing whatever they were doing, and I didn't want to be caught doing what I was doing. So there was a lot of connection and disconnection from the Imperial Mind. They had the advantage of numbers, of course, but often it was only Jipru and Marmro who would follow Charoz's lead, and though Tyrtho said she was neutral, in fact she often helped me.

I also found a new strategy to help me attack Charoz when I discovered that once I had reached twenty-four demerits, I wasn't given any more, at least not until the old ones had expired. So I could always be slightly late for every class and in those few minutes wreak havoc on Charoz's locker, uniforms, or equipment. The others, who were fearful of demerits, always left the barracks on time to make sure they weren't late for the next lesson, parade, or whatever.

I wondered *why* I wasn't given more demerits after I got twenty-four racked up, so I followed some interesting lines of research through the great mass of data the Imperial Mind served up on Naval regulations. The Mind was like that—it often wouldn't answer a direct question but just give pointers to where the answer might be found and dump a huge amount of unsorted data that had to be actually read or mentally arranged. In this case, I discovered that if a cadet received *more* than twenty-four demerits every quarter, then there would be an investigation from a higher headquarters. Further research indicated that in my case this investigation would come from the sector admiral, a Prince Elrokhi, who belonged to House Tivand. Presumably an investigation from his headquarters would not at all suit Commandant Huzand.

But there were other punishments in addition to the demerit system, and I was soon introduced to them. The most basic were simply extra drills or lessons to be undertaken in what was notionally a cadet's free time, and included semiofficial humiliations, like being ordered to scrub floors or to shadow the mekbi trooper guard, doing everything they did—which was mostly standing next to a door all night, occasionally snapping to attention as a Prince came through.

I didn't mind the extra drills and lessons too much, as I discovered that while I didn't want to do them, they helped my classwork and drill scores—and I learned things that the other Princes never would.

For example, hanging out with the mekbi troopers turned out to be very educational, though I hated having to salute my treacherous classmates. Charoz and Jipru in particular would often spend an hour just walking backward and forward in front of the guard to make me spring to attention and salute a hundred times.

But it turned out I learned a lot more about the troopers from the interminable guard sessions than from the official direct download lessons like "An Introduction to the Command and Deployment of Standard Mekbi Infantry." As far as a Prince would know from that data and the accompanying virtual experience, mekbi troopers were not much more than combat automatons who only communicated battlefield information and had no personalities at all. But spending hours and hours with them on duty, marching as one of them, and even (as an additional punishment) lying down with them in their replenishment chambers, I found that there were individual differences and, very importantly, that they did communicate among themselves. In fact they kept up a constant, simple Psitek chatter that most Princes sensed only as an irritating mental humming, a side effect of commanding the troopers.

But the troopers' mental hum, if you could understand it, contained comments about themselves and the tasks they were undertaking, and constant speculation about how many enemies they would kill before they were killed themselves. Troopers who had already killed enemies were known to all, their serial numbers assuming the place of honored names.

Interestingly, the mekbi troopers assumed they *would* be killed, and that it was only a matter of time. This didn't concern them; it was their destiny. As far as I could tell from my eavesdropping, they never considered anything else as being possible. They would do their duty, follow orders, kill and be killed. But they wanted to die good deaths, which meant killing enemies first.

Preferably *lots* of enemies.

Unfortunately, the cadet under-officers who particularly targeted me soon worked out that I didn't mind hanging out with the troopers, and they varied my punishments. I annoyed them and got even more punishments by cheerfully accepting whatever they threw at me.

After all, I still thought that I was going to be taken away on some special mission for the Emperor. Except, as each week went past and I got more tired and more harassed, I didn't get taken away. No special mission was forthcoming, and I started to think that maybe I'd gotten a bit overconfident . . . again. After all, the arch-priest hadn't said I'd get a special mission. Only that I shouldn't join House Jerrazis.

Just to piss me off even more, I had accumulated so many demerits that I was permanently on duty. I couldn't go and relax in my comfortable off-duty chambers every seventh day, which for the other cadets was a holiday. I had to stay in the barracks doing extra duties, either additional downloads, classes, or drills or once again tailing along with the mekbi troopers as they eternally changed guard.

As this continued and the weeks became months, I came to the reluctant conclusion that I had made a big mistake. I should have taken Huzand's offer, joined House Jerrazis, and learned to fit in with all the other Princes.

In fact, I was on the brink of asking to see the Commandant and basically groveling to try to make amends when everything changed.

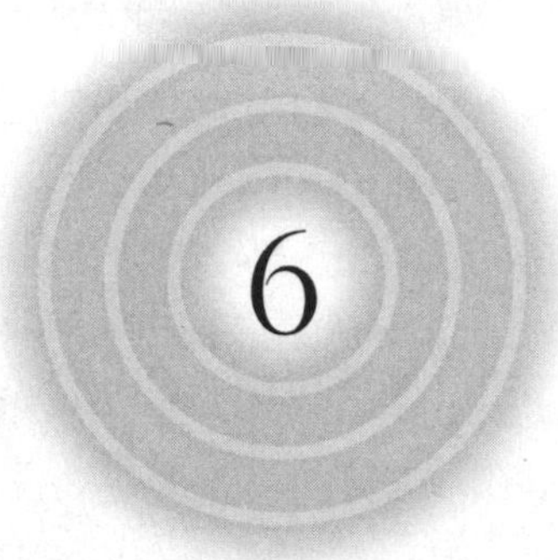

6

THIS BIG, BIG change in my circumstances came in my fifth month at the Academy. I was standing guard with the troopers, listening to the hum of their "2378FDE98X98 slew six rebels" and "9854AAD871F burned down four pirates," and like I said, I had just about decided that I would ask to see Huzand and see if total subservience would work where rebellion had not.

Changing my miserable life was uppermost in my mind right then because it was a seventh day, and almost every other cadet was on the off-duty side of the base, enjoying their rooms, their mind-programmed servants, their chosen food, and so on. And I was the unnecessary fifth wheel joining a quartet of mekbi troopers guarding a door that didn't even rate a cadet officer and an extruded desk.

It wasn't just missing out on relaxation and fun I was worried about. Being confined to barracks also seriously limited my access to Haddad and my priests. I could speak to Haddad via mindspeech, but I was often too tired to do so, and I was also mindful of his earlier advice that other people could potentially listen in. So I still hadn't discussed the arch-priest with him, what she had said, and so on. My mental conversations with Haddad were always too brief and limited to me asking his advice on how to deal with Charoz's latest stupid trick, or scheduling my priests, or on some very rare occasions planning how I might let down my constant witnessing for the Imperial Mind so that I could get some real rest.

I was thinking about this, and how I was going to get myself out of the hole that I had largely dug myself, when Haddad's familiar mental voice suddenly broke in.

:Highness. Procure Psitek protection suit, Mektek communicator rig, and dislocation rifle from <<locker map identifier>> Sad-Eye incursion alert:

I was already moving as I sent back a very surprised query.

:What incursion? There's no alarm!:

:There will be. Hurry!:

The emergency weapon and equipment cache was behind one of the larger metal plates in the Bitek wall, about ten meters away down the corridor. Naturally it was alarmed and monitored in several different ways, and in my sensory overlay there was the warning that any cadet who opened it unnecessarily would face frightful punishments, not just demerits from the Academy but also the Navy proper.

This time I didn't wonder what else they could do to me. I knew by now that there would be all kinds of things I hadn't even thought of.

I feared the potential punishment. But I trusted Haddad.

I sent a Psitek command and slapped my hand on the ID plate, which first scanned my palm print and then bit me for a taste of blood. All three tek measures confirmed my identity. The door swung open, alarms went off everywhere in both physical and tek space, and at that same instant I felt a strange sensation in my head as I lost touch with the Imperial Mind, Haddad, and everyone else.

Every Psitek connection had dropped out. I froze in place, my mouth open, finally processing what Haddad had in fact already told me was about to happen.

A Sad-Eye incursion.

As with almost every other subject of importance, I didn't know much about Sad-Eyes beyond the basic "Enemies of the Empire: An Introduction" lesson a few months back. They were an alien race, masters of their own version of Psitek. Physically they were parasitical brainbugs with a boring-drill snout and really short legs. They drilled into the head of a chosen host, and then from that comfy spot a single Sad-Eye would psychically dominate and control fifty or sixty puppets. They liked humanoids for their host position but could use their Psitek to control almost any living organism that had a developed brain.

These head-drilling monsters were called Sad-Eyes because the only part of a humanoid body they had difficulty controlling were the tear ducts. Sad-Eye hosts and their puppets, if human, tended to look as if they were crying or holding back tears. Which was bad news for ordinary people suffering allergies, or crying at a spaceport or somewhere sensitive like that. Sad-Eyes were greatly feared, and many Princes would order wet-eyed suspects killed as a simple precaution.

Apart from shooting anyone with tears in their eyes from a great distance, the basic Imperial technique for dealing with Sad-Eyes was to turn off every tiny little bit of Psitek, so that they couldn't suborn it or worm their way into your brain, and then kill them using Mektek or Bitek.

A microsecond after this went through my head, all the auditory alarms in the corridor began to wail and the locker that I had just illegally opened jerked as its automatic opening mechanism cycled again. Farther along the corridor, other doors sprang open, but there was no sudden pounding of feet on the floor of eager cadets coming to pick up weapons and equipment. They were all off duty.

"Ultra Alert! Ultra Alert!" said a voice. "Prepare to repel Sad-Eye boarding force. All cadet officers report to designated battle stations. Other cadets report to your barracks. This is not a drill."

The voice kept repeating this as I ran into the emergency armory and practically dived into the robing chamber. Nothing happened till I remembered I needed to speak, as all Psitek comms were down.

"Psitek defense suit, Mektek comm gear, flash!" I shouted, raising my arms.

Ports opened and Bitek facilitators aimed their spinnerets. As they wove a Psitek defense suit around me, robot arms positioned a headset over my ears and, with a slight tap, stuck a throat mike just below my Adam's apple. A few seconds later, the grubs spun up a hood, pulled it closed so that only my mouth, nose, and eyes were free, and retreated back into wherever it was they came from.

I bounded out of the robing chamber, slapped on a nice heavy Mektek armor helmet, grabbed a dislocation rifle from the rack, and checked it, suddenly grateful that a good part of my extra punishment lessons had been spent interminably breaking down and assembling all standard Imperial small arms, a subject that we had not covered in the official curriculum as yet.

Three minutes after Haddad's original alarm I was suited and armed and back in the corridor. My mekbi guard companions were now really guarding the door, which meant that they had stripped back the Bitek paneling to occupy defensive niches in the rock that gave them some protection and a good field of fire for their energy projectors.

Voices crackled in my ears from the Mektek communicator. Belatedly, I listened to them. There were lots of Princes talking over each other, so it was difficult to sort out. Particularly since I was used to the clarity of mindspeech, where I knew just who was sending.

"It came in riding the supply ship, must be suborned—"

"Don't recognize the type of vessel, but it's very heavily armored—"

"It's got a phased-field drill, they're boring, we've lost guard post five and four in Huzgar, they're almost through three—"

"How did it get past the system patrol? Achmir must have let it through, curse him; I will protest—"

I recognized that last voice. It was the Commandant, complaining and whining as per usual. I didn't know who'd spoken before, but what they were saying was a lot more relevant. I was in Huzgar quadrant of the base, and even though I'd lost the Psitek schematic, numerous punishment drills had engraved the base layout on my memory.

Guard post three was directly above my head.

A new voice came on then. A commanding female voice that

cut through everyone spouting off whatever was in their heads.

"This is Captain Glemri, Marine Garrison Commander, assuming tactical command. Clear the voicenet now."

I didn't know Prince Glemri, though I had seen the Marine specialists around a few times. They commanded the mekbi troopers and were, as far as I could ascertain, looked down on by most of the Naval Princes and by extension, the cadets. Real Navy Princes fought in space, in ships, not with mekbi troopers, who most Princes considered to be an even lower form of life than normal humans, which was kind of unfair since the troopers were superb at what they were made to do, which was kill enemies of the Empire.

Typically, the only voice that didn't stop talking was Huzand's, which kept ranting on about Achmir and treachery and so on.

"Commandant, shut up!" barked Glemri. "Any cadet officers in Huzgar, report status."

There was a deafening silence. After a few seconds, I hesitantly transmitted.

"Uh, I'm in Huzgar, sir, level four, guard post two. Cadet Khemri, with four mekbi troopers."

"Cadet Khemri? Is there a cadet officer there?"

"No, sir. I was on an . . . extra duty with the troopers."

"Okay, listen up, Cadet. There isn't much time—we've got a shipload of Sad-Eyes boring down. Get to an emergency armory and get a Psitek protection suit and—"

"I'm suited up and have a dislocation rifle," I reported.

Glemri sounded surprised.

"You are? Uh, good. About fifteen seconds from now the ceiling is going to come down above your guard post. Pull your troopers back to the Huzgar-Jeresk bulkhead and stop anything trying to come through. Got it?"

"Huzgar-Jeresk bulkhead! Got it—"

I would have added "sir," but all I could hear now through my headset was the horrible electronic squeal of successful jamming. Which meant that the Sad-Eyes had picked up some puppets who knew at least something about our Mektek.

I ran to the nearest mekbi trooper, intending to tap out an emergency instruction on his chest plate, since these troopers weren't currently fitted with Mektek comms. But as I got closer, I realized that the low-level Psitek hum of their own talk was still going on, though I could only pick it up when I got close.

Since I could receive it, I could also send. So I sent them a simple message in their own mindspeech.

:Follow me. Glory. Killing. Death:

Technically, it shouldn't have worked, since there was nothing in it to identify me as their commanding Prince. But as one, they swung out of their defensive wall niches and ran toward me. I spun about and was twenty meters down the corridor when I was blown forward off my feet by the shock wave of something massive smashing through the ceiling behind us.

I rolled over and sat up just in time to cop a wave of dust across my face. The mekbi troopers, who had not fallen thanks to the spurs in their feet, propped to either side of me and opened fire with their energy projectors. Blue beams of intense ferocity shot through the dust, making tiny crackling pops as they passed.

Something the size of my own head but traveling at supersonic speed shot over me and went shrieking down the corridor. Hastily I threw myself flat and found that I had the dislocation rifle already at my shoulder. The sight and target acquisition was active, the small screen showing multiple moving organics coming straight at me, emerging from whatever it was that had come from above and was now filling up the entire other end of the corridor.

I picked the closest enemy and pressed the firing stud. There was the characteristic short, eerie whine, and though I couldn't see clearly for all the dust and the light bloom from the energy weapons, the scope confirmed the dislocation rifle had hit the target and had basically turned whoever or whatever it was inside out. This was one of the main reasons that dislocation weapons were preferred for fighting Sad-Eyes. If there was one of the remarkably durable master puppeteers inside the braincase of a puppet, it would be flung out by a disco hit instead of potentially lurking inside what otherwise appeared to be a corpse, where it could continue to direct its puppets.

The mekbi troopers were firing but also shuffling back, obviously in response to the sheer number of enemies. Another one of the big projectiles boomed over my head, the dust eddying in its path. In that brief moment I saw dozens and dozens of armed and dangerous life-forms, most of them nonhuman, boiling out of the wide hatch of some kind of earth-boring attack ship.

The mekbi hum was all tactical discussion now.

:Back, back. Keep minimum energy distance:

:Agreed. Back, back. Too many. Who will stand?:

:I am oldest. I am 8734DDD871F. Go:

Three of the mekbi troopers stood and fired as the fourth ducked forward, energy filament blades extended from each hand. Whirling like a top, he spun into the onrushing wall of enemies, the blades arcing and sparking as they met armor and bone.

I slithered back, twisted around, and ran for the corner,

crouching low. The mekbi troopers followed, walking backward and firing. The last one was hit just before it turned the corner, yet another of the big projectiles taking off the entire top of its body. Its legs kept walking back for a few paces, then the spurs locked in and the remnants fell, Bitek juices spraying out of severed lines.

A second later, there was an explosion back where we'd come from. Flames and fragments blew past, a few ricocheting down our arm of the corridor. The shock wave came through the floor and made me bite my tongue, which despite all efforts of my candidate priests, nerve programming and all, I still stuck out a little bit when I was concentrating.

:8734DDD871F antimatter battery self-overload. Good death: remarked the two surviving troopers, both at the same time.

They did not pause, trotting past me to each rip out a Bitek panel and move into the defensive niche behind.

I tried to do the same thing, but either I didn't have the knack or I was in the wrong place. All I got was a handful of crumbly material and the sight of a bare patch of rock behind.

Apart from the niches the troopers already occupied, there was no cover in this corridor. There was only the bulkhead door at the end, which I must not open and through which the enemy must not be allowed to pass.

"Defend," I said aloud to the troopers. "The enemy are not to pass this point."

Then I lay down on the floor and readied my rifle as the next wave of mind-reamed puppets came rampaging around the corner.

I can't say I really remember what happened next, though I have replayed my internal visual and auditory recordings. It all happened too quickly. The enemy employed no tactics at all.

They didn't do anything sensible, like fire guided projectiles from around the corner, or throw grenades. They just charged, wave after wave of them. Most of them didn't even have distance weapons—the big projectiles had evidently been fired from a turret or mount on the driller. They were swinging charged axes and electro-rapiers and the kinds of stuff you see in a gladiatorial demonstration, not in modern combat.

Maybe that's what it was, for the Sad-Eye who was controlling them all. A gladiatorial show.

A little more than three minutes after we got around the corner, there were only good old 95E6711AD19 and me left, and the mekbi trooper was hopping about on one leg and wielding just one filament blade because it had lost the hand that had been holding an energy projector.

I wasn't a lot better off. I fired from the prone position until a bellowing ursine creature cut the front end off my disco rifle with what could only be described as a plasma-arc meat cleaver. Jumping back, I discharged my Bitek phage emitter at the bear thing and his closest companions, but it wasn't fast-acting enough. Even as his fur and flesh melted, that cleaver came whistling across. I raised my hand to block and had every internal system flash emergency warnings as I saw my arm from the elbow down go flying across the corridor.

The next thing I knew, I was ten feet back, the deintegration wand in my right hand, the stump of my left arm tucked into my side. The wound had been cauterized by the plasma burn, and my own systems had also closed the blood supply, and I felt no pain. But it was disturbing.

Particularly as I only had three shots in the deintegration wand, my mekbi companion had just gone down with his head as well as his limbs missing, and there was a whole new wave of enemies coming around the corner, waving their glowing, pulsing, sparking hand weapons of great destruction.

When in a situation like that—essentially being about to die—it wasn't helpful to suddenly realize that without a connection to the Imperial Mind, I really *was* going to die, like *permanently.*

There would be no weighing up of my service by the priests of the Aspect of the Discerning Hand, no rebirth.

I just wasn't that special after all.

And as I discovered, right then, I *really really really* didn't want to die. It was all very well thinking about death in the abstract, secure in the knowledge that in the very unlikely event that something lethal did happen to me, I would almost certainly come back, compared to the finality of it all when it was actually happening.

But on top of these sudden, mortal terrors, I also grasped at one slim hope. Perhaps the directing Sad-Eye had been mentally walled off by the priests of the temple. Maybe I could connect to the Imperial Mind after all. I just had to remove my Psitek defense suit hood in the few seconds remaining before the horde descended on me.

Lacking a left hand, I found this easier said than done. Holding the wand with three fingers, I reached up and ripped the hood apart with my thumb, hoping that I would feel the sudden flowering of a connection to the Mind.

But I didn't. Instead, I felt a cold, loathsome touch, almost as if something had plunged their frozen fingers into my brain and was feeling around for something it had lost. I knew instantly it was the Sad-Eye puppeteer, and more than that, I could sense a kind of illusory Psitek tendril leading back into the pack of attackers, and suddenly I knew exactly where the thing was located—inside the head of a humanoid creature who was moving slowly in the rear ranks of the assault, taking care to be shielded by a large creature, with gray folded skin and a trunk, whose ancestors might well have been uplifted elephants from old Earth.

My first shot from the deintegration wand took out the elephant creature. The second shot was more difficult, because the mental fingers in my head were stabbing everywhere now, no longer looking for something, just causing me intense pain and disorientation. But I managed it, and the humanoid's head was blow apart.

I nailed the Sad-Eye itself with my third and final shot as it was hurled out of the remains of its host. It had probably been hoping I'd miss so it could scuttle away on its horrid little feet and find a new home inside the head of one of the dozens or perhaps even scores of its puppets who still remained.

But it wasn't going anywhere.

With the death of the Sad-Eye, the terrible pain inside my head disappeared. The puppets also regained control of their senses, but not in quite enough time to do me any good. I'd fired just as the leading wave reached me, and I went down under multiple charged weapon blows. I think I lost my other hand then, trying to shield my head, but I can't be sure. Certainly many blows struck my body and legs.

But as I lay dying against the bulkhead that I had defended with my life, there was a sudden, blissful buzz at the base of my skull.

:Connection reestablished Prince Khemri <<identifier>> and running. Check. Check. Save for rebirth assessment:

7

THAT WAS MY first death.

The next thing I knew, I was lying on a broad and very comfortable bed. I had the sensation of having just woken up, allied with the wooliness of being half asleep and not quite knowing where I was.

Then I remembered. I'd been dead. I mean, I was dead; I'd been dismembered by Sad-Eye puppets. . . .

I checked my internal systems. Everything was working. I could feel all my limbs. All augmentation was operational.

:Welcome back Prince Khemri II <<identifier>> You have been weighed in the balance by our Priests of the Aspect of the Emperor's Discerning Hand and found worthy of rebirth <<Sigil of the Imperial Mind>>:

The Imperial Mind's mental voice faded, but the connection

was still there, that buzz at the base of my skull. I let the Mind keep witnessing, raised my head, and saw that I was in my own bed, in the off-duty rooms that my demerit load meant I wasn't supposed to be in for at least another month. Haddad was waiting at the foot of the bed, with all my twelve priests arrayed around him . . . only there were more than twelve. . . .

I sat up properly, yawned, and wiped my eyes, happily removing sleep, not tears. That small act was a delight, not least because this allowed me to physically confirm what my various natural and assisted senses told me. I had both arms and I was alive!

"Welcome back, Highness," said Haddad.

"Thank you, Haddad," I replied. I looked around at all the blue-paned shaved heads. There were eighteen of them now. "Who are these other priests?"

"You have been granted another six priests as part of your gallantry award," replied Haddad. He made a gesture at the ceiling. I looked up and saw that each corner was occupied by a spread-eagled assassin's apprentice, holding themselves up by sheer physical strength and dexterity, not with antigrav. "And four of my apprentices have arrived from Jadekha Seven."

"Uh, good," I said. "What gallantry award?"

"Your courageous action in defending the access to the base-temple interface has resulted in you being made a Hero of the Empire, Second Class, Highness," said Haddad. "Which typically comes with an additional allocation of priests or other resources, such as a ship."

"I've been granted a ship?" I asked excitedly.

"No, Highness," said Haddad. "That was purely an example. But please allow me to introduce Uncle Hormidh and Uncle

Gorrakh from the Aspect of the Kindly Gardener. Hormidh is a battle surgeon, and Gorrakh's particular expertise is in nanoscopic Bitek—phages and so forth; Uncle Rerrunk and Aunt Viviax from the Aspect of the Rigorous Engineer—they have considerable experience in small Mektek systems and weapons; Aunt Waldhrun from the Aspect of the Instructive Father, who is a specialist in Mektek/Psitek information system and interfaces; and Uncle Naljalk, from the Aspect of the Cold Calculator, who is a probability forecaster. My apprentices above you are known for the moment as U-One, U-Two, U-Three, and U-Four. The *U* stands for useless, a state that I trust will be temporary."

"Ah, hello, everyone," I said. "Welcome to my service."

I gave a kind of wave, which stopped halfway as I looked at my hand. It was the same as ever, visually and to my internal audit, which meant that under my skin, the bones were much tougher than any normal human's, grown that way by Bitek genetic manipulation, but also strengthened with Mektek sheaths and overlays.

All of which had taken years and years when I was a child. . . .

"Haddad," I asked. "How . . . how long ago was I killed?"

"It has been twelve days since your heroic action, Highness," replied Haddad. He made a sign with his hand, and the priests all turned and filed out of the room. The apprentice assassins lightly leaped to the floor and followed them.

"Twelve days? Is that all? But how can . . . how is it possible that I have my old body . . . I mean the augmentation, everything that took all those years . . ."

"It is a mystery of the Empire," said Haddad. "Sometimes a rebirth is fast, like your own, Highness. Sometimes it may take several years. You could inquire of a Priest of the Aspect of the

Emperor's Discerning Hand, but I do not think you would receive an answer."

I filed that away for later inquiry while I thought about the whole rebirth thing. It was such a basic foundation of being a Prince, but I'd never really given the matter much attention before. Now I was wondering if there were other Khemris kept on ice somewhere, completely augmented clones, ready to have my personality transferred into them. Presumably at the cost of whatever proto-Khemri already existed inside that brain, however dormant.

Later I would think more about that, and what my rebirth might be costing someone else. At that moment, I was simply elated to be alive, and there was also this business of an award. I was a hero?

"So how come I'm getting a medal?" I asked Haddad as I got up and flexed, checking further that everything was operational. "I didn't think any of it was witnessed by the Mind."

"It wasn't witnessed by the Mind," said Haddad. "But everything was very comprehensively recorded by the Mektek security in the corridors, and also in the visual cortexes of the troopers, three of which were retrieved and the data extracted."

"I'm still surprised Huzand would put me in for a medal," I remarked, wrapping myself in the Bitek robe from the end of my bed. It purred a little and adjusted itself to fit, while also lifting its temperature to provide a pleasant warmth. Haddad handed me my phage emitter and deintegration wand. I checked both, then stowed them in the appropriate pockets of the robe, at the same time thinking that I must add a few more weapons to my personal armory. Weapons that held more ammunition. A lot more ammunition.

"The Commandant didn't, Highness," replied Haddad. "Your commendation came from Commander Glenn, the Marine officer, and went via Marine channels."

"Meaning Huzand would have stopped it if he could," I said bitterly. "I suppose I still have to go straight back to duty and keep working off my demerits."

"Actually, Highness, the approval of your decoration by the Imperial Mind has cleared all demerits," said Haddad. "And you have three days of post-mortality leave."

That cheered me up. Three days' leave! I hadn't had such an expanse of peaceful, untrammeled time for so long, and I had not yet been able to experience the pleasures that I'd planned for my off-duty hours.

"Haddad," I said briskly, "what mind-programmed servants do I have here?"

"Two cooks, two waiters, two porters, a valet, two female courtesans, two male courtesans, and you also have a nonhuman masseur, a Vivarkh, who is not mind-programmed but has had loyalty conditioning."

"Excellent!" I clapped my hands, thinking exactly how I would allocate my time. "First, have the cooks make a feast. Something of everything I've missed for the last five months, just in tasting portions, with appropriate wines and other stimulants. The courtesans can come along to that, and I shall make a selection for later. First, however, that Vivarkh masseur, while my valet can lay out some clothes—anything that is not a cadet uniform!"

The blue fluid in Haddad's head roiled, and I caught the edge of a communication.

"You have a visitor, Highness," said Haddad.

"Tell them to go away!" I snapped. "I'm on leave!"

"It is the Commandant, Prince Huzand," said Haddad. His eyes narrowed, just a fraction. "This is very unusual. Naljalk is calculating possibilities. The most likely scenario is that now that you have become noticed by higher authorities, he wishes to invite you again to join House Jerrazis. This could in fact be a sensible course for your Highness to adopt."

"Uh, I never told you the reason I refused," I said. "I've been wanting to talk about this, but . . . um . . . are we completely secure here?"

"As far as possible," replied Haddad.

"Keep this to yourself, but the fact is, an Arch-Priest of the Discerning Hand told me not to join any House, and not to tell anyone about that, except . . . and this is interesting . . . she did say I could tell you. . . ."

If I thought that was going to surprise Haddad, I was wrong. His face remained as inscrutable as ever.

"Did the arch-priest give you their name?" he asked.

"Yes, Morojal."

"Where did you meet her?"

"At my connection to the Imperial Mind. It wasn't the ordinary priest you saw later."

"This greatly modifies the possible outcomes," said Haddad. "Because you *must* refuse any invitation to join House Jerrazis. But another refusal will incense Huzand. In my opinion he is already in a less than optimal mental state. The probability he will do something . . . ill-advised . . . is . . . Naljalk?"

:Probability of illegal action 0.145: sent Uncle Naljalk.

"Considerably higher than I would like," continued Haddad. "But we can't refuse him directly. I suggest you meet the Commandant in your reception room. My apprentices and I will be on hand, and you should take care to witness, Highness. If it is an invitation to join Jerrazis, ask for time to think about it. Even a few days could be crucial."

"What can he do?" I asked anxiously. "I mean, you said before he can't assassinate a cadet, or challenge me to a duel."

"He cannot legally do anything, and if he does anything against Imperial law, there would be dire consequences for him," said Haddad. "However, there is an element of irrationality at work in Prince Huzand, which has been rising over time. U-Two is watching him in the antechamber now and reports unusual facial coloring, likely the side effect of a drug."

"A drug!"

I'd thought Huzand's red flushes to be a visual preference, not a side effect of something else. Also, while Princes off duty could consume whatever drugs they wished, as their internal systems could usually flush the effects within minutes, the use of mood-altering or mind-bending Bitek was totally forbidden when on duty. It was also supposed to be nearly impossible for a Prince to become addicted to something, provided you kept an eye on your own internal biochemistry and adjusted it accordingly.

"The Commandant is believed to be very fond of raziskiba," said Haddad. "A minor drug that enhances self-belief and good feeling, but in extreme doses also increases the possibility of uncontrolled bouts of rage."

"Great," I said. "I thought he was bad enough before. Is this an official visit?"

I hadn't actually queried the Mind, but it answered anyway.

:Huzand <<identifier>> off duty <<Sigil of the Imperial Mind>>:

"Maybe he's come to congratulate me on my medal," I said

as we went through to the reception room. "Should I change out of my robe?"

"Given his history with Your Highness, he would be unlikely to offer congratulations now, informally. Naljalk calculates that as a 0.02 chance. The official medal presentation is scheduled for your return to duty in four days," said Haddad; at the same time he mentally transferred the details to me. "As you can see, the award will be made not by the Commandant but by Vice Admiral Elrokhi, the sector commander, who is en route here from Lastamen. I doubt that this visit is something the Commandant will be pleased about."

The reception room still had its original decoration scheme, as I had not had time to order changes. The previous Prince who had occupied it had chosen to fill it with large, inflatable cushions stacked in tiered columns according to color density, darkest to lightest. It made it a kind of bulbous rainbow forest and was in my view a complete waste of space. If you leaned against a column you bounced off, and there were so many of them that you had to weave a zigzag path just to get in and out of the room.

One of Haddad's apprentices held up a viewer to show the entrance hall of my chambers. Huzand was waiting right near the inner door, alone, unaccompanied by cadet officers, priests, or his assassins.

The Commandant did look even more red faced than usual, and shorter, too, since he was off his ramp. He was in basic field uniform, camouflage set to ship gray, but he was still wearing powered miniatures of his medals and many specialist badges, and he had the Gift of the Emperor sidearm on his belt.

"I don't like this. Perhaps you should communicate that you are not able to receive visitors," suggested Haddad. "Some disorientation is permissible after a rebirth."

I thought about that for a second. But I was feeling overconfident again. After all, I had survived the mass assault of Sad-Eye puppets *and* I was a Hero of the Empire, Second Class.

"Let him in," I commanded.

Huzand marched into the room as if he owned it, stopping with the crash of boots only when he saw me standing in front of him, clad only in my highly disrespectful purring Bitek robe.

"Cadet Khemri," he said. His mouth twitched strangely as he said my name, and all of a sudden I knew for sure that he wasn't there to reinvite me to House Jerrazis.

"Yes, Commandant," I replied warily.

"I knew you were up to no good from the start," said Huzand. "You looked too much like Atalin. I didn't know what it meant at first, but now I do, and you're not going to get away with it."

"Um, get away with what, sir?" I asked.

"Substituting yourself for a good cadet!" shouted Huzand. "A good Jerrazis cadet!"

I glanced at Haddad out of the corner of my eye.

:I do not know what he is referring to: sent Haddad. :You recall Atalin was the cadet who met us when we first landed here; there is a strong physical resemblance:

"I really don't know what you're talking about, sir," I said soothingly. Encouraged by the fact that the Imperial Mind was observing all this, I gestured at a tray of silver goblets. "Can I offer you a drink?"

Huzand was not to be soothed. He advanced closer to me, and I saw that there were bubbles of what could only be froth in the corners of his mouth.

"Don't play stupid with me, boy," he hissed. "I know Vethethezk is behind this, probably with Tivand or Youngre as well, and I'm not going to let you put one over on me or my House."

I still wasn't worried about all this posturing, until all of a sudden I was cut off from the Imperial Mind and Huzand went for the ivory-handled revolver at his side.

I would like to say that I reacted instantly, drawing my own deintegration wand. But I didn't react instantly. I was slow. I gaped in disbelief, and the wand was stuck in the stupid purring robe, and Huzand got the revolver out and pointed toward me as I hurled myself aside into one of the inflated columns, and then his finger curled into the trigger guard and pulled, and he missed me because I was bouncing back the other way, and I had the wand out and fired it as he fired again, only my shot burned a dinner plate–sized hole through his head while his shot only grazed my shoulder.

I stared down at the headless body of the Commandant of the Academy and flinched as I felt the Imperial Mind reconnect and resume witnessing. Huzand, who naturally had far more priests than a mere cadet, had been blocking. With his death, that had ceased.

I wondered how many demerits a cadet could get for killing their own Commandant . . . if such a thing had ever happened in the past.

I also wondered how he'd missed his first shot. At least until I saw Haddad bend over and remove a small dart from the deceased Prince's neck.

"Paralysis dart," replied Haddad, answering my unspoken question. Perhaps I'd mind-sent it without thinking. "However, it was also slow, for which I apologize, Highness. Fortunately I think his aim was affected by the drug."

"What happens now?" I croaked. Uncle Hormidh was already pulling away my robe to check out the bullet wound. I could hardly feel it, the shock of having a dead superior at my feet rather overriding everything else. Uncle Rerrunk saw my expression and went and got one of my sheets to put over the dead Commandant's body.

"There will be an inquiry," said Haddad. "But the facts are quite clear. The former Prince Huzand came to your private quarters, and his priests blocked the Mind witnessing, not yours. Why would he have done that save to avoid the inconvenience of it being a witness to murder? Without direct evidence, he hoped to get away with it."

"He's going to be really cross when he gets reborn. . . ."

I stopped as I caught a very faint change of expression in Haddad's normal eye. Just the flicker of something that I probably wouldn't have noticed except that I was watching him so closely.

"*If* he comes back," I said slowly. "You think he won't be found worthy by the Discerning Hand?"

"I do not wish to speculate, Highness," said Haddad. "In any case, we already know that Admiral Elrokhi is on the way here, and so she will conduct the inquiry. It would be wise to stay in your quarters until she has arrived, and admit no visitors. Also, do not tell anyone what has occurred. It may appear that Huzand has simply vanished."

"But his priests, his Master of Assassins, they must know," I said.

"They will not speak of an unofficial attempt at murder, coupled with an illegal order to block witnessing by the Imperial Mind," said Haddad. "Besides, they will have already been reassigned—"

"What?" I asked. "You mean you *know* he's not going to be reborn?"

I queried the Mind on Huzand's status.

:Prince Huzand <<identifier>> lost in action against Sad-Eye incursion. Insufficient connection for rebirth permanent honorable death:

"But that's not what happened!" I protested. "Everyone knows he survived the Sad-Eye attack!"

"Some Princes will know he wasn't killed in the incursion," replied Haddad. "But they will not inquire further, because they will not want to know that Huzand came here secretly to kill a cadet. Even if someone from his House does suspect some strange occurrence, they will know it is better to leave him dead with honor."

"I didn't know the Imperial Mind could lie to us," I said somberly.

"There are levels of information veracity, Highness," Haddad replied. "In a sense, Huzand *was* killed by the Sad-Eye intervention. I doubt he would have determined on this crazed course of action if you had not distinguished yourself and been noted by higher authority."

"The Sad-Eye incursion . . . that reminds me. How did you come to warn me a minute or more before the base alarms?"

"I have various sources here and in the wider system, Highness," replied Haddad. "As should a good Master of Assassins."

"And how did they get here, anyway, from the wormhole, past the guard there?"

"That is under investigation, Highness," replied Haddad gravely.

He wasn't telling me everything, I knew, but I also knew that

I wouldn't get anything else out of him. At least on that subject.

"What was Huzand on about with that stuff about me replacing Prince Atalin?"

Haddad became very still.

"Have you looked at Prince Atalin's visual reference from the Imperial Mind?"

I shook my head and called it up.

Prince Atalin was three years older than I, not that I could tell from the image. She had brown skin like mine; a slightly hooked nose like mine; almost-black hair like mine; almond-shaped eyes with dark-brown, almost-black irises like mine. . . .

"We look very similar," I said slowly. "She could be my sister, if that were possible. . . ."

Princes don't have siblings. Or parents. At least not ones they know about. So it was very weird for me to be looking at someone who really could be a physical relation, sharing the same genetic heritage.

I felt decidedly strange. If she was my sister . . . what did that mean? How would we behave if we were to meet again?

"It is not impossible, Highness," said Haddad. "It could occur if your birth parents chose erasure when Atalin was selected, resettled elsewhere, and had you."

"But what are the chances of that?" I asked. "I mean, surely they would have been resettled somewhere that wasn't on a candidate-seeking list for decades?"

"They could have moved again, through choice or circumstance," said Haddad. "Though you are correct that it is highly improbable."

"But I still don't understand Huzand," I said. "I mean, sure, I look like Atalin. Maybe she even is my sister, not that it means anything. But I couldn't replace her! I wouldn't even know how to start to act like 'most successful cadet ever' Atalin. And the Imperial Mind would know, for a start."

"Indeed, Highness," said Haddad. "I fear Prince Huzand was suffering some form of delusion and found your physical similarity to a favored cadet as an unfortunate focus."

"Yeah, unfortunate all around," I snapped. "I guess I'm going to be a big fat target for all those Jerrazis out there. Huzand must have recruited ninety percent of the Academy by himself."

"If they find out what happened," Haddad reminded me.

:Priests of the Aspect of the Emperor's Discerning Hand

<<identifier>> present for collection of deceased Prince:

One of my apprentice assassins held up the viewing screen. There were four priests outside the door, dressed in their normal day-to-day robes, so it was impossible to tell what Aspect they belonged to. They could even be assassins. Maybe Huzand's Master had stayed loyal to him after death . . . if that was possible. As per usual, I didn't know.

"Retire to your chambers, Highness," said Haddad. "I will deal with the Discerning Hand."

"Are you sure that's who they are?" I asked.

"Yes," said Haddad. "No one would dare use their identifier in mindspeech with you witnessing for the Mind. But it is best you retire for now."

"Why?" I asked. "What do they do with the body?"

On the screen, I saw one of the priests take out something that resembled a small energy saw, and the one next to him was unfolding a Bitek bag of the kind used to contain and preserve organics.

"I'll retire," I said hastily.

"Do you still wish your feast to go on as ordered, Highness?" asked Haddad.

"No . . . uh . . . I mean, yes," I said, just before I slipped through the doorway.

After all, it might be my last opportunity to enjoy myself for a very long time. Though Haddad seemed confident, I couldn't believe that I really would go unpunished for killing the Commandant of the Academy. Even if he'd come to kill me, I was sure that I was going to cop something from someone higher up, whether it was official punishment or private retribution.

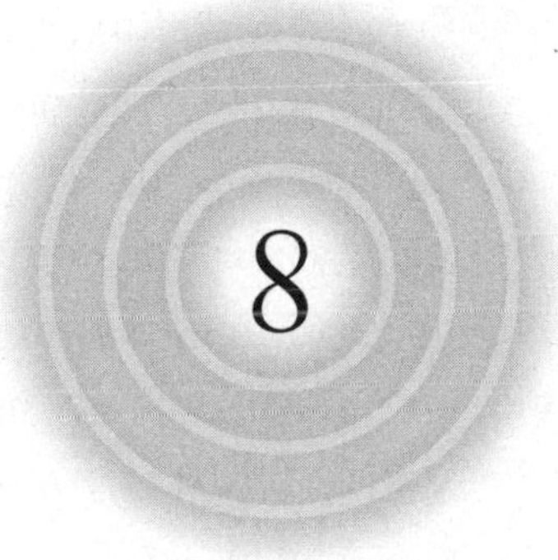

BUT I DECIDED not to worry about the things I couldn't change, so the next few days were among the most enjoyable I had ever experienced. I finally got to sample all the delights of my private apartment and household, for the first time feeling like I actually was a Prince of the Empire. Particularly as I had adopted the ancient motto "Party like there is no tomorrow" and had tried to indulge in every possible stimulant, relaxant, intoxicant, hallucinogen, and sexual experience that was available and permissible, and could be recovered from in time without major intervention from my priests or the temple.

This brief but very pleasurable interlude came to an end with a summons to the Commandant's office to report to Vice Admiral Elrokhi. That was when I really did feel like there might not be a tomorrow. I had been detoxed by my own priests with

Bitek nanocleansing and was entirely sober, but I felt washed out and uncomfortable in my own skin. Part of that was probably nervousness about what was going to happen rather than a classic hangover, which Uncle Hormidh assured me was not possible after the recovery procedure I'd been through.

I expected trouble, but when I fronted up in my full ceremonial uniform, complete with the stupid one-and-a-half-meter-high fur busby, I had a pleasant surprise. Vice Admiral Elrokhi V was nothing like Huzand. She welcomed me as one Prince to another, not from on high, and congratulated me on my defense against the Sad-Eye attack. Then she placed the Hero of the Empire order over my head herself and pinned a Scarlet wound badge to my chest. Apparently you don't get a wound badge for being killed, but since my arm had been cut off before my death, I did qualify for the lowest level. Now that I knew how much it had felt strange and horrible, if not exactly painful, I didn't want to qualify for the higher levels, like the Sable wound badge, mark of more than fifty individual wounds.

Since we were alone, not counting the various priests about the place, when I'd finished stepping back and saluting and doing all the things I had now been trained to do, I stammered out something about an inquiry.

"Inquiry?" asked Elrokhi. "Into what?"

"Uh, the events after the incursion," I said. "Concerning the former Comm—"

"Oh, that inquiry! It's been done, all has been signed off," said Elrokhi. "I don't think there's any point revisiting that, do you?"

"Not if you say so, sir," I replied.

"I do say so. Now, why don't we take tea while we wait for the new Commandant, Captain Kothrez, to finish up some of her administrative . . . ah . . . reforms. I'd like you to meet her before you return to duty."

I called up the new Commandant's details as Prince Elrokhi poured the tea, which was brought in by a programmed servant of some nonhuman species, whose broad back doubled as a tea tray while its multijointed arms laid out the crockery. The tea service, I noticed, was translucent china decorated with pale-blue flowers. It was very old and beautiful, and possibly even from ancient Earth, or was some ultra-high-quality Bitek reproduction. As I fumbled my cup slightly and saw Elrokhi's brow tighten, I realized that dropping one of those cups would be a great sin in the Vice Admiral's eyes, even though killing the former Commandant hardly rated her raising an eyebrow.

I held on to my cup very carefully as I went through the information from the Imperial Mind on Prince Kothrez XXII. Like Huzand, she held the rank of captain in the Imperial Navy, but she had clearly seen much more combat service, having been awarded the Imperial Star of Valor; Hero of the Empire First, Second, and Third Classes; and a Conspicuous Gallantry Medal. And she was a Grand Adept of War (Sensors) and a whole lot more. But the most relevant part as far as I was concerned was her House affiliation.

Kothrez belonged to House Tivand. Not Jerrazis. I hoped that could only be good for me.

When Kothrez showed up, I was instantly impressed. She definitely had more immediate presence than most of the officers I'd met, something greater than the natural arrogance of a Prince. Some of this was probably due to the tattoos on her shaved head, marking service in Imperial Survey, each tattoo commemorating a new and viable wormhole discovered by her, something few Princes could boast of. Otherwise she looked unremarkable, and unlike Huzand (who had had far less to boast about), she wasn't wearing powered versions of her medals, just the cloth ribbons in the smallest size issued, on a plain service shipsuit with the coiled gold epaulettes of her rank. Also unlike Huzand, the only visible weapons she wore were twin energy lances mounted under her wrists, excellent modern personal armament, instead of some affected antique awarded for dueling.

I resolved that now that I also had medals, I would follow Kothrez's example rather than Huzand's and make as little show of them as possible. I also thought I'd like to get the same kind of wrist-mounted energy lances and learn how to use them properly.

Kothrez wasn't friendly like the Vice Admiral, but she wasn't unfriendly like Huzand, either. She was just all business. She congratulated me on my award, asked me a few details about the Sad-Eye incursion, looked into my teacup to see if it was empty, and promptly sent me on my way.

"Back to duty, Cadet Khemri. You've done well. But don't let the excitement distract you. Your job is to study hard and equip yourself to serve the Empire. Dismissed."

I put the cup down very carefully, stepped back to salute, spun on my heel, and left. Back to my duty barracks, that hellhole from which I had had only the briefest escape, and most of that time I'd been dead. Or wherever it is Princes are before they are reborn.

I didn't have high expectations of my classmates, so I entered the barracks very carefully, looking out for traps or tricks, with my connection to the Imperial Mind up and witnessing.

A few steps inside the barracks, I stopped. Not because of a sudden trap or attack, but because apart from Tyrtho, Aliadh, and

Calzik, I didn't recognize any of the other Princes. For a moment I thought I'd wandered into the barracks of another class group that Tyrtho and the others were coincidentally visiting. But that wasn't possible. This was the right room. There was my bed and locker.

"All hail the conquering hero," said Tyrtho with a cheery wave. "Welcome back."

The others all saluted in welcome. Or saluted my medal, or maybe even the wound badge.

"Thanks," I said. "Uh, what happened to Charoz and his mighty legions?"

"Reassigned," said Tyrtho. "All the class groups have been split up and changed. Let me introduce you."

I checked them out with the Imperial Mind as they came over. None were from House Jerrazis.

Even our cadet officer was different. Instead of the surly Jesmur, we had the very tall and very composed Prince Hocozhem, who came in to gravely congratulate me on holding up the honor of Class 2645 and to let us know that we had seventeen minutes to don flight-rigged shipsuits for our next lesson, a practical session flying some of the Academy's antiquated singleships that had been reconfigured as trainers with two pilot seats.

Later, as we lined up to be assigned to individual craft and our instructor copilots, I asked Tyrtho what had happened while I was dead.

"Not a lot," she answered. "No lessons. We were on clean-up duty mostly, tidying up after the Sad-Eyes trashed the place. Make and mend. Just to keep us out of the way and busy, I guess, while heads rolled in the background."

"Heads rolled?" I asked casually. "What do you mean?"

"Come on! The Academy attacked out of the blue by a Sad-

Eye raid, with almost every cadet officer off duty, the long-range sensors unmonitored, no patrols up, and the autoweapons down for maintenance? No wonder Huzand got himself killed without the option of rebirth."

"What?"

Tyrtho gave me a considering look. Some of the other cadets were listening, so she either took pity on me and played along or she really thought I didn't know.

"Yeah, Huzand got it in the raid and was 'out of communication with the Mind.' No loss to the Navy. Liked dueling but not much good at anything else. I don't know how he got the Commandant job here. Jerrazis looking after its own, I guess."

Several cadets looked murderously at her for that, but far fewer than would have been the case only a few weeks before. I wondered how many cadets had switched allegiance from Jerrazis as soon as they caught the shift in the wind. It was possible to do this at least once, though of course changing Houses earned you the instant enmity of everyone you left behind.

"Khemri!" called out a lieutenant, Prince Loghrezk, who had been my instructor pilot before, on my very first practical launch. Like the other instructors, he was detached to the Academy from the system defense flotilla. He hadn't been at all friendly in the past, but as I marched up this time and saluted, he actually gave me a very smart salute back.

"Good to see you again, Cadet Khemri. Let's see if you can do as well in this exercise as you did against those Sad-Eyes on the ground."

I actually enjoyed my next six months at the Academy. While there were occasional moments of trouble from some of the die-hard Jerrazis and one notable full-on brawl with Charoz that got us both half a dozen demerits, it was nothing like my earlier experience. I got on pretty well with my new classmates and became as much a friend of Tyrtho as it is possible for Princes to be friends, outside of being allies within a House.

My interactions with officialdom also improved, though I still copped extra drills and lessons here and there. I suppose I'd got into the habit of being a bit late, a bit outspoken, and a bit too smart for my own good. I got some leeway in the first few weeks back, because of my medal and the Sad-Eye battle, but only so much. As soon as I overreached this latitude, the Commandant came down hard, so my zero-demerit score didn't last long. But I never came close to building up dozens, either, so I usually got back to my off-duty quarters at least once every two or three weeks.

Then, much to everyone's surprise, we all found ourselves in the last month of our initial year, faced with having to decide whether to come back or not. After the first year at the Academy, a cadet could go and join a ship for on-the-job experience and further training; or stay on for an additional two years to do the advanced courses, which were necessary for higher rank; or just leave with the reserve rank of ensign (essentially meaningless unless the Empire engaged in a major war and recalled you to the Navy) and do something else entirely different.

I, of course, was still waiting to find out what the special service was that I was supposed to do for the Empire. But I'd had no communication from Arch-Priest Morojal, so I had to start thinking about the alternatives.

Surprisingly, staying on at the Academy was not totally out of the question. I liked some parts of Naval work. I enjoyed piloting singleships, the heavy intrasystem fighters that were ferried through wormholes on various types of much bigger starships. Even the 120-year-old Jerragor-class singleships we learned on were still very capable craft, though they were Mektek-heavy compared to more recent Imperial craft, which had a more finely tuned balance among the three teks.

I was also very interested in Imperial Survey and their pathfinder vessels. Princes of the Imperial Survey took their multifunctional craft through newly discovered wormholes and, if they survived whatever they encountered at the other end, found a route back. This was the problem with wormholes—they were all one-way, so the trip home could be very long indeed. However, if there was a wormhole in, there was always at least one wormhole out, a fact that lent credence to the theory that the wormholes were actually constructs of some long-vanished galactic civilization.

It also made interstellar strategy fascinating, another subject I enjoyed. Systems with multiple useful wormhole entrances and exits were of supreme importance in galactic warfare. Or at least of the same importance as the rapid transfer of information. This was one of the Empire's great advantages. The Imperial Mind, and the Psitek network of communication, meant that as long as there were priests somewhere in range, Imperial forces would be in communication with each other and with headquarters.

Only the Sad-Eyes had a similar form of interstellar communication, and fortunately for us, they didn't seem to use it in as organized a fashion. In fact, they rarely organized themselves into groupings larger than two or three hundred Sad-Eyes in hosts, with fifteen or sixteen thousand puppets. Raids and surprise attacks were the Sad-Eye's modus operandi, not the massive fleet battles that were standard against the suicidal Deaders or to a lesser extent against the Naknuk rebels and their Bitek hordes.

But I didn't think I'd stay on at the Academy. I still wanted to strike out on my own. Head out to the fringes of the Empire, commandeer a ship, and go and seek my fortune.

But I kept this to myself. Particularly keeping it from the senior Princes who came to talk to me in the final few days before our graduation, when we cadets had to choose our future paths.

There were more visitors than I expected, starting with the Marine garrison commander, Prince Glemri. She dropped in while I was hanging out with the mekbi trooper door guard at station seven, punishment for what would probably be my last fling at tardiness.

"Cadet Khemri, I'm glad to find you here," she said. "I've been meaning to talk to you."

"Yes, sir," I said stiffly, standing at attention in line with the motionless troopers.

"Stand easy," she said. "This is just a chat. I wanted to talk to you about possibly signing up for Marine training. What are your plans?"

I had got smarter over the course of my year, so I didn't spit on the ground and declare I'd never be a Marine or anything dumb like that. Instead I wrinkled my forehead thoughtfully before answering.

"I'm not sure, sir. I'm evaluating all possibilities."

"You did well against the Sad-Eyes. And I know you can understand trooper talk."

"Uh, yes sir, I can," I replied.

"That's not all that common—maybe only one Prince in ten

gets it," said Glemri. "And it is a prerequisite for the Marines. With that, and your early start in combat, I bet you'd be a full colonel inside ten years. Have a regiment of your own."

"I'll seriously think about it, sir," I replied.

I would think about it, but I really doubted that I'd take up the offer. I liked the mekbi troopers; they were straightforward and kind of soothing to be around. But Glemri and the few other Marine officers I'd met were a bit too deadly serious. They seemed to come from the end of the Princely spectrum that lived for their profession and rated nothing else as important. I didn't want to become a useless kind of do-nothing Prince that came at the opposite end of the spectrum, but I wasn't ready for the kind of dedication the Marines had either.

I also wasn't all that keen about ground combat. I still woke at night sometimes with a sudden phantom sensation in my elbow, and images stuck in my head of that bloody fight in the corridor.

No. I would fight where necessary, of course, but I wasn't going to join up with the Imperial service that did the most of that kind of fighting, and to no small degree actually went looking for it.

Commandant Kothrez didn't come and see me, but she did order me into her office for a discussion about my career. She thought I had a good future in the Navy and encouraged me to stay on for the advanced courses. A pair of cadet officer's bronze epaulettes lay on the table in front of her, mine for the taking if I accepted.

Once again, I had learned a little tact. I expressed interest and reserved my decision to the last possible moment, which would be the evening after our graduation parade.

The morning before that parade, we all sat on our beds

in our ceremonial uniforms, minus boots and fur hats, and discussed the choices we had decided to make. Unspoken, but present in all our thoughts, was the knowledge that once we left here, we would be rejoining the survival-of-the-fittest world of Imperial Princes. Even those Princes returning to the Academy or joining a ship would be eligible for duels and liable to assassination, at least for the three months or so till their active service resumed. It was even possible that some of the Princes I was listening to in my barracks already had plans to eliminate me or other classmates. Haddad had told me that it was not unusual for dozens of duels and assassination attempts to take place on the first shuttle from Kwanantil Nine to Kwanantil Four.

Tyrtho, not unexpectedly, obviously knew this. I was intrigued to discover that she had not only already signed up for the advanced course and would be continuing at the Academy, but that she had somehow wangled a job for the three-month vacation period. She would be assisting a lieutenant commander who was redesigning the base defense systems, and so wouldn't be leaving the Academy and wouldn't be at risk from duels or assassination.

I didn't bother asking how she'd managed it. Like Tyrtho, the lieutenant commander in question was House Tivand, and so was the Commandant. But I was impressed with the forward thinking. I might have tried to do something similar, only my desire to get out into the greater galaxy was rather stronger than my fear of assassination or dueling.

Possibly because I was, once again, overconfident. I'd already been killed once and come back to life, and it hadn't been so bad. . . .

Aliadh and Calzik had volunteered for ship duty, asking for the same ship. They'd left House Jerrazis, and Aliadh had told me they would start their own House when they were senior enough. They were very unusual among Princes, totally devoted to each other from the very beginning, though of course there was no sexual component to their relationship. Princes are not only forbidden sexual liaisons among ourselves but programmed not to be able to indulge. We have our mind-programmed courtesans or other normal humans to take care of that.

Back then, I do not think I ever considered that what Aliadh and Calzik had might be love. I had no experience of what normal humans called love. I had never seen it or been taught anything about the concept by the priests in my childhood temple. There was sex, of course, which was done with inferiors for the fun of it. There were mutual assistance pacts, as between Princes of the same House. There were ties of obligation and service, such as a Master of Assassins owed to his or her Prince and to some lesser degree in return. There was loyalty, as given to the Empire, because anything else was unthinkable.

But love?

I did not know what love was then, but I think perhaps Aliadh and Calzik had something like it, some deep feeling that made them place each other's concerns even above their own. Somehow a small, remnant piece of basic humanity had lasted all through their candidacy: they had an instinctive ability to love, so that when they encountered each other, they fitted together in a way that made the two of them more than each could ever be on their own.

Back then, everyone thought they were weird. Some of the others even thought it was a kind of psychological game they were playing just to freak out everyone else and consequently give them an edge.

"So what are you going to do, Khemri?" asked Tyrtho. "You can't put off making a decision much longer."

I didn't answer. Instead I sent yet another message to the Imperial Mind.

:When am I going to get a special mission?:

I had expected to get back a typical "study hard and shut your face" message. But I got something else entirely different this time.

:Prince Khemri <<identifier>> promoted lieutenant
Imperial Navy effective immediate on graduation.
Transfer immediate Imperial Supply Station Arokh-Pipadh
<<identifier>> appointed aide Commodore Prince
Elzweko III <<identifier>> board INS *Zwaktuzh Dawn*
<<identifier>> inbound Kwanantil Nine eta 2315 CT
etd 0415 <<Sigil of the Imperial Mind>>:

I had a moment of total shock. My special mission was to become a secretary to a supply clerk?

The shock was quickly followed by an urgent inquiry to the Mind, which revealed that Commodore Elzweko was nearly two hundred years old, had been reborn only twice, had no significant decorations, and hadn't been promoted in sixty-eight years. Supply Station Arokh-Pipadh was in a very peaceful, very boring quadrant that had very few combat elements in it and so very little supplying to do.

Following lines of information, I was not greatly surprised to see that the newly appointed admiral commanding Rozaxra Domain, in which Arokh-Pipadh was one of the most minor outposts, was none other than Prince Jerrazis himself, very recently promoted to full admiral.

Further millisecond inquiry showed that Jerrazis had actually put in a request for my services to join him at his headquarters, and that normally I could have just refused and gone on my merry way. But then the Grand Admiral of the Imperial Fleet herself had promoted me and the Imperial Mind had confirmed the promotion, instantly signing me on for another year, whether I liked it or not. But the Mind had also changed the orders so that instead of going to Rozaxra Domain Headquarters, I was being sent to this supply outpost that, while in Rozaxra, wasn't directly under Admiral Jerrazis's command but instead came under the Supply Directorate on the Imperial Core.

I had no idea what this meant. All I knew was that I couldn't refuse. I'd just been suckered into another year in the Navy. Transferred to a supply station on an asteroid in the middle of nowhere, the move at least in part initiated by someone who had good reason to be my enemy.

"So what are you going to choose, Khemri?" repeated Tyrtho.

I picked up my fur hat and stuck it on my head, then reached for my boots before I answered.

"Yeah, what?" asked Aliadh.

"It seems," I replied as I stood up and brushed a nonexistent fleck off the ribbon of my Hero of the Empire medal, "that my services are so important to the Emperor that I have been promoted to lieutenant immediately."

I felt the sudden flurry of queries to the Imperial Mind, followed immediately by several looks of disbelief, one smile (from Tyrtho), and a sneer.

"So from this afternoon you can all call me sir," I said.

Before I collected more sneers, or perhaps a bunch of

busbies thrown at my head, I added, “And just to temper the blow of injustice for those of you who quite rightfully think that I shouldn’t have been promoted ahead of your good selves, I’m being sent straightaway, without graduation leave or any time off, to be the jumped-up secretary of a passed-over commodore in charge of a supply station in the middle of nowhere.”

9

WHILE I WAS not pleased to be caught up in what appeared to be a Jerrazis trap, or at best some awful sideline for a year, I was delighted to discover that the INS *Zwaktuzh Dawn* was an automated ship, crewed only by two Priests of the Aspect of the Rigorous Engineer and half a dozen mekbi service drones. Which meant that I could assume command instead of just be a passenger.

As I'd wanted a ship since basically forever, I immediately took advantage of this and swore myself into the command with the Imperial Mind, whose laconic confirmation couldn't match the excitement I felt.

:Prince Khemri <<identifier>> taking command INS *Zwaktuzh Dawn* <<identifier>><<date stamp>>:

The *Zwaktuzh Dawn* didn't hold up very well compared to

the ships of my childhood daydreams or the Prince Garikm sims. She wasn't much to look at, specification-wise or in actuality, being just a cargo hauler. Her hull was a hollowed-out piece of millennia-old space junk, a million-tonne spheroid of some long-extinct star-faring culture's industrially created material that was of a similar toughness to our best Mektek hulls. A relatively modern command-control-habitat module had been stuck into a tunnel bored into the top of the sphere, and a series of Bitek thrusters had been grown onto it around its equatorial ring.

The wormhole drive was the old Mektek one. While it had the advantage of needing far fewer priests than a Psitek drive, this was more than counterbalanced by the fact that it was considerably slower in wormhole transit; and even more significantly, if the Psitek drive failed, you lost only the priests, whereas a Mektek wormhole drive failure usually resulted in an antimatter explosion. On the bright side, according to Uncle Rerrunk, this was very unlikely to happen, and even if it did, the command and accommodation models would probably survive.

The ship was armed with a number of traveling turrets that moved on a railway system around the hull into different configurations as required, but I soon discovered that only half a dozen of the full fifty turrets were operational, and these six contained short-range interdiction guns, suitable just for intercepting low-grade missile or projectile attacks.

More usefully, there was a launch tunnel with a mothballed Kragor-class singleship inside. Though even older than the Academy's Jerragors, a Kragor-class singleship carried serious armament, and while it was mothballed, there was a full fit-out of stores for the ship aboard.

There was also plenty of room for the extra priests I had

collected. Getting promoted to lieutenant had earned me four more, this time two from the Aspect of the Joyful Companion and one each from Roving Seeker and the Wrathful Foe. I don't know where Haddad got them, or how they were vetted, but by the time it came to launch, the night of my graduation, they were all aboard, along with another dozen of Haddad's apprentice assassins who had mysteriously arrived aboard the *Zwaktuzh Dawn*, even though they must have got aboard well before I was informed by the Imperial Mind that I was going to be traveling on her.

I asked Haddad about this as Kwanantil Nine dwindled in the viewscreen of the bridge. I glanced once at what I suppose was my first real adult home, but I felt no twinges of homesickness or regret. I was glad to be out of the place. The only person I would miss on any level was Tyrtho, but that was tempered by the knowledge that at some time in the future we were far more likely to be rivals than allies. I might have to kill her, or be killed.

"My apprentices traveling in on the *Zwaktuzh* is simply a coincidence, Highness," replied Haddad. "This ship was the first available transport from Bereskizh Five, their temple. However, it has proved fortuitous, as I had tasked these apprentices with the training exercise of surveying the ship they came in on and ensuring it was secure for Your Highness. That has allowed us to board more swiftly and depart ahead of time."

"Are you sure you didn't know about my transfer in advance?" I asked again. I often felt not only that Haddad was smarter than I, which was of course not possible, but that he was also somehow leading me down a particular path, or at least could see a lot farther ahead than I could.

"No, Highness," replied Haddad.

"Well, we have three weeks of nothing much to do," I replied. "I think I shall retire to my quarters with my courtesans and masseur, while Lazkro and his chefs cook up a feast."

Haddad coughed.

"I regret that this will not be possible, Highness. I thought you were aware when you made the decision to command this vessel, rather than be a passenger, that this made it an on-duty activity for the duration, and consequently we have left the civilian component of your household behind, to join us by other transport in due course."

"What!" I shrieked. "You . . . you should have warned me!"

"I regret I did not, Highness," replied Haddad, his head bowed.

I smashed my fist into my hand, truly angry for a moment, before I wondered if my face was going red like Huzand's used to, and breathed my anger out. I didn't want to be that kind of Prince.

"Oh well, I suppose I'll find something else to occupy my time," I said.

"May I suggest dueling practice, Highness?" asked Haddad. "And I would recommend reactivating the singleship aboard, a process you will need to oversee personally."

Like I said, Haddad was always looking several steps ahead. I'm sure if I hadn't taken command of the ship, Haddad would have found some other way to leave my courtesans, cooks, and masseur behind.

He was right that I needed the dueling practice. We had lessons at the Academy, and I did the required practice, but lessons with Haddad were much more intense. He took over one of the empty holds, a space as big as an amphitheater, and had it rigged for rapid configuration of different habitats, terrains, and structures. Our duels ranged across all manner of possible fighting grounds and all the traditional weapons, like sword, pistol, and nerve-lash, and some of the stranger ones that Haddad said were sometimes chosen for advantage, like bolt-and-cable guns or roulette blasters, which, though apparently random, could be gamed.

I also worked with one of the ship's engineers and my own Aunt Viviax and Uncle Rerrunk activating the Kragor singleship. Many of its Mektek modules had to be replaced and its Bitek components regrown, and I learned more about singleship engineering from helping the three priests than I had from all the download lessons at the Academy.

Particularly since the official experiences I'd been imprinted with were sometimes simply wrong. I couldn't believe this at first and argued with the priests the first time it happened, but it was brought totally home when I was assisting with the armament load and tried to maneuver a kinetic sliver into its launcher the wrong way around, the overlay in my head completely at odds with the reality of the missile.

The mere fact that it was possible to load it completely the wrong way around, and that my imprinted knowledge was incorrect, shook me quite a lot. I wondered what other data that had been put in my head was false, and I resolved that in the future, I would always try to get practical, actual experience of my own to test the downloaded learning experiences.

I also spent time with Haddad talking about my immediate future, and what my strange promotion and posting actually meant.

"Prince Jerrazis very likely requested your transfer to his headquarters in order to have you assassinated or killed in a duel, in retribution for the death of Commandant Huzand," explained Haddad. "The Grand Admiral almost certainly owed Jerrazis a favor and promoted you to assist Jerrazis in this aim, removing the option you had of leaving the Navy. But then other influences came to bear. It is unclear what purpose, if any, the Imperial Mind has in shunting you from Rozaxra HQ to this supply station. Uncle Naljalk has calculated that the highest probabilities are roughly equal for two scenarios: one, that the Mind has placed you somewhere out of the way so that Jerrazis will forget about you; or two, that it has done so to facilitate your removal by Jerrazis."

"Great!" I muttered. "I get a boring job and I have to be extra-careful!"

"You will always have to be extracareful, Highness," said Haddad. "This is the life of a Prince."

"When you say the Mind might be facilitating my removal by Jerrazis, what exactly do you mean?" I asked. "The Emperor might want me dead?"

"While the Imperial Mind does express the will of the Emperor Hierself, it is not always the specific personal will of the Emperor," said Haddad. "Most of the time it simply adjudicates between the competing interests of Princes to achieve the best result for the Empire. It may be that in this relatively small interaction of Jerrazis revenge versus your future potential, it has come down on the side of Jerrazis. But it is equally possible it is trying to preserve you, or there may even be some other explanation."

I thought about that for a minute. I'd hoped that Huzand's death would get me out of this unearned Jerrazis enmity, but it seemed I'd attracted the negative attention of the boss man of that House himself. If he was really out to get me, and deployed the full assets of House Jerrazis, I didn't have a chance.

Unless I could somehow counterattack. I had an idea about that, though it was typically a not very practical or well-formed notion.

"Haddad, tell me what you know about how a Prince is chosen to be the next Emperor."

"I know very little, Highness," said Haddad. "The abdication is in less than a year. Three months before Abdication Day, a cohort of one thousand Princes will be announced as Imperial candidates at the Imperial Core. But what happens after that is a mystery. None of the candidates are ever seen again, but they are not recorded as permanently dead or missing, just listed as candidates forever after. One of them becomes the Emperor. It is not known what happens to the others, nor is it known who ascends to the Imperial Throne. Considerable analysis is always ordered by Princes at the beginning of a new reign to see if patterns of decision making or favoritism indicate the successful Prince of the thousand candidates. Sometimes particular Houses have been favored in new reigns, but I do not believe the analysis has ever been able to narrow down this sort of data to conclusively establish which particular candidate has ascended the throne."

"So I can't count on becoming the next Emperor," I said. "As a means of getting Jerrazis before he gets me."

"It would be best not to make any actual plans based on that eventuality," agreed Haddad, without apparent humor. "Given the disparity of experience and power between you and Jerrazis, Highness, perhaps the best course of action is simply to be on guard, present a small target . . . and continue with your dueling practice. There are two thousand three hundred and five members of the Jerrazis House who currently hold the rank of lieutenant or its equivalent in other services, and every one of these is a potential challenger. A duel is the most likely way that House Jerrazis will target you."

"Let's practice, then," I agreed.

At least it took my mind off my bleak future.

The future looked no less bleak as we made our fifth and final wormhole transition into the Arokh-Pipadh system. There was only the one wormhole exit and only one wormhole entrance, which was fairly unusual. Most systems had multiple wormhole exits and entrances. Arokh-Pipadh was really out of the way, and having only one pathway back to Imperial space made it feel even more like a trap to me.

The system itself was also very uninspiring. It had no planets as such, just a bunch of big asteroids and two broad bands of much smaller rocks and dust. Its star was blue, and too damned bright, even way out in the tenth orbit where the wormhole spat us out into local space.

I was sitting in the command seat of the Kragor singleship as we emerged, on the advice of Haddad. An armed and hostile reception committee was unlikely, but even at the 0.01 possibility calculated by Uncle Naljalk, that was enough for Haddad to be cautious.

As per standard procedure, the first thing I did was to connect to the Imperial Mind. At least that was the first thing I tried. But nothing happened.

:Haddad. No connection to the Mind! Are we being blocked?:

:No, Highness. It appears we are too remote and have

insufficient priests for the relay distance:

:Are there any hostiles in system? Do we have communication with the supply station? Why isn't there a guard ship on this wormhole exit?:

:No hostiles on ship scans or Psitek reach. We're deep in Imperial space, Highness. It is not unusual for the wormhole to be unguarded. Frekwo and Aleakh are sending to the station now, and will relay if we achieve comms:

:Should I launch?:

Of course, I just wanted to fly the Kragor. Even six months before, I would have just launched without asking for Haddad's advice. But I had learned a little caution. Day by day, in a small way, I was getting smarter.

:Strongly advise against launch, Highness. We have connection with the station . . . and they are now relaying to the Mind:

I could almost sense an undercurrent of relief in Haddad's mindspeech. Or maybe it was just an echo of my own feelings. After all, it could have been a big, nasty trap. Jerrazis could have had a ship waiting to take us out and, with no connection to the Mind, would probably have gotten away with it.

I guess I wasn't worth that much trouble.

We docked at the supply station twenty-six hours later. I'd managed to get one short, seriously high-G flight in the Kragor, which was fun. And I'd blown up a chunk of cometary rock with a kinetic sliver, ditto.

Now, as I waited for my welcoming interview with Commodore Elzweko in my newly fabricated field uniform with a lieutenant's green epaulettes and (unpowered) medal and wound badge, I internally said good-bye to all things fun.

The station was a metallic asteroid some two hundred kilometers long and eighty kilometers in diameter at its widest point, with the addition of an exterior layer of ice a few kilometers thick along two-thirds of its length. The ice had been removed in the last third in order to emplace various Imperial installations like the starship dock, though as per usual most of the base was bored deep into the asteroid itself.

The first thing I noticed on arrival was that the place stank, and I really mean stank. It had a stench that was worse than the Bitek sludge I'd fallen into at the Academy, and for a similar reason. The initial information I'd gotten from the Mind had failed to include the salient point that the Arokh-Pipadh Supply Station was a Bitek Resource Growth Center, not a general storage facility.

In other words, the whole place was a cross between a vast botanic garden, a zoo, and a compost pit. It smelled of fertilizer, animal excrement, and the Emperor knew what else. Most likely some kind of horrible alien shit.

And lucky me was going to be one of the two Princes in charge of the whole place, as I discovered when I delved further into the Mind. There was just the Commodore and myself, some three thousand priests from the Aspect of the Kindly Gardener and the Aspect of the Companion of Life, an equivalent number of mekbi drone workers, and a single company of mekbi troopers, which would undoubtedly come to be my particular responsibility, bringing an awesome load of additional administrative tasks and the danger of being tracked into future Marine assignments.

"Please enter, Highness," said the priest who opened the Commandant's door. He appeared to be wearing a kind of smock and was holding a spraying device, fortunately pointed at the ground. I looked at it carefully for a moment, wary of some Ditck attack, but I was connected to the Mind and witnessing, and Haddad was close to me. I went in. The priest turned aside and began to spray a large trefoil plant near the door with nothing more complex than water.

The Commodore's office smelled as well, but even more strongly, with good reason. It was a big room, but one half of it was occupied by a banked-up pile of earth in which there were numerous growing plants. There was also a pile of what could only be some form of animal manure.

The Commodore—and believe me, I checked his identity broadcast twice—was digging into the pile with a shovel. He was taller and broader than me; in fact he was considerably larger than most Princes, and as he was wearing only a pair of field uniform shorts, his impressive muscles were well displayed. He grunted as he lifted a shovel load of dung and flung it between a row of plants, then drove the shovel back into the pile and turned to me.

He smiled as I saluted, and waved several fingers in the air. Like many Princes of an older generation, he had a full beard and a long mustache, both of which had quite a lot of dirt caught in the yellow hair. At least I hoped it was dirt.

"Lieutenant Khemri," he said jovially. "Welcome! Welcome!"

I snapped my hand down.

"Thank you, sir. It's . . . uh . . . good to be here."

"Excellent! Excellent!" boomed Elzweko. "Nice to meet you. Now I suppose you'd best go straight on through."

He pointed to the far end of his vegetable patch or whatever it was. There were taller plants there, and even a luxuriant stand of bamboo. Looking closer, I saw a path made from wooden slats between the bamboo, a path that led into a darkness resistant to all my various visual faculties.

"I see," I said, even though I couldn't see.

I turned back to Haddad to ask him if he'd known about this all along. But he had gone, and so had the other priest.

"Hurry along, Lieutenant," said Elzweko. There was no cheer in his voice now.

Still I hesitated. Could this be a trap after all?

:Take the path through the bamboo Prince Khemri <<identifier>> it is our command <<Sigil of the Imperial Mind>>:

There was no arguing with that. Avoiding the spread dung, I clomped through the loose earth, got onto the path, and went into the darkness between the overarching strands of bamboo.

10

I FOUND MYSELF ONCE again in a bamboo forest, following a stream. After a few steps I was sure it was the same stream from the temple sanctum back on Kwanantil Nine and that this was the same bamboo forest, the same small bridge; and by this stage not unexpectedly, the Arch-Priest of the Aspect of the Emperor's Discerning Hand was waiting for me.

Morojal.

This time she didn't have a fishing pole, and instead of standing on the bridge, she was sitting on a folding chair by the stream. There was another chair next to her.

"Welcome, Prince Khemri," she said. "Come, sit by me."

I sat, while looking cautiously around.

"How can this place be here and at Kwanantil, Great-Aunt?" I asked in a very respectful tone of voice.

I'd learned a lot in the year since we'd first met.

"This sanctum is a vehicle that goes where it is needed to be," replied Morojal, which didn't really answer my question. How did it travel? How did it end up in the middle of an asteroid, or deep underground in a planet?

"You have been brought here to be offered an opportunity, Prince Khemri," continued Morojal.

After my discussion with Haddad about how a new Emperor was chosen, I thought I knew what was coming. Surely I must be one of the chosen thousand Imperial candidates due to disappear over the next year? Which was both exciting and unnerving. Exciting because *I could be the Emperor.* Unnerving because no one knew what happened to the 999 candidates who didn't make it. . . .

"A rare opportunity to serve the Empire," said Morojal, her calm voice lapping on the shores of my imagined promised land, where I had been elevated to the Imperial crown. "You are aware of the seven Imperial services?"

Her question snapped me out of my daydreaming.

"Uh, *seven*?" I asked. "I know of six. The Navy, Marines, Survey, Diplomatic Corps, Imperial Government, Colonial Government . . ."

"There is a seventh, secret service. It is called Adjustment. You have been selected to become an Adjuster."

So I wasn't an Imperial candidate after all. The Imperial crown in my imagination fell off my head and dissipated into nothing.

"What does that mean?" I asked grumpily. "What does an Adjuster do?"

"An Adjuster does what is required by the Imperial Mind

to maintain the balance of the Empire," said Morojal. "Usually this means interfering in the plans of other Princes, sometimes to assist them in their objective, sometimes to deny them the same. To enable Adjusters to do this, they have particular powers not granted to regular Princes. For example, more priests, better access and communication with the Mind, the ability to present as more than one identity to other Princes, and so forth."

"To what? To present as more than one identity? What does that mean?" I asked. I was deeply shocked. That meant the Imperial Mind really could lie to us, and not just in Haddad's "levels of veracity" way.

"When necessary, the Imperial Mind can . . . recalibrate the information you broadcast to other Princes, indicating that you are in fact a different Prince or hold a different rank that is more useful, and so on."

"But what about if it's to a Prince who already knows the Adjuster?"

"Adjusters are also permitted to change their physical appearance, unlike other Princes. Under controlled conditions."

"I never understood that," I muttered, thinking of my own slightly too long nose. "I mean, the tek is there. Why not just let us all look however we want?"

"Face sculpting allows surgeons—even priest-surgeons—to get far too close to a Prince's brain," replied Morojal. "That is why it is only allowed even to Adjusters in circumstances where the entire medical team's loyalty is both beyond question and under close observation."

"In case of what?"

"In case of the introduction of alien or enemy Psitek components into a Prince's brain," said Morojal. "Which might then invade other Princes or even the Imperial Mind."

"So even priests can't be trusted?"

"Not all the time," replied Morojal. "Most priests who are not relay communicators are not regularly in contact with the Imperial Mind, and some are only mentally inspected and adjusted on an annual or even less frequent basis. Loyalty conditioning breaks down. Things happen."

"That's for sure," I said feelingly. "Or they don't. Happen, that is."

"You are a very young Prince," said Morojal. "However, unlike many Princes who never bother to learn anything beyond satisfying their immediate desires or ambitions, you appear to be capable of wider thought. I think you have the capacity to be a much more significant Prince of the Empire, should you choose."

"What happens if I don't want to be an Adjuster?"

"Nothing," replied Morojal. "You go to work here at the Supply Station. In a few months, you will probably be assassinated, or die in something that appears to be an accident but will in fact have been engineered by Admiral Jerrazis, who *knows* that you permanently killed his protégé Huzand."

"What?" I yelped. "How does he know that?"

"He was informed," said Morojal, her eyes cold, the blue fluid roiling around and around inside her head.

"You told him. To bring pressure on me," I said. "To make me choose to be an Adjuster."

"Yes," agreed Morojal. "Partly. An Adjuster had been working at the Academy to remove Huzand in a way that would dishonor House Jerrazis. Assisting you on your path to becoming an Adjuster was a second objective. Elegantly, she used you to achieve both objectives."

"I suppose I don't really have a choice, then," I said, furious at being manipulated in this way.

"There is always a choice," said Morojal. "Even if the alternatives don't appear to be equal. In the interests of your making a fully informed choice, I should tell you that if you do volunteer for service in Adjustment, you must pass a graduation test."

"What test?" I asked. I was wondering who the secret Adjuster at the Academy was. Morojal had said "she," but this could be misdirection. Who could have made me more of a target for Huzand? I mean, more than I did myself?

"It is not an easy test," replied the arch-priest. "First, we transfer your consciousness to an unaugmented version of yourself."

A what? I thought.

I opened my mouth to ask a question, but Morojal didn't pause to let me speak.

"Then we put you in an obsolete one-person life capsule of inferior, copied-Imperial tek and drop you in some sparsely inhabited system well beyond the borders of the Empire. For a year, or thereabouts."

I shut my mouth with an audible click, nipping the end of my tongue.

"If you can make it back to the Empire, you will be returned to your augmented physicality and welcomed into Adjustment. In your case, we would probably also give you a Naval cover story and promote you to lieutenant commander. You might even get another medal. Questions?"

Questions? I had enough questions to keep the arch-priest busy for the next three days, but since I doubted I'd be allowed that time, I rapidly sorted them out into the top three or four.

"Does this happen straightaway? I mean, I get 'transferred'

into a . . . nonaugmented body . . . and *wham!* Off I go?"

"No. The transfer is immediate, but you would then have a period of training and orientation, to become used to the lack of augmentation and also to be familiarized with how ordinary humans live, or typically live, outside the Empire."

"What about the genetically programmed Bitek improvements I grew up with, and my natural Psitek ability?"

"The unaugmented version will have some of the viral programming of your early growth, but not all, as some sequences can be detected and identified. All the additional Bitek organs and glands that you have now will not be present. You will have whatever your latent Psitek ability was, which may be considerable in your case. You will have no internal Mektek shielding or reinforcement, of course, nor will you have the internal monitoring you are used to."

I shuddered at the prospect of losing all of this, and remembered the feeling I had when my arm was cut off. Could I deal with a whole year of being even more reduced? But if I didn't take on this graduation test, I would be shoveling shit, or at least watching shit being shoveled, for months before getting killed anyway, and now I could not be at all confident I would be reborn. Somehow I didn't think that Princes who knew about Adjustment but weren't Adjusters were allowed to wander about and potentially inform the Princely community about what was really going on.

"If I'm in an nonaugmented body, no one will know I'm a Prince," I said slowly. "How could I get anywhere near an Imperial post, or inside a temple?"

"Indeed," said Morojal. "I believe I told you this is a graduation *test*?"

"If I still have some Psitek, will I be able to communicate my real identity to priests?"

"If you're close enough," said Morojal. She paused and then added, "Perhaps."

"Great. No Mektek or Bitek ID and only maybe Psitek. It's impossible!"

"Is it?" asked Morojal. "Commodore Elzweko managed it, as have some forty-six others in the last twenty years."

Elzweko the manure spreader was an Adjuster? I made a mental note, once again, not to judge by first impressions.

"Yeah, but how many failed?"

"You do not need to know that number. It is not an impossible test. Merely very difficult. Now, I must ask you for your decision."

I rested my face in my hands and tried to think it through. Either way looked like a death sentence. But at least if I stayed a Prince, I'd be better equipped to handle whatever might happen. I mean, what if assassins tracked me down while I was in a nonaugmented body?

Surely it would be better to stay on the supply station? Maybe Haddad could think of something—

"I need a decision," said Morojal. "One way or another."

"I'll try out for Adjustment," I said. It just sounded more interesting than moving manure about while waiting to be assassinated, and at least there would be a chance, however slim, that I could stay alive and prosper.

"Good," said Morojal. "We would have been sorry to lose you at this point."

"But . . . but you said I could go back to the supply station. . . ."

"I lied," said Morojal. "That is part of the test. You mean

you didn't figure that out?"

I didn't answer. I hoped this would be taken to mean that of course I had it all figured out.

"So what happens now?" I asked.

Morojal pointed at the stream.

"All right," I said. I stood up, took off my clothes, and waded into the water that was not water, and once again I found myself falling into darkness lit by a multitude of beams of light.

When I returned to my body, or at least to *a* body, I was in total darkness, and as far as I could tell, I was alone. I felt incredibly weak, and it took an extreme effort to crawl out of—not the creek—but some sort of low bath full of a very salty fluid, which was irritating my eyes and mouth.

I collapsed onto the ground, which was cold and unrelenting, clearly a Mektek deck or installation floor. I lay there for quite a while, trying to stem the panic that I was barely keeping at bay. My body felt weird and clumsy, and my mind was slow and disoriented. I don't know how long I lay there, because I no longer had an internal clock to tell me the time.

My senses were also greatly reduced, but after a while I noticed that I could see the outline of the bath I had crawled out of and a thin strip of light some distance away at floor level. But that was as good as it got. I no longer had the capacity to shift my sight across a variable spectrum. I wasn't going to see any more unless I could find a source of light.

It was also very quiet, particularly inside my own head. I was used to being connected to the Mind, being able to query it, to pick up information, to view overlays about the world around me, to luxuriate in a constant flow of information, picking out whatever I wanted to know. Not to mention mentally chatting with Haddad and my other priests and fellow Princes . . .

All of that was gone. To all intents and purposes, I was no longer a Prince of the Empire.

It suddenly came home to me that perhaps I never would be again.

Slowly, I started to crawl toward the strip of light. At first, my muscles were so weak I could barely manage to drag my sorry self along the floor. I found myself trying to initiate Bitek glands that I no longer had, glands that would have provided stimulus to those pathetic muscles and glands that also helped a Prince overcome fear. Without the hormones and other infusions, I was thrown back to a primitive state, and I was faced by the two great fears that have always threatened humanity.

Fear of the unknown and its dread companion, fear of the dark.

A small sob caught in my throat. I swallowed it down, acutely aware of the sound it made. Until I knew where I was, and what threats I faced, I did not want to draw any attention. Particularly since I wasn't sure if I even had the strength to stand up, let alone defend myself.

Slowly, ever so slowly, I inched and wormed my way to the light. It seemed to recede as I approached, and I mourned the loss of all my target acquisition and ranging augmentation. I could not tell if the light was a weak one ten meters away or a powerful one at a much greater distance.

I struggled on and found myself growing stronger. It was as if my muscles were awakening from a long sleep. Eventually, I stopped crawling on my belly, and reaching above me to make sure I didn't hit my head, I stood up.

As I did so, the thin band of light suddenly expanded into a doorway of blinding brilliance. I shielded my face with my arms and half shut my eyes, as I no longer had the additional eyelids of a Prince, nor the systems that would compensate and adjust my vision.

Slowly, the brilliance paled, and I made out a humanoid shape in the doorway. It raised one hand in welcome and spoke. The voice sounded familiar, but I could not quite place it—nor match the voiceprint against internal records.

"You have done well to get so far, Khemri. Or as I will call you now, Khem."

"Khem?" I croaked. My voice sounded strange. Everything sounded strange, for it was no longer filtered and ordered as it had been.

"Khemri might be recognized as an Imperial name. Khem is suitably short and speaks of no particular origin."

I nodded. This made sense.

"Where am I?"

"Arokh-Pipadh," replied the figure, and at last I recognized the voice. It was Commodore Elzweko. "Deep inside, at the Adjustment facility that is hidden within the supply station."

Elzweko stepped through the doorway, and I peered at him, my eyes adapting very slowly to the light. He wasn't in any kind of Imperial uniform, instead wearing a stained and patched coat with a fur-lined hood, padded trousers, and knee-high boots with metal knee plates. He had a weapon on his belt, but it was in a closed holster, so I couldn't identify it.

He touched his hand to a panel on the wall, and the door closed behind him and lights came on overhead. I looked around to find myself in a large chamber of Mektek construction, typical of ship interior plating. The bath I had emerged from was no longer present, but a panel some three meters long and two meters wide was closing in the floor, marking the bath's exit.

There was nothing else in the room. I looked down at myself and saw that I was naked. Apart from that I looked exactly the same as I had before, at least as far as I could tell.

But I did not feel the same. I felt weak, and small, and incredibly vulnerable.

:Can you hear this?: asked Elzweko in mindspeech. It sounded distant, even though he was only a few meters away, but it was clear.

:Yes!:

I answered in a mental shout, like a man calling for a lifeline.

:Good. Your latent psychic power is excellent. Follow me:

I followed him to the other side of the room, where another door sprang open. That led to a corridor that gently curved for a hundred meters or so, ending in an airlock hatch that was covered in warning signs. Doubtless it also had an overlay that would have been visible in tekspace.

The signs read DO NOT ENTER. WORMHOLE DRIVE RADIATION HAZARD. EXTREME RISK CATEGORY EIGHT.

Category Eight meant instant death for ordinary humans, slow death for hybrids like the mekbi troopers, and very unpleasant but probably not terminal sickness for a Prince.

Elzweko waved to the door, and it rumbled back. He went into the airlock and turned to face me. I followed very slowly, still learning to move my weaker, slower body.

"It's not actually a Cat Eight risk, is it?" I asked. "Only now . . . it would kill me straightaway."

"No," rumbled Elzweko. "There is no Mektek wormhole

drive present. It is just to slow down the inquisitive. Tell me, when you were in your Princely body, would you have thought so much about that warning?"

"No," I replied. "No. I am suddenly all too aware of how easy it is to die."

"Good," said Elzweko. The door shut behind us, warning lights flashed red for several seconds, then the inner door whined as it began to open. "Keep that in mind. Stay behind me."

We exited the airlock, entering a guardroom. Six unusually equipped and strange-looking mekbi troopers watched us, not springing to attention. They were taller than any troopers I'd seen before, less thin waisted, and instead of energy projectors they carried short, gleaming tubes that were obviously weapons but not ones that I knew.

The tubes were pointing at us, which was also completely at odds with normality.

Elzweko made a complicated gesture with his hands and muttered something I didn't catch. My hearing was dull now and could not be turned up or down.

Whatever he said, combined with the gestures, made the troopers raise their weapons and stand aside. As we walked past, I tried to hear their Psitek chatter, but either there was nothing or I just couldn't pick it up.

In the corridor beyond the guard post, I asked Elzweko about the strange troopers and their mental silence. I was afraid that my inability to hear them meant that my natural Psitek was very weak indeed, and as it represented my only hope of getting into a temple sanctum, I really needed to know.

"They have limited neural capacity and all Psitek is blocked," he answered. "So they cannot be suborned or commanded. They answer only to certain visual and auditory stimuli or particular situations."

"And their weapons? I've never seen those tubes. . . ."

"They are shock tubes," said Elzweko. "Designed to immobilize a Prince's tek systems."

I thought about that as we walked on. Mekbi troopers that could fire at a Prince? With weapons specifically designed against Princes? I was beginning to realize that the test assignment might be only the beginning of the challenges that came with joining Adjustment.

"You understand why?" asked Elzweko.

"I can guess," I said slowly. "I do not think most Princes would like the idea of Adjustment. Nor the knowledge that a Prince can be . . . unmade. If a Prince were to learn of this, and come here to find evidence—"

"They would find no evidence," interrupted Elzweko. "But we would prefer to lose a suspicious Prince than this Adjustment headquarters. Now, we are about to come to your home for the next four months. You will not leave it, under any circumstances, without direct permission from myself or the Imperial Mind. Note that shock tubes will simply kill an unaugmented human. You understand?"

"Yes, sir."

A door slid back ahead of us, and we walked out onto a platform or balcony that was built into the side of a truly vast cavern. I could no longer tell exactly, but I visually estimated it as at least ten kilometers long, ten kilometers wide, and ten kilometers high. Lit by a small auxiliary sun high above, the vast space was quartered into four areas.

One was rich in plant life, a riot of both terrestrial and galactic trees, shrubs, and other forms, though here and there I also saw constructions of Bitek or Mektek origin, small huts or cabins, half hidden in what was basically a jungle.

The second quarter was a junkyard of crashed ships and vehicles, piled upon a desert landscape of red sand. I saw no complete ship, but there were hundreds of partial hulls, both Mektek and Bitek, mixed up with ship components; ground, air, and sea vehicles in various states of disarray; and many other bits and pieces that I could not even begin to identify from afar.

The third quarter was effected by a zero-G field—and other transformations—to create a cube of space. A partially complete orbital station hung there, a small one, perhaps three hundred meters in diameter and one hundred meters high. Construction vehicles floated near it, but there was no work going on.

The fourth quarter was directly below us, about five hundred meters down. It had been made to look like a planetary surface, one of cold tundra. There was ice and snow in abundance, and a large lake. On the shore of the lake there was a sprawling settlement of repurposed, grounded spacecraft and shanties of various materials set around an area of quick-set Bitek huts built in streets radiating out from a very large Mektek dome, probably the core of the original, ordered settlement that had succumbed to later, more careless development. Some distance away an orbital shuttle sat on a basic prefab runway, a long, straight line of dark Mektek surrounded by snow and ice.

Looking down at the frozen land below, I realized that I was very cold, that I could not regulate my temperature, and that I was still naked.

Elzweko opened a locker near the door and took out two contragrav harnesses and a pair of insulated coveralls with built-in undergarments, gloves, and a hood that were of an unfamiliar Bitek construction and definitely not Imperial issue. He handed the coveralls to me and put on one of the contragrav harnesses himself before handing me the other. I noticed that his was the standard Prince model, with the extra power supply. Mine was a lesser model, for servants and the like engaged in domestic activities, not even the heavy-duty mekbi trooper version.

I got dressed quickly, thankful for the warmth and the illusion of protection. I had never been all that fussed about clothes, or the absence of them, being secure in myself. Now, even though I knew that these coveralls wouldn't stop so much as an anesthetic dart, they felt like armor to me.

"Your harness has enough power to take you down," said Elzweko. "But not to come back up. You will be fetched when necessary."

"What am I going to do?" I asked.

"Learn how to be a normal human outside the Empire," said Elzweko. "And gain some basic skills that might serve you in the wider galaxy."

"You're going to teach me?" I asked as I put on the harness and checked it out.

"No," said Elzweko. "I am going to guide and observe and, if necessary and possible, save your skin."

"Save my skin?"

"We're dropping into a simulation, one that we try to make as real as we can," explained Elzweko. "You'll spend a month, or thereabouts, in each quadrant. First of all, you go to a typical Fringe settlement on a marginal world, where spacers pass through. If you survive that, we move on to the jungle, which has few humans but lots of inimical life. Then the junkyard, where you can learn more about the kind of tek you'll see outside the Empire, most of it copies of old Imperial tek, with a few Sad-Eye and Naknuk examples. There are sentients there too, with a more organized social structure that will present a challenge. Finally you spend four weeks working construction on the Feather, the orbital station, so you know about native zero-G as an ordinary human. A lot of places out in the galaxy don't have gravity control."

"A simulation?" I asked. "On what level?"

"On every level," said Elzweko gravely. "It starts about fifteen minutes after we land. We have ten thousand mind-programmed individuals down there, human, alien, various levels of sentience. But they are only mind-programmed to stay within the bounds, to not notice the artifice of their environment or tek they don't have, like our zero-G rigs. Otherwise they behave as they would behave if it were real."

"So I could die as easily here as I might out in my 'test,'" I said. "Some training."

Elzweko shrugged. "Train hard, fight easy. I'll be guiding you, like I said, and providing some backup, at least to begin with. But yes, you can easily get killed down there."

"Do I get a weapon before we start?" I asked. "And, uh, what's it called? A balance of negotiable units for obtaining goods and services?"

Princes never paid for anything. They requisitioned, and unless it was already under the aegis of another Prince or requisitioned for Imperial purposes, they got whatever they asked for.

"You mean money," said Elzweko. "Nope. No weapon, either."

"But I get fifteen minutes before the people . . . activate, or whatever you call starting the sim."

Elzweko smiled and nodded.

"Where do we land?"

"The spaceport. They'll think we came out of that orbiter, down from the station, recently arrived into the system."

I looked over the balcony. The spaceport was a good two kilometers from the dome and the other buildings. As a Prince I could run that in a couple of minutes. As an ordinary man, who still felt a bit uneasy in the knees . . . maybe I could do it in six or seven. That left about the same time to find a weapon, and items of value, or both.

I wished Haddad were with me. I could really do with his help. A flash of anger toward him ran through me because he wasn't at my side, where he belonged. But the anger faded quickly, as I had to concede that this current situation was beyond Haddad's control.

Then, rather surprisingly, I found myself wondering what would happen to Haddad and the rest of the household. Would they be reassigned if I didn't make it back from this training, or my test afterward?

It was an odd feeling, thinking about servants and their potential fate. Fortunately, it passed fairly quickly and I resumed concentrating on myself. After all, I was the one who was in the life-threatening situation.

"Ready to learn?" asked Elzweko. He waved his hand, and the railings of our platform retracted, so we stood on what was basically a diving platform.

"Yes," I said, and jumped.

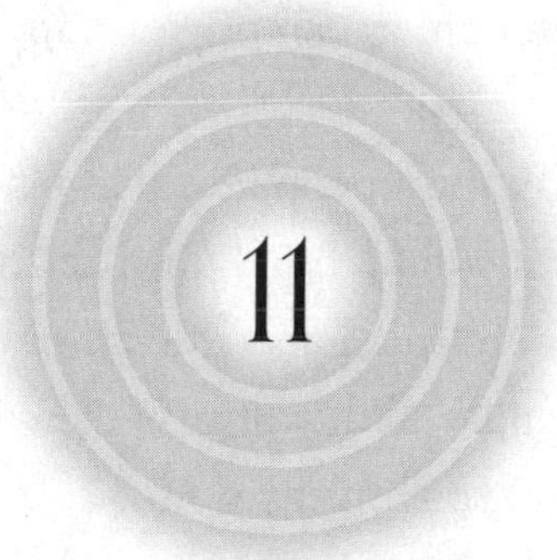

11

I LEARNED MY FIRST lesson very quickly indeed. I had thought myself quite smart to realize that I would need to take a weapon and valuables from one of the sim participants before they were activated, and I achieved that. I even made the run in from our landing spot in six minutes, so I was able to ransack the pockets of two people in the "main street" of the settlement and also take a sidearm from the holster of a man who was standing outside one of the dome buildings.

What I hadn't thought through was what would happen when the sim did start a few minutes later and the man whose weapon I'd taken let his hand fall on his holster, clearly an instinctive reaction. Finding it empty, he took only a moment after that to look around and see the new face in town, which happened to be me, because I was still standing in the street taking in the ambience.

I also had failed to take the basic precaution of putting the weapon out of sight. With Princely arrogance, I had simply checked it over once to see how it worked and then tucked it into my belt, where it was clearly visible. So the next thing the man saw was his own weapon, apparently pickpocketed in a moment of inattention.

As I would learn, most people in that place carried multiple weapons. He drew a stubby handgun from inside his coat and began to raise it toward me. I also drew the weapon I had taken, all the while being amazed that it wasn't already in my hand, my detuned reflexes now so absurdly slow.

I would have died then, permanently, if it had not been for Elzweko. Something boomed off to my right, there was a susurration of displaced air, and my attacker was flung backward and down to the muddy ground before he could fire. My own shot, a moment later, carved a line of molten dirt some distance behind where he'd been standing, indicating that I would have missed anyway.

Elzweko grabbed my arm then and hustled me away into a dark lane that ran between two buildings that had once, long ago, been spacecraft.

"Move!" he ordered. "He's got friends."

As we ran through the narrow, slushy streets, Elzweko told me that I had chosen a very bad target to rob. The dead man was a ship captain who had not only friends but a whole crew who were also his relatives.

"Think of it as if you had killed a Prince of an important House, with many allies," said Elzweko when we finally stopped. I had no idea where we were, apart from the fact that it was still in the jumbled shantytown and not among the more ordered extruded cabins near the center.

"What do I do, then?" I asked.

"Change your appearance," said Elzweko. "Keep that weapon hidden. Chances are that no one got a good look at you, or won't tell his crew anyway. Try to stay alive."

"How do I change—" I started to say, but Elzweko just smiled and suddenly shot up into the sky, the faint, disappearing whine of his contragrav harness sounding to me like the tromp of doom.

I thought about what he'd said for a second, then stripped the top half of my coveralls down and tore out the pale blue undershirt liner. I put this over the top of the white coveralls. Then I put the stolen gun inside a thigh pocket and checked out the "valuables" I'd stolen. They turned out to be a tin of emergency rations and some kind of entertainment device that lacked a power pack.

Fifteen minutes later, after some arrogant experimentation on my part almost ended in further disaster when I started out by ordering someone to give me information, I found a kind of market made of many small stalls near the central dome. There, I swapped the rations and the entertainer for a better disguise, a hooded fur coat that was probably real animal hide rather than extruded Bitek, with six orreks thrown in to close the deal. This was the currency used in the startown, amazingly in the form of actual physical hexagons of some kind of non-Imperial Bitek imprinted with Mektek fibers that held data indicating the value of the hexagon in "orreka rounds" or "orreks," which apparently was the money of some Fringe polity that was nearby. In the simulation, of course.

Six orreks were not enough to buy anything useful, I soon discovered. I considered theft and murder to get some more, but after my initial experience I concluded that it would not be wise.

Everyone in the startown was armed, it seemed, and many of them might well belong to family groups, crews, or gangs. I certainly didn't need any more enemies looking for me, presuming that the dead ship captain's crew were already doing so.

Which they were, as I soon discovered, overhearing two men and a woman asking the people walking ahead of me if they'd seen a young man in a one-piece white coverall carrying a Prang & Virl energy beam with blue Bitek grips. They answered in the negative, as did I—but I was trembling as I strode past, expecting at any moment to feel the sudden, savage pain of some impact or piercing shot in my back.

I spent the next three days constantly on the move, only one step ahead of a group I eventually observed to total two women and three men. This gave me quite a lot of time to think about the fact that even my smallest action among ordinary people would have consequences, possibly dire consequences, which was quite an alien concept for a Prince.

The startown was not very large, with only a few thousand inhabitants packed into an area the size of a middling Imperial battlecruiser, so it was difficult to avoid my pursuers.

Fortunately, no one seemed particularly inclined to help them. Most of the population of the startown were transients, ship crews passing through (or so they thought, doomed as they were to eternally repeat the simulation), leavened with those who had been left behind by their ships for various reasons and a very few who had chosen to stay on this frozen world.

All of them helped each other only if there was some reason to do so, either for commercial or emotional reasons. Like being family, or ship crew, which as far as I could tell meant much the same thing.

After a few false starts I found that I could earn sufficient orreks to pay for food and shelter simply by reactivating or doing minor repairs on old Imperial Bitek or Mektek, most of which was simply a matter of using my remaining Psitek abilities to turn the devices on. Again I almost made a bad mistake the first time I did this by not making enough of a show of looking at it, opening the case, and so on.

But I learned to disguise my abilities and to stay ahead of my pursuers, who weren't really sure who they were looking for, and to get on after a fashion with the various people in the startown.

In many ways, the most important thing I learned in that cold, falling-down settlement was to readjust my thinking. I had to act as if everyone else around me was a Prince, not an ordinary human. Furthermore, I had to force myself to slow down and always evaluate what was going on instead of just reacting, for my immediate reactions were as suspect as I was now in this environment.

It wasn't easy, and I was very glad when one afternoon Elzweko suddenly appeared in the doorway of the cargo container I was living in, which I paid three orreks a night for the privilege of doing so to one of the local bosses who controlled what was either a crew or a family, or some combination of the two.

"Don't shoot," said Elzweko as he twitched aside the blanket that served as a door.

I kept my handgun trained on him until he was inside and I was sure he was alone. It wasn't the Prang & Virl energy beam I'd stolen on my first day. I'd gotten rid of that long since. This one was a simple chemical powder weapon that fired a slug of some superdense metal.

"You changed your appearance pretty well," commented

Elzweko. He sat down on a control chair that had probably once graced a long-ago paid-off passenger liner.

"Yeah," I said. "Most of it's dirt."

I still had the fur coat, but the coveralls had gone the way of the energy beam, traded for a much less warm but much more ordinary two-piece shipsuit of the kind worn by most of the inhabitants of the startown. I'd also picked up a soft helmet liner with a visor of amber-colored translucent Bitek and was wearing that as well.

"It's been twenty-seven days," said Elzweko. "Time to go to the next quadrant. You can bring whatever you're carrying right now."

I was only carrying the handgun, and there was a knife in my boot. My spare ammunition, other clothing, a basic medikit, and some concentrated food and other stuff was all in a small pack. I had been thinking ahead, you see, and picking up useful items whenever I could.

I'd just made the mistake of not carrying all that stuff with me.

"I'm touching my pack with my foot," I said. "Does that count?"

"No," said Elzweko. "Come on out. The sim is stopped here."

I followed Elzweko out into the cold, shivering as the chill air instantly bit through my clothes, fur coat and all. I had learned very quickly that cold can kill a normal human, as I was now.

I had also just learned that it would be a good idea to have all the essentials of survival on my person. Not in a pack.

I shivered again, this time not so much from the cold.

Elzweko misunderstood my second shiver.

"You'll like the jungle," he said. "It's hot there."

I didn't like the jungle. It *was* hot, and very humid, and to make matters worse there were trace elements in the atmosphere that made the moisture slightly astringent. It wasn't dangerous by itself, or so I supposed, but I was glad of my visor. Pausing to wipe eyes was not a survival trait in this environment.

Elzweko didn't even bother to hang around at all this time. As soon as we landed in something that could be laughably called a clearing, he took off again.

"Watch out for the sto—"

"The what?" I called after him, but whatever he said was lost in the boom of my projectile weapon, as I had to open fire on something that swung down from one of the surrounding trees, coming straight at my head.

I ducked aside as it swung by, and I put another few rounds into its midsection, since the first few I'd put into what I thought was its head hadn't appeared to do anything. I wasn't sure if the follow-up had done anything either, because it continued its swing, up into the jungle canopy, where it was immediately lost to sight.

I didn't know what I'd seen, except that it was vaguely humanoid and the same color purple as the trunks of the enormous trees that surrounded me, holding up a vast canopy of intermediate plants that mostly blocked out the (artificial) sun and filtered the light to a kind of bluish haze.

On the way down I'd seen a larger clearing that might or might not have had a building or habitation of some kind in it. I hadn't seen it long enough to be sure. But I'd kept a careful eye on it and taken a rough bearing by the sun. The sun in the previous simulation quadrant had moved in a predictable fashion, so I was hoping that this one would too, though it was quite difficult to see through the canopy.

I figured if I could make it to the bigger clearing by nightfall, I might survive.

In previous times, before I was made mortal, I might have wasted a good ten minutes complaining and yelling abuse up at the sky. All that was gone now. Keeping my handgun ready in my right hand, I drew my knife from my boot, took a line from the sun, and set out through the dense undergrowth.

By nightfall, I was out of ammunition and had three deep scratches on my arm that felt bad, as if there was some poison in them. A vine had done it, or something I'd thought was a vine, before it lashed out and tried to draw me into a suddenly yawned open seedcase the size of a singleship.

But I reached the clearing. There was a building there, right in the middle. I ran for it as the sun went down, and with its absence came a darkness deeper than any I had ever experienced, accompanied by terrible noises from the jungle behind.

In a panic, I ran straight into a wall and almost knocked myself out. The few seconds of disorientation calmed me as I lay on the ground, panting. The jungle was behind me, the thrashing and squishing and slashing noises had not followed beyond its fringe, and the wall I had run into felt like the familiar Imperial Bitek of standard Naval construction.

Unable to see at all, I slowly felt my way along the wall. Eventually, I came to a doorframe. Following its rim up, along, and down, I came to a control unit. There was a socket for a Bitek analyzer, but I thought it might not be a good idea to put my finger in it. I was no longer unequivocally a Prince, and I remembered something about this body not having a typical

Prince genetic profile. If this was an Imperial building, it would likely have anti-intrusion measures in place.

Instead, I reached out with my diminished Psitek senses—and immediately encountered a Psitek lock that was represented in my mind by a three-dimensional hexagonal grid of multiple levels, with over a hundred playing pieces, already in various positions beyond their usual start. A gold piece flashed, awaiting my orders for it to move.

I groaned aloud, which was stupid, but I just couldn't help myself.

It was a puzzle lock, the game was unknown to me, and I had to beat the single-minded Bitek brain that lurked somewhere deep inside the building in order for it to open the door.

Something large whirred over my head. Without my augmented senses I had no idea how close it was, how large, or how dangerous it might be. I crouched lower against the door, listening, but the sound faded.

I focused on the game again, looking over the visualization. The game appeared to derive from something like chess, for there were a dozen different types of pieces, some of them present in multiples, some of them unique. As I looked them over, it dawned on me that they were all starships of various kinds, ranging from classic Mektek projectile and spheroid shapes of the very early Empire to the more artistic and varied forms of more recent times.

I even recognized some of the ships from my candidate days of gazing at gazetteers of Imperial vessels and from *The Achievements of Prince Garikm*. There were twenty Kwygrel singleships, fast and deadly, but unarmored; eight Jorgnul monitors, which were quite the reverse, being massively protected but slow; another eight ships that looked like they might be the progenitors of the Yaotin battleships I knew. . . .

The piece that was illuminated was not a ship I recognized, but I could guess its class from its shape. It was a scout vessel, made to seek out wormholes . . . and as I thought that, I saw faint lines emanating from the piece, cutting through the various levels of the playing board.

I ordered it to follow one of the lines, and it sped through a dozen hexagons, rising up six levels. More lines, revealing other wormholes, sprayed out from its passage. Some of them connected with enemy positions, and some led to my own pieces.

A silver battleship moved, and one of my singleships vanished in a flash of rainbow light.

The game was on! I forgot about the noises in the jungle, and the astringent moisture that clung to me, and my empty gun and all too short-bladed knife. Instead I calculated position and possibility, and moved my pieces as if they were a fleet and the future of the Empire depended on my command.

Sometime later, the final silver piece retreated into the darkness off the board, and I felt the door make the merest move away from my shoulder. I pushed, and it gave way before sliding aside.

A bright light flicked on, almost blinding me. It was followed a moment later by a terrifying cacophony from the jungle edge, the sound of something . . . or several thousand somethings . . . scrabbling over the bare earth of the clearing to race toward the light.

I ran inside, almost gibbering with panic, instinctively reaching out for anything that might be a rapid-close button, while my mind was stabbing out *close, close* Psitek instructions.

My fingers touched a panel, or maybe it was the Psitek, for the door slid shut. I backed away from it and held my knife ready as the door and the wall and the roof above boomed and rattled with the sound of the assault of hundreds or thousands of crazed creatures.

Then, as quickly as they had come, the assault ceased. With the door closed, the light that had drawn them was gone, and they went back into the night.

I looked around, blinking.

I was inside one big, empty room. Right in the middle there was a pack—my pack that Elzweko hadn't let me bring, which looked as if it still had everything in it, hopefully including the medikit that I needed for the poisonous scratches on my arm. I walked over to it suspiciously, keeping a wary eye out for some kind of trap.

There was a message cube on the bag. It glowed as I approached, so I backed off in case it wasn't really a message. But it didn't explode or anything. Instead the image of Elzweko rose up from it.

"Good work, Khem. This building will fold itself up fifteen minutes after sunrise. You will be killed by this process if you are still inside. It will restructure itself again fifteen minutes before dusk. But you'll have to beat the Bitek intelligence every time to get in. You've probably seen what gets attracted to the light here, so I've taken the liberty of removing the illuminator you had in your pack and given you a timer instead. Good luck."

12

To cut a long story short, I survived the jungle, albeit with several scarred welts on my arm from that poisonous vine and a few other thankfully minor injuries. I even got kind of used to the panicked departure in the morning, of waking up in a frenzy, thinking I'd missed the timer only to find it had an hour or more to go. Then there was the almost equal panic at the end of the day as I wrestled with the game, desperate to get inside.

One evening, I didn't win, so the door didn't open. I spent the whole night awake, constantly creeping about the building, moving along whenever it sounded like something was coming close.

But like I said, I made it even through that, gaining an even greater perception of the mortality of myself and other ordinary humans. Also I learned to really hate hot, humid environments and not being able to see in the dark.

I never did find out what it was that roamed in great packs through the night, though I learned that what they followed were the luminous eyes of some larger creature that moved in small groups. I only ever saw the clustered, shining eyes once, but I think they belonged to arachnids of some kind, judging from the wisps of web that they left behind.

Elzweko gave me a zero-G harness on the thirty-second day, just when I was starting to get a bit panicked about being left there, which was probably the intention. I'd learned the earlier lesson, too, and had everything I possessed on me, which of course Elzweko had anticipated, so when I was dumped into the third quadrant, the junkyard, it was to the new-arrival processing, where some newtlike quadrupedal aliens I'd never even heard described before confiscated everything I owned, though they called it "compulsory purchase," and gave me a credit chip in a finger ring that I could use for what they called a "grubstake," which was working capital.

The junkyard, despite appearances, was very highly organized. The aliens, who were from a world called something that came out like "Shube," and so were called Shubians by the human populace, held commerce in a very high regard. Everything had value to them and could be traded, including such basic necessities as being allowed to stay alive. A Shubian deathmaster came around every noon, and you could either pay to stay alive or die. Or fight the deathmaster, I suppose, though this seemed likely to be unprofitable since the Shubian deathmaster was nine feet tall, wore an armored suit, and carried a chopper with a blade the length of my arm.

But the Shubians were fair, which is why they gave everyone

who arrived on their asteroid (or what they thought was an asteroid) a grubstake based on whatever the visitor had on them. Then it was up to the new entrepreneur to turn that grubstake into sufficient funds to stay alive and prosper.

I would have been in trouble if that had been the first quadrant of my training, for I would almost certainly have tried to manage entirely on my own. But I had grown a little wiser from my experiences in the startown, and certainly wearier of my own company in the jungle, so I found a group of mostly humans—in that most of them were derived from some kind of old Earth stock, plus a few aliens—who had bought the rights to restore an ancient Imperial troop carrier, and I offered my services helping repair and reactivate its various components.

After demonstrating that I did in fact know something about several devices, and also surreptitiously using my Psitek to activate a Mektek-Bitek hybrid logic array they had thought completely defunct, I was given a contract.

All I had to do then was get along with a group of people who I still, at heart, thought were totally inferior and should do what I told them to do. Resisting this impulse took a lot of energy and thought, and one wearisome day a week later I told the two main shareholders in our little enterprise how I really regarded them.

Five minutes later I had a very bruised face and was looking for another contract or business opportunity, with only a few hours before the deathmaster's noontime visit and my cash reserves denuded by a penalty clause I hadn't noticed in my contract because I had arrogantly not bothered to read it all the way through.

But I had been picking up a few small odds and ends of Imperial tek while I'd been working on the troop ship. Things that the others thought were dead or burned out but I knew could be repaired, recharged, or reactivated.

One of them was a Mektek cutting beam that could be tuned to drill a hole as fine as a hair or fan out to burn a hand-sized hole in anything short of modern hull armor.

I took it over to a crew that was salvaging the contents of some kind of courier vessel fitted out with hundreds of small lockboxes, demonstrated what the beam could do to one of those locks, and was in business again.

This time, I kept my thoughts about my innate superiority to myself. I had to, because my jaw had swelled up so much I could barely talk.

Likely the enforced silence saved my life, and I got so used to the regular routine of not talking about how great I was, burning into lockboxes, and cataloging the contents that I was actually annoyed when Elzweko turned up to move me on to the next quadrant. Because it could only be worse.

"You like it here?" asked Elzweko as I slipped on the contragrav harness.

"Better than the jungle," I replied. "And the startown was too damned cold."

"Last one's easy," rumbled Elzweko. "Long as you don't get a hole in your suit, forget to tie on, or have a booster malfunction."

"I'll handle it," I said. I gave him the sneer I'd kept bottled up for the last few weeks, but he didn't notice.

"We'll stop by the launching platform to get you a suit," said Elzweko. "Do you have any preference what kind?"

I opened my mouth to say I didn't care what kind of suit, I was rated on all types, but shut it again to let my thought processes catch up.

"Yes," I replied. "I want to choose it, and test it first."

Elzweko smiled and gave a small nod of approval.

"Onward and upward," he said, and launched.

It was odd to be back up inside an Imperial ship, even just up on the viewing platform above the vast cavern that contained the sim. That sounds weird, I know, since all the simulated quadrants were also inside the ship. But they certainly didn't feel like it, and now I found myself feeling kind of out of place, so close to Imperial normality, but separate from it forever unless I could pass the test I was training for. Not for the first time, I regretted ever being picked out by the Arch-Priest Morojal.

Elzweko opened the locker that my original coveralls had come out of, but this time he let me walk inside. There were a dozen vacuum suits hanging along one wall. They were of many different types and origins, though all were old and well used.

"You have fifteen minutes," said Elzweko. "Choose wisely."

I ran along the row of suits, turning them on, which in each case took ten to fifteen seconds fumbling at switches and panels, save for the last one, which was a Naknuk Bitek suit that had its own rudimentary intelligence. I didn't even bother with that one, because it would have been made for a single user, recognizing its authorized wearer via a blood test or skin scrape.

But ten minutes later, as I ran through the test routines of the other suits and they all failed for one reason or another, I had to return to the Naknuk suit.

Naknuks basically spoke and wrote Imperial standard, because they only split off from the Empire four or five hundred years ago. I'd never been able to get the full story from the Imperial Mind, or from anyone else, but the available authorized version basically said that a whole House of about three thousand Princes had fled the Empire to set up a Bitek-only confederation way across the galaxy, shunning Psitek and Mektek. Of course, the Empire had kept growing, and the Naknuks hadn't gone as far as they might have, so in recent decades there had been numerous clashes along a border region that contained several thousand disputed systems.

So I could read the information that scrolled across the suit's external vision-skin without difficulty, but that only confirmed what I already suspected. The suit, which called itself Ekumatorozikilinee, was fully operational. But it would work only for its authorized wearer, one Star-Major Druzekh. Who was probably long since dead, as the suit was over two hundred years old.

"Three minutes," said Elzweko.

I ran the schematics again. The egg-sized Bitek brain that ran the suit was in a small hump at the back, just below the helmet neck rim. I bent close to it and focused my Psitek upon it, reaching out to make a connection.

It was like diving into warm mud, enfolding and closing over me, blocking out all exterior sensation and causing an intense feeling of claustrophobia that made my mind shriek to withdraw. But this was only a typical defense against Psitek intrusion, something I had encountered as a child in my Psitek lessons. I kept on, and broke through into the simple consciousness of the suit, impressing on it that I was its rightful owner, Star-Major Druzekh, replacing the genetic profiles it had for the Naknuk with my own.

I came back out of the suit's mind as Elzweko said, "Two minutes."

I sent Ekkie, as I had rechristened the suit, a command to open, and stepped inside. The suit closed up after me, the helmet visor slid shut, and various telltales glowed and flickered just above my eyes, displaying patterns of meaningful information. I'd have to work out what they were later, but for now, I could just interrogate Ekkie's small but literal mind directly. It said the suit was sealed for vacuum, and all systems were operational.

"Good," said Elzweko. "We go in through the topside airlock of the Feather, which is actually the connection for the zero-G projector; the sims are programmed not to use it. You have a meeting with your shift boss and will go straight into your first eight-hour shift. You ready?"

"Of course," I said. "I just can't wait."

The Feather, as the people in it called the orbital station, really wasn't that bad. It was well organized, so I didn't have to worry about people trying to kill me, or about inimical life-forms. And as long as Ekkie worked, it was comfortable enough, not too hot or too cold.

Sure, it was hard work, which didn't come naturally to me. Mektek construction in zero-G and vacuum isn't the easiest thing in the galaxy. I wondered why they didn't use automatons of some kind until I saw the first accident with a reaction unit explosion. People were a hell of a lot cheaper to replace than any kind of automaton.

The hardest part for me was sharing a dormitory. Luckily we had our own sealed sleeping tubes, which afforded some measure of privacy. It was all I could do to put up with the inferior life-forms around me when I was working, let alone having to listen to them or watch them in the off shift.

I usually went into my sleep capsule instead and studied technical manuals. It passed the time, though again it was much slower and more difficult than the direct implantation I was used to. Mind you, I did find it easier to work out when they were wrong. With the direct-experience stuff you always had to fight against what it was telling you, even when the evidence that it was wrong was staring you in the face. Like the kinetic sliver loading on the *Zwaktuzh Dawn*.

So I got used to the eight-hours-on, eight-hours-off shifts, and the constant repetition of simple tasks performed in a difficult environment, and I even got somewhat used to living among other humans, though I kept myself as apart as possible.

In fact I got so used to it, I stopped counting the days until it would be over, fully expecting that Elzweko would leave me there for at least a month. But after only three weeks or thereabouts I was paged to meet an incoming shuttle—at the topside airlock, the one the people in the sims couldn't even see. I went over there, still wearing Ekkie, and met Elzweko, who was wearing a sleek Imperial suit that made mine look like something from the pre-starflight era of old Earth.

He gestured for me to follow and led me through the airlock up into the internal ceiling of the training cavern.

"So you made it," said Elzweko as we climbed out into the familiar Imperial corridor.

"Yes, sir."

"You learned faster than some," remarked Elzweko. "Though of course a fair few never learn at all. You still need to be careful. Think about what a Prince would do . . . then do the opposite."

I nodded. It was good advice.

"We're sending you straight out," continued Elzweko. "There's a storehouse ahead; you've got thirty minutes to pick out whatever you can find and fit into a survival capsule. The capsule piggybacks on an automated courier, preprogrammed for at least ten wormhole transitions, straight out toward the Lokowhik rim. After ten transitions, it'll keep going until it drops you in the first system where it picks up enough tek transmissions to indicate a permanent presence of some kind, not just other passing ships."

"What if they're Sad-Eyes, or Deaders?" I asked. "Or Naknuk?"

"You'll be in Fringe space," replied Elzweko. "Not in the domain of any of our enemies. But it is possible you'll encounter an enemy ship. If it's Sad-Eyes, I suggest you overload the power plant on your capsule. Deaders don't take prisoners. Naknuks . . . Naknuks you might survive. There's nothing about you their Bitek will pick up as Imperial, and they do work with Fringe humans and the like. You got a Naknuk suit to work, I see. They'll respect that."

"Speaking of the suit, can I keep it?" I asked. I'd gotten used to Ekkie.

"You can take whatever you have on you, plus whatever you can pick up in the storeroom," said Elzweko. "Just go through that door and keep going. Good luck, Lieutenant Khemri. Or should I say Khem, a trader originally from the Raboghad system, a place of no particular account? You'll find some background details on yourself in your capsule's info system, by the way."

"Khem it is," I replied. I held my hand up, palm out, in the fashion I'd learned in the training sim, a salute apparently common among humans in the Fringe.

Elzweko returned it, spun on his heel, and went out a door that led to the Empire and everything I really wanted to get back to. I continued on into a long hall loaded with what looked like the flotsam and jetsam of a hundred worlds, laid out on and under three lines of tables that stretched the full hundred-meter length of the hall. At the far end, the outline of a door fluoresced green, then immediately turned yellow as I entered. I knew I must pass through it as soon as it turned red.

Thirty minutes later, that door slid shut behind me, and I walked down a ramp to a small, deep internal dock where a slim, nonstandard automated courier ship sat on a launching rail. A disturbingly small, five-meter-long, three-meter-diameter cylinder was mounted on the courier's back, the hatch on the end flipped open so I could see the acceleration couch inside.

This was my lifeboat capsule. I looked at it and wondered how I was going to survive the five weeks or so it would take to transit ten wormholes, let alone however long I'd be in space afterward.

I also wondered how I was going to stuff my loot inside. I'd taken Elzweko literally and brought with me everything useful I could find in the storehouse that I was able to carry.

All of it was very old, and mostly it was copied Imperial tek, and ancient copies at that, but all kept in good repair. I had managed to find:

A needlegun, a sidearm that shot slivers of ultradense metal at very high speed. It was a very effective weapon, limited in my case by the fact that I had only been able to find three compatible magazine/power packs, each loaded with a hundred needles.

A Bitek medical symbiote applicator and a living symbiote pack that still had three dormant symbiotes. Again, properly fed and watered, this could be a lifesaver for human or near-human patients. The symbiote could deal with a huge variety of diseases, poisons, and contaminants, and repair minor injuries or maintain life in the face of major ones.

A shipsuit made from a Mektek-Bitek composite somewhat

resistant to puncture and energy weapons. Ekkie, my vacuum suit, was pretty good armor against a variety of weapons, but I would probably need something more casual to wear when a full-on Bitek spacesuit that made me fifty centimeters taller and fifty centimeters wider was inappropriate. The shipsuit was probably Imperial Survey issue of a century ago, but all the insignia had been replaced with the faded badges of Five World Shipping, some kind of merchant company from a Fringe polity of, I guessed, five habitable worlds, part of the false background that had been established for me that I would have to study en route.

And last but probably not least, a stasis box of Bitek templates for a whole bunch of useful items. Though trickier to activate, as they took careful handling and attention, not to mention various raw materials, with the templates I could grow a reentry manta like the one I'd used before; a kind of watchdog; two types of reconnaissance flier (nocturnal and diurnal); and an aquatic rescue beast. It was unlikely I'd need to use all or even any of these, but I knew from my training that they were very valuable trade goods.

There were other items already in the survival capsule, a pretty standard load-out of rations, water, atmosphere-regeneration equipment, and some very basic and limited planetary survival gear. I checked through all of this and ran the diagnostics on the capsule. Like everything else I had, it was old but operational. As far as I could tell, it had been made on a Fringe world but was a direct copy of an Imperial Mektek model, with a few bits and pieces of Bitek here and there.

The capsule didn't have any modern communication devices, only ancient Mektek rayder, wide- and narrow-band, line-of-sight, and so on. But they worked and were active.

When I'd finally loaded everything in, done my checks, and clicked the restraints over the top of Ekkie, a toneless Mektek voice from the automated courier we were piggybacking on came through the rayder, warning me of imminent launch.

A minute later, the countdown began, and ten seconds after that the launch rail fired us out into space, on the first step of my voyage into the unknown.

It did not start well, as I discovered once again the limitations of my unaugmented body. The courier had gravity control, but it didn't or couldn't extend it to the capsule during launch. I was subjected to at least 7 G's and was immediately knocked out.

I came to when the courier lit up its own drive and finally did extend its field, adjusting everything back to a comfortable single gravity. My nose was blocked and there was salty fluid in my mouth. I had a moment of panic till I realized my nose was bleeding and that Ekkie's internal suit cilia were clamping my nose and suctioning the blood away.

Once the nosebleed was taken care of, I noticed that my head and back also ached, and as I tried to shift about to get comfortable, it was brought home to me again that this was going to be one long and tedious voyage.

The tedium was possibly the worst thing of all. Lying in a suit on an acceleration couch with barely enough room to stretch was bad enough, but there also just wasn't enough to do to keep my mind occupied. I was on edge for the first wormhole transition, constantly watching the shortsighted, slow-to-update scans that were all the capsule could manage, but the courier was so fast and small that the few times I picked up any other craft, we'd left them behind before they could do anything, even if they'd wanted to.

By the fifth transition, I didn't even bother watching the screens. I knew the courier would tell me if there was anything I needed to know.

By the ninth transition, I didn't even try to stay awake. I'd been a month inside my suit, inside the capsule. While I was in reasonable physical shape thanks to the suit's massaging cilia and my own exercise routines, mentally I was a mess. If there had been any drugs available to let me exit my own brain for a while, I would have taken them, but there was nothing of that kind aboard. There were painkillers, but they didn't help. All I could do was try to sleep, do my boring exercises, and attempt not to go over and over all the possible scenarios by which I could return to the Empire, get into a temple, enter the sanctum, and become who I was supposed to be instead of the pathetic remnant of a Prince whose greatest feat of the moment was doing two thousand toe curls in an hour.

Finally, the courier exited the tenth wormhole.

I woke with a start as the automated pilot suddenly spoke to me for the first time since we'd left, yanking me out of a dream where I was a Prince again, on the command deck of a ship that was a million times nicer than the interior of my crappy capsule.

"Destination reached. Inhabited world life signs positive. Ship traffic positive. In-system combat within mission parameters. Releasing capsule on mark. Ten . . . nine . . . eight . . ."

"Wait!" I shouted. What did "in-system combat within mission parameters" mean? I didn't want to be dropped into *any* in-system combat!

The automaton ignored my shouting.

"Five . . . four . . ."

I flailed at my restraints. I'd been sleeping with just the waist belt loosely fastened. Now I slapped the emergency Bitek foam button above my head. Nothing happened for a terrible second; then a grayish web sprayed out over my body, everywhere but my head. When the capsule left the courier's gravity field, it would be with a sudden deceleration, maybe even more than the 7 G's I'd experienced on our initial launch.

"Three . . . two . . . one . . . mark."

A massive hand came down on me, smashing me against the couch. The emergency web set fast, holding me there. The capsule flipped, or maybe I just got turned inside out.

Everything went black.

13

I CAME TO WITH the familiar sensation of cilia sucking away at my bloody nose and the unfamiliar beeping, wailing, and screeching of various alarm systems within the capsule. But the capsule was no longer decelerating, I was in free fall, and the restraint web was loosening. Woozily, I brushed the webs away, reached up, and snapped on the main control screen, a holographic cube that was supposed to appear in front of my face but had been made for someone shorter and defied all adjustment. It projected on top of my chest, so I had to crane my neck to get a proper look.

The warnings were all about dangerous objects on high-velocity paths that intersected our own current trajectory. It didn't take even my dimmed-down wits more than a second to work out that first of all they weren't fast enough or directed enough to be missiles or other projectiles and that as they had a wide variety of characteristics, what I was looking at was a whole bunch of fairly recent debris, some of it still venting atmosphere or other volatiles. In other words, I was tracking a rapidly expanding cloud composed of the remnants of a ship or ships after a spot of space combat.

We weren't in any imminent danger from the debris, so I immediately pointed and dragged and flicked my fingers over the holo to make the capsule sensors have a look for something or somethings that were much more important than the leftovers of war: I needed to know if there were any intact and maneuvering ships, or any power sources.

Not that the capsule had the sensor capacity to pick up an Imperial or other high-tek warship that wanted to stay hidden, but it should—eventually—find any of the usual sort of Fringe pirate or small polity vessel that might have been the cause of the recent fracas.

I waited what felt like a really long time before the display refreshed. No active ships came up, but there was a fading power source relatively nearby, in what appeared to scan as an almost motionless, but intact, hull. It was either a damaged ship or possibly one of the combatants attempting to stay quiet in a low-tek way.

Interestingly, the updated scan also showed power sources on a planet in the fourth orbit, both on the surface and in its immediate space. The cloud of debris lay between this planet and the wormhole entrance I'd come out of. There was also another, smaller cloud of debris somewhat farther out across the system from my position, most of the bits and pieces having a vector toward what the capsule guessed but could not confirm was a wormhole exit, though it very likely was, since there was a trail of wormhole-drive radiation typical of a ship or ships taking that exit.

All this suggested that the battle had taken place between an attacking force that had come out of the same wormhole I had and a defending force, probably from the planet, attempting to intercept the intruder. I'd thought that the more distant debris cloud might have been that intruder, but as the capsule built up a data image of the debris and found it likely to come from the same style of ship as the other defenders, I formed the opinion that the intruder hadn't given a rat's ring about the defense. It had come in, blown the shit out of them, and left. Quite possibly nothing would have happened if the defender had just avoided the intruder altogether.

This was merely my hypothesis, of course, based on very limited data. Later I would discover that it was, as you might expect, not entirely correct.

For the moment, I was most interested in the power source and the undamaged ship. The capsule had a pathetic propulsion system, a Mektek fusion thruster that could eventually wind up to a mighty 0.1 G. But even though it was slow, it would enable me to match velocity and dock with the target ship, provided it didn't start moving of its own accord.

There was no other visible traffic in range of my scan, and the capsule wasn't picking up any transmissions, lagged or otherwise, though there was a lot of suspicious noise from the planet that suggested some sort of ultra-broadband Mektek comm shield or scrambler was in use. I suspected there might be a bunch of point-to-point stuff going on as well, but the capsule was useless for intercepting those comms.

It was also pretty useless navigation-wise, but that was clearly part of my test. Once upon a time it would have had a navigation unit of some kind, and I could have worked out where I was from the type of star, the planet orbits and type, and so on. But there was nothing like that now.

I had no idea where I was, or how far away the nearest Imperial possession might be.

I thought about heading for the planet, but that dying ship was too close to resist. If I could get aboard and get its power plant fully operational, it might well be my first step back to the Empire and my real life.

Of course, it might also be a quick trip to oblivion, if the ship still had enough power for its targeting and weapons systems, and had a trigger-happy crew or automatics. While my capsule was obviously a lifeboat, that might not count for anything, depending on who had been fighting here.

I thought it was worth the risk.

My fingers flicked the holo. The capsule calculated an interception course. A faint, gentle pressure tickled at my stomach as the drive lit up. I let my head fall back and activated Ekkie's self-test as I reached over to extract my various weapons and place them in suitable outside pockets of the suit.

It took a couple of hours to reach the other ship. As we got closer, the data on it resolved. I looked at the images and information and discounted the crappy guess from the capsule's own ill-informed information store. It thought the ship was a clone of an Izhkhik-class battlecruiser, which even though it was six hundred years old would not be something to mess with. But I was sure the ship in question wasn't a warship, or at least it hadn't started out that way. It was about the same size as an Izhkhik, that was true, and it had a Bitek hull, but the similarities ended there.

This ship was, I thought, a cargo hauler that had had one of its main cargo bays ripped out in order to emplace what seemed to be some sort of very large missile launcher, and I mean *large*. I had only a partial scan, but the single projectile that was sitting in the launch bay stuck out a good fifty meters from the cargo bay doors (which were long gone), and that was probably just the actual warhead, some kind of penetrating fusion charge. The rest of the missile, hidden inside the cargo bay, was one big old fusion torch.

This was a strong hint that the ship wasn't built as a warship, because if that missile lit up anywhere within a few hundred thousand meters of the ship, the torch would wreak almost as much havoc on the firer as the fusion warhead would on whatever it hit.

No, this ship wasn't so much a missile launcher as a missile hauler. It would take the missile to a launching position, maneuver it out of the bay, and skedaddle before it actually fired. All of which would take forever, so the missile would only be useful for shooting at something static.

Not that they'd had any chance to do anything with it. There were some telltale scabs and blisters across most of the Bitek hull, marks I recognized from my Academy training. It was no wonder that the ship was pretty much dead in space—it had been hit with a relatively new and powerful Imperial weapon expressly developed to take out the personnel and systems of Bitek ships. Sometime in the past few hours, this basically civilian conversion had been hit with a Null-Space concussion wave that had instantly killed anything with a pulse that wasn't shielded. As the ship was essentially a living organism, and this kind of vessel didn't have backups of other tek, that meant both crew and ship systems were killed at the same time.

Except, I thought, I was still picking up a fading power supply. Any Bitek power source should have been knocked out instantly. I didn't know what this meant, but there was only one way to find out.

The ship had half a dozen typical Bitek envelopment docks. I simply piloted the capsule into the smallest opening in a line of what looked like huge pockmarks in the hull, fortunately on the opposite side from the Null-Space burn. Even so, I was a bit surprised when the hole closed behind us as the capsule settled into the landing cradle, and more surprised when ship cilia made it fast and the dock was repressurized, indicating not only that there was sufficient power but that some part of the ship's nervous system was still operating.

From the available evidence it looked like the Null-Space wave had only intersected with part of the ship, delivering a mortal wound if not an immediate death blow. But it was still dying, and I couldn't depend on its maintaining atmosphere. So I kept Ekkie sealed when I clambered out, needlegun in my right hand and a light beam in my left, to supplement the suit's headlights. It was dark in the dock, with only the emergency luminescents glowing here and there in the floor. I expected it would be darker still deeper inside the ship.

There was no gravity, but this kind of ship might not have had any gravity control anyway. Having just had a month in training on the Feather orbital station, I had no trouble with zero-G. Ekkie had grippers on its boots that quickly adapted to the Bitek surfaces of the ship, allowing me to walk without the stop-stick-swear-jerk-rebound motion common to zero-G movement with mismatched tactile aids.

It took me a few moments to overcome the airlock's natural reluctance to allow an unknown visitor aboard, but as it lacked a connection to a higher authority, I was able to use my Psitek to manipulate the nerve cluster. After some trial and error, it dilated and let me through, as did the inner door.

I found the first bodies floating on the other side of the lock. Half a dozen men and women and one nonhuman alien, though it was clearly an accepted part of the group. All of them were in suits, and some of the suits were heavily armored, but not the kind of armor that would do anything to stop a Null-Space compression wave. Every blood vessel in their bodies had exploded in an instant, so I was grateful that the suits were sealed. There were enough globules of Bitek nutrient/waste exchange fluid floating around as it was without the addition of human blood and other liquids.

The various weapons of the group were floating near them, indicating that they were probably a Marine boarding or defense party. But like the ship itself, they were clearly not professional military. Every one of them had a different kind of suit from a different manufacturer, and all the suits had been heavily personalized or repaired in nonstandard ways, as had the eclectic mix of weapons.

The only indication that they were even pseudomilitary was from the insignia that had been painted on the sides of helmets or chest plates. They all had a kind of winged animal in blue and red, evidently painted by an automaton from a stencil, and done very quickly, which pointed to them being part of a militia rather than regular forces.

I made my way through this cloud of bodies and started

checking the hatches on either side of the entrance chamber. I'd thought I might have a hard time finding my way to the bridge—it was a big ship and could be easy to get lost in—but I was helped by its essentially civilian nature. Unlike in a Naval craft, there were color-coded signs at every intersection, hatch, ladder, or ramp. I quickly worked out the code and, with it, the fastest route to the bridge.

There were a lot more bodies on the way, floating loose, strapped into seats and couches, even wedged into corners. Most of them were in armor with the stenciled winged animal insignia, and were not crew but the same kind of militia as at the airlock. There were so many that I guessed the ship had expected a boarding attack. It was too slow and ill equipped for any boarding to be done from it, unless it was an assault on something that didn't maneuver, like a station or a moonbase.

The bridge was sealed off, as I'd expected. The door nerve cluster took a bit more Psitek tickling than the outer airlock, but eventually it gave in and opened up. I entered cautiously, because the short entrance corridor ran through some kind of diamond-hard Bitek stone. I didn't recognize the material, so there was a chance that this might have shielded the occupants from the Null-Space wave.

Inside, I saw that the shielding had worked, but only to a degree. The six bridge crew hadn't died instantly. They'd had a minute or two before the massive hemorrhaging inside them had gotten too much for their suit medical systems. I noticed that two of the six had died out of their web cocoons, both of them with medikits in their hands but attached to other people. Surely they should have had the sense to use the paks themselves rather than trying to save others?

Not that it made any difference. But it is indicative of my Princely mind-set that back then I could not understand why anyone would sacrifice themselves for other people.

Most of the control panels were dead, liquid bubbling out of burst fluid transport lines and cracked vision-skins. But a couple of panels on the right-hand side of the bridge were still functioning to some degree, lending credence to my theory that the Null-Space concussion wave had hit only part of the ship with full force, and though a glancing hit was enough to kill everyone on board, it hadn't taken out all the Bitek systems.

After some quick tapping and plucking on the nerve strands of the surviving panels, I managed to get a status report up on the vision-skin. What I found was very encouraging. The vessel had two ship-hearts. The main one was dead, dead, dead, but the smaller, auxiliary heart was still working. Most of its output was being lost due to severed lines, and if that continued, it would effectively bleed to death. But if I could get to it quickly enough and reroute its fluid supplies, that would hold it for a while. Then, with power, I could repair or regrow enough of the command system, get at least some of the Bitek thrusters back online, and then . . .

My next steps would depend on how the situation changed. There might be more ships back on the planet I'd observed, already boosting out toward me. Others could come through the wormhole at any time.

I tried not to think about that as I hurried out of the control room and started down and rimward, heading to the auxiliary ship-heart. If I could save the heart, anything was possible. If I couldn't, there was always the capsule for a low-G getaway. It would at least take me to the planet, and I would be no worse off.

I was in a hurry, and so I was also a little careless. By the time I got to the auxiliary engineering space, I'd made my way among hundreds of floating, suited corpses. So I was rather surprised as the door ahead of me dilated and I saw a moving figure working by the side of the huge, pulsating orb of green and pink that was the ship-heart.

Whoever it was had their back to me, and I almost shot them, just as a precaution. But I stayed my hand, tapped the nerve cluster to make the door stay dilated, pressed myself against the wall, and keyed my external speakers.

"Attention!"

The suited figure started, and one hand went to a sidearm.

"Do not move or I will shoot" boomed out of my suit.

The right hand stopped and rested on the suit belt. I couldn't see what the person was doing with their left hand, which was in front and hidden.

"I have the ship-heart main nerve exposed," crackled a voice. A woman's voice, tense and aggressive. "I will explode the heart, pirate!"

I thought about the situation for a second. My needlegun might not penetrate her suit, which looked like a considerably newer Mektek model than most of those aboard. Even if it did, she might not die instantly and could trigger the heart to destruct.

Negotiation seemed called for at this point, even though negotiation goes against the grain for Princes.

14

"I'M NOT A pirate," I said. "I'm a survivor. You may turn your head slowly. I won't shoot. For now."

"I'm keeping my hand on the nerve; my fingers are around it. If you shoot, I'll clutch and it'll blow."

"I understand," I said. It would be very annoying to lose that ship-heart now. Belatedly I realized that the explosion might also kill or seriously wound me, a jolt of sudden fear making me speak faster. "We can work this out."

She turned her head. I couldn't see her face, as she kept her visor silvered. I twitched to make Ekkie turn my visor transparent. Part of my domination training was to fix the subject with my eyes. Not that they were what they'd once been. For instance, I could no longer do any mimetic imprinting via eye blinking, or accurately measure someone's pupil dilation to check if they were lying, or gauge minute shifts in blood flow and temperature and so on.

"I'm not a pirate," I repeated. "My ship got hit with something on wormhole emergence. I was the only one who got to a life capsule. This was the closest ship."

The woman's visor slowly cleared. I couldn't see much, as she had a breath mask covering her nose and mouth, but her eyes were a very dark blue, and very bright, in contrast to her skin, which was very pale.

"How . . . how do I know that's true?"

She spoke slowly, and with some effort. Either she was exhausted or in pain. Or both.

"If I was a pirate, you'd already be dead," I said.

"Point," she replied. "I guess . . . it's too early for the pirates to be here, anyway. What . . . what was your ship?"

"Merchant vessel *Zimit*, Five Worlds Shipping," I lied, using the fake background name Elzweko had left for me in the capsule's information system. "What do you mean, 'it's too early for the pirates to be here'? Who blew your ship and the others?"

"An Imperial!" She said it like it was a curse. "It sliced through the wormhole picket, then the Fleet, and took out the exit wormhole picket on its way out. Nineteen ships destroyed in less than ten hours . . . and not a thing we could do."

"How do you know it was an Imperial ship? I thought you said pirates."

"What else could have done that kind of damage? Besides, the Prince told us who she was, and that she would destroy us."

Not exactly standard Imperial tactics, but quite plausible. I supposed there must be some reason the Imperial Mind or even just some senior Naval officer wanted these Fringe dwellers destroyed. But it was odd the Prince's ship hadn't stayed to complete the task.

"So what do pirates have to do with it?"

"The pirates come a day or two later," she said. "This has all happened before. Twice. Four years ago, and five years before that. Exactly the same thing. An Imperial ship clears the way, and then the pirates come in and loot everything they can before the Confederation fleet can get here."

"The Confederation fleet?" I was feeling a bit short on data here. There were lots of Fringe polities that called themselves federations, so this wasn't a clue as to my location. But why would a Prince do favors for pirates?

"We joined the Confederation after the first raid," said the woman. She didn't sound too good, and I noticed there was now pink foam leaking around the corners of her mask, indicating internal bleeding in her lungs. "It helped, the second time. At least the Confed fleet made the pirates leave without finishing the job. This time . . . I'm guessing there'll be even more pirates. The Confeds might not think we're worth the effort to save a second time. . . ."

"You're wounded," I said as I thought about salvaging her for future use. She was working on the ship-heart, so presumably was a Bitek engineer or had some training that could be useful to me.

"I'm *dead*," said the woman with a bitter laugh. Pink froth bubbled out around the mask, more than could be whisked away. Her voice was almost lost as she drowned in her own blood. "I was out of the hull, inside the comm-beam mast . . . but I still got the edge of whatever . . . whatever hit the ship."

"But you're still trying to save the ship-heart," I remarked. "Why?"

A coughing gargle answered my question, and the woman's helmet slumped forward. I tensed for an explosion that did not come, then ran to her, quickly grasping her fingers to uncurl them from the tangle of nerves in the uncovered control ganglion.

The medical symbiote and applicator was in my thigh pocket, which opened at my command. I spent a few seconds looking over the woman's suit for an appropriate port but didn't find one, so instead I unsealed her forearm. Blood misted out in a cloud of tiny droplets. I ripped the tab on the symbiote and loaded it into the applicator. For a moment it looked like the symbiote might be senescent, but after a few seconds the wrapper turned gold. I applied the applicator to the skin of the woman; it bonded, and the symbiote launched itself into her bloodstream, there to replicate and do good works.

I hoped it was in time, and that she was human enough for the symbiote to work. She looked human, but appearances can be deceptive.

The applicator shivered in my hand, and the square of display skin glowed with a demand for additional biological materials that the symbiote needed in order to effect repairs. I went back out and found the nearest corpse, dragged it down, and connected the feeder tube from the applicator.

I'd learned enough about humans in my training months to turn the woman's head to the side, so when . . . or if . . . she regained consciousness, she wouldn't see her former shipmate being scavenged in order to keep her alive.

Then I turned my attention to the ship-heart. The woman had already clamped off most of the outputs, keeping the fluid levels high. I quickly ran around and sealed off the ones that were still connected and then started the heart's self-check and repair routines. Interestingly, this heart had a Mektek restarter in place of what originally would have been a purely Bitek system. Like the ship-heart itself, it was a copy of old Imperial tek, and so was very responsive to my Psitek commands. I told it to stimulate the ship-heart and accelerate the process of self-repair.

I followed this up by encouraging all the auxiliary automatic repair nodules and shiplouse hatcheries to their highest efforts, which was not easy, since I had to get close for my Psitek to work and most of them were in service conduits in the floor, walls, and ceiling. Many were simply inaccessible while I was wearing Ekkie, but I wasn't going to take off my suit. The ship was maintaining a breathable atmosphere, but there was no knowing when that might fail. In the end I worked out a leapfrog system where I spoke to one nodule and ordered it to work on the next nodule in line, and so on.

An hour later, two important things happened.

The first was the appearance of an operational shiplouse, a Bitek drone assistant the size of my hand. It came scuttling in on its thousand legs from one of the inaccessible hatcheries and immediately went to work rebuilding a nerve complex with its tissue spinner. A ship like this would usually have hundreds of shiplice at work, but they had all been killed and most of the hatcheries destroyed, so even one was a good sign. A working hatchery could make a few every hour, given enough organic material and some inorganics, and there was no shortage of either on board now. Bodies, suits, and weapons would all be recycled in time.

The second important thing was that the woman woke up. I had removed the corpse already, as soon as the symbiote no longer needed additional material, and moved the woman to an acceleration couch in the crew alcove near the ship-heart. The symbiote had reported via the applicator's image skin that she would live but would need to rest for some days while the symbiote continued its work. I was disappointed by that, since she would not be able to do much if any work on the ship, but provided we were left alone, there would be plenty to do even after she recovered.

I was not thinking of her as a person, you see, even despite my months in training with normal humans. Caught up in an emergency, I had reverted to type. She was just another mind-programmed asset, or at least that's how I thought of her. At that stage.

"What's your name?"

I started at her voice, something that wouldn't have happened while I was still a proper Prince. I would have heard the difference in her breathing seconds before, a change that announced consciousness.

I left the command ganglion I had been studying and went over to her. She had opened her visor and removed the mask. Now I could see her entire face. She was still pale from loss of blood, but I thought that she could have had a place among my courtesans, for she had an unusual beauty. Most of it was in her eyes, which though weary were still bright and had the hint of a smile in them, though it was a sardonic smile.

She was also younger than I had thought, or was the recipient of very effective anti-aging treatments. We were probably of a similar age, somewhere around nineteen Earth-standard years, though of course my chronological age was somewhat misleading, as I had so much directly downloaded training and experience.

"My name is Khem. What are you called?"

"I get called lots of things," said the woman. The girl. "But my name is Raine."

"Rain?" I asked. "As in planetary precipitation of liquid?"

"Yep. Only with an *e*. *R-a-i-n-e*."

"Raine," I said it again, grappling with the feel of it in the corners of my mouth. Like a lot of names outside the Empire, it felt peculiar to say and sounded even stranger to my ears.

"Yes, I know it's a stupid name." Raine sighed. "You don't have to carry on about it."

"Why is it a stupid name?" I asked. I was curious. Princes' names were generated by priests according to a particular formula; there could only be one Prince who held a given name.

"I said enough already!" cried Raine. "I get it."

I shrugged. Ordinary humans were puzzling creatures. At least the mind-programmed ones just did what they were told, no more and no less. The others were unpredictable, more unpredictable than my fellow Princes. But I didn't intend to stay among Fringe humans long enough to learn more about their quirks and foibles. Which meant getting on with fixing this ship.

"You are a Bitek engineer?" I asked.

"Me?" replied Raine. "No. I'm a communication specialist. Well, a student. Second year."

"Ah," I said. This was disappointing. A communication specialist wasn't much use to me. "But you were working on this ship-heart. You'd stopped some of its fluid loss."

It was Raine's turn to shrug, an action that obviously hurt. She gasped and her face went even whiter before she continued. "I've done the damage-control course, and I had a reserve tour on the old *Heffalurp* last year. One of the exercises was to bring the secondary ship-heart up."

"The *Heffalurp*?" I asked. "Oh, that is the name of this ship. What system are we in, by the way?"

"What *system*?"

"I'm not an astrogator," I said patiently. "We did a lot of transits quickly, the last week or so. I don't know which one we were up to when we got hit."

"This is Kharalcha," replied Raine. She spoke slowly and with effort. I looked at the vision-skin on the applicator. The symbiote wanted her to sleep now, to conserve energy.

"It isn't much," she continued, her eyes drooping shut. "But it's home."

Not for much longer, I thought as I turned back to my work. Not if she was right about the pirates coming in.

Home. That was a curious concept I'd learned a little bit about from the humans in the Adjuster training simulation. Something to do with a place, a family, and accepted status in a particular society. Not having a family, I supposed the Empire was my home, but not any particular part of it, nor with any particular people. Though it would be very helpful to have Haddad and my household back. Particularly if there was the possibility of pirates turning up.

This line of thought led me back up to the bridge. There were shiplice working there too now, another positive sign. I caught two of them and, using my Psitek, prioritized them to work on the ship's long-range scanners. The actual sensory nodes appeared to be undamaged, missed by the concussion wave since they were basically feelers that stuck out some six hundred meters from the hull. But all the nerve lines between the feelers and the bridge were dead and had to be restrung.

I didn't want to wait that long to get scan data, so I returned to the dock and jury-rigged a system that would repeat the scans from the capsule to Ekkie, with particular attention to the wormhole. If it looked like something was about to emerge, at least I would know about it.

I also took the opportunity to eat from the capsule stores and have a drink that wasn't recycled water from Ekkie's internal reservoir. It was still recycled by the capsule, but it tasted better. I was still getting used to being tired and hungry. It had never affected me as much before. I thought I had been tired at the Academy, but in the training simulation and now, I had found out that the weariness of the ordinary human was a much harsher thing than the lassitude of a Prince who can tweak their mind and body chemistry at will.

On the way back to the auxiliary ship-heart, I stopped by the wormhole-drive control room—and got a very nasty shock. I'd expected this craft to have a Mektek wormhole drive, because there was no Bitek equivalent and only the Sad-Eyes and the Empire had Psitek wormhole engines. That being the case, it should still be operational, the concussion wave only eliminating biological organisms.

But there was no wormhole drive. The *Heffalurp* just had a great big hole where a drive used to be. Somewhere along the line, the drive had been ripped out and the space turned into a cargo hold. The *Heffalurp* was a purely interplanetary, not interstellar, craft. I had been wasting my time all along.

Furious, I slammed my fist into the wall, forgetting that my hand was no longer as tough as a ship hull and I wasn't in Imperial-grade armor. Ekkie protested that I had bruised its gauntlet, and inside, my fingers ached. The pain brought back the wise words of Commodore Elzweko.

"Think about what a Prince would do . . . then do the opposite."

Smashing the wall in fury was a Prince thing, and very stupid in my current circumstances. Reacting in anger would not help me. I had to assess the situation and plan ahead. Sure, the ship had no wormhole drive, so I couldn't use it to start back toward the Empire—wherever that was.

But maybe there were interstellar ships on the planet, or at its station. If I could salvage the *Heffalurp* and get it back to Kharalcha Four, maybe I could swap it for a smaller, faster, wormhole-capable ship.

That sounded like a sensible plan. At least to someone like me, who had no experience in dealing with small planetary governments that were in fear for their very existence and would hang on to ships, any ships, like glue.

Feeling slightly happier, I had just reached the auxiliary ship-heart, noted that Raine was still asleep, and was about to resume repair work when Ekkie brought a relayed message to my attention.

The wormhole's energy signature was increasing. Something was going to come out of it very soon. Within ninety minutes. Given what Raine told me had happened before, it seemed very likely that what would emerge would be the pirate fleet, and we would be a bonus prize ripe to be picked up en route to the sack of the planet.

I must have cursed aloud, because Raine woke up.

"What is it?" she asked, stress in her voice.

"The entry wormhole is radiating," I said.

"The pirates," said Raine.

"Probably," I agreed. I looked at the vision-skin that was

reporting the ship-heart status. It was improving, but there was no chance of reaching operational power within the next six to eight hours, and whatever was coming through the wormhole would be able to strike or even board us long before that.

Raine followed my glance.

"How is the ship-heart?"

"Eighteen percent," I replied. "Not enough to run the command systems, even if the thrusters are working."

It had been a worthwhile gamble, but it was not going to pay off. It was time to cut my losses. I looked at Raine, or more particularly at the rectangular box on her arm.

"I'm going to have to take the symbiote applicator," I said calmly, going over to her and removing the box in one swift motion. "You can keep the symbiote, of course."

"You're going to evacuate? In your capsule?"

"Of course," I said. "What else can I do? Stay here and be killed or captured?"

Those were now Raine's options, of course, since I wasn't offering to take her with me. But she had a different idea.

"Help me fire the missile," she said.

I stared down at those dark-blue eyes and wondered how the symbiote had let her brain chemistry get so out of whack.

"The fusion torch?" I asked. "It would never hit anything, at least anything that can maneuver. Waste of time."

"It can hit the wormhole exit," said Raine. "That's what it's for."

I tilted my head to one side, at least as far as Ekkie's rather large helmet interior permitted, thinking about that. The wormhole exit wasn't something that you could hit, at least physically. It was a kind of point of possibility between space and

Null-Space that didn't mean anything until particular energies were applied to make it connect to some other potentiality with similar characteristics.

But I knew Raine wasn't being literal. I'd obviously been mistaken about the missile's warhead. It must be what was colloquially known as a "stopper," and it didn't need to hit the wormhole exit as such. It just needed to detonate its peculiar energy payload within a certain radius of a wormhole that was in the process of opening.

If it did so, that wormhole would lose its potentiality, at least for a while. In other words, it would be shut off, and no one could get through for the weeks or sometimes months it would take for the effect to dissipate.

It wasn't a weapon the Empire used very often, if at all, and the strategy behind it was dubious. Closing a wormhole cut off potential help as well as enemies, and in any case, most systems usually had more than one entry wormhole. But I supposed in this case, with the system's entire Navy wiped out and the near certainty of imminent enemy arrival through that particular wormhole, it made sense.

"It's a stopper," I said.

"You got it. And I have the launch codes."

"It would have to be fired soon," I said, working it out. "No time to move it out of the ship. Its torch will finish off what the conc— the Imperial weapon did. And it will kill anyone left on board."

"How big's your capsule?"

"It's a solo module."

"But you *could* squeeze two people in, right? For a short transit at least?"

I supposed it was possible, and it slowly dawned on me that she expected me to take her along. She hadn't even caught on that a minute or so before, I had planned to leave her behind. Once again I was reminded that I was thinking like a Prince and thinking of her as a programmed servant or something equally disposable.

How would it look if I turned up on Kharalcha and they knew I had left one of their own behind? Particularly if she did manage to fire the missile and close the wormhole? I had been weighing up her potential use all wrong. It was not her immediate technical skills that were valuable; it was the potential debt her society might owe me if I returned her. After all, I would no longer have the salvaged *Heffalurp* to trade.

And how much would the planetary government owe me if I closed the wormhole and gave them a breathing space to prepare against the pirates?

"So how about it?" asked Raine as she levered herself up. "We prep the missile to fire in thirty or so and bug out in your capsule?"

"All right," I said.

She surprised me by taking my hand and shaking it. I almost drew my needlegun with my left hand but managed to desist. I'd met a few hand shakers in training.

"Welcome to the Kharalcha Space Forces," said Raine, and smiled.

I FROWNED. I'D NEVER said I would enlist in what must be a largely defunct militia.

"It's a joke," explained Raine. "Uh, meant to ease the tension of a stressful situation. You know, you laugh because otherwise you'd cry?"

"Oh, right," I said. Princes made jokes—jokes were for equals. I was still having difficulty adjusting to my changed situation. "Can you walk?"

There was only a narrow window of opportunity to launch the missile.

"I think so," replied Raine. She clapped a hand on my shoulder and stood up, remaining slightly stooped. Then she slid a foot out and took a step, and then another. I found myself walking by her side, partially supporting her weight. It made for slow progress, and I knew that I should leave her to make her own way and speed ahead to the missile bay.

But for some reason I didn't.

The missile bay control room must have been a hastily rigged lash-up of Mektek and Bitek modules even before the concussion wave took out its Bitek components. I set Raine down on the command chair, where she tried to get a status report on the vision-skin, while I went and caught as many shiplice as I could find.

Raine watched as I dropped an armful of the creatures in the room and they scuttled into various access ports.

"How did you program them?" she asked curiously. "I thought all the louse-coding wands would be as dead as everything else."

"Uh, I've got my own," I said hastily, patting one of Ekkie's pockets. "Just had to recalibrate. Is that control array working?"

Raine forgot the shiplice and turned back to the Mektek control panel. It was lit up now, drawing power from the ship-heart.

"It's functioning on the tertiary backup level, without a holo," she said, drawing with her finger on the emergency input slate that had slid out when the holographic controls failed. "But the missile isn't responding."

"The lice need to reweave the nerve lines," I said.

Raine nodded. Her suited fingers danced on the input.

"I've loaded the launch solution. It'll begin to count down as soon as communication is established with the missile. Is there . . . is there any more activity at the wormhole?"

I checked Ekkie's internal vision-skin. There had been no further report from the module. I couldn't interrogate further as the comms were all one-way. I hadn't had time to rig up anything fancier.

"Nothing yet," I said. "The last scan I got, it looked like a little time till something comes through."

"I guess we just hope that the shiplice work fast," said Raine.

"If you've set the launch, we could go now," I suggested. "Get a head start away from that fusion torch."

Raine didn't answer immediately. Then she turned to look at me, fixing her eyes on my face. She blinked a couple of times. I found her gaze weirdly fascinating and wondered if the blinking was some kind of hypnotic domination effect, and cast my own eyes down. I was tempted to reach out with my Psitek, but if she had even a trace of psychic ability herself, she would feel it, and that might complicate matters far more than I would like.

"No, I . . . I have to be sure the missile is okay," she said. "It's my duty as the only surviving officer. I'll . . . I'll wait till the nerve lines are up and the missile reports green. But if you want to leave now, Khem . . . I understand."

I did want to leave. But the calculation I'd made before hadn't changed. I needed to bring Raine with me to gain credit with the Kharalchans, and doubtless even more credit if we managed to stop the wormhole and thus the pirate attack.

Also, there was something about her . . . I didn't want to look bad in her eyes. I was starting to think of her as a fellow Prince. I could not do less than she did.

"We stay then," I said.

Raine turned back to her controls. I watched her for a second, then went out to gather more shiplice and check a couple of things. The quicker contact was reestablished with the missile, the happier I would be. If even one pirate got out of the wormhole before it was stoppered, we would be—to use an expression some of the humans were fond of back on the Feather in the training simulation—totally in the shit tank without an environmental recycling unit.

But thirty minutes later, even with a dozen shiplice, we still hadn't reestablished communication with the missile. There had been no further scan report from the capsule, but our window of opportunity was closing all too quickly. There couldn't be more than an hour before the first pirate came through, and maybe less.

"How long are you giving us to get clear?" I asked Raine as I returned with yet more shiplice and hurried them into action.

"The delay is set for twenty minutes," replied Raine. She was hunched over in the command seat, watching several vision-skins that were intermittently updating.

"And at maximum acceleration, how long for the missile to get in proximity range of the wormhole?"

"Twenty-one minutes, fifteen seconds."

Forty-one minutes in total. Too long. The pirates might get through.

"Better make the delay twelve minutes," I said.

"I'm not sure if I can move very fast . . . your capsule's in L Dock, right? The smallest?"

"Yes," I replied. "I just timed it, walking. Six minutes there. Two minutes to get in. One minute to launch. Three minutes at max acceleration . . . it should put us clear, given that the missile's torch will have to burn through what's left of the ship first. But we need to launch the missile at the wormhole as soon as possible—"

A vision-skin flashed, and the input slate flickered. I felt a sudden tremor pass through the ship.

"Connection established," said Raine calmly, as if reporting to the bridge. "Target acquired. Launch routine initiated. Twelve-minute countdown begun on . . . mark!"

I grabbed her as she staggered out of the chair and lost her foot grip. I managed to stay upright and stuck on, and we half floated, half walked out the door. But in the corridor, Raine lost traction again and pushed me away as I tried to pull her up.

"No! I'm too slow; you go!"

I didn't reply, but in trying to pull her up, I lost my foot grip too and ended up near the ceiling. I hung there for a moment, till I triggered the directional jets on Ekkie's maneuver rig and came back down, getting my boot soles stuck back on the floor and giving me an idea at the same time.

"Lie flat!" I ordered. "Arms outstretched."

Raine obeyed, tearing her boots from the floor. She bobbed up slightly, enough for me to lean over and wrap both arms around her middle.

"What are you doing?" she asked.

I didn't answer. I was sending a Psitek order, pushing every bit of my mental strength into it. Shiplice poured out of their accessways and spilled into the corridor, then turned to race away from us, their tiny minds imprinted with my desperate instruction.

:Open all doors and hatches between this point and L Dock and keep them open:

Then I pushed off, breaking my own grip, at the same time twitching to activate Ekkie's main backpack thruster at a very low level. Bitek glands pulsed out reaction gas, and we shot along the corridor at a far faster speed than I'd anticipated, overtaking all but the leading shiplice.

I dropped my foot to try to slow us down with some minor drag, but it worked too well. My foot stuck for a moment, sending us careening into the wall just before the next hatch. I caught the blow on my shoulder, Ekkie protesting about bruises again, and tried to correct with my directional jets. It kind of worked as we started off again, but with a corkscrewing motion that got worse as we went through the open hatch, a shiplouse waving its feelers from the control nerve as we flashed past.

Raine shifted in my arms, dropping her arm and leg. I held her more tightly till I realized she was trying to compensate for the spin. We steadied and managed to take a sixty-degree turn and fly up a ramp with only minor collisions. The hatch ahead dilated, letting a veritable swarm of shiplice pour through seconds ahead of us. There were scores of them, far more than I knew were around.

"Nine minutes to launch!" shouted Raine. I hadn't been checking the time with Ekkie and didn't now. I was too busy negotiating the next ramp and then the door at the top of it, which barely dilated in time, parts of Ekkie scraping the door edges as we rocketed through.

There was only the airlock ahead now. I saw a shiplouse jump at the control nerve, and the inner door stretched open. Then I realized they couldn't open the outer door unless the inner door was shut, a basic safety measure even though the dock was pressurized.

Hastily I killed the jet and dropped my feet, just enough to slow us down, or so I hoped. But again my soles stuck, jerking me to a much more sudden stop than I expected. Raine was torn from my arms and went barreling along the corridor and into the airlock. I followed after her in a stumbling, sticking run. As soon I was inside, the shiplouse shut the inner door and another one opened the outer door.

I never knew they were that smart. I pulled Raine up and we staggered over to the capsule.

"Seven minutes," panted Raine. She was hunched over and holding her stomach. I guessed the medical symbiote had cut back on painkilling, correctly reading that the adrenalin level in her blood meant she needed to move.

I boosted her up and she crawled into the capsule. I jumped more than climbed in after her and immediately slammed the control to shut the hatch. A few shiplice came in with me, but I couldn't be bothered with them.

"Lie down!" I ordered Raine, who had hunched up at the other end of the acceleration couch.

"What about you?" she asked.

"Lie down!" I bellowed, unwittingly sounding like every cadet officer I had ever known. "That's an order!"

Raine lay down. That left about sixty centimeters of acceleration couch free. I crouched there, activated the holo control, and ordered an emergency escape launch and the crash webs.

Web hissed out over Raine and a bit wrapped itself around my middle in an uncertain way. The stuff had very limited programming, and it couldn't cope with someone hunched next to the hatch instead of lying down where they were supposed to.

"Three minutes," said Raine.

The capsule lurched, breaking free of the docking tentacles. I hoped the dock sphincter was still working; I'd forgotten to check it. But as I'd got the capsule in all right, it should open up automatically for anything trying to get out.

There was another shudder as the drive activated to maneuver us up and away from the cradle. I tapped the holo to get an exterior view from the front, and breathed a sigh of relief as I saw stars and space and the edges of the dock. It was open and we were heading out!

But all too slowly.

"Call this emergency launch!" I screamed uselessly at the capsule, my fat, suited finger dancing over the holographic keys. "Come on!"

The capsule shuddered a little more, and I felt a very minor acceleration shoving me sideways. But it was still too slow, and not for the first time I wished I was in an Imperial singleship. Or in fact anything better than the ancient slug I'd been saddled with.

"Two minutes thirty," said Raine urgently. From her angle she couldn't see the holographic view. "Are we clear of the dock?"

"Just out," I said with relief. "Two minutes to go; we should get—"

I never finished what I was saying. The holoview flashed white, and an instant later we were hit by a sudden explosion of gas and debris and a massive surge in exterior temperature. The capsule spun end over end, sending me tumbling about as the crash webs lost their grip on my middle. Alarms shrieked and the holographic display shifted from an outside view to a sea of red symbols, reporting system failures and extensive damage.

The missile had launched early. The only thing that had saved us—for now—was the fact that the blowback from its fusion torch had to cut through several hundred meters of the *Heffalurp*'s hull. So instead of being vaporized, we were just hit by a whole lot of superheated ship atmosphere and lots and lots of the tiny bits of what used to be the ship and its systems.

Something clanged on the hull, sending a severe shock through the whole capsule. A hole as big as my fist appeared above the acceleration couch where Raine was wrapped in webs. Our atmosphere went out through it, spewing forth as frozen crystals and incidentally messing up the capsule's attempts to right itself with its thrusters.

I lunged forward, ripped open the emergency locker amidships, found a Bitek seeking patch, and threw it in the general direction of the hole. The ball of goop exploded into a plate-sized circle as it left my hand and was sucked onto the hole by the departing air. Though there wasn't enough pressure left inside to keep it in place, its own tiny suckers were already hard at work bonding to the hull.

Unfortunately this almost instinctive action of mine meant I lost my bracing position, and once again I was tumbled about, crashing into Raine and the sides of the capsule. She cried out in pain, Ekkie complained inside my helmet, and the holo display added some more problems as I tried to reorient myself and not throw up. I'd never had this problem as a Prince, but now the spin and tumble was making my gorge rise in my throat.

I bit back bile, pressed my feet and one hand hard against the sides of the capsule, and with the other hand took control of the module away from its rather stupid automated flight controls and started to fire the maneuver jets in a sequence that would get us stable again.

At least that was the plan. It proved harder than I thought, particularly as several thrusters were not responding to commands. I overcorrected, undercorrected, and made us spin and tumble in several different directions in quick succession, all of which was too much for my inner ear. I threw up several times, pointing my chin so the vomit would go down the suit and be dealt with there rather than collect in my helmet. Ekkie was pretty quick at clearing away fluids, but I really didn't want to drown in my own spew.

Finally, I got the capsule under control and could actually

take stock of what was going on.

"Are we going to make it?" asked Raine as I gingerly lowered myself back to a sitting position and looked down at her. Her face looked clean. The symbiote had saved her from vomiting, or else her suit was better at tidying up.

"I'm not sure yet," I replied as I went through the damage report. It didn't look too bad at first. We'd lost some maneuvering ability, but the main drive was fine. All our existing atmosphere had blown out, but we had our suit supplies and there was a Bitek air regenerator . . . or actually, as I read on in this status report, I saw that this was no longer true. The air regenerator was defunct, as was the small reserve tank of oxygen. The debris that had made the hole I'd patched had come through the hull, the air tank, and the regenerator and then the inner compartment lining.

That still might not be a problem, depending on what else was happening and how long it would take us to get somewhere with breathable air.

"Is the wormhole stoppered?" asked Raine.

"I don't know yet!" I snapped.

Raine shifted around but didn't speak. My fingers were sliding over the holo, calculating our trajectory toward the planet and the transit time, as well as trying to get the sensors to make a sensible report instead of trying to track all the myriad bits of debris that were accompanying us away from what used to be the *Heffalurp*. There was nothing we could do about them anyway—if they hit us, they hit us.

Very slowly the data picture resolved.

"The missile deployed to the target area and something just happened a moment ago," I said slowly. "I'm waiting on the wormhole energy signature. No ships showing up on scan so far."

Raine didn't answer. I looked over and saw that her eyes were screwed up tight and her lips were moving without making a sound.

"What are you doing?" I asked.

"Praying," she said without opening her eyes.

"What? Preying? I don't understand."

Raine opened one eye to look up at me in puzzlement. I guess I didn't look too good—there was still vomit caked around my mouth—because she shut it again pretty quickly.

"Praying. You know, quietly asking an invisible, probably nonexistent higher power to ensure that the wormhole is closed."

"Uh, I see," I replied, though I didn't see. While we had priests in the Empire, they were not go-betweens to some invisible entity who might or might not exist or have any power; they were agents of a completely real power. Princes didn't pray to the Emperor. We just communicated with the Imperial Mind.

"Does it ever work?" I asked after a moment. I was still waiting for the scan to complete.

"I don't know," replied Raine. "Maybe."

She hesitated, then added, "I was praying back in the *Heffalurp*, at the ship-heart. Then you came along."

"Not conclusive," I said. Most of my attention was on the scan as it slowly reported the wormhole energy state. The numbers were climbing, but hadn't reached a level that indicated the wormhole was opening.

"I know," said Raine. "I never really had prayed before. I'm not a believer like—"

She stopped in midsentence.

"Like who?" I asked. The numbers were static now. Was the wormhole actually closed?

"Like some of the crew on the *Heffalurp*," she said.

"So they probably prayed?" I asked.

"Yes," said Raine.

"But they all died. So this prayer thing clearly doesn't work."

"I guess not," said Raine softly.

The wormhole energy signature started to fall.

"On the other hand . . ." I said, a smile slowly spreading across my vomit-stained face, "the wormhole is closed. And I'm not picking up anything as having come through before it did."

"All right!"

Raine pushed one hand out of the restraining web and held it up near me, gloved palm out. Unsure of what to do, I shook the top of her fingers gently. My smile was already fading as I looked back at the holo and our best possible trajectory toward Kharalcha Four.

It didn't look good. At our maximum thrust of 0.1 G, it was going to take fourteen standard days—336 hours—and that presumed they had a deceleration web to catch us, which was probably unlikely. If we had to turn over halfway and decelerate, we were looking at twenty days.

Ekkie could keep me alive for about ten days without an infusion of fresh atmosphere. Raine's suit was Mektek. It might have a Bitek air scrubber, but even so, I doubted it had an endurance beyond a few days.

"Uh, how much atmosphere do you have in your suit, Raine?"

She dipped her head inside her helmet, looking at a readout near her chin.

"Eight hours, give or take."

"Oh," I said.

"I . . . TAKE IT THAT is going to be a problem?" Raine asked. Even without my augmented hearing I detected a tremor in her voice, though she was trying her best to sound calm and in control.

"Yes," I replied. "We've lost the capsule's atmosphere reserve and the regenerator, and with the pathetic drive this capsule's got, it's going to take at least three hundred hours to get to Kharalcha Four. Is there anything closer? Or have your lot got any ships left?"

"There are other ships," said Raine. "But I think they'd be kept close, to try to protect the Habitat. Even at full boost . . . eight hours is just too short. How long have you got?"

"Around two hundred and forty hours," I said. "On full recycling, if Ekkie . . . my suit . . . keeps working."

"You call your suit Ekkie?" asked Raine. I noticed she had a dimple when she smiled.

"The previous owner called it something unpronounceable; I call it Ekkie for short," I said. I repeated my earlier question. "Is there anywhere closer than Kharalcha Four? A mining station or something? I can't resolve anything in those rings around the gas giant in the sixth orbital."

"I don't know," said Raine. "I mean, I think there was some kind of palace thing there when this was still part of the Empire—"

"*What?*" I spat.

"Still part of the Empire," Raine repeated. "Uh, do you mind if I sit up? It's kind of weird looking up at you like this."

"Sit, lie down, it doesn't matter," I replied. "What do you mean, *used to be part of the Empire*?"

Raine struggled to push the restraint web aside till I helped her shove it back into its dispensers. The stuff was supposed to retract automatically, but of course it wasn't working properly.

"I mean 'part of the Empire,'" she said. "Why is that so hard to understand? This was an Imperial system until about three hundred years ago. For some reason Prince Xaojhek left, with all the priests and everything, and that was it. No one took over; no one came back. There wasn't even a visit from an Imperial ship till that first attack, nine years ago."

I tried to take this in. I *knew* that the Empire never retreated from anywhere, never gave up a system or world. The Empire was always expanding, in a perpetual, triumphant conquest of the galaxy.

Or was it? Yet another of the pillars that had underpinned my early life was looking a lot less solid. I'd thought that Imperial Law was sacrosanct, that Princes always obeyed the Imperial

Mind . . . perhaps the continued expansion of the Empire was about as true as all that was.

"Kharalcha Four was once an Imperial world?" I asked, thinking of the basically rural, undeveloped planets that were most typical of the Empire. "I mean, a rural food producer and so on?"

"Sure," agreed Raine. "It still is, kind of. I mean, it's all yokels and farms, and pretty countryside and not much of anything useful. Except food variety, I guess."

"So you're not a planetsider."

Raine laughed.

"A dirtgrubber? Of course not. I'm from the Habitat. Gryphon torus."

She tapped the symbol of the winged creature on the shoulder plate of her suit, and her laughter faded.

"All of us on the *Heffalurp* were from Gryphon. But the other rings will have suffered too, with the rest of the fleet destroyed."

"The Habitat is an orbital environment, from Imperial times?" I asked.

"It was," said Raine. "There's been a lot done to it since."

I was beginning to think ahead again. If I could stay alive and get to the Kharalcha Four orbit, there might be some Imperial tek I could salvage. Princes typically had secret caches. Maybe there was even a ship hidden away that would answer to my Psitek.

But I had to get there first, before the air ran out.

"What kind of comms do you have?" asked Raine. "If I can get in touch with KSF headquarters . . . there might be a ship somewhere close that can pick us up."

"Not much that's any use," I replied. The capsule had once

had a superior comms system, but it had been ripped out before I got it. "Wide- and narrow-band rayder, basically. Nothing real-time."

"I'd better try now," said Raine. "We're about a billion kilometers out from the Habitat; that's a fifty-minute lag or thereabouts."

I nodded. Almost an hour for them to get our message, another hour to get a reply, or for a nearby ship to be dispatched, if there was one. . . . It wasn't very promising.

Something moved in the corner of my eye. I turned quickly, reaching for a weapon, but it was only a shiplouse. I'd forgotten a few had come on board with us.

"Hey, maybe the shiplice could fix the regenerator!" exclaimed Raine.

I shook my head.

"Different Bitek," I said. Which was true. I realized I needed to lie about how I worked with them, though, so I mimed patting my pocket and added, "Besides, I dropped the coding wand after I had programmed them to open the doors. Here's the rayder hand unit."

I pulled the comms control unit out of its socket, flicked it on, and handed it to Raine. She looked it over, adjusted a few settings, rotated the connections to the one she wanted, and plugged it into her suit. That was the best thing about most of the tek lying around the Fringe being Imperial tek or copies of it. Connectivity across teks and generations of tek was a fundamental part of Imperial design.

"Calling KSF Tac-Command and any KSF ship beyond sixth orbital, any KSF ship beyond sixth orbital, this is Raine Gryphon, survivor of KSFS-17 *Heffalurp*. I am in a civilian life capsule; coordinates and vector are . . ."

She looked at me. I flicked the holo display to bring up our position, tilted it toward her, and she read off the coordinates, heading, and acceleration.

"The capsule is damaged and we have limited atmosphere. Rendezvous and retrieval urgent, any KSF ship, KSF TacCommand."

Raine repeated the message five times, while I thought about the situation. We were continuing to boost toward Kharalcha Four, but there was no question that even I wouldn't make it. And Raine had far less air. I had to work out something that would save both of us.

I glanced across at her, still sending her message. I did need to save her, but I didn't know why. I mean, there were logical arguments about the Kharalchans' gratitude and so on, but that didn't explain the almost overwhelming feeling I had that I must not let her die. It was an inexplicable, emotional response, one I had never felt before.

I didn't like it, because it felt weak, but somehow I couldn't stop it. I tried to tell myself that she was just like a mind-programmed servant of my household, but she wasn't. They were all the same. She was . . . *different.* More interesting . . . and she was different from all the humans I'd met in my training. I'd gotten on well enough with some of them, but I'd certainly never felt like I needed to protect them.

What had she done to me? There wasn't any real possibility that she had somehow introduced a behavioral virus into my mind. Whatever I was feeling had to be coming from inside me. . . .

But there was no time to conduct any self-analysis. I had to work out what the hell we were going to do.

Raine stopped sending and looked at me looking at her. I looked away.

"Now I guess we wait for a while," she said. "I'll resend every ten minutes until we get a reply."

"What's your exact atmosphere supply?" I asked.

"Oh, like I said, around eight hours," replied Raine. She didn't look at her readout.

"Exactly," I repeated sternly.

Raine's nose twitched, but she inclined her head to check the readout.

"Seven hours, twenty-three minutes," she replied. "Presuming minimal activity, which I think is a given, considering."

She indicated the lack of room, patting the hull and my suit. We were crammed in very close together.

"The symbiote could probably put you in a trance state," I said, thinking aloud. "But that would only be good for another eight hours or so, at most . . ."

"No fun, either," said Raine.

I gave her a puzzled look, then I caught on, and smiled.

"So you do have a sense of humor," said Raine. "I wasn't sure if you were just one of those all-business-all-the-time military types."

"Me? A military type?" I asked. I'd have to watch that. "I'm just trader crew. You're the KSF officer."

"Uh, that's not exactly true," said Raine. "I was kind of not meant to be on the *Heffalurp*. I mean, I am a cadet officer in the KSF Reserve, but . . . I was sort of a stowaway. That's why I was inside the comms mast."

"Sort of a stowaway?" I asked.

"I was on the *Heffalurp*, dockside training, when the alert came. I was supposed to disembark, but I didn't. When Uncle Lymond—the captain—saw I was still on board, we were under way, so he had me locked up in the comms mast lifepod station."

"'Uncle' Lymond?" I asked cautiously. The only uncles I knew were randomly assigned priests. I had a vague recollection that in familial terms, an uncle was a male parental sibling, but I wasn't completely sure about that.

"My dad's brother," said Raine quietly. She shut her eyes for a second. "He was so angry . . . and now he's gone . . . all my cousins . . ."

She was silent for a while after that. I edged past her and examined the patched hole and the atmosphere regenerator, just in case there was some chance of repair. The shiplice came over and looked with me, their feelers running over the lumpy mass of the regenerator. But it was completely dead. I shuffled back to my sitting position. Raine was repeating the rayder message.

I thought about how I could get her additional air. Ekkie had a small, highly compressed reservoir that was mostly oxygen, and its regenerator was working well. Maybe if I bled the atmosphere from my suit into the capsule, and ran Ekkie's regenerator with my helmet off . . .

I ran the numbers. There was some remnant atmosphere in the capsule, about 18 percent of normal. In my augmented days I could cope with that for hours, but only for a few minutes in my current state. However, adding all of Ekkie's reserve would lift the pressure to 54 percent normal. The problem then wouldn't be lack of atmosphere but carbon dioxide buildup, as Ekkie's regenerator wouldn't be able to cope with two of us breathing for as long as it would cope with just me in the smaller, suit environment.

But it would give us both seventy-two hours, give or take,

instead of Raine's seven hours.

"I've worked out a way to get you some more air," I said. "I can partially repressurize the cabin from Ekkie's reserve, and then run the suit regenerator with my helmet and joint seals open. It'll be thin, but it'll give us three days."

"Are you sure?" asked Raine.

"The calculations are pretty straightforward," I said. "I mean, three days, give or take a margin of two hours either way—"

"No, I mean are you sure you want to do that? Three days might not be enough, and you said your suit could do ten days just for you."

Was I sure? No, I wasn't. In fact I was wondering why I was even suggesting it. But she was looking at me again. . . .

"I'm sure," I said. I braced myself and instructed Ekkie to vent its atmosphere reserve into the cabin.

When the pressure had built up sufficiently, I unsealed my knee joints, removed my gloves, and took off my helmet. Almost immediately my nose started to bleed. I pinched it closed and breathed slowly and shallowly through my mouth. The air was thin, and colder than I'd expected. But it was survivable.

"Id's all right," I said to Raine. "You cad take your helmed off."

She took off her helmet and shook her head. Her reddish hair wasn't as short as I'd thought, and was only kept back from her face by her comms headband, which she kept on.

Ekkie's cilia kept my hair trimmed to some degree, but I was aware that I had the rough equivalent of a three-day beard, now caked somewhat with vomit and blood. I grabbed one of the shiplice and held it to my face, instructing it via Psitek to clean up the extraneous matter.

"I didn't know . . . you could do . . . that with a shiplouse," remarked Raine.

It was hard to talk in the thin air.

"Uh, it's in their basic response programming, but it's not recommended," I said. "Got to . . . hold them just the right distance away."

Its job completed, I set the shiplouse down and it scuttled away.

We sat silently for a while, adapting to the atmosphere. I watched the scans, and Raine repeated the rayder message. I tried not to keep looking at her, but I couldn't help myself.

"What? What is it?" asked Raine when she caught my eye for the third or fourth time. "Is something wrong?"

I started to laugh and then I couldn't stop laughing, and Raine was laughing too, then both of us were sobbing and that turned into coughing and panting for breath, and eventually I leaned back at one end of the capsule and Raine leaned back at her end. Later I learned that this was a reaction to severe shock, something Princes didn't usually have to contend with, their systems automatically adjusting body chemistry to cope.

"Yes," I said finally. "There is something wrong."

That started us giggling again, and coughing, and then all of a sudden, a crackling voice sounded in the capsule and we were instantly quiet, all focus on the audio.

"Raine Gryphon capsule, this is KSF *Tormentor*, outbound from K6. We have you on scan, will rendezvous eighty-one hours if you maintain course and acceleration. KSF Tac-Com reports wormhole stoppered, relay from KSF Top Mark 'very well done Heffalurps' and 'why are you there Raine?' Report status soonest."

Eighty-one hours. A mere nine hours more than we could stay alive.

17

"I'LL TELL THEM we don't have that much time," said Raine. She breathed out hard, and coughed as she couldn't get enough air back in. "So close . . ."

"No," I said. "We can do it. I have another medical symbiote. If we both trance out . . . we should make it."

"But if anything happens, we won't be able to do anything," protested Raine. "What if you put me under, but you stay conscious?"

I shook my head.

"The margin is too tight," I said. "We both have to consume less oxygen and add less carbon dioxide. Tell them we're going to trance out and we're depending on them to get to us as quickly as they can."

"The *Tormentor* is a fast corvette with a Gryphon crew,"

replied Raine. "They'll be pulling maximum G's for sure."

"No gravity control?" I asked.

Raine shook her head.

"None of our ships have it, not anymore. Can't get the modules, or the engineers to fix the systems."

That meant the *Tormentor* really was going as fast as it could to get to us. Without gravity control the crew couldn't take more than two or possibly three gravities' acceleration for any length of time.

"Tell them then," I said.

As Raine sent the message, I got the symbiote applicator out and reattached it to her arm. Its vision-skin flickered, then updated. She was still low on blood, and the reduced atmosphere pressure and oxygen content wasn't helping, but the symbiote had the internal bleeding under control.

I told the applicator to order the symbiote to put Raine into a medical coma, as low as it dared go with her injuries. It sent back an interrogative, requesting additional blood before it could proceed.

Raine finished sending the message for the third time. She bent her head down close to mine. I realized I was holding her hand in order to get a better view of the applicator vision-skin. It was telling me she needed at least another liter of blood.

"Shouldn't you load your symbiote first? In case there's a problem?"

"No," I replied. "I've got two more. It'll be fine. You ready?"

"I guess so," she said. She closed the gap between us and set her lips very lightly against the side of my cheek. "I never said thank you, Khem. Thank you."

I sent the command to put her to sleep and gently pushed her back down into the acceleration couch, still holding her hand.

"Good night, sweet prince," Raine whispered.

I jerked her back up in surprise.

"*What?*"

How could she know I was a Prince? Even if we did manage to get rescued, if anyone else found out, I'd be killed, or taken apart to study, or who knew what. . . . I'd have to kill her first. . . .

Raine's eyes slowly closed, and the hint of a smile drifted across her face.

"It's a line from . . . an old, old Earth story," she muttered. "'And flights of angels sing thee to thy rest.' See . . . you . . . later. . . ."

I sighed with relief and laid her back down. She was already unconscious, drifting deeper . . . but she needed that blood.

I opened the port in the applicator and was about to put my finger in to let it draw blood, and then I had a better idea.

Shiplice were Bitek organisms. They had a kind of blood. The symbiote could probably use it.

I used my Psitek to order the closest shiplouse over, and held it while I queried the applicator. The louse wriggled as the applicator's probe sank in to test it. I quelled the little beast's alarm, lulling it to sleep as the applicator thought about the matter before agreeing that it could indeed use the shiplice's biological matter.

I connected both shiplice up and, when the applicator was finished, took the husks and shoved them in a locker. Then I removed the applicator and loaded it up with a symbiote. Then I waited . . . and waited . . . for it to flash gold.

It didn't. The symbiote was senile, no use to anyone.

The second one flashed orange. It wasn't senile, but it wasn't fully operational either. Generally speaking, introducing a half-dead or possibly crazed symbiote into your own bloodstream isn't a recommended course of action.

I sat there, wondering what I was going to do. I simply had to breathe less and exhale less carbon dioxide, or we wouldn't make it. Lying back and thinking shallow thoughts wasn't going to cut it. Even a normal or drug-induced sleep wouldn't be enough.

If I had still been augmented, I could just have dialed down my metabolism, telling everything to hibernate. But that was no longer an option.

Or was it? My Psitek facilities still functioned. I'd had no problem programming the shiplice, or commanding Bitek nerve ganglions. Could I use my Psitek coercion abilities to tell my own body to go into a coma for eighty-one hours?

There was only one way to find out.

I tried to visualize myself as an enemy to be dominated, just as I would perform a Psitek attack on someone else. I made my consciousness separate and then sent out psychic feelers to my . . . no . . . *my enemy's* mind, searching for the nodes that maintained the body.

I felt my senses withdraw. My sight faded, and my hearing, and I was both inside and outside my body. I was acutely aware of my nervous system, the synapses firing impulses along immensely complicated routes. I could sense blood flowing, and oxygen interchanging in the lungs.

I followed the nerve impulses into the brain and tweaked a little here and a little there. My breathing slowed. My heart slowed. Everything slowed down.

I felt a surge of triumph. I had succeeded in putting my body into a coma.

But I was still conscious, somehow separate from my body.

Blind and deaf to the outside world, all I could sense was internal. I knew nothing of anything beyond my own skin. There was just the very slow drumbeat of my heart, but even that faded into the background.

I had no sense of the passage of time. Maybe five minutes had gone by while I was trying this out, maybe five hours or even longer.

This didn't bother me at first. It was quite peaceful being a disembodied mind. I was relaxed, just floating along, calm and content. But after a while—how long, I don't know—a nasty thought began to clamor for attention.

What if I'd been in this coma for much longer than I thought? Maybe I'd been in it for days?

I felt panic rising, but not in my body. My heart rate didn't change, but I couldn't tell whether it was fast or slow, as I'd lost any frame of reference. My blood pressure didn't feel high. The panic was all mental, all within this separate consciousness I had somehow established.

Then I started to wonder about something else. Not how long I'd been under, but if I could even get "back" inside my body.

I tried to stay calm, but I couldn't. The panic rose and overwhelmed everything else, and all of a sudden nothing else mattered. I didn't care if I was going to slowly asphyxiate—I just had to return to my physical existence.

Desperately I retraced the nerve paths I'd followed, plunging along them, trying to find whatever it was that made my mental persona stay within my flesh. I felt like a shiplouse racing through maintenance tunnels in a frenzy, programmed to reach a critical malfunction but never getting there . . . and then . . .

I was suddenly back in my body, gasping and coughing,

my heart racing and my head aching. There was a bright light above my head, and some kind of alarm was emitting a high-pitched buzz.

I blinked and tried to lift my head, but there was something across my temples. My wrists were restrained as well, and my ankles. I growled and tried to break the bonds, but I was weaker than I'd ever been, and I just flopped back onto my bed.

Bed? I blinked again and turned my head sideways. I wasn't in the capsule anymore. I was strapped to a bed, in a Mektek ship compartment, a ship with artificial gravity . . . or under boost close to 1 G.

I took a tentative breath of air. It was ship air, but it tasted sweet to me. Judging from my restraints, things weren't as promising as they might be, but even so, it was a lot better than being in a capsule with a slowly spoiling atmosphere.

The door opposite the bed slid open. I couldn't raise my head, so I couldn't see who it was.

"Raine?" I asked.

"No," said a much less pleasant, male voice. The owner of the voice came into view a moment later, bending down to look at me and then at a display panel on the bed. "I'm Medtech Kilgore. How are you feeling?"

I had to think about that for a moment.

"Uh, I'm all right," I said at last. "Am I aboard the *Tormentor*?"

Medtech Kilgore gave me a sideways look.

"You need to rest," he said, and touched the panel.

I felt a drug infuse into my arm.

"No! I just woke—"

The next thing I knew, I was staring at the light again, and the beeping alarm was going off again. I tensed my arms and legs.

The restraints were still there. So was the band around my head.

"What is your name?" asked an unseen voice. Not Medtech Kilgore. It was a female voice, but not Raine's.

"Khem," I replied. Weirdly I felt a compulsion to add the missing *ri*, but I swallowed it.

"Do you have any more names?"

"N . . . no," I croaked. What was going on?

A woman's face leaned over me. I blinked it into focus.

"Why am I tied down?" I asked. "And that Kilgore drugged me. After everything I did for you, with the wormhole stopper and all."

"We're grateful," replied the woman. Her hair was silver, but her face was younger and didn't match. Rejuvenated in some way. There were lots of rejuv teks. Some worked better than others. "There's just a question of your . . . identity and motivation."

"What?" I asked. "I'm a trader. My ship blew—"

"We know what you told Raine," said the woman. "But there is something that doesn't fit."

"What?" I asked.

"Why do you look exactly like the Prince who destroyed our fleet?" asked the woman.

"What?" I asked again, trying not to overdo my puzzled frown. Inside I was thinking furiously.

A Prince who looked exactly like me? That wasn't possible. . . . Then my slow brain reconnected a few more neurons and I remembered Atalin from the Academy. The perfect cadet, who did look like me, who was maybe even my sister . . .

But if it was Atalin, why would she have trashed the fleet here, of all possible systems? And why would she have broadcast her face?

I felt a cold feeling spreading in my guts as I thought this through. None of this would be a coincidence. Morojal was manipulating something here, setting me up, and maybe Atalin as well. Making my test more difficult? Or something deeper?

"You look exactly like the Prince in the message sent from the Imperial ship," repeated the woman. "She said her name was Atalin. Why do you look like her?"

I could feel the pressure of drugs in my arm again. Truth serum of some kind, I supposed, but not working as effectively as it should have been.

"I don't know," I replied quickly, to try to answer before the drugs overcame me. Would they work properly on my non-augmented form? I didn't feel overwhelmingly compelled to tell the truth, or at least not yet. "Maybe it's a joke. My ship must have come in only minutes before the Imperial. Maybe she scanned me and just used my face. I mean, I'm not a woman, am I?"

"Are you a Prince?"

Not right now, I thought, and had a moment of panic as I wondered if I'd said that aloud.

"A Prince?"

I laughed, and tried to laugh harder. Hysteria would be better than truth. "A Prince? You must be joking. They're like . . . supermen. . . . I'm just a trader. . . . Scan me, you'll see—don't they have like power plants inside and blaster fingers and armored heads and I don't know, all sorts of amazing . . . I wish I did have that. . . ."

"We have scanned you," said the woman. "Several times."

Morojal had assured me there was nothing to find in this body. But what if she'd lied? I didn't want to consider the possibility that she might be wrong.

I could feel the drugs working deeper into me, but I hadn't lost control. I knew I'd feel so good if I just unloaded everything and babbled. But I resisted it and tried to convey half-truths at best.

"Are you an agent of the Empire?"

"No," I said. That was true, as far as it went. I wasn't an agent. I was a principal.

"Are you an enemy of Kharalcha?"

"No." I shook my head.

"What is your age in old Earth years, subjective?"

Why did they want to know that?

"Nineteen, I think. Maybe twenty."

There was some muttering behind the questioning woman. I thought I recognized that voice.

"Raine? Is that you? Are you all right?"

"I'm not asking that!" said my interrogator. She had her head turned away and wasn't talking to me. She obviously thought I couldn't hear, or wouldn't remember. "I think we're done here. He scans human normal. I guess that Prince *was* just . . . I don't know . . . appropriating a face. Maybe they don't like us mere mortals knowing what they really look like. Or it was some kind of sick joke."

I almost answered that, but I managed to turn it into a coughing fit. As I coughed away, I felt my restraints retract. I sat up and saw that Raine was there at the foot of the bed, looking fresh and clean in a dark-blue shipsuit with a single twisted line of gold on each sleeve. She smiled at me, the dimple appearing.

The other woman was in a green shipsuit, with three gold lines on her sleeve.

"I'm sorry about that, Khem. My name is Commander Alice

Gryphon. Raine has told us how important your help was in stoppering the wormhole and in her own survival. But we have to be careful, particularly in the current situation, and the Prince's image thing was . . . odd. In any case, I believe that you can be transferred to the civilian side now. Welcome to Kharalcha Orbitplex One, or as it's more commonly known, the Habitat."

The commander looked at Raine and said, "He's all yours now, Raine," before adding to me, "I mean that somewhat literally. Visitors must be sponsored to leave the docks here. Raine is sponsoring you; she will be held responsible for your actions. In any case, you're cleared to go, from both a medical and a security perspective."

She left, and I sat there with my mouth open and my mind working feverishly away. Raine came over and stood near my bed, and I finally got my question out.

"I'm at the orbital habitat on Kharalcha Four? I thought this must be the *Tormentor*. . . . What . . . what happened?"

"You've been out for eight days," said Raine. "When the *Tormentor* picked us up, the medtech said you'd rejected your symbiote after it put you into a coma, and they couldn't wake you up. Even back here they couldn't do anything. Just wait and see. I'm . . . I'm really glad you woke up, Khem."

"So am I," I said. Eight days? I shuddered. I wasn't going to abandon my body again, that was for sure. I was lucky I'd made it back. "Uh, what do I do now?"

"I thought . . . you can stay with me and my parents to start with," said Raine. "I think we owe you quite a lot—"

"Your parents?" I interrupted. I didn't mean anything in particular. It was just the whole concept of parents and knowing who they were, let alone living with them. But Raine blushed.

"Yes, uh, I still live with them. I'm a student as well as a reservist. I mean everyone is pretty much and . . . I've only just turned eighteen."

"And *you* wanted to know how old I am?"

She smiled, and I smiled back. I couldn't help it.

"Well, why shouldn't I stay with you?" I said, and swiveled my legs off the bed. "I have to go somewhere."

Raine looked away suddenly as I got out of the bed. It took me a moment to work out that this was because I didn't have any clothes on. Many human societies were peculiar about nudity, I knew from my training.

"My father is making a feast to celebrate," Raine said, still looking away. "I hope you like Kharalchan prawns. From the planet, not the vat ones."

"I probably will," I said. I opened the locker next to the bed and was both delighted and surprised to see my vacuum suit. All the rest of my gear looked like it was there too, noticeably minus all the weapons.

"Ekkie!"

Raine turned around when I said that.

"You can't wear Ekkie," she said. Then she hastily turned around again as I bent over and rummaged about in the bag next to Ekkie, extracting underclothes and my shipsuit with the Five Worlds insignia. At least someone had washed me while I was in bed, and shaved me too. I hadn't been so clean for weeks.

"I'll get a trolley for your gear," said Raine hastily as I straightened up and put the clothes on the bed. She was half out the door as I put my foot through one leg of my underpants and started hopping about while I tried to get the other leg in.

"Back in a minute!"

BEFORE RAINE COULD take me to her home I had to endure the new-resident briefing, but at least it was from the civilian administration of the Habitat rather than the KSF, and without chemical assistance.

I was still a bit zonked by the interrogation, so I think I came across as mentally substandard. The guy who was showing me the schematics of the place had to keep stopping to make sure I was following, and a couple of times he looked at Raine as if to say *Why are we letting this freak move in?*

What it all added up to was the Habitat was an old Imperial Mektek orbital city, constructed to very high specifications some eight or nine centuries ago. The structure was built as a series of five stacked rings, each composed of a circled tube about two kilometers in diameter, with a dozen six-kilometer-long, two-hundred-meter-diameter spokes leading to the central hub. Each of the rings was named after some kind of old Earth animal, so there were Gryphon, Dragon, Basilisk, Sphinx, and one named after a mythical animal, Dolphin.

The hub was imaginatively called the Hub, and it was where most of the administrative and military offices were located, the ship docks, and so on.

Unlike the Kharalchan ships, the Habitat still had functioning gravity control and excellent climate conditioning, which made it a pretty nice place to live. Or so the briefer assured me.

Even better, he continued brightly, I was to be given a week to acclimatize myself before I would have to get a job and make my contribution to the community.

"We have no freebreathers in the Habitat," he pronounced. "What shall I put you down for? Do you have any special skills?"

"Uh . . . yeah . . ." I answered vaguely. I was trying to get out that I was pretty good at making any kind of former Imperial tek work, but the drug haze wouldn't let me.

"I'll just put you down for hull patching to start with," continued the briefing clerk without waiting for my answer. "It's not too difficult."

"Oh, come on, Ganulf," interrupted Raine. "Khem is—"

I was about to agree with Raine and tell this functionary what he could do with his hull patching and demand a position suitable to my status . . . then I remembered Elzweko's words of advice.

Think about what a Prince would do, then do the opposite.

"It's all right," I said. "Hull patching is fine. Uh, inside or outside?"

"Inside," said Ganulf. "We still have a functioning meteor

shield, and a self-sealing outer hull. But we do get pinprick leaks, so it is a very important job—well, it is important, Raine; don't give me that look—we need hull patchers to patrol with a leak detector and a bag of patches, and fix up all the not-so-dangerous holes that crop up here. It's a good way to learn your way around as well. I was a hull patcher once, you know."

"It's fine," I said. In fact it *was* fine. It could even be a good job, because it would let me roam about and have a look around for any secret Imperial caches the locals had never realized were there. Besides, it wouldn't be for very long. "No problem. I like hull patching."

"Good," said Ganulf. "Now, I have your full ID scan here from KSF Int . . . from the military . . . hold out your hand, no, palm down, and I'll just insert your tag under the skin. There we are. That will tie in with our information center and activate the payment and credit system. I presume you are familiar with this kind of ID solution? I know some traders prefer more . . . archaic—"

"It's fine," I mumbled. It was basically the same as the Shubians used in the junkyard, back in the sim. Besides, even though I'd been in a coma for days, I felt incredibly tired. I just wanted to get to a bed, preferably one where I wasn't restrained at a dozen points across my body.

"You've been given some initial credit for your life capsule, and most of its contents have been transferred to your personal storage," said Ganulf. "No weapons, of course."

"What? My capsule?" I asked. They'd taken my capsule? Not that it was much use, being badly damaged and all, but I might have been able to repair it.

"All private spacecraft have been requisitioned by the KSF," said Ganulf. "We are in a state of emergency, you know."

"Yeah, I did know, amazingly enough," I said.

Ganulf sniffed and looked at a checklist.

"Welcome to the Habitat, Khem," said Ganulf. "Or Khem Gryphon, I should say, though of course you will be able to change your name later, if you move to a different ring."

I nodded. I'd got that from the briefing. Everyone who lived in a ring took the name of it, and most of them were actually related in some way as well. So I was Khem Gryphon, for now, because I was going to be living with Raine and her parents.

Which was a pretty weird concept, but not one I was capable of grappling with in my current state. As with the hull patching, I told myself it wouldn't be for long. As soon as I got my brain sorted out, I'd start looking for the serious Imperial tek that was bound to be hidden away here somewhere. Then I was going to get out and get on with the business of returning to the Empire. Returning to my proper self.

"Come on, Khem," said Raine. She took my arm and helped me out the door. "You look absolutely wrecked."

"I am," I said. "It's probably shock from discovering I'm not dead after all."

Raine stopped and looked at me, very seriously. I didn't meet her eyes, not because I was really worried about some sort of mimetic imprinting from her eyelid flutters. She just made me feel different, and I didn't like it. Or I did like it, but I felt like I shouldn't, because it was distracting me from my mission, which was to get back to Imperial space as quickly as possible.

"We would both be dead if it wasn't for you, Khem," she said. "And so would a lot more people. The pirates would be here, right now, looting everything, killing anyone who resisted. And

I know we haven't treated you as well as we should have, but we *are* grateful. I'm grateful."

"I know," I said. "Now I need you to take me to a bed."

"Uh, I know there are societal and communication differences with people from different systems," Raine continued after a slight pause. "When I said 'I'm grateful,' I didn't mean that I was offering—"

"I mean show me to a bed," I interrupted. "Otherwise I'm just going to collapse here in the corridor."

"Oh. It's a bit of a walk to Gryphon ring. . . . I guess I could call us a traveler. . . ."

I sat down with my back against the corridor wall to emphasize my point about collapsing.

"Or a medical team—"

"I'm just tired," I mumbled. "Need sleep. Proper sleep."

Raine spoke into her bracelet, a personal communicator, and I noted I had not been issued one. Perhaps I was supposed to buy one myself.

A traveler turned out to be a narrow four-seater antigrav cart, obviously as old as the Habitat itself but still working. I pretty much collapsed across two seats and went out like a light.

When I woke up the next time, I was lying on top of a comfortable, wide bed with a bright red-and-blue coverlet. The bed took up most of a room that could almost have been the quarters of one of my servants back in Imperial space, since it was very clean and bright and comfortable. There was a Mektek vision system on one wall, a personal refresher cubicle was visible through a partially frosted privacy shield in one corner, and generally speaking, it was a 1,000-percent improvement on living inside Ekkie inside a life capsule.

There was a retractable shelf next to the bed, with a translucent cube on it. I picked it up, and the cube unfolded into a thin panel the size of my chest. It glowed with a blue tinge, then color ran across it, and a picture formed, a young woman who at first I thought was Raine till I realized this woman was somewhat older. She waved, then ran away from the device that had captured the picture and down a corridor, turning to wave halfway to the hatch at the end. From my limited waking experience, it looked like a Habitat corridor.

"See you soon!" she called. "It will seem like forever, but when I'm back it will feel like no time at all!"

The picture vanished with the last word, then started again. I touched the corner, and the panel folded itself back into a silent, translucent cube.

The door made a humming noise and a soft pearly light spread across its surface. I got up and waved it open. Raine was on the other side, in a communal room that had several doors like mine leading off it.

"I heard something," she said, looking in. "Are you okay?"

I gestured at the memory cube.

"The woman in the picture spoke."

Raine's face froze into immobility, then she dashed forward and picked up the cube, retreating back out while I stood watching.

"I forgot it was there," she said. "I hope it didn't . . . I hope it—"

"Who is it?" I asked.

"Was," said Raine. "It was . . . my sister, Anza."

"She's dead?" I asked.

Raine nodded, not speaking.

"How?" I asked. I was curious, and despite my training, hadn't quite learned that sometimes humans are unable to process questions that have deep emotional resonance.

"The pirates, last time," said Raine. "Please . . . please, don't ask any more, and don't . . . don't mention . . . don't ask my parents about her."

"Sure," I said. From some previously observed but inadequately understood exchange between humans, I added, "I'm sorry."

Raine nodded, and took a deep breath.

"This will be your room, obviously," she said, talking quickly. Her face was red on the cheekbones, which could be an indication of anger or other emotion. I thought "other emotion" in this case, probably relating to her dead sister. "It connects with our living room, which is shared by my parents and myself. That is the door to their room, and that one over there is mine. The general door to the corridor is there, and the emergency exits are located topside—that hatch you can see—and downside, though that hatch is under the carpet there. Uh, are you hungry?"

I didn't have to think about that. I was very hungry. I'd probably been fed via a tube up my nose to my stomach for the past few days.

"Yes!"

"Good. It is almost dinnertime, on the primary cycle," said Raine. "Breakfast for secondary, but we're on the primary cycle. Um, my parents are both in. They want to meet you, obviously. Is it all right to eat with them?"

"Sure," I said. The whole concept of parents was weird but would undoubtedly be interesting. And again, I thought I'd be out of there within a few days. Maybe a week.

Dinner was more interesting than I'd even expected, mainly because while Raine's father, Larod, was very quiet and had something to do with shipping foodstuffs from the planet, her mother, as I might have guessed if I'd known anything about how families interacted, was the Commander Alice Gryphon in KSF Intelligence who'd done my hospital interrogation. As her leading questions continued through the meal, I though perhaps she'd let Raine bring me to their home so she could keep an eye on me as a potential enemy.

I also found Raine peculiarly fascinating. I liked talking to her, and I even wanted to hear her thoughts and opinions, something that I had not found with anyone save Haddad and Elzweko, and with them I had simply needed to know what they thought in order to stay alive. With Raine, I wanted to know whatever she wanted to tell me. Even if it was information of no apparent strategic, tactical, or survival value whatsoever.

"We have a few months' breathing space before the pirates can come through," said Alice. "And there is a reasonable chance that the Confederation fleet will get here first through the other wormhole entrance. If that happens, what will you do, Khem?"

I shrugged and spooned up some more of the sweet, pale-purple, semiliquid stuff they called jelbery, swallowing it down before I answered.

"I'm a trader," I said. "I'll sign on with the best trading vessel available and head out."

"If there was a trader here now, would you go with it?" asked Alice.

I looked at her, wondering if this was some sort of trick question. If there was a trader, and they were letting it go, maybe I should go with it.

"Depends where it's going," I answered, which was true. I needed to head back toward Imperial space. "Is there one? I thought you'd confiscated all ships."

"We have," said Alice. "I was just curious."

I looked at Raine. She wasn't eating her jelbery; she was looking at me.

"You know," she said to her mother, "that's not really true."

"What's not true?" asked Alice.

"That there's a reasonable chance the Confederation fleet will come in time," said Raine. "They probably won't arrive in time, or won't commit enough strength. The *most* likely scenario is that the tenth-orbit wormhole will reopen in a few months and the pirates will come through and we'll try to stop them with the pathetic remnant—"

"Raine," cautioned Alice. "These are operational matters."

Raine stopped talking. There was a long silence. Larod gave me a direct look with a slightly raised eyebrow that I was obviously meant to understand but didn't, then went on eating while also watching some kind of information feed that was scrolling across a patch of vision-skin on a kind of bracer or Bitek prosthetic reinforcement on his left wrist. It was all symbols that I could not immediately decipher.

"Do you have family, Khem?" asked Alice.

"Family? Uh . . ."

I hesitated. I suppose it would sound too odd to their ears if I said I had no family. It might even give my true identity away, or make Alice even more suspicious than she already was.

"I have a sister," I said, sticking to something that could be true. Alice might have a voice stress analyzer on me even now. It might be the device Larod kept looking at. I couldn't give

Atalin's real name, for obvious reasons, nor anything that sounded too Imperial.

"Tyrthos," I mumbled through a mouthful of jelbery. "Haven't seen her for quite a while. Different ships."

"And your parents?" asked Alice.

"Dead," I said, again with a high probability of truthfulness, as I thought of a man and a woman giving up their child to the selecting priests and the monofilament blades whipping across their necks. "Killed by Imperial mekbi troopers."

"I'm sorry," said Alice. "Was this long ago?"

I nodded, looked down at my plate, and said, "Yes. I'd rather not talk about it."

I had learned that from Raine, and it worked. Alice stopped asking me questions and soon left for some urgent duty.

"You're a survivor in more ways than one, I see," said Larod as he got up a few minutes later. He clapped me on my shoulder, and I restrained myself from automatically grabbing his wrist and twisting him to the ground, to then stab him with the not very sharp end of my spoon. I just wasn't used to being touched without permission. But it showed as no more than a flinch.

"I have to go downplanet, Raine," continued Larod, unaware of how close he'd come to death. "Check on some crops. Twenty-four hours, I think."

He clapped me on the shoulder again, this time leaving his hand there as he bent down close.

"Welcome to the Habitat, Khem. And thank you for what you did. Stoppering the wormhole . . . and . . . for saving my daughter."

Before I could speak, he had gone, but not before I saw the look on his face, and the glistening in his eyes—and even with my decreased Psitek ability I could feel the strength of the emotion he was holding in check. An intense feeling of relief that was at the same time still threaded through with stress and fear of the future.

"So," said Raine brightly. "What would you like to do now?"

19

WHAT I WANTED to do was grab her, kiss her, tumble to the floor with her, and have sex on the carpet that covered the downside emergency hatch. But I didn't know how to initiate this. If she had been one of my mind-programmed courtesans I'd have just told her to lie on the carpet and prepare to receive her lord and master, but I knew both that this was somehow wrong for Raine and, more importantly, that it wouldn't work.

I didn't think offering her credit or taking over one of her shifts would work either, which was how matters had sometimes been arranged in the training sim, in the startown and the Feather, respectively. But I knew from both those places that there were also much more mysterious arrangements, where the couples involved didn't exchange credit or take on shifts, but I didn't know how that worked.

"Um, I'm not sure," I said. It was an odd feeling to say that. Even in the sim, I'd pretty much always known what I wanted to do, and how to get it, or at least I'd tried and either succeeded or learned otherwise. But now I didn't want to risk making a wrong move, because . . .

Because Raine had somehow become important. I didn't want her to become an enemy, or to hate me, even though I knew this was a tactical error. I shouldn't be caring about any human. I should be focusing on my mission.

With an effort I turned my thoughts toward that mission.

"Maybe you could show me around," I said.

"Good idea," said Raine. "You okay to walk now?"

"Yes. . . . I think it was mostly a reaction to being drugged."

"Sorry about that," said Raine, and made a face.

For a moment I thought she was having an attack of some kind.

"Uh, that's meant to be a funny face," said Raine. "Again, making light of a bad situation."

She did it again, making her eyes goggle and her mouth twist.

This time, I laughed. I couldn't help myself. I wanted to stop, but I couldn't for at least a minute, and then when I finally got under control, Raine made the face again and off I went.

It was another alarming thing, to not even be in control of my *breathing*.

But I liked it. When I laughed, I could forget everything else, and it was a wonderful feeling, something I had never experienced before.

I felt free.

A few days later, Raine and I did manage to overcome our different societal programming, culture, and mores and get past the early stages of being deeply attracted to each other but without a clue about how to go about expressing this properly.

It started badly, though. I had just been for my initial employment orientation, and found it to be as dull and boring as Raine predicted. I was forced to watch a holo show of how to find a leak and then patch it, and then had to practice said procedure several times over, even though it was incredibly basic and I could have done it in my sleep.

I also missed Raine. We'd spent all our waking moments together and had even fumbled a kind of almost, not quite kiss the night before. Only I wasn't sure if it had been intentional on her part, or if she had really slipped and just happened to fall into my arms and then our faces had met in an uncoordinated way and then . . . we'd sprung apart, even though no one else was there.

When I got back to our living quarters, I looked for Raine immediately. She wasn't in the shared living quarters, so I tapped the inquiry panel on her door, but it remained frosted and there was no answer. Somewhat let down, I went to my room, slid open the door and went inside, and—

There was a silver box on my bed, just like the one the assassin had held, the novice in my candidate temple. The flower-trap that fired the sunbeam.

"Khem!" said Raine, close behind me.

I stepped back, whirled around, and flung Raine to the floor, covering her with my body so that there was a slim chance she would survive when the sunbeam burned a hole through my chest.

"Khem! What are you doing?!"

I tensed, waiting for the sudden, sharp moment of my death.

After a second or two, when it hadn't happened, I pushed up with my arms and looked back into my room. The silver box was still on the bed. It hadn't risen up and flowered to become a lethal weapon.

"Khem?"

I looked down at Raine, lying beneath me.

"Uh, that silver box . . . it looks a lot like a . . . I thought it was a . . . kind of . . . bomb."

Raine blinked.

"It's a present," she said. "From me. Go and have a look."

I stood up sheepishly and went over to the box. My mind was a roiling mess because I'd just done something incredibly stupid and incredibly un-Princelike.

I should have used Raine as a shield. Not the other way around. It was the second time I'd thought to save her no matter what the cost to myself.

I had to be losing my mind, but somehow it was voluntary!

"Open it," said Raine. She'd come in behind me and shut the door.

I opened it. As far as I could see, there was nothing inside. I showed her the empty container as she came into my arms and kissed me square on the mouth, leaving no doubt this time that it was intentional.

I kissed her back and, as we subsided onto the bed, asked her, "So where's my present?"

"That kiss," said Raine as she slid her finger down the fastener on my shipsuit. "It's a tradition here: we wrap a kiss and leave it on the bed of whoever we're interested in."

"So you're *interested*," I mumbled into her hair.

"*Very* interested," she replied. "What about you?"

"*Crazily* interested," I said.

I feared that the crazy part was true. But right then, I just didn't care.

With Raine, I discovered that while my courtesans were perhaps *technically* more skilled, once again there was something different about her. Or perhaps there was something different about me. It wasn't just the sexual activity I wanted with Raine. It was everything, even just holding her while she slept and I looked at her and listened to her quiet breathing.

I had never known anything like it before, and I was both immensely happy and absolutely terrified.

Terrified because I knew that I would have to give Raine up. I might be in a normal human body for the moment, and subject to all the ailings of a human heart, but I was a Prince of the Empire. I had to get back to who I really was. Didn't I?

When I was with Raine, I could forget about everything except just being with her. But after a week Raine was recalled to the KSF, like all the reservists. The Kharalchans were desperately preparing everything they could, for the wormhole was going to reopen in an estimated three to five months. Fortunately Raine wasn't assigned to an active ship, but to a destroyer refitting in the shipyard, so she could come home. Even so, she had to sleep on board four nights out of seven.

I missed her, and I was also deeply conflicted about what I was doing when I wasn't with her, which was hunting for hidden Imperial caches while also doing quite a lot of hull patching. Because if I found a means to leave the Habitat, there could be no further delay. I would go . . . but that meant leaving Raine.

In addition to my searching and patching, I spent a lot of time just observing what was going on, since any information might be useful to me, either in my preparations or when it came time for me to get the hell out.

The major topics of conversation among the Kharalchans were all related to the current situation. The most challenging for me were their hatred of the Empire and just how much they despised Princes, who they thought of as being hostile aliens, no better than Deaders, who also shot up everything they came across (though Deaders then blew themselves up if it looked like they might lose, so I thought this was a pretty stupid comparison).

Quite a few times I had to clench my fists to stop myself striking some ignorant Hab dweller who was going on about the Empire being a sick organism that was spread by a horrific disease vector called a Prince. But I did manage it, which would not have been the case before my training. I had come to terms with my current reality, however much I didn't like it—except of course for the time I spent with Raine.

Apart from slagging off the Empire, the next favorite topic was when the wormhole was likely to open, and when the pirates would come through, and whether or not a reinforcing fleet would get in first from the Confederation that Kharalcha had joined. They had a lot of hope invested in this rescue fleet coming through the system's other entry wormhole, the "safe" one that came in from an area uninfested with pirates. Almost everyone I talked to would begin by asking if I'd heard anything about the Confederation fleet, or offer some gossip that suggested their arrival was imminent.

I didn't believe it was, myself. As far as I could tell, this Confederation was a small grouping of only a dozen or so systems. They'd sent a fleet the last time, but I reckoned that made it *less* likely they would again. With limited Naval strength, they'd be asking what was in it for them. The Kharalchans already owed for the help they'd got the last time, and they hadn't paid anything back.

I tried not to think about the pirates. Because if they came, then Raine would go out to fight them, and most likely die somewhere in the utter cold and dark. Without me. Because I planned to be back in the Empire as soon as possible, a Prince again, with all these difficult thoughts washed away.

But in the meantime, the only way not to think about the future was either to be with Raine or to physically wear myself out traveling all over the Habitat doing twice as many hull patches as any hull patcher before me. While also, of course, looking for hidden Imperial tek.

In my first month I spent a lot of time in the Hub, at least in the parts where I was allowed to go. It contained all the docks, the main power plants, and so on, so at first I thought it the most likely place to find anything hidden away by the former ruling Prince. But after I'd managed to visit as much of it as KSF Security would let me, I changed my mind. The Hub was too much in constant use. As the most secure part of the Habitat it would be where the Prince would have deployed all his or her *obvious* ships, the mekbi garrison and so on. The temple would also have been in the Hub.

So where would a sneaky Prince park some secret stuff and, most important of all, a secret ship?

I kept my ears open for any hints, but the Empire had been gone a long time, and if there were any myths about old Imperial tek, I didn't hear them amid the general abuse of Princes, the Empire, and so forth. Leak detection let me look into odd corners and spaces, but only a small part of my mind was intent on finding leaks. I was also reaching out with my Psitek senses, hoping that I'd get a reaction from something hidden away, something that was just waiting for a Prince to activate it.

I got nothing for a month, except very bored with patching tiny pinprick holes. I decided I had to narrow down my search and really examine the Habitat structure for some likely hiding places.

It took me a while, but when I eventually figured it out, I wondered why it had taken me so long. After all, I'd wandered past the visible part of it several times before. But once I'd targeted it as a likely locale and spent more time probing it with my Psitek, I was finally rewarded with the faintest whisper of a response from an Imperial Psitek system. I felt the slight frisson in my head as I looked out at a section of the Habitat that was perfect for hiding just about anything.

The reservoir in Dolphin ring.

This was the biggest single source of fresh water for the Habitat, occupying the lower fifty meters of a whole octant of the ring. A small part of it was open as a ten-meter-deep lake, which people could swim in if they wanted, but most of it was hidden under a nicely shaped hill loaded with broad-leafed atmosphere-renewal trees.

I reckoned that somewhere deep inside the closed part of the reservoir was where I'd find something interesting. It would be easily accessible for a Prince, who didn't need to breathe for a half hour or so. But very forbidding for a human. Even recreational divers would not be tempted by the dark depths of a reservoir, and since it was used for drinking-water storage, there would be health barriers as well.

As soon as I found it, I thought about having a look in Ekkie, but I wouldn't even get to the lake if I was seen wandering about wearing a vacuum suit, or even carrying one. I was sure that a number of citizens had been alerted to look out for me, and the Habitat's security systems were programmed to keep an eye on me as well. Though both the human and system surveillance had holes I'd identified, I couldn't get a suit all the way to Dolphin.

But in the box of stuff the KSF had let me keep from my life capsule, I did have the Bitek template for what was described as an aquatic rescue beast. I read the data ribbon on it and discovered that dolphins weren't mythical after all. This template was a distant development of an Earth dolphin, and it would grow a six-foot-long finned hybrid air/water breather with a tentacled snout and, best of all as far as I was concerned, a breathing spigot for a rider, with automatic oxygen regulation. It could swim along at thirty kilometers an hour with me aboard, dive to seventy meters, and fetch things.

All I had to do was grow one from the template somewhere in the lake—somewhere that wasn't under the Habitat's watchful eye. Plus I'd have to feed it about a hundred and fifty kilograms of organic material over ten days.

And after all that, I could well be wrong. There might not be anything very interesting there, or the Kharalchans might have found it long ago. But I couldn't think of anywhere else old Imperial tek might be hidden—and the faint Psitek echo suggested it would be something good.

Fortunately, the answer to how I might hide and grow my aquatic rescue beast was presented the very next time I prowled along the shore, pointing my leak detector at the floor. Several people were lined up on the bank, about ten meters apart, each with a fishing pole. After the usual discussion about the wormhole, the pirates, and the Confederation fleet, I found that fishing was a popular pastime among many Karalchans. You just registered a spot on the shore and off you went. There were lots of fish, one of the better anglers told me. He showed me the five-kilogram salrout he'd caught. For a small fee, anglers were allowed to take fish home to eat. Or as I planned, not to take anywhere but feed to the template.

When I took it out there, I studied the sky high above, and the Habitat wall, and tried to work out where the long-range lenses were. Then I looked about for a spot that was awkward to reach and most sheltered by the oxygenating trees, registered that as my fishing place, and sent in an order for fishing gear and a training course. Not a direct mind download as in the Empire, but an interactive holo simulation that worked reasonably well. Interestingly, the fishing gear that arrived wasn't extruded Bitek but had actually been made on the planet, the rod from some kind of native wood and the reel and line from primitive Mektek metal and petroleum-derived substances. Apparently they fished in earnest down there.

A few days later, my aquatic rescue beast was growing nicely in the shallows a few meters out from my fishing spot.

Weirdly, even though it could only cause trouble, I really wanted to tell Raine about what I was up to, particularly as the aquatic beast neared its full growth. It took an effort not to blurt it all out in bed when we were chatting about what we'd been up to in the previous few days while Raine had been on duty.

"Patches, patches, and leaks," I said with a smile. "What about you?"

Raine turned in to me.

"Does it bother you? The patching thing? I'm sure you'll be able to get a better job soon . . . maybe join me on the *Firestarter*."

"I don't mind," I said hastily. "Or not too much, apart from not seeing you every day."

"You should be in the KSF," continued Raine. "I mean, you know more about ship systems and combat and everything than I do. More than the other officers, too, come to think about it. Even our captain."

She didn't mention that was because most of the veterans had been killed when Prince Atalin swept through the system. There was also a hidden question, which Raine was hinting at. We'd kind of moved on from being all about unspoken modes of communication into some actual verbal stuff. Raine had begun to want to know more about me and my past.

I hesitated for a moment, then I told her a little bit of the truth.

"I . . . ah . . . I *was* trained as a Naval officer, pretty intensively. I left to become a trader."

"I knew it!" exclaimed Raine, jumping on top of me. "You should tell Mother! We can get you on *Firestarter* for sure."

"Raine . . . I left the . . . Five Worlds Navy . . . because I didn't want to be a Naval officer. That's still true."

It was true. If—when—I got back to the Empire, I was going to leave the Navy if it was at all possible. Surely there would be another suitable cover for me as an Adjuster. Imperial Survey, maybe. I quite liked the idea of going exploring.

"But we need you!" protested Raine. "We need everyone."

"The Confederation fleet will arrive before the pirates," I reassured her. "Everyone says so."

"That's because we want to believe it," said Raine. "It doesn't mean it's true."

"If the pirates do come through before the Confederation . . ." I said slowly, "I'll do whatever I can to help."

Raine smiled and hugged me tight. I put my arm around her, hating that I wasn't telling her the truth, because if it was at all possible, I would be gone long before either the Confederation or the pirates arrived.

Later, while Raine slept, I wondered if I could take her with me. But as I watched her, I knew that this couldn't happen. Raine could only be my courtesan back in the Empire, and Haddad would quite rightly insist she be mind-programmed for obedience. She would die in the Empire, or be as good as dead, since the Raine I knew would no longer exist. I could not do that to her.

Even worse to my mind, if she was not mind-programmed, she would not want to be with *Prince* Khemri. I had to acknowledge that the Empire had done too much harm to her people, and as a Prince, I was the Empire. Or so it would seem to Raine.

I thought about that quite a lot, because while I wanted to be a Prince again, I did not want to lay claim to everything the Empire did. But it was an insoluble problem, for the two could not be separated. Prince and Empire. Empire and Prince. I was what they had made me.

The next morning Raine was called back on duty, with her ship about to launch. The KSF had cut short everyone's leave, but there were no official announcements for the reason behind this, and no reliable rumor, either.

It was yet another measure of how far I had departed from the normal behavior of a Prince that I made Raine take Ekkie for herself, with some sleight of hand covering a quick Psitek injunction to the suit to let itself be worn by her. Ekkie was by far the best vacuum suit I'd seen anywhere in Kharalcha, and I should have kept it for myself. But as I had now demonstrated twice, first in the capsule and then with the silver box I'd thought was a flower-trap, I was more concerned for her safety than my own.

Raine left with Ekkie. I forced down the feeling that I was somehow being broken in half—my Imperial self tearing away from some other identity that was emerging—and went to do my leak detecting and patching, and then to my fishing spot.

I queried the rescue beast's growth with Psitek and was startled by its reply. I'd thought it needed another few days, but it was fully operational, reporting that it had caught additional fish on its own to complete its growth.

I waded into the lake, letting the cool water lap against my knees, and then my waist. The rescue beast came up next to me, still submerged so it could not be seen.

I started to reach my hand out to it but stopped. This was now the point of decision, come upon me unexpectedly, ahead of time.

I didn't know what to do. This was my first step back toward the Empire, back to being Prince Khemri. If I went into the lake now and found, as I hoped, a ship, my former life would be within my grasp once more.

But it would also be the first step away from Raine. The step that could not be taken back. Did I really want to leave Raine and return to the Empire?

"I love her," I whispered, trying the words out on my tongue. I had not yet said them to Raine, and now that I wanted to, it was too late.

Or was it?

I took a step back, the water coiling around my knees, settling back into its equilibrium.

Who did I really want to be? Khem, who had found the universe to be a far more varied and marvelous place than he had ever supposed? Or Prince Khemri, who I suddenly saw clearly was a cog in a vast machine? A massively overprivileged cog, to be sure, but those privileges disguised the fact that we Princes were not free. Not free to be anything other than what the Empire desired us to be.

I stood there for what felt like a very long time but was probably only seconds, torn between my past and my possible futures.

I pushed a foot back, the water swirling, and began to turn for the shore, beginning a decision that I was still not entirely sure would be my final choice.

As I turned, the artificial sky of the ring flashed from blue to a sunset red, accompanied by the sound of a long-drawn-out electronic scream followed by three short blasts, repeated over and over again.

I knew what it meant. It was the signal for all KSF to report to battle stations and civilians to Evacuation Drop Points. Not that there was much chance of getting a hundred and fifty thousand Hab dwellers down to the planet in time, but I supposed they had to try.

There was only one possible reason for the alarm. The wormhole must have reopened earlier than expected.

The pirate fleet was coming through.

20

FOR A FEW seconds I was frozen by that alarm. All my thoughts were now with Raine. Her ship would be flung out to try to stop the pirates, along with the few others that had been at least partially refitted over the last four months. A forlorn hope, the too young and the too old, in ancient, undergunned ships. They wouldn't stand a chance. . . .

"Khem! Khem Gryphon!"

Startled, I looked around. A man and a woman were coming through the trees. Both wore green-and-black security shipsuits and carried synaptic scramblers at the ready.

I guess I'd been under closer surveillance than I'd thought.

"Stay still and raise your hands!"

My mind changed again. I wasn't going to hang around as a prisoner. If I stayed free, and there was a ship under this lake, I might even be able to do something useful. For Raine, if not the ungrateful Kharalchans.

I waved to the security agents and dived into the lake. The rescue beast, as per its training, dived underneath me and rose up so I was on its back. I let my breath go in a cloud of bubbles and closed my mouth over the breathing tube. Then, following a sharp Psitek command, the rescue beast took me down, down through the bright upper waters into the dark depths of the lake that led to the inner reservoir.

Unless the agents had artificial gills, they wouldn't be following me anytime soon, and I would be really, really surprised if the Kharalchans still had that tek. If I was lucky, they wouldn't even have seen the rescue beast and would be scouring the edges of the lake, waiting for me to reemerge somewhere along the shoreline.

There was a rigid, water-permeable membrane between the lake and the reservoir to keep fish and presumably swimmers out of the drinking water, but I knew there had to be some other access point. As the rescue beast had a sonar imager that I could tap into, it didn't take long to find an interestingly broad airlock, much larger than any technical access required. It was locked, but I bypassed the security with a direct Psitek command that opened both doors.

It was completely dark inside the reservoir, and not for the first time I missed my augmented eyes. But the beast had its sonar, and using that, I began a search routine, building up an image of the reservoir interior.

I was most interested in the outer wall, because this was also the outer wall of the Dolphin ring. If the reservoir narrowed at any point and this wall got thicker than its usual five meters or so, it would be a giveaway that something was hidden there.

But when I found it, it wasn't in the outer wall. It was right out in front of me, in the very middle of the reservoir, sitting on the floor as brazen as anything. I supposed it could be mistaken for some sort of huge filter system, but I recognized the round dish shape immediately.

It was a Khorkrek-class Mektek-Bitek hybrid slingship, a design only three or four hundred years old. Which, if it was fully fitted out, not only had a Mektek wormhole drive and Mektek *and* Bitek interplanetary drives, but also carried a Kragor singleship, which could be launched at very high acceleration via its "slingshot," a weaponized extension of Imperial gravity control that could be used to pick up and throw space junk as well as launch fighter craft.

It was *exactly* the kind of ship I'd always wanted for myself, in those daydreaming years in my candidate temple. It was highly automated, so I could fly it alone, at least for a while. It was precisely the sort of ship a Prince would hide away as a fast personal escape vessel that also had its own very nasty kick if it came to fighting.

I rode the rescue beast to where the hatch would be, even though nothing showed up on the sonar, laid my hand on the smooth metal hull, and sent my command.

:Report status immediately Prince Khemri <<identifier>> assuming command:

I almost forgot to breathe from the tube as I waited for a reply. It wasn't immediate, and I felt a vibration through the hull before I sensed the Psitek response, but at last it came.

:Welcome Prince Khemri <<identifier>> to *Khorkrek 1118*. Status is alert from rest, rising, all systems going to full operation:

The hatch beneath me opened, and a cascade of water carried me and the rescue beast inside.

:Hold outer door open:

I held my breath and instructed the rescue beast to swim back and out into the lake, where it could survive and perhaps even prove useful to the Kharalchans. Plus it would distract the security duo and their inevitable reinforcements who would be looking for me.

The second the rescue beast was away, I told the ship to shut the outer door and pressurize. This took less than two minutes, but it felt a lot longer. Once again I'd forgotten that without augmentation, even a simple thing like holding my breath deep underwater was a considerable challenge.

Spluttering a little, I left the airlock and entered the ship. It had a Mektek hull, but that wasn't apparent, because the last Prince who had commanded it had obviously had very particular ideas for starship interior decoration. The floors were of some kind of pseudo-marble, veined with gold, and the walls paneled in Bitek reproduction chestnut, with a deep-yellow sheen that would never need polishing. The hatches and doors, though actually Imperial Mektek armor, were also clad in Bitek fireproof timbers, so the whole ship interior looked and felt like a house of antiquity from ancient Earth. There was even a spiral staircase up to the bridge, though as I ascended, I picked up a Psitek overlay showing controls to retract the stair, and it would become a drop shaft.

I liked it. Whoever had decorated this ship had experienced a lot of the same kind of Psitek bios as I had. It even could have been modeled on one of the ships from an episode of *The Achievements of Prince Garikm.*

I entered the bridge through a double door of studded bronze and green leather that swung open noiselessly on my approach. Inside, a fireplace lit itself and a huge scarlet leather armchair rotated to face me. I sat down in it and felt the presence of the ship's Bitek intelligence, eagerly awaiting my attention.

:I am in command:

There was an odd delay before the ship answered.

:Psitek confirmation. Bitek confirmation anomalous.
Request code phrase:

I felt a sudden apprehension. In this body I didn't have the correct Bitek signature, and I certainly didn't know any code phrases relevant to this ship.

:I am an Adjuster operating in nonaugmented physicality.
Allow command on interim basis until connection to
Imperial Mind possible for confirmation:

I sent that with some vehemence, putting all my mental strength behind it. Hopefully this would help convince it. Or it might know about Adjusters, with some secret instructions hidden away in its intelligence base.

There was another delay. I could almost feel the Bitek brain deep inside the ship thinking this through.

:Acknowledged. Temporary command confirmed.
Relay to Imperial Mind not possible. Priest complement
incomplete. No priests in stasis:

I let out a small sigh of relief and relaxed back in the big chair. It was interesting that the ship had stasis chambers. Few Imperial ships of this size had the facility to store personnel in cold sleep until they were needed. The technology did have its drawbacks, with a loss rate of some one in ten revivals, but it saved on life-support consumption and you could stack a lot of personnel into a small space.

:Report stasis complement:

:In stasis fourteen mekbi servitors model Kergekh-Alish; ten mekbi troopers model Gilgakhr revised II; six mekbi small-access drones model Leeish; three mind-programmed humans class courtesan, gender male; three mind-programmed humans class courtesan, gender female. Seventeen empty stasis pods, fully functional. Four empty stasis pods, compromised:

That was interesting. I'd definitely found a Prince's personal escape ship, given the servitors and courtesans. It also begged the question of why Prince Xaojhek hadn't taken this ship when he'd left almost three hundred years ago. I'd asked Raine and her parents about the sudden Imperial departure, in as roundabout a way as possible, but they hadn't shed any light on the matter, and as I couldn't look into the Hab's knowledge base without Alice wondering about my choice of information retrieval, I'd not pursued it. All I could find from general sources was that the immediate period after the Prince bugged out had been very problematic, with few surviving records and no clear indication of what had happened.

So I thought I might as well ask the ship.

:Was Prince Xaojhek your former commander?:

:Yes. Prince Xaojhek <<identifier>>:

:Report last confirmed status of Prince Xaojhek and how long ago:

:In transit for system Jeghre aboard INS *Lorghra*. Time elapsed since report 262 years, four months, three days, six hours, and forty-five min—:

:Report rank and service Prince Xaojhek:

:Planetary Governor, Kharalcha Four, Imperial Government:

:Was Prince Xaojhek recalled by a superior Prince or by the Imperial Core?:

:No information:

:Do you know why Prince Xaojhek left the system and did not return?:

:No information:

I decided to let the past go and concentrate on the present.

:How long until systems are operational for launch and maneuver?:

:One hour thirty-three minutes fifteen seconds . . . fourteen sec—:

:Show available scan data for system:

:Null-space scan single pass done eighty-two percent confidence continuous scan not yet operational projecting now:

I looked at the wall and then at the ceiling but couldn't see anything. Nor was there a direct Psitek neural feed.

:Uh, where is the scan projection?:

:The fireplace. Prince Xaojhek liked to see data presentations in the fire:

Unusual, but each to his own, I guessed. I started to turn to look at the fireplace. The chair, equipped for biofeedback, swiveled around. Sure enough, there, framed by actual flames, was a holographic representation of the system, in great but tiny detail that I couldn't see without augmented eyes. Impatiently, I reached out and pulled the holo out of the fire and then, using the standard swipe-and-pinch technique, enlarged and scrolled it until I could see what I wanted to see.

Sixteen ships had come out of the wormhole, in four

formations of four, showing considerable military precision. They were boosting toward Kharalcha Four at five G's, indicating that they had gravity control and so were *not* beaten-up old hulks. They were on an interception trajectory that would meet the five considerably slower outbound ships of the KSF in about forty hours. One of those KSF ships was the *Firestarter*, and on board was Commtech Lieutenant Raine Gryphon.

I highlighted the pirate fleet.

:Get me all data on these ships and estimated interception time at full combat acceleration . . . uh . . . do you have an operational singleship aboard?:

:One Kragor III-class singleship is being crash-prepped from stand-down. Permission to revive mekbi servitors to accelerate preparation?:

:Permission granted. Ah, revive the mekbi troopers and the drones as well:

:And MP-human courtesans?:

:No . . . keep them on ice:

I looked at the holo again. I was out of practice for ship command, and I knew my brain just wasn't working as quickly as it used to. I was also a bit distracted by the water dripping off my nose.

:Uh, report combat capabilities and send a servitor with a towel:

:Servitor revival in fourteen minutes. Weapon bays one to six topside no weapons in place. Weapon bays twelve to eighteen downside no weapons in place. Weapon bays seven to ten operational, in place Lixgur Standard Fourteen Mektek missile load Bitek penetrator kinetic sliver:

The ship droned on in my head, basically telling me that half its weapons had been removed, but we still packed enough missiles and two reality-stripping beam weapons to cause someone a lot of trouble, and the singleship was almost fully armed and would have a complete combat load in a few hours.

But I wasn't giving it all my attention. I was looking first at the KSF fleet, and in particular the ship I thought was the *Firestarter*, and thinking about Raine. However things turned out, I would never see her again. That little orange ship icon was my last connection to her. I stared at it and wiped my nose again, and then my eyes for good measure, because some of the water had dripped into the corners and was making my sight blur.

The ship was still droning on in my head when I noticed something else in the holographic display. A tiny green icon amid the great swath of asteroidal dust and debris that made up the ring around Kharalcha Six, the gas giant.

I touched the icon.

:What's that?:

The ship stopped telling me about its armaments in too great detail. There was another curious pause before it answered.

:That is Imperial Survey Watch Post Lozhren-Wassek:

:And what's at this watch—:

The icon under my finger faded out of the display.

:Hey, what happened?:

:Query not understood:

I stabbed the holo with my finger.

:What happened to the Survey watch post in the gas giant ring just there?:

:Information base update lag. Null-space/real space dissonance. There is no Survey watch post:

I guessed that was possible, but I was suspicious. That IS watch post was there, for sure, but a Prince—or maybe the Imperial Mind—had just told my ship not to notice it.

The whole thing smelled to me. Atalin sent in to wipe out the defenders, a pirate fleet with relatively modern ships and training, a Survey post hidden in the gas giant ring . . . even my own appearance in this, of all systems. But I couldn't be sure whether this was all set up as part of my test to join Adjustment or whether someone else was involved, pulling other strings.

"Whoever you are, I hope you enjoy the show," I muttered.

:Query?:

"Not you, ship," I answered aloud. "Which reminds me, do you have a name?" :What did Xaojhek call you?:

:Ship:

:Uh, do you have a name on the Navy list?:

:Reserve Vessel *Khorkrek 1118*:

I sighed. I'd gotten used to conversing with humans. Communicating to the Bitek brain of a starship was all too like talking to a mind-programmed servant.

:I'm going to call you *Korker*:

:*Korker*. Kore-ker:

:Very good, *Korker*. I want a course that will take us out of here with no or at most minimal damage to the Habitat, then at maximum acceleration past the KSF fleet here, staying beyond their weapon range, to attack this fleet here, first launching kinetic slivers to be followed up by singleship to mop up, which I will pilot. I will then loop back to rendezvous for retrieval and we will depart through the exit wormhole here:

I tapped the holo as I gave *Korker* these directions.

:Bring up wormhole connections from that exit to the

closest Imperial possession according to your information base:

I'd looked at the Kharalchans' star maps, but they weren't very useful. They had good data spinward to the Confederation and for some parts beyond, but very little coreward to the Empire. Apparently ships just didn't go through that wormhole exit anymore, or if they did they didn't report back.

Korker, on the other hand, had all the star maps I might need, even if they were a few hundred years out of date. According to this information, the nearest Imperial possession was a mere three wormhole transits away. An alien world called something unpronounceable by its inhabitants and Xinxri by the Empire, it was under Colonial Government, which meant there would be a Prince in residence, and a temple. This was unlikely to have changed in the few hundred years since *Korker*'s information base had been updated. I still didn't understand why the Empire had left Kharalcha, but alien worlds of worth were relatively rare, and I was sure Xinxri would still be firmly under Imperial control.

Getting into the temple there might be interesting, but I was content to leave tomorrow's problems for tomorrow.

Today's problem was the pirates, and as per usual, I had been somewhat overconfident about that, as *Korker* soon told me.

:Preliminary analysis of inbound fleet suggests lead vessel has gravitonic field suppression capabilities sufficient to divert kinetic slivers from fleet:

Typical. Just when I got my hands on some advanced tek for once, the enemy turned out to have some as well.

:Report enemy capability and any identification. Are they communicating?:

:Enemy vessels self-identify as belonging to Porojavian

Co-Prosperity Collective. They are Imperial copy-Mektek of unknown origin. Capabilities of basic equivalence to one Lyzgro-class light cruiser, three Dyshzko-class destroyers, twelve Leolekh-class transports:

I sat back in my chair and thought deeply. The Lyzgro light cruiser was a real fly in the ointment. The transports would be mere chaff to my divine wind, the Dyshzkos not much more opposition. But the Lyzgro was a ship type only thirty or forty years old. I was very surprised there was a copy of it out in the Fringe, as at the Academy I'd been taught it took more than seventy-five years on average for an Imperial design to be successfully copied. Of course it wouldn't have the Psitek enhancements of a real Imperial ship, but the basic design had all the Mektek trimmings: gravity control, gravitonic screens that could shield the fleet against kinetic sliver attacks, and also very heavy armor, so the reality strippers *Korker* mounted wouldn't do much except at very close range. . . .

I'd have to take the Lyzgro out first with the singleship, and then *Korker* could destroy the other ships with kinetic slivers, missiles that accelerated up to 0.2 light speed.

Singleships were made to be piloted by Princes. I could control one with my Psitek, but I hadn't counted on having to go up against real opposition, requiring full acceleration. The Kragors used most of their power for maneuver, so their internal gravity control was far less powerful than that used in larger ships, and it reduced rather than nullified gravitational stress. To successfully assault the Lyzgro and avoid its weapons, I'd have to do an attack run at 40-G acceleration, which meant the effect of 10 G's in the cockpit, for at least thirty minutes. As a Prince practicing that sort of run, all I'd had were momentary blackouts.

As a normal human, I'd have a brain like a squashed fruit and all my blood squeezed into my toes and then sprayed all over the cockpit.

But I simply couldn't coast in, not against a modern ship like the Lyzgro.

I thought about this for a few seconds. The obvious solution was not to attack the pirates at all, but just to bug out through the exit wormhole back toward Imperial space. That's what any sensible Prince would do.

However, I was no longer a sensible Prince, and it was *possible* for me to survive 10 G's for thirty minutes, with suitable precautions.

:*Korker*, I presume there is a Bitek cornucopia on board?:

:Three. Two general-purpose, one gourmand food specialist. There is a shortage of some specialized precursor materials:

:Okay, manufacture enough Bitek accel gel to fill a singleship cockpit plus twenty percent, and I need a medical symbiote implanted immediately:

:Done:

I felt a slight sting on my arm and looked down. A panel was closing in the armrest, an advanced symbiote applicator withdrawing inside. In one swift motion it had cut away a square of my shipsuit and introduced the symbiote. It was a much more advanced model than the one I had used on Raine. It didn't need the applicator as an interface but had already grown a patch of vision-skin over my own flesh. This was now displaying my general condition—and an alert that was flashing red.

I focused on the alert at once. It said there was an alien object the size of a pinhead in the flesh between the knuckles of the third and fourth fingers of my right hand. I'd forgotten about the ID tag, which had to also be a tracking device. I told the symbiote to destroy it. I guess the KSF and Commander Alice weren't as trusting as I'd thought. Or maybe it was a parental thing. But it meant they knew that I'd gone into the reservoir and had vanished, as it would appear, as soon as I got behind the ship's protective screens.

They'd be looking very seriously for me now, given that I'd inadvertently timed my disappearance to coincide with the pirates' arrival in system.

:How soon till launch?:

:One hour forty-five minutes fifteen seconds:

I hesitated for a moment, unsure of the best course of action. Or rather, the best course of action given that I'd gone totally mad and wasn't just going to depart Kharalcha forever.

:Scan shows small parties of aquatic-equipped humans approaching through the reservoir. Tracking with close-interdiction RS beam. Fire?:

:Don't fire! Patch me into the Habitat communication system. Find location of Commander Alice Gryphon and open a channel to a comm at her location:

Another holographic panel sprang up in the fireplace, partially overlapping the scan display until I flicked it across and closer to me. It showed a very busy control center, with around fifty KSF and other uniformed personnel all working away at individual command stations that were hybrid tek, each with three or four holographic screens on top of Bitek stalks that funneled power and provided nerve relays for data transfer.

The command stations were arranged in five concentric rings, and it was easy to see that the outer rings were junior stations, growing more senior as you progressed inward. Alice Gryphon was standing at her station in the innermost ring. Like most of the others, she had a headset on and was listening intently to something.

:Patch in and project my image and voice on the holo unit in front of Alice Gryphon:

My screen flashed and my viewpoint changed. I was now looking directly at Alice, and she was looking directly at me. Her jaw dropped for an instant, before she suppressed her surprise.

"Hello, Alice," I said. "Uh, I wanted to call to . . . to update you on some stuff you need to know."

"You're in that ship in the reservoir," said Alice slowly.

"Yes," I replied. "Look, it's not exactly—"

"Gold Taiga Rosamond Latchkey Execute," said Alice, but not to me. She shut her eyes and added in a whisper, "Forgive me, Raine."

21

"UH, IS SOMETHING supposed to have happened?" I asked Alice nicely.

This time she couldn't hide the shock on her face.

:Nuclear fusion initiation stifled in close proximity: reported *Korker.* :Device rendered inoperative:

:What device?:

:A fusion mine copy of model Fyrrez-Waltav 231, fixed to the reservoir floor under my hull, emplaced there thirty-two years ago, replacing an earlier device. Nil threat:

So the Kharalchans had pretty much always known this ship was here. They just couldn't get into it or do anything about it. Though obviously they'd hoped the fusion mine would take it out in extreme circumstances, like someone trying to use it against them. As Alice had clearly presumed I would.

"Just wait!" I said hurriedly as the shock passed over Alice's face and I saw determination sweep back in. "Don't do anything rash. I actually want to help you."

"Help us?" replied Alice bleakly. "To ensure more loot survives for you and the other pirates?"

"I'm not with the pirates, Alice," I said firmly.

"Then you serve the Empire, which aids the pirates."

"Ah, not that, either," I replied. Some other KSF officers, including a man I recognized as Admiral Wylliam Sphinx, their commander-in-chief, had come in close to Alice's station. "I had no prior knowledge of the pirates, and while it's true I am . . . um . . . I am temporarily working for a Prince, he's not involved here either. And I doubt that it was an Imperial order to clear the path for the pirates. That's some private initiative."

"A *private initiative* to kill more than twelve thousand men and women and leave thousands more to be the prey of pirates and slavers?" spat Alice.

"I'm not going to discuss how the Empire works right now, or its morality," I said. "I just wanted to tell you not to do anything stupid, because this ship will react against any attacks, and also . . ."

I bit my lip for a moment and hesitated. I could still change my mind. But somehow saying to Raine's mother what I was going to do made my choice irrevocable. It was stupid, and irrational, and I didn't know why a few simple words could bind me to a course of action, but there it was.

"Also," I said, taking a deep breath, "I have asked the Prince in command of this ship to destroy those pirates . . . and he has agreed to do so."

"There's a Prince there?" asked the Admiral, butting in as

Alice stared at me without speaking, her eyes looking like they would burn a hole through an Imperial battlesuit.

"Yes," I said, thinking fast. "He's been in stasis. I was sent to find him and wake him up."

"We want to talk to the Prince," demanded Admiral Sphinx.

I shook my head.

"He's . . . busy. You should be grateful he's agreed to attack the pirates. They've got some recent tek, and it's not going to be easy."

"Who are you?" asked Alice, her voice overriding something the Admiral was going to say. "What are you?"

Who was I? What was I? I didn't really know myself.

"You *know* I'm just an ordinary human; you scanned me," I said, doing my best to look her in the eye. "A Fringe trader. I trade with some Imperial worlds. A Prince on one of my regular stops made me an offer I couldn't refuse—I mean really couldn't—to come here and retrieve the sleeping Prince and this ship. I don't know why she wanted it done on the quiet. Princes . . . Princes work in inexplicable ways to us ordinary people."

Then I did look Alice square in the eye.

"I didn't know I would meet Raine. I didn't know that I would . . . that I would fall in love with her."

Love. I'd said it now, and now I knew what it meant.

Alice might have said something then, but the Admiral had pretty much edged her out of the way.

"The Prince . . . he really will attack the pirates?"

"Yes," I said. "He owes me."

"How quickly can you engage the enemy?" asked the Admiral.

I asked *Korker* this via mindspeech at almost the same time and relayed the answer. It was a hell of a lot faster than the KSF, because *Korker* could maintain 25-G acceleration and a nice single gravity inside the ship.

"Twenty-one hours," I replied. "Well ahead of your fleet, Admiral."

He blinked, but it wasn't surprise at the speed of my ship. They'd seen Imperial craft in action before. I knew it was relief, that he had given up hope and now here was a straw to clutch at.

"You don't have to go with the ship, if the Prince has agreed," said Alice suddenly. "We'd detain you, until things work out as you say and the pirates are defeated, but then . . . you'd be welcome here. Right, Admiral?"

"Of course!" snapped the Admiral. "You'll have done us another great service, on top of your part in shutting down the wormhole."

So they had known how involved I'd been in that and just pretended otherwise. These Kharalchans were more cunning across the board than I'd thought.

I shook my head, not bothering to try to hide my regret.

"It's not up to me. The Prince has given his orders. I have to go with the ship. It's old, and has been on standby a long time. There are things I can do to help prepare for the combat."

"Khem, I didn't want to . . . the standing orders were to fire that mine," said Alice.

"I understand," I replied. "If things were different . . .. but they're not. I'll do what I can against the pirates."

"Thank you," said Admiral Sphinx.

I almost said "Thank Raine" but held my tongue. That might cause her problems; they might think she knew more about me and hadn't reported it. Besides, while it was true, it wasn't the whole story. I did want to save Raine, but I also wanted to save the whole sorry Habitat, even including the stupid, annoying people like Ganulf, simply because they had become people to me, not just subservient pawns to be used for my own purposes.

A Bitek servitor arrived at this point and handed me a towel. Alice and the other Kharalchans tried not to stare but couldn't help it. I guess they'd never seen the insect-human hybrids in a current context instead of in old recordings, and as mekbi servitors weren't hidden under armor like the troopers, their narrow waists, chitinous thoraxes, and limbs were glaringly obvious.

:Terminate transmission:

Korker obeyed, cutting Alice off as she was about to say something. I didn't want to keep talking. There wasn't anything left to say.

Besides, I hadn't been lying when I said there was work to be done on the ship. There were many preparations to be made.

We left the reservoir on schedule, a little less than an hour later. I'd thought we might have to cut our way out through the Habitat hull, but Prince Xaojhek had prepared everything very carefully. There was an emergency hatch beneath us, big enough for the ship. It opened slowly, water boiling off into space for a good fifteen minutes, creating a nice diversionary cloud if we'd needed one. But not as much water as I'd expected, since various membranes like the one between the lake and the reservoir proper changed to their emergency properties and no longer allowed even water through.

The ship slid out of its long hiding place with a gentle push from its thrusters and maneuvered away from the Habitat at a sedate 0.25 G. The Kharalchans didn't even bother to track us with the meteor protection laser grid in case I was lying. I guess they knew that it would be a waste of time anyway.

A suitable distance from the Habitat, we kicked into high gear. *Korker* went from an amble to a sprint, accelerating up to its full 25 G's and twenty thousand kilometers a second in less than an hour.

Not that I noticed inside. With internal gravity control, allied with Null-space sensors and a Bitek artificial consciousness to operate them, this velocity and such things as minor relativistic effects were of no consequence.

I had twenty hours or so before we would be in launch range, but that was only just enough time, because in addition to the symbiote who I hoped would help me live through serious singleship maneuvers and anything else that might happen, I also had to fill the Kragor's cockpit—and myself—with Bitek acceleration gel.

This disgusting, translucent material was roughly the consistency of snot. Highly oxygenated and engineered to be breathable, it broke down carbon dioxide and did a whole lot of other useful things. But to get the full effect, you had to be immersed in it and breathing the stuff.

And as I discovered, if you have a normal human body, you definitely need a medical symbiote to keep you calm as the stuff slowly flows into nostrils, mouth, throat, and lungs. It hurt, and it felt like drowning, and even though I knew it was designed to be breathable, I just couldn't believe it.

Nevertheless, quite a few hours later, I was in the Kragor cockpit, in an Imperial flight suit, totally restrained by crash webs, and completely saturated and immersed in acceleration gel. Not to mention mildly sedated by the symbiote.

Everything depended on my Psitek now. I couldn't move, and I couldn't talk. I could fly the Kragor using direct Psitek commands, and I could communicate with *Korker.* At least I hoped I'd still be able to communicate with *Korker* after I launched. But my Psitek felt strong, so I was reasonably confident.

Korker kept me updated on scan, but there wasn't a lot to tell. We'd long since shot past the KSF fleet, and the pirates were just barreling in, without any tricky tactical maneuvers. There was a slim possibility that *Korker*'s stealth capabilities were hiding us, but it was more likely that they did not see me as an enemy, and thus saw no need to change their course or plan.

I hoped this would give me another small edge in what was to come.

I also hoped I would survive the launch. The point of greatest stress on my body would be when the singleship was launched by *Korker*'s slinging gravitor and at the same time went on its own gravity control.

:Let's just go over the plan one more time, *Korker*:

:Yes:

:As soon as we enter extreme effective range, you fire one salvo of kinetic slivers at the Lyzgro and launch the Kragor immediately behind. With the cloaking package, it should look like a defective missile. They'll think it will get taken care of by the gravitic screen, so they won't bother shooting. As soon as I'm in close effective range, I launch the Kragor's slivers. I'll be inside their screen by then, there'll be nothing they can do, and the Lyzgro will be knocked out. At the same time I launch my sliver, you launch slivers at all the other ships. Without the Lyzgro's screen, they also explode into little bits. Got it?:

:Affirmative:

It was either a brilliantly simple plan or a remarkably stupid one. Unfortunately the only way to discover which one was to carry it out. Most of it would depend on just how up-to-date the Lyzgro's tek was. If their sensors could see through *Korker*'s cloaking and spoofing systems, they would see me coming, and though they probably couldn't hit a singleship with a sliver, they had reality strippers, fusion beam cannon, and other stuff that certainly could.

I also had to survive the brutal acceleration and high-velocity maneuvering long enough to not only pilot the singleship but coordinate the strike.

:Fourteen minutes fifty seconds to launch:

:Acknowledged:

I wondered if there was anything else I should do, or order *Korker* to do. But I couldn't think of a single thing.

:Anomalous rayder message received "For Khem":

:Relay it:

It was from Raine. Even though it was the ship relaying it to me via Psitek and so it was straight into my head, I could have sworn I heard her voice.

"Khem. It's Raine. I just got a message from Mother about what you're doing, and how you came to be able to do it . . . and I wanted to tell you I don't care who you are, or where you're from, or why you came here. I know you'll do what's right. I love you."

:The message is looped. Do you wish to receive it again?:

:No . . . but keep it. I may . . . I may want to listen to it again, when . . . if I get back:

:Ten minutes thirty seconds to launch:

I lay in my sea of goop and *didn't* wonder what I was doing, or why I was doing it.

I knew it was right.

Eleven minutes later, I wasn't so sure. Barely able to stay conscious, I had a terrible pain in my chest and guts, despite the symbiote's efforts. The acceleration gel around me was stained pink with blood from my nose and ears and who knows where else, and I couldn't tell if I still had any hands or feet since I couldn't feel anything below my elbows or knees.

On the positive side, my Kragor singleship was streaking toward the enemy at incredible speed, Null-space sensors had detected no launches toward me, and even better, one of *Korker*'s preliminary kinetic slivers had got through the Lyzgro's screen and taken out one of the Leolekh transports already. Analysis suggested that many of the bits and pieces trailing along in the funnel-shaped cloud where it had been were people or bits of them. That transport and probably most of the others had been packed with ground troops. Many hands make light work of serious looting. If they got through, they would strip the Habitat bare, taking all useful tek, and they would plunder the world beneath as well, stealing all the crops, livestock, and stores, thus sentencing everyone they didn't kill in the first place to a lingering death through starvation.

My Psitek was also working, though it took a supreme effort to focus, to rise above the pain and the terrible sensation of being crushed to death. But I had no problem reaching *Korker*, and the singleship continued to answer to my mental controls.

:Enemy launch: reported *Korker*. Simultaneously, I ordered evasive action and discovered that in acceleration gel, it is impossible to scream. I managed a mental one, though.

A second later, we were struck by the passage envelope of a kinetic sliver.

I knew it was only the envelope because I was still alive and the singleship was still sort of in one piece around me.

But the drive had been damaged. Dozens of status reports flickered through my brain, all of them negative.

I felt the pressure on my body lessen. We were still moving at an incredible speed toward the enemy, but the singleship was losing acceleration as the drive failed.

There was other damage too. We were venting something, a trail visible to *Korker*. I pretty much knew what it was even before I checked, or *Korker* chimed it.

:You are losing acceleration gel:

:I know. Time to optimum firing position?:

:Forty-four seconds:

I knew, all right. I'd been here before, with Raine. My acceleration gel was my atmosphere, and it was going fast. Too fast to be survivable. No induced coma can help you survive a total lack of air. There had to be a biggish hole somewhere behind me, and all my precious atmosphere was spewing out of it.

I really was dead this time.

I just had to live long enough to make sure I took out the pirate flagship so *Korker* could take out the rest.

It was a long forty-four seconds.

:Screen perimeter passed. Launch:

All my slivers flew, followed only seconds later by *Korker*'s.

The singleship's acceleration faded again a moment later. The pressure on my body eased, though the pain didn't, and the feeling didn't return to my arms and legs.

But I didn't care about that. All my attention was focused on waiting for the sliver impact, which came some three seconds later.

The singleship and *Korker* reported at exactly the same time, a chorus inside my head.

:Target destroyed. Lyzgro destroyed. Dyshzko 1 destroyed. Dyshzko 2 destroyed. Dyshzko 3 destroyed. Leolekh-class transports 1 through 10 destroyed. One transport severely damaged:

So we didn't quite get them all, I thought wearily. But I couldn't do anything now. I was too tired, and everything hurt. I wanted to rest. . . .

But I knew I couldn't yet, not quite. The task had to be finished. Raine and her people had to be protected.

:*Korker*. Close and . . . destroy remaining transport. Pick up singleship. Carry on planned course . . . to Xinxri:

My eyes were already shut. They had been all the time. But I felt a darkness come as if I had squeezed my eyelids tight, a spreading darkness that brought with it a biting cold.

I guessed I'd failed the test to become an Adjuster.

But I'd passed the test for being human.

So this is the very precipice of death, I thought. *It feels different when it's final.*

:Highness. Reach for the Mind:

I think I tried to smile, though my face was frozen. It seemed appropriate that Haddad would be with me now, here at the end. Even if only as a figment of my imagination, the last gasp of electrical impulses in a failing cerebellum—

:Highness! Reach for the Mind!:

It wasn't just Haddad. It was all the priests of my household, all my uncles and aunts. I could feel them reaching for my mind, trying to grab me and reel me in, all the way from that little observation station in the ring around the gas giant. . . .

They were actually *in the system*! I could connect!

Dying, I reached out, and though I felt no buzz at the back of my head, the Imperial Mind was suddenly there, in all its cold glory.

:Connection reestablished Prince Khemri <<identifier>> and running. Check. Check. Save for rebirth assessment:

22

THAT WAS MY second death.

As previously, the next thing I knew I was lying on a comfortable bed. This time, I had the brief feeling that I was emerging from some long, calm sleep, but it vanished as I came to full consciousness with a snap and instantly I was back in my augmented body, a flood of reports rushed through my head, and hard on the heels of these updates came the familiar presence of the Imperial Mind.

:Welcome back Prince Khemri III <<identifier>> You have been weighed in the balance by our Priests of the Aspect of the Emperor's Discerning Hand and found worthy of rebirth <<Sigil of the Imperial Mind>>:

I sat up, and while I did not recognize the large and lavish chamber in which I found myself, I was greatly pleased to see

Haddad and my original twelve priests, with Uncles Frekwo and Aleakh at the front.

"Welcome back, Highness," said Haddad gravely.

"Where are we?" I asked. "The observation post in Kharalcha?"

"No, Highness. We are at the Imperial Core. You were returned to physicality here. However, your household and I did indeed come in from the system Odkhaz, which you may know as Kharalcha."

I raised an eyebrow. The Imperial Core was a world essentially reserved for ceremony. Long ago the Emperor and the Imperial Mind might have been located here, but it was well known that this was no longer the case. Whatever infrastructure the Imperial Mind needed was spread across the Empire, and the Emperor—well, no one knew who the Emperor was, let alone where he or she might be at any given time.

"How long was it this time?" I asked. "I mean, how long since I died?"

"Four months and one day, Highness."

Four months. So whatever had happened at Kharalcha was long done, already beyond any intervention from me.

"Did . . . did the pirates get through?" I asked.

"The fleet that you engaged was completely destroyed, Highness," said Haddad.

I looked away from him for a moment to hide my emotion as best I could. Raine was alive! The Habitat wasn't plundered . . . or at least it shouldn't have been . . . provided Atalin hadn't swung back again. I suppressed a surge of sudden fear.

"What is the current status of Kharalcha?" I asked. "What happened after . . . after I died?"

"As I mentioned, your household, including myself, returned

to Imperial space almost immediately," said Haddad. "However, knowing your interest, Highness, I have monitored system Odkhaz and can report that no further military engagements have taken place and that the system is on track to regaining its lost economic potential—"

"Why am I here, at the Imperial Core?" I interrupted, as another thought struck me.

"The Imperial Mind has announced that you are to be presented with the Imperial Star of Valor, and to be promoted to lieutenant commander in the Imperial Navy."

:I'm getting the Imperial Star of Valor?: I asked the Mind. The ISV was the highest decoration the Empire gave, and I certainly hadn't done anything to be honored with one. :Why?:

: Citation for ISV. On 272-4456 Prince Khemri III <<identifier>> in command of obsolete vessel ISN *Khorkrek* on recovery and salvage mission encountered a pirate fleet of eighteen vessels including light cruiser of recent copy-tek intent on looting Imperial Protectorate Odkhaz. Prince Khemri III engaged the pirate fleet in a close action personally piloting obsolete singleship Kragor 2, destroying all the pirates despite being mortally wounded:

"Imperial protectorate? Recovery and salvage mission?" I started to mutter to myself. What was this crap? And the pirates were only there because Prince Atalin had wiped out the KSF. I wouldn't mind betting that the Lyzgro light cruiser clone had been a present from a helpful Prince as well.

Why was the Imperial Mind treating what I did as a successful Naval action? And what was the Imperial protectorate about?

:Query effect of Imperial protectorate status for system Odkhaz:

:System Odkhaz directly reserved by Imperial Mind for future unspecified use. Off limits for Princes. No claims, no transit without specific orders. Imperial Survey watch post to maintain vigilance:

That was odd. The whole Kharalchan thing was strange. But at least the system was relatively safe now, to some degree at least. Atalin could not go back to clear away the remnants of the KSF without direct permission of the Mind, and with the main strength of the Porojavian Co-Prosperity Collective destroyed, the pirates couldn't do it alone. Maybe the long looked-for Confederation fleet might actually have turned up as well.

Despite trying not to, I thought of Raine again. I felt a pang as I visualized her back home in the Gryphon ring, perhaps lying on the bed we had shared. . . . These thoughts were not helpful. I was no longer Khem. Khem the trader was four months dead, buried with the past. Prince Khemri was a few minutes into a new life. I simply could not afford this sentimental reverie. I dismissed the memory, locking it away.

The past *is* another universe, and to all intents and purposes, Raine was dead to me.

"The reception before the presentation will commence soon, Highness," said Haddad tactfully, breaking into the silence. I realized I had been staring into some distant space. "Your valets are ready to dress you."

"All right," I grumbled, climbing out of the bed. I jumped a little on the spot and shadow-boxed to reacquaint myself with my enhanced muscles and reflexes. It was a heady, intoxicating feeling to once again be superhuman.

"What is the etiquette about assassination here at the Imperial Core?" I asked Haddad as my two mind-programmed valets entered with my ceremonial uniform, now with the red epaulettes of a lieutenant commander.

"It is expressly forbidden, and the Imperial Mind is constantly witnessing," replied Haddad. I nodded, suddenly noticing the familiar buzz at the back of my neck. "However, it cannot be totally discounted, so as always you must remain on guard. There is also another danger you will not be used to, Highness."

"What's that?"

"Princes at the Imperial Core are not considered as being on duty, so dueling is permitted between those of equal rank and those who do not hold rank in an Imperial service. There are many Princes here now, and with the abdication to come very soon, many see dueling as a means to bring themselves to the attention of the Emperor."

I knew that last was a figure of speech. No one knew who the Emperor was, or how he or she might be physically manifest in the Empire, because of course they could not go on as the Prince they had been. But they could have assumed any number of new identities, I supposed. In any case, as the ruler of the Imperial Mind, the Emperor could oversee anything, anywhere in the Empire where there was a Prince connected to the Mind. A number of notable successes in dueling would doubtless be noted by the Imperial Mind, and that in effect meant by the Emperor.

Now that I knew that it was possible to transfer a Prince's consciousness into different bodies, I wondered if I had in fact already met the current Emperor and just didn't know it. The Emperor might even have a number of different bodies and different identities. . . .

It was an interesting thought, but I dismissed it as I took my usual weapons from Haddad and hid them away before buckling on my ceremonial sword and putting on my hat. At least as a lieutenant commander I had a modest peaked cap instead of the ridiculous busby of the cadets.

An overlay of the route from my chambers to Grand Reception Palace Eight appeared in my head, annotated with an etiquette summary. Apparently I was to join 999 other Princes in the reception hall of this particular palace for drinks before we organized ourselves into a single line by level of decoration and proceeded to the Award Chamber, where we would be given our medals by either Grand Admiral of the Imperial Fleet Itzsatz or Domain Governor Leshakh, depending on our service.

Haddad accompanied me, a trusty and very welcome shadow. I realized that Haddad was in many ways the only one of my household whom I had always considered as a person, even before my Adjustment training. In some ways, he had a kind of similar place in my life as Alice had for Raine . . . once again, I had to stop myself thinking such thoughts. There could be no comparison. Haddad was merely my Master of Assassins, assigned to me and replaceable. It was a fault in me that he felt like something more, and I would have to suppress that feeling.

Only Haddad left the room with me, but on the way out I met another twelve new priests who had been assigned to me with my promotion, and six more apprentice assassins.

Unlike the Academy and my candidate temple, most of the Imperial Core was not underground. Or at least, the accommodations and public areas for visiting Princes were sited for aesthetic effect rather than for security. My rooms turned out to be in a small building of its own, situated in a charming park dotted with similar four-story houses built in a style imitating a region of ancient Earth that favored high gables and curved extensions thrusting out of multiple, stacked rooflines.

Other Princes, resplendent in the full dress uniforms of their various services and each accompanied by their Master of Assassins, were emerging from the nearby houses and setting out along the broad, paved path toward the Grand Reception Palace. I didn't need the overlay to find it, for it was the only structure of significant size within sight, a vast white building adorned with multiple turrets and onion-shaped domes that had been brightly gilded. It was not at all in the same architectural style as the Princely houses. In any case, underneath the different stylistic touches, it would all be the same, extruded Bitek composites and Mektek armor.

As I joined the main path between two groups of Princes, a sudden rain of cherry blossoms fell from the apparently empty sky, bringing a sweet scent. I held my breath, closed my nostrils and mouth, and looked at Haddad.

:Routine ceremonial. No danger:

I nodded but still kept my nose filters operational and my mouth shut. I also maintained my distance from the group of Princes ahead of me and the one behind. They were all older, and higher ranking, and there was at least one Rear Admiral in the group ahead. I caught their ID transmissions, lots of names, ranks, and services washing through my mind, but none meant anything to me until I entered the Reception Room. This was a vast chamber several hundred meters wide and long, with an arched ceiling high above painted with a star map of the Empire's earliest conquests. Mekbi servitors in white and gold robes were bustling about, offering drinks from silver trays to Princes who seemed to mostly be percolating into groups of their own service.

I took a drink and was idling my way toward a group nearby that was all Navy when I caught the ID broadcast of one of the officers whose back was toward me.

:Prince Atalin I <<identifier>> Lieutenant Commander, Imperial Navy. To be awarded Hero of the Empire First Class:

I queried the Imperial Mind.

:Citation. On 212-4456 Prince Atalin I <<identifier>> in command of ISN *Khouresk* on routine patrol was attacked by an illegal squatter fleet of twenty vessels in system Odkhaz, and destroyed the squatters without loss:

"That's a lie!" I said aloud, anger boiling up inside me.

Atalin turned around, and all the Naval officers stopped talking and looked at me, and then back at her. We did look remarkably similar, though Atalin had longer hair.

We stared at each other for a moment.

"Were you speaking to me, Prince Khemri?" she asked finally.

"The citation for your decoration is at odds with my experience," I said. The anger had become stronger than my common sense. I already knew where this was going, but I couldn't turn back. "I think you must agree my reaction is understandable."

"You said something about a lie," said Atalin calmly.

"I think it was the part about being 'attacked by an illegal squatter fleet,'" I said. "I personally wouldn't call a preemptive attack with a Null-Space Concussion Wave on a bunch of primitives being 'attacked' by them. Hardly the stuff of heroism."

"I think perhaps you are confused," said Atalin. "The Imperial Mind recorded, as always, the true facts of the matter."

There wasn't much of an answer to that. I knew what had happened, but if the Imperial Mind said otherwise, that was that as far as actually proving anything else.

"Perhaps the Imperial Mind was . . . distracted . . . in this case," I said. "But whether it was or not, I don't see anything very heroic in your space 'battle,' Prince Atalin."

Atalin shrugged and handed her glass to a servitor.

"You seem determined to give offense, Prince Khemri," she said. "It is a common fault among recent graduates of the Academy. Perhaps you think that your face too much resembles my own, and seek any excuse to have it altered? Very well, I will teach you a lesson you obviously did not get at the Academy. Name your weapons."

A duel. That was all I needed. In my candidate temple I had thought duels the stuff of Princely life, to be sought out at all times and relished. At the Academy, where duels were forbidden, the only obvious duelist was the Commandant, and I had no desire to be like him. Now, in the heat of anger, I simply wanted to beat Atalin, to teach her a lesson, to punish her for her destruction of the KSF fleet.

My dueling practice with Haddad aboard the INS *Zwaktuzh Dawn* on our way to Arokh-Pipadh seemed like a lifetime ago, but his advice about choosing uncommon weapons in a duel was suddenly uppermost in my mind.

"Bolt-and-cable guns," I snapped.

Atalin did not appear to be fazed. She turned to her Master of Assassins, a tall, very thin woman with long, sinewy arms. "Vivaldra? You will arrange matters with . . . Master Haddad? For after the ceremony?"

Vivaldra bowed and glided over to meet Haddad. They bent their heads together, blue fluid roiling in their temples, so close together they were almost but not quite touching.

:Honorees gather in decoration order now <<Sigil of the Imperial Mind>>:

"Till we meet again," said Atalin. She saluted me, and automatically I saluted back. I hated her for killing Raine's uncle and all those thousands of other Kharalchans, but at the same time, I couldn't help admiring her poise and coolness. I had to admit that even six months previously, I would have killed the Kharalchans too, without compunction.

I also couldn't stop thinking that she was almost certainly my sister. There was something about her, some Psitek whisper that spoke to me, saying that we were of the same blood. That she was to me what Anza had been to Raine, or could have been, if we had grown up together.

But even if this was true, and even if she did feel something similar, it could not and did not mean anything. Not for Princes of the Empire.

"Congratulations, Prince Khemri," said a voice at my elbow. A captain appeared next to me, his uniform a dazzling display of medals and ribbons, including the huge orb of the Imperial Star of Valor hanging from around his neck. "Welcome to our small but select order of companions."

"Thank you, sir," I muttered. But the words stuck in my throat. My own decoration was as false as Atalin's in its way. I wondered what this Captain Garuzk had got his for, but I didn't query the Mind. I really didn't want to know if he'd burned off an inhabited planet or something equally horrendous.

I thought about Atalin as I took my place near the very front of the long, long line of Princes. I'd provoked the duel in anger for what she had done, but really, I was angry at the Empire. Besides, fighting a duel wouldn't bring back the dead of Kharalcha, or stop something like that happening again. It wouldn't resolve anything. Even if one of us actually got killed, we'd be pretty certain to be reborn. I mean, how could the Aspect of the Discerning Hand find a Prince unworthy immediately after he or she had been decorated? And the Mind was witnessing constantly here at the Imperial Core, so there was no chance of error there.

Besides, what was I doing trying to be the instrument of the Kharalchans' revenge? I'd never see Raine again, and even if I did, what could I say to her? That I'd fought the Prince who'd killed her uncle and her family, and by the way, she was my sister and I killed her, but only for a little while, because she was reborn? And then we both went on being Princes together, doing whatever we felt like to all the Kharalchas of the universe, simply because we could. With rationalizations—and medals—to come afterward.

I felt sick at heart at the whole thing. But I couldn't show it. I was back in the machine, a moving part that had its role to play and could do nothing else. Except take my own life, I suppose, and I didn't want to do that. Certainly I couldn't see any way of escaping, of leaving the Empire. There was no escape from the Imperial Mind, nor from all my fellow Princes.

Cheerful thoughts like this occupied me on my way up to the dais to meet the Grand Admiral of the fleet. Prince Itzsatz was a charming fellow who didn't look anything like his 157 years, until I got up close and saw his eyes. They were old, and very, very cold—and the smile on his face never touched them.

"Well done, Prince Khemri," he said as I put my cap under my arm and knelt on the cushion provided. He draped the ribbon with its heavy medallion around my neck. "The Empire needs more young Princes like you. Straight into the enemy with a singleship, that's the way! I saw good things about your ground action against the Sad-Eyes, too. Keep it up, keep it up, haw-haw!"

I stood, replaced my cap, saluted, and executed a perfect right turn to march out of the side door—and saw Arch-Priest Morojal standing there, just out of sight of the main chamber.

I almost hesitated, but training took over. Without conscious direction, I marched through the doorway. Morojal beckoned to me, and instead of continuing along the broad main corridor the other Princes had taken, which led back to our waiting compatriots and Masters of Assassins, I followed the arch-priest along a much narrower passage.

I was not overly surprised when the light began to change and the sharp edges of the white palace corridor began to transform into the stands of bamboo, through which I could see a forest. A few minutes later, the corridor was entirely gone, and I was following Morojal along a slatted path through the green forest.

The stream burbled through the clearing, and the two chairs set there might not have been moved since I had last sat in them, when I was given the choice of joining Adjustment.

"Sit," said Morojal.

"Only if you answer my questions," I said belligerently.

"I will answer what I am able to answer," said Morojal. "Sit."

"Why was I given the Imperial Star of Valor for killing pirates that Prince Atalin cleared the way for and that had also obviously been given Imperial tek as well?" I said. "And why is Kharalcha all of a sudden an Imperial protectorate?"

"We thought you would like it done," said Morojal, answering my last question. "Consider it a reward. It is not particularly meaningful, but it will make it more difficult for someone like

Prince Jerrazis to send a Naval force to attack it."

"So Atalin was following Jerrazis's orders?"

"Yes. Prince Jerrazis has been building his influence in that part of the Fringe, using the Porojavian Co-Prosperity Collective as his tool. That is over now. He will direct his ambitions elsewhere."

"So that's why you sent me to Kharalcha. It wasn't just a test; it was an Adjustment. You, or the Imperial Mind, wanted those pirates defeated."

"Yes," replied Morojal. "The Mind does not consider it in the best interest of the Empire to allow Admiral Jerrazis and House Jerrazis to build up a strong independent force in the Fringe. However, the primary purpose was to test you, Highness."

"And since I've been reborn, I'm guessing I passed," I said. "But why did you let me think I would permanently die in my nonaugmented body?"

"To test you properly, we needed you to think of yourself as being alone, with no chance of rebirth," replied Morojal. "But you are correct. You have passed the test to become an Adjuster."

I felt a small, slight hope come to life inside me. If I could work as an Adjuster to save systems like Kharalcha from the depredations of Princes like Jerrazis and Atalin, perhaps my life would be worthwhile. Perhaps I could be someone that I wanted to be; I could become someone Raine would respect, someone that I could respect myself . . . though deep inside I doubted whether it would be possible. Being a Prince precluded so much else.

"So what happens now?" I asked.

"In a normal year, you would be given Adjustment assignments by the Imperial Mind," said Morojal.

She paused and looked at me with her ancient, triple-pupiled eyes.

"But this is not a normal year. You have been selected not only to be an Adjuster but, as will be announced later today, an Imperial candidate. Congratulations, Highness."

"What?"

Every time I got almost used to what as going on, Morojal changed the situation.

"An Imperial candidate," repeated Morojal. "To be the next Emperor."

"One of the thousand," I said slowly. "Announced at the Imperial Core—and there's a thousand of us being decorated. . . ."

"Yes. All will be announced as candidates shortly."

"One becomes Emperor and the others . . . get listed simply as 'candidates' forever after. What happens to them?"

"One ascends," said Morojal. "As for the others . . . you will find out, Highness."

"What if I don't want to be a candidate?" I asked, though I knew it was no more than a formality, because I knew the answer. "What if I don't want to be Emperor?"

"It becomes one step easier for those who do," replied Morojal. "However, I would urge you not to take such a foolish action. As you must be aware by now, you are not merely one of a thousand candidates. You are the favored candidate of the Emperor and thus of the Imperial Mind."

Before Kharalcha I would have taken this entirely at face value, and entirely as my due. Now I was suspicious.

"Why?" I asked bluntly. "And why am I a candidate at all, out of all the Princes who could be chosen?"

There were ten million Princes in the Empire. Choosing one

thousand to become candidates couldn't be easy, and knowing the Empire, it was almost certainly more complicated than it might appear.

"The latter question is relatively easy to answer, though it is of course an important secret. First of all, very few Princes have the extraordinarily high degree of native Psitek ability needed to ascend the throne and direct the Imperial Mind. Even fewer have the proven ability to exist without connection to the Mind, which is necessary again to dominate the Mind as opposed to being subsumed by it. You have proven ability in both."

"So only a thousand Princes every twenty years qualify?" I asked.

"No," replied Morojal evenly. "Two thousand years ago, it was a thousand Princes, and that number is chosen and announced as a matter of tradition, and also to cloak the real facts."

"How many are there now then?"

"Five," answered Morojal.

I stared at her for a long, long second.

"Five!"

"You will not, of course, be able to reveal this fact to any other candidate at the ceremony," said Morojal.

I felt a slight pain deep behind my right eye as she said this, and blue fluid swirled around her head. Psitek intervention, to make sure I couldn't talk about it even if I wanted to.

Which I didn't. I was still taking it in. Ten million Princes and only five candidates who could become Emperor?

"There is a mutation involved," said Morojal. "One that we cannot yet induce or breed for. Once it was more common. Now it is rare."

"Why change Emperors at all then?" I asked.

"We do not exactly change Emperors," said Morojal. "Have you ever wondered what the Imperial Mind actually is?"

"No . . ." I said slowly. Why hadn't I wondered? The Imperial Mind just was . . . whatever it was.

"That is part of the making of a Prince," said Morojal. "In the same way that we mind-program servants, Princes are made not to question certain things."

"Who is 'we'?" I asked sourly.

"The Imperial Mind and its most important servants, the Arch-Priests of the Sixteen Aspects," replied Morojal.

I sat silently, taking this in. I was neither appalled nor greatly alarmed by this revelation, which I suspected would not be the usual reaction of most Princes. I hadn't felt like I was the ruler of anything much, and I had begun to question whether the apparent power of a Prince was to be wished for anyway.

"The Imperial Mind," continued Morojal, "is a gestalt identity of all the previous Emperors, directed by the present incumbent. However, typically after twenty years the directing identity begins to be subsumed, and a new directing identity is needed. A new Emperor."

"So if I become Emperor I just . . . *join* the Mind?" I asked.

"You retain your mental identity for twenty years," said Morojal. "And in that time, you have total power to direct the Mind, and through the Mind, every Prince and every priest. You command the totality of the Empire. It is *absolute* power."

I felt something surge up inside me as she said that, an almost overwhelming desire. I wanted absolute power. I wanted to become the Emperor. I had to become the Emperor!

I fought against it, because I knew it was not my feeling. It was something implanted in me, something *done* to me.

"You said there are five candidates," I said, my voice husky, my throat dry. "How exactly is the Emperor chosen?"

"In the time-honored way of the Empire," said Morojal. "Survival of the fittest. There is a test. Only one of you will survive.

"You can even get a head start. Kill Atalin in your duel. She will not be reborn. Then there will only be four."

"Is Atalin my sister?" I asked.

"Of course," said Morojal. "Though this is not relevant. She is merely an opponent. It is you who are the favored candidate. You have the best chance of the five to become the Emperor. You must take your rightful place."

It was what I had always wanted, what I had believed for so long was my rightful destiny. I should have been ecstatic, overjoyed by the news.

Part of me was electrified and joyous. But there was another part of me, perhaps the greater, which recoiled from the news, and I experienced a strange, momentary hallucination, as if a shadow had suddenly fallen inside my head, shutting me off from any hint of open space and sunshine.

23

HADDAD WAS WAITING for me when I stumbled out of the bamboo forest, rejoined the line of exiting honorees, and came into a garden full of gloating Princes toasting themselves and perhaps their peers with the best vintage champagne that Bitek cornucopias could produce.

"I was delayed by the arch-priest I met before," I whispered to him as he bowed to greet me, his head close.

"I understand, Your Highness," said Haddad. "The duel with Prince Atalin has been scheduled in one hour, in Dueling Chamber Erodh-Azkhom. Do you wish to proceed there now?"

The duel. The present and its needs broke through the warring parts of my personality that were grappling with what Morojal had told me about my future.

I was to become the Emperor. . . .

"Do you wish to proceed there now?" repeated Haddad.

His words were accompanied by a data overlay indicating that the dueling chamber was within easy walking distance. I could stay and toast my decoration, and probably be toasted, since there were few Princes who had received the Imperial Star of Valor that day. But I didn't want to stay, and I knew from Haddad's lessons that it was always advisable to be early to a duel, to allow plenty of time for everything to be checked out in case of dirty tricks. Also, as always with Haddad, just by asking the question he was also suggesting a course of action.

I forced myself to focus on the moment.

"Yes," I replied, and strode out through the crowd, acknowledging the occasional waves and salutes as I went by, nearly all of which came from members of other services, or the few other Naval officers who also wore the Imperial Star of Valor. Most of the other Naval Princes seemed keen to ignore me, so they might celebrate their own, lesser decorations without comparison.

Outside the garden, away from the crowd of Princes, Haddad led me across a lawn toward a sunken pathway bordered by hedges.

"My apprentices have secured this path," he said quietly as we approached. "And I have another team at the dueling chamber now—as does Prince Atalin's Master Vivaldra. Can you tell me what was the import of Arch-Priest Morojal's meeting with you?"

"Yes," I said. I trusted Haddad more than anybody else. In the Empire at least. "I have been selected as a candidate for the Imperial throne."

"Ah," said Haddad. "I wondered."

"Did you?" I asked. "I had no idea."

"My first Prince was a candidate, twenty-two years ago," replied Haddad. "Prince Emzhyl. She was chosen for Adjustment and then a few years later became a candidate. I notice similarities in your own capabilities and career path, Highness."

"She could be the Emperor now!" I exclaimed.

"Perhaps," agreed Haddad.

"Do you know anything about the challenge that candidates face?" I asked eagerly.

"No," replied Haddad. "Prince Emzhyl told me she was chosen as a candidate . . . and then the next morning she was gone, and I was reassigned."

"Oh well," I sighed. "I guess it was too much to hope for some advance knowledge."

"You should concentrate on the forthcoming duel, Highness," said Haddad. "Though you have had some practice with bolt-and-cable guns, I fear that you are far from a master. Do you recall the basic strategies?"

I nodded. Bolt-and-cable guns fired penetrating bolts that would stick in almost anything—flesh, bone, rock, Bitek building materials—and trailed an immensely strong but thin cable that remained connected to the gun until it was released by the firer. A duel with the weapons was conducted on a miniature mountain two hundred meters high built within a dueling chamber. The mountain, with its four peaks and many cracks and crevices, provided a challenging battlefield where the bolt-and-cable guns were needed for climbing, swinging, and moving about as much as for shooting at an enemy. Each gun contained ten bolts and Bitek spinnerets that would produce five hundred meters of cable.

We would each start on top of one of the minimountain's peaks, just out of the bolt-and-cable gun's range. Whoever was better at maneuvering their way around the mountain and could get close enough to the other and get off an effective disabling or killing shot would win.

In Atalin's case, I knew that a killing shot of mine would probably mean a final death for her, if Morojal's words could be trusted. I couldn't stop thinking about this as I walked with Haddad. It changed the whole nature of the upcoming duel.

Could I kill my own sister? My anger toward her had cooled, and I had to recognize that she was no worse than any other Prince. Perhaps she had the same potential that I did, to try to become something better. Maybe, like me, she even harbored secret dreams of breaking free of the mold of a Prince, escaping from the strictures of the Empire. . . .

I stopped in midstride to think about that, Haddad moving swiftly around me, expecting to see some threat that I had just perceived.

"Nothing's wrong, Haddad," I said. "I'm just thinking."

Thinking. Thinking that now that I was back in my augmented body, back as a Prince of the Empire . . . I didn't want to be.

I had been *happy* back in the Habitat, as Khem the trader. . . .

I certainly did not want to become the Emperor and join the Imperial Mind, whether I was in charge of it or not. Even the temptation that I might be able to do some good as Emperor was false, I knew. The way the Empire did things was too entrenched, and I doubted that I would be able to wrangle the hundreds of minds of past Emperors in the Mind to make any effective changes.

Against these rational thoughts from the part of me that I considered to be genuinely myself there was still that persistent, programmed chorus from some other part of my brain that insisted that becoming Emperor was everything I had ever wanted and that I must do my best to become Emperor as soon as possible.

I clamped down on those thoughts and tried to work out what the hell I was going to do.

The alternative to ascending as Emperor was clearly death or something even worse, and I didn't want to die. Or experience whatever the "worse" might be.

There had to be some other way. Only I couldn't see it.

Reluctantly I tried to focus on the upcoming duel.

At least I had developed one certainty with that. Despite my anger earlier when I'd seen that she was to be decorated for killing my Kharalchan friends' families, I decided that I should do my best *not* to kill Atalin. This would make the duel even more difficult, but I wanted to try to stay the kind of person that Raine thought I was and that I aspired to be. Atalin might deserve to die for what she had done, but she was my sister.

I was not the right executioner.

Of course, *she* might kill *me*. . . .

"You do recall the basic strategies?" Haddad asked again as we left the sunken lane and crossed a courtyard toward a characteristic Imperial cube, marking the entrance to an underground facility that I saw in the overlay was the Dueling Chamber.

"I do," I replied. "Fire as few bolts as possible, and use short cables. Make the mountain do the work."

"I advise against the fancier moves," continued Haddad. "Keep it simple, Highness. No swinging decapitations or the like."

"No," I agreed. I doubted I could even do a swinging decapitation—where you looped a cable around your opponent's neck and swung off the mountain while still connected.

Haddad's apprentices appeared out of the hedgerows and rose up out of the grass as we crossed to the cube, so that I had an entourage around me as we entered the building. After the customary checking of the dropshaft, we descended to the reception area. There, in a hall decorated with huge pictures of mountains from many different worlds, Atalin's Master of Assassins and a dozen of her apprentices were waiting, though my opponent herself was not yet present.

"We have inspected the mountain, Prince Khemri, and accept the ground," announced Vivaldra. "Prince Atalin requests snow and ice, at your pleasure."

I waved my hand negligently.

"Snow and ice by all means," I said. "Let's have a blizzard."

Haddad looked at me. Though his face was impassive as always, I detected an aura of censure, or perhaps disappointment. But I had a reason for asking for a blizzard. If after the duel began either one of us accidentally fell off the mountain without the other's intervention, and was injured or unable to proceed, the duel would be declared a draw. To me, this was an attractive outcome. Though I would prefer it if it was Atalin who fell off.

"Prince Atalin will accept a blizzard," replied Vivaldra.

"With your permission, Highness, I will check the mountain now," said Haddad. I nodded. He gestured to his apprentices. Four followed him, and six moved closer to me. He went toward the ornate ceremonial door opposite, and as it opened, I caught a glimpse of the mountain, and the snow that was beginning to swirl down in answer to my request for a blizzard.

Haddad returned five minutes later, just as Atalin arrived, accompanied by half a dozen more of her Master Vivaldra's apprentice assassins.

"The ground is acceptable," said Haddad. "Though I must point out that the blizzard has reached only ninety-five point six percent of the standard laid down in Prince Euthrax's *Code Duello*, the prescribed rulebook on the Imperial Core."

"I'm sure that is sufficient," I said. "Prince Atalin?"

"It is of no consequence," replied Atalin. She did not look at me but held out her arms so Vivaldra could take off her uniform coat. I did the same, allowing Haddad to remove mine. Atalin then handed over several weapons, which were taken by the apprentices, and I followed suit with my own armory.

In shirts, breeches, and ceremonial boots we faced each other.

"I testify before the Imperial Mind that I carry no weapons into the duel," announced Atalin, repeating that in mindspeech.

I gave the same declaration.

A priest of the Aspect of the Stern Adjudicator emerged from a smaller door tucked away at the side of the dueling chamber. She wore full ceremonial robes, including the ridiculously tall wicker hat that looked like an upturned basket on her head, and carried two bolt-and-cable guns. These she handed to Haddad and Vivaldra, who examined both, then handed them back to the priest. She approached Atalin and me, bowed, and presented the weapons.

"You choose first," said Atalin.

"No, after you," I said, determined to be no less courteous.

Atalin shrugged slightly and took one of the weapons, immediately checking it with disturbingly fast motions.

I hefted my gun, examined the charge indicator, the Bitek reservoir, the safety switch, and the grips. It all appeared okay, exactly the same as the guns I'd practiced with.

"As the challenged, you shall begin upon the northwest peak,

Prince Khemri," the priest said to me. "And Prince Atalin upon the southeast. Are you ready?"

"Yes," we both intoned. Our voices were so similar they sounded like one voice. I looked at Atalin, but she did not look at me, instead languidly examining the ceiling.

"Steps have been activated to your peaks, Highnesses," said the priest. "They will retract when you reach your positions. The Imperial Mind will announce the start of the duel. Begin."

Both leaves of the massive ceremonial door swung open. An overlay indicated that I should go through the left and Atalin the right. Ten meters apart, but in step, we marched into the snowstorm at the foot of the miniature mountain of jagged rocks.

Through the snow I saw the beginning of my steps, and I immediately ran and jumped onto them. Whoever got to the top first would have precious time to check out the mountain and plan strategy before the duel began. I intended that this would be me.

Taking the steps four at a time I dashed upward. The snow swirled around me, and I had to adjust my skin, body temperature, and vision as I ran. After thirty or so steps I also took the risk of pausing for a few seconds to remove and throw away my boots. They did not have sufficient grip for the icy steps, let alone for the bare rock. I could take the cold, and the minor abrasions and cuts, better than I could take a fall. Particularly since a fall before the duel properly began would not result in a draw, only a postponement.

Bootless, I climbed even faster, my bare feet providing much better traction. But even so, when I arrived panting at the top of my peak and looked across, I saw Atalin arrive at exactly the same time.

The steps retracted below me, and the Imperial Mind spoke inside my head.

:Commence duel on mark three two one mark <<Sigil of the Imperial Mind>>:

Immediately I fired my first bolt across to the northeast peak, which was the closest. Stopping the cable at fifteen meters hanging, without cutting it, I launched myself into space, swinging across the gulf between the peaks and onto a rocky ledge I'd indentified in the split second I'd had to evaluate the ground. Cutting free the first cable, I leaped across to a narrow outcrop from the eastern peak and fired again, this time sending a bolt up and over to come down on the southeastern peak from above. I cut the end of this cable at fifteen meters and, taking the end, whipped it sideways and down. Atalin had almost certainly moved, but if she hadn't, this might knock her off her feet.

A bolt striking the rock just above my head indicated that she *had* moved. I threw myself down the mountainside, firing a bolt back toward where I thought she was, but also using it to arrest my fall. Swinging across on the line, I scuttled into a shallow cave, eyes frantically scanning the snowstorm.

A dim silhouette leaped above me. I fired twice, sending a bolt ahead of where I thought she was jumping and then another immediately behind, both with short cables. The bolts struck the mountainside opposite, but sudden tension on the second cable announced that I had caught her between them. I dropped the gun to my feet, snatched up the end of the first cable, and pulled the cables together, desperately twisting them around.

Atalin spun a few meters above and five meters across from me, her legs enmeshed in the cable. But as she spun, she took careful aim. I dodged aside as a bolt smashed into the rock behind me. She spun back and I used that second to fasten my two cables to her bolt, pick up my gun, and dodge again.

Before she could fire for a third time, I fired myself, sending a bolt into her right forearm, where it lodged in the reinforced bone. Yanking the cable back, I pinned her arm to her side, and the gun with it, at least till she swapped it to her left hand.

But that took precious seconds and allowed me another shot. This time, I sent a bolt through her left arm at the wrist. Pulling that tight, I fastened both cables to her own bolt again.

Despite this, she continued to struggle, trying to bring her gun up, which was impossible.

"Concede!" I called.

Atalin looked down at me, her face furious. Blood was dripping from her wounds. Not much of it, for her internal systems had shut off the flow, but enough to make some of the snowflakes pink.

"I concede nothing!" she spat. "Kill me if you can!"

"You're my sister!" I shouted over the howl of the blizzard. "I don't want to kill you. Particularly since—"

I tried to say "you won't be reborn," but the words wouldn't come out. Obviously Morojal had restricted that information as well. I simply couldn't tell Atalin.

"What?" shrieked Atalin. She was trying to flip herself up and bite the cables through. She might even be able to do it, I thought, so I spoke quickly.

"We are going to be announced as Imperial candidates!" I shouted, rapidly trying to think what I could tell her to make her listen. "Of the . . . the thousand! But not if you die now."

"How do you know?" asked Atalin. She hadn't stopped swinging her legs up and trying to bend her head down. But she didn't sound quite as angry.

"Arch-Priest Morojal of the Aspect of the Emperor's Discerning Hand told me," I replied.

:This is correct <<Sigil of the Imperial Mind>> You are both to be announced as candidates:

I hadn't asked, but clearly Atalin had.

She stopped trying to swing her legs and looked down at me in what I could only describe as how I must look when I was really thinking hard about something.

"Why tell me?" she asked. "Why not just kill me? It would be one less candidate for you to contend with."

"Because you *are* my sister," I said. I meant it too, and I think she could tell that. Even if she couldn't understand it.

Atalin stared at me for a full three seconds, but her face remained expressionless and I had no idea what she was thinking behind that familiar but at the same time strange visage.

"I concede," she said aloud, repeating it in mindspeech.

:I concede to Prince Khemri:

:Duel concluded <<Sigil of the Imperial Mind>> Prince Khemri Duel Victory count one. Prince Atalin Duel Loss count one:

The wind immediately stopped howling, and the snow lessened and petered out. Steps appeared near me, leading off the mountain. I didn't start down them.

"Do you have any memories of our parents?" I asked.

Atalin scowled.

"Of course not. And I am not your sister. It is not possible."

"It is," I said. "Arch-Priest Morojal confirmed that too, though I suppose the Imperial Mind won't. Tell me . . . how did you come to spend time disconnected from the Mind?"

Atalin turned her head away.

"It's a requirement for a candidate," I said. "So I know you must have done it."

"You seem to know a great deal more than you should," said Atalin. She let herself spin back to face me. "More from Arch-Priest Morojal, I warrant. I spent a year in Imperial Survey. A year disconnected, as far out as you can get."

"Then you've probably seen normal human families in the Fringe," I said. "Brothers and sisters and so on. Parents and children."

Atalin eyes narrowed.

"I am your brother, like it or not," I continued. "And I spared you for that reason. Maybe one day you might return the favor. Sister."

Atalin continued to stare down at me, much as a nonsentient might look at a holographic control display, unable to comprehend it at all.

Priests were coming up the steps, ready to provide medical aid. So were Haddad and Vivaldra and their various apprentices.

I went down the steps toward them. Atalin swung above me, silent and brooding, like a spider caught in its own web.

My feet hurt, but inside I was happy.

I had finally worked out the beginnings of a plan for what lay ahead.

24

WHILE I HAD the beginning of a plan, I certainly didn't have the middle, or most important, the end. Nor did I get the time to develop my plan any further. After the duel, I returned to the guest house I had been allocated, had my feet treated by Uncle Hormidh, and then suffered a number of semiofficial visits from Princes who wanted the newest winner of the Imperial Star of Valor to join their Houses. All of them had to be offered drinks, and I forced myself to listen to their "compelling" reasons why joining their particular House would be of enormous benefit to me.

Unsurprisingly, there was no ambassador from House Jerrazis. When the tenth Prince, a member of House Izhwall, left, I collapsed back in my rather thronelike armchair and ordered Haddad to admit no more. Night had fallen outside, and I wanted time to think through my plan before the announcement of the Imperial candidates was made.

But I did not get that time. I had barely sat back and taken the proffered goblet of wine from Haddad when I received a priority communication in mindspeech from the Imperial Mind.

:Hier Imperial Highness has chosen the thousand candidates who will contend for the throne. The Princes chosen are . . .:

I tried to tune out as the long list of names rolled through my head but gave a start when I heard my own name. Right up until that moment there had always been the slight possibility that Morojal had lied for her own purposes, or even that she was wrong. That slim hope was now denied to me.

I took a sip of the wine. It was chilled and delicious, something based on an old Earth variety that was both fruity and dry, and that left a slight tang in the mouth after you swallowed.

But after that swallow, I couldn't move. I tried to turn my head without success. Even my eyes would not move in their sockets. Yet none of my warning systems had alerted me. They still said the wine was only wine.

Haddad moved into my field of vision and bowed his head. Leaning forward, he stripped me of my weapons, carefully tucking them away in the pockets of his own robe. Then he put a pair of light slippers on my recently tended feet and stepped back.

:Haddad? You have poisoned me?:

"I regret that this is so, Highness," confirmed Haddad.

:But you're my Master of Assassins . . .:

"I am foremost a Priest of the Emperor, in Hier Aspect of the Shadowed Blade," said Haddad. "This is part of becoming a candidate, Highness. It is not a poison but a nanoinhibitor tuned particularly to you. The effects are temporary. You will soon be mobile again but will be weakened for a short time, your augmentation and some internal systems turned off."

:Weakened?:

"Princes have been known to attempt unauthorized winnowing of other candidates before commencement," said Haddad. "This . . . pacification . . . ensures that all candidates embark upon the initial test."

I tried to move my hand and was rewarded with a twitch of two fingers. I followed that up by clearing my throat, and found that I could move my tongue clumsily and talk, after a fashion.

"I would have complied without this," I whispered. "I always thought I could trust you, Haddad. Always."

Haddad sighed and looked down at me.

"We are what we are made to be," he said. "I am utterly loyal to you, Highness, in all matters save the direct order of the Mind. As in this circumstance, my Prince, I could no more disobey than you could yourself. Try to stand up now."

I stood up, very shakily. I was as weak as when I had emerged in my nonaugmented body and would have fallen, except Haddad caught my arm. He held me up and propelled me toward the front door. We passed through the reception hall, which had been populated with my priests and Haddad's apprentices only a short time before. Now it was empty.

Outside, the moon was up, hanging huge and low on the near horizon. Not just any moon, but a pale disk that I knew from long-ago history lessons in my candidate temple. Bright but cold; the pattern of its craters and mountains signified that it was the moon of ancient Earth.

Haddad watched me gaping up at this unexpected satellite

and foresaw my question.

"It *is* the moon of Earth," he said quietly. "The fifty-fourth Emperor had it brought here. It is in an eccentric, guided orbit and is illuminated only on the night the candidates go forth, once every twenty years."

I looked around me, across the gardens. Out of every guest house nearby, a stumbling, weakened Prince was being led and supported by his or her Master of Assassins.

"You lied about Prince Emzhyl," I croaked. "You took her, as you are taking me."

"Yes, Highness," said Haddad. "Again, upon the orders of the Mind."

We did not speak after that. It took all my energy to lift and move my feet. Without Haddad I would have fallen and lain on the grass, twitching like a bug that has reached the end of its short season of life.

All of us shuffling Princes were being herded in the same direction, toward the moon. Its light fell like a silver highway across the gardens, drawing us along, over lawns, through courtyards, down converging lanes and paths.

We probably traveled no more than a thousand meters, but to me it felt like one of the longest journeys I had ever undertaken. I was weary in both body and mind, and bitter, because I had always trusted Haddad, and at least some part of me had built up the irrational feeling that he really was my friend, one of my family, and that he would take my part even against the Empire.

If I had examined this feeling, I would have known it was false. Haddad was as much a creature of the Empire as everybody else, as all we Princes were. He could not escape the strictures and conditioning of his calling any more than I could.

We came to the top of a low hill. Though I could barely turn my head, I saw that there were many Princes to either side of me. Some were in worse shape than I, their Masters of Assassins practically carrying them. Yet again, Haddad had proved to be a most superior assassin, dosing me exactly as required and no more.

All the Princes were being lined up in one long, extended rank along the ridge of the hill. I looked down and saw dark water below. A broad lake, whose far shore I could not see, as my eyes suffered the same weakness as my muscles.

The light of the moon fell only on the closer shore below us. It was a sandy beach that stretched to the left and right as far as the line of Princes was long, perhaps two thousand meters. Drawn up on the beach there was an answering row of one thousand slim, sharp-prowed boats, each not much wider or longer than a man.

"The candidate boats," said Haddad quietly, close to my ear. His fellow Masters were telling their Princes the same thing, at the same time, making an odd noise, like the shuffling of many leaves caught by a slight and momentary breeze.

We advanced down the hill, the thousand Princes and the thousand assassins, each pair going to a particular boat that was straight ahead, so there was no need to cross paths or shuffle sideways. Everything was perfectly arranged.

:Welcome to the first stage of the testing, Princes <<Sigil of the Imperial Mind>> Masters of Assassins, place their Highnesses in the candidate boats:

Haddad had to lift my feet to get me into the boat and then help me down. As I lay back, and pseudopods rose up and lashed around my legs, chest, and arms, I realized that it was not exactly a boat, though it was dipping and floating on the water. It was some kind of Bitek organism, and it was holding me very tightly indeed.

"Good luck, Highness," whispered Haddad. He laid his hand very lightly on my chest, then slowly withdrew it, his fingers curling as if he had reluctantly let go of something that he had once treasured. Then he stepped back and was gone.

A translucent membrane closed over the top of the pod, sealing me in, and the Imperial Mind spoke inside my head. Only it felt slightly different from the way it usually did, with a more distinctive mental voice that somehow came across as being very weary.

> :The candidate boats are controlled by Psitek <<Sigil of the Imperial Mind>> After they are launched, you will need to guide your craft through the central channel of the waterfalls that lie ahead, and then through the subterranean river beyond. Those of you who succeed in doing so will reach the second stage of the testing. There will be no witnessing: if you die here, it is a permanent death:

That was the Emperor Hierself, I thought. Not the collective voice of the Imperial Mind. Taking a personal interest in whichever Prince would replace them and allow them to sink into the gestalt entity. From the weary, resigned feel of that communication, I thought the Emperor was looking forward to that outcome.

This only further confirmed that I really did not want to become the Emperor.

But my choices had narrowed. I had to compete or die.

The pod shuddered under me, a vibration coming from the sides as whatever propulsion system it used sprang into life. The boat began to rock more as it headed out into the open waters of the lake.

Though I was still physically weak and none of my Mektek systems or Bitek glands were operational, my Psitek senses did appear less affected. I reached out, seeking the echo of a Psitek system. But I caught nothing from the boat, though I did pick up several Princes nearby, catching angry mental swipes as they sent Psitek probes all around them.

I started to get seriously concerned. But as I mentally searched the boat again, I did feel a response, an echo that reminded me of *Korker*'s Bitek brain. I focused on it, exerting my mental strength, and eventually it answered. It was not self-aware, like *Korker*, or anywhere near as sophisticated, but after a few minutes of exploration and experiment I worked out how to stimulate different parts of its simple brain to regulate the speed and pitch of the flippers that were the boat's propulsion and steering systems.

Not that this did me a lot of good, because I was held down by the pseudopods and couldn't see anything except the sky above me. A sky almost totally dark, save for the faint sliver of a moon rapidly disappearing behind my boat. So how could I steer the boat to a middle channel of the waterfall ahead?

It occurred to me that I could just do nothing. After all, Morojal had said there were really only five possible candidates out of all the thousand who were now launched upon the lake. Surely they wouldn't risk losing one of the five so early and, if Morojal was to be believed, their favorite candidate?

If Morojal was to be believed . . . that was not something I was prepared to stake my life on.

I needed to be able to see, or use some other senses to steer, as I had done when I had accessed the rescue beast's sonar in the reservoir back in the Kharalcha Habitat.

Someone else's senses. Best of all, someone else's eyes.

:Haddad. Are you there?:

:Yes, Highness:

:Will you obey me?:

:In anything I am permitted to do by the Imperial Mind, Highness:

:I need to see through your eyes, so I may steer my boat:

:Yes, Highness. That is why we remain here, on the shore. Please proceed:

He didn't explain to me how to proceed. But I instinctively knew. I shut my own eyes and followed the mental trail established by our communication microseconds before. I felt myself enter Haddad's mind, or some contained portion of it, and then the darkness behind my eyelids was suddenly replaced by a clear vista: a view of the lake, all the way across, for Haddad's vision was greatly enhanced by his Bitek eye. There was even a map overlay, and a grid, and a pointer indicating my own boat and the desired channel I must take.

The channel was almost straight ahead of me, at least partly confirming that Morojal had spoken the truth. I had been placed in a very favorable candidate boat. Several hundred of the others, far to my left and right, would have no chance of making the central channel, even if they did work out how to see and steer. As I looked through Haddad's eyes, it was clear very few of them had figured out how to use their assassins' eyes, or if they had managed that part, had not discovered how to steer.

Even in this contest, the Empire was trying to adjust things the way the Imperial Mind wanted.

But I had little time to think about my fellow Princes. There were a number of strong currents rushing my boat toward the waterfall, but *not* toward the correct channel. I had to urge my boat to swim hard, its flippers digging deep as it drove diagonally across the lake, sliding this way and that as various currents pushed it off course.

I found that in my weakened state even the mental effort of directing the boat and looking through Haddad's eyes was exhausting. It took all my willpower to keep my Psitek focused on both activities, and for a moment I thought I would faint with the effort. But I hung on, and then all of a sudden I saw the pointer for my boat was in the right channel and that I was on the very edge of the waterfall, and then—

Everything went black as I lost the connection to Haddad. I opened my eyes, but all I could see was darkness, and there was water roaring all around the boat as it suddenly flipped up on its end, and the pseudopods released me. I was hurled against the transparent membrane, which was now as hard as if it was an armored shell. The boat corkscrewed violently, and I felt water strike my face and legs.

:Hold your breath. This really is farewell, Khemri. Either way:

The mental voice was very faint. It was the last thing I ever heard from Haddad. I suppose in many ways he was like the father I'd never had, or perhaps some wise uncle, saddled with a foolish nephew. At the last, I caught some thought like this from him as well, a moment of sadness that we were both caught in our Imperial roles. The sadness was for himself, as well as for me.

I followed Haddad's final advice at once, gulping several great lungfuls of air before I held it in, a moment before the water I could feel bursting into the boat completely filled it. As it reached my head, I scanned the pod's brain again, searching for a nerve impulse that would free me from the clutches of its pseudopods. I had not found one initially, but now it was there, as plain as day. I mentally stabbed at it, and the entire boat fell apart around me, the pseudopods shriveling back as if withered by acid.

I flailed about in deep, lightless water.

All around me, I felt the Psitek screams and rantings of Princes as they drowned. There and then I knew what happened to most of the thousand Imperial candidates.

With my Mektek navigational systems and sensors out, I had no idea which way was up. But rather than swimming in some random direction, I simply stilled my limbs and let myself float. Even with the armored bones and other odds and ends inside me, I knew I was buoyant, and should be even more so than usual with my lungs fully inflated.

That was the theory, anyway. After two minutes—calculated by slow counting, since my internal clocks were not responding—I began to become afraid. The fear came very close to panic, but I kept it in check, and gradually the fear subsided, to be replaced by something that was almost acceptance.

Perhaps drowning wasn't so bad after all, compared to becoming the Emperor. If I did win this competition, I would be bound to something I had come to despise, essentially imprisoned within the Imperial Mind. Having ultimate power in the Empire would be no compensation for the limitations that would be imposed on . . . on what I supposed was my soul, an archaic word whose meaning I had never really understood before now.

But whatever philosophical thoughts my drowning mind was having at this stage, my body didn't share them. My eyes caught a glimmer of light, above and to the right. Instantly I was thrashing toward it, arms and legs kicking wildly, using up every last shred of energy, but it seemed to recede before me, continuing to get farther and farther away until suddenly my head broke the surface. Coughing and spitting, I gasped for air; at the same time I looked around for whatever new and terrible threat was undoubtedly about to appear.

25

THE LIGHT I had seen was a strip of Bitek luminescence several meters long that was stuck on the rough stone ceiling high above me. In its soft light I saw that I had surfaced in a cavern that was either natural or had been made to look as if it was. It was basically round, about twenty meters in diameter, and at first it appeared as if the only way out of it was to go back down through the water, something I really didn't want to do.

Then I noticed there was a small dark patch to my right, just above water level. I slowly swam toward it, or more accurately floated with intent in that general direction. I eventually got there and saw it was the mouth of a tunnel that sloped sharply upward. The tunnel was about as wide as my shoulders, and smoothly bored, pretty much indicating that this was where I was meant to go.

Naturally, I distrusted it. But after looking around several more times, I couldn't see any alternative. I also needed to get out of the water. It was very cold, and the nanoinhibitor Haddad had given me in the wine had not worn off. I had regained a basic human level of fitness but none of my higher functions. Most importantly, I couldn't regulate my temperature at the moment, so I was feeling the effects of immersion. I needed to get dry and warm. Or find some means to reactivate my augmentation.

Very slowly, I hauled myself into the tunnel and began to worm my way up. It was dark at first, as soon as I'd blocked the light from the cave with my body, but after five meters or so, there were two little dots of Bitek luminescence, and another pair five meters after that.

I followed the glowing dots for a long time and, after a while, noticed that I was no longer cold, and I felt less tired than I had. My augmentation still hadn't come back online, but I was used to that from my time in the Adjustment training and on Kharalcha. Heartened, I crawled onward, questing ahead with my Psitek senses, as well as keeping as sharp an eye as possible out for traps.

Eventually, the tunnel began to widen. I slowed down and advanced even more cautiously till I arrived at a door set in the stone. It was of old Mektek, complete with visible rivets, and had a purely mechanical wheel to operate it. I knelt close and checked it over, even listening with my ear against the steel, but I didn't discover anything. My Psitek senses also didn't pick up anything on the other side.

I spun the wheel and cracked the door open. Nothing horrible happened, so I eased it open a little more and looked through the gap. It was totally dark beyond the door, and I couldn't see anything, but I felt a soft breeze upon my face, indicating open space.

I pushed the door open far enough to allow me to slide through and gingerly stepped out of the tunnel. As I did so, an artificial sun suddenly blossomed high above, making me squint and blink as sunshine illuminated everything around me. I had stepped out onto the sandy floor of an ancient circular arena, a vast coliseum made of white stone.

Apart from the sound of my own breath and the soft brush of sand as I moved my feet, the arena was totally silent. There was no audience—the benches that extended high above my head were empty—and there was no one else in the ring. But I noted that there were many doors all around the inner wall, just like the one I had come through. A thousand doors, I would say, which made me immediately look for weapons. Clearly this was where we Princes who had made it through the waterfall and the underground river would fight each other to the death.

A nice, old-fashioned way of finding out the fittest Prince to rule.

The weapons were in the exact center of the arena, about two hundred meters away. As soon as I saw the shine of steel, I started to run. At almost exactly the same time, a door opened on the far side of the arena and a Prince staggered out. Then off to my right, another door opened, and there was another Prince. They were moving slowly, but both immediately looked at me, then at what I was running toward, and instantly reacted.

Another door opened to my left, though no one immediately came out. I was halfway to the pile of weapons, closer than any of the others. I tried to run faster, but I was still weak, and several times I almost fell, my slippered feet losing their grip in the sand. It was exhausting running through that stuff, too, for it was quite deep. More like a beach than just a layer of grit laid down over stone or dirt.

Out of the corner of my eye I saw a flicker of colored light up in the stands of the arena. I turned my head to glance at it, quickly, and saw that there was someone there, after all. A single figure, sitting alone in a box that was halfway up the stands but projected out to the inner wall that surrounded the ring. I had no time to look. Gasping for air, I hurled myself forward to that central cache of weapons.

Because of my head start, I got there first, but only by a few seconds. Just time enough to take in that there were three swords, two tridents, and two nets. I immediately snatched up a trident and swung around just in time to skewer the Prince who had come up on my left. He was a fast runner, all right, but his speed didn't serve him at the end, because he ran right onto the trident, throwing me back as the three sharp points speared right through his chest. Judging from the look of shock and surprise on his face, I guess he was too used to his augmentation, which would have allowed him to side-slip at the last second.

There was no time to think about what I'd done. Dropping that trident, I picked up the second one and the net that went with it. I'd never trained with this combination, but I figured it would not be dissimilar to using a sword and nerve-lash.

The next Prince slowed as she approached. She was taller and obviously stronger than me, and she grinned as she circled around, and I matched her movements. I flicked the net to test her, and she swayed back but then lunged in again and grabbed it, yanking it as hard as she could.

Again, she was too used to her augmentation. The net didn't jerk out of my hand, and in that second while she was still holding it, I stepped forward and threw the trident. It struck her in the neck, and down she went, bleeding out into the sand.

But even dying, she still held the net. I let it go and raced back to pick up a sword just as a third Prince I hadn't even seen coming did the same.

Both of us went for a shortened stab as we rose up, blades in hand, and both of us missed, each twisting aside and jumping back. I stumbled a little as I landed, and she attacked me immediately, thrusting at my thigh. I parried, stepped aside, and hesitated even as my reflexes began a riposte, which went wide with the hesitation.

It was Atalin. Like me, her ceremonial uniform was muddied and her face and hands were covered with small, bloody abrasions. Her feet were also cut, for she must have left her guest house wearing something heavier than my slippers, and she'd had to abandon them in the water. Again, Haddad had prepared me better than perhaps I deserved.

"So here we are, *brother,*" she said, and stepping forward, she cut at my head. I ducked under the swipe and slashed at her arm, but she was too quick, spinning away. Panting, we backed off and circled. I kept most of my focus on her but also tried to look around the arena. Morojal had said there were five real candidates, and I was sure we had all been helped to get to this, presumably final, round. Two Princes lay dead already, but where was the third?

Atalin saw me looking.

"Morojal told you five real candidates?" she asked, her focus all on me. Before I could answer, she lunged, the tip of her sword almost reaching my belly as I sucked it in, arched back on my toes, and belatedly parried.

"Yes," I grunted. I opened my eyes a little, as if startled by something I could see behind her, hoping to distract her in my turn. But Atalin did not even glance aside.

"I got the fifth as she came out her door," said Atalin. "There's just the two of us, Khemri. Soon to be one."

She attacked again. I dodged and parried, giving ground.

"So . . . Morojal . . . talked to you . . . too?" I gasped out in between another round of stabs and cuts from Atalin and parries and dodges from me.

"I talked to *her* after our duel," said Atalin. She didn't seem to be out of breath at all. "She told me you're the favorite. I'm supposed to let you win."

I counterattacked, driving her back a few steps so I could rake in a long, shuddering breath.

"She told me, too," I said. "But I don't—"

My words were cut off and my head almost went with them as Atalin spun and whipped her sword around at the full extension of her arm. I ducked beneath it, felt my knee tremble and then suddenly collapse, and I was on my back on the ground. Instantly, I rolled away as Atalin's spin stopped as if arrested by a wire, and she drove her sword point into the sand where I'd been a split second before.

As she pulled it out, I rolled back and struck at her arm. The tip of the sword sliced down and across her forearm, drawing blood, but it was not a decisive blow. Atalin stepped back, raised her sword, and saluted me as I scuttled back and gingerly stood up, testing my knee.

"First blood to you," she said. "Not that it makes any difference. I don't care what the priests want. I *will* be Emperor, and you will be—"

She struck in midsentence, but I was ready for that. We

exchanged blows. I parried a lunge and riposted, and when we both stepped back a few seconds later, Atalin had another scratch, this time across her shoulder. Unfortunately, I also had one, a cut along my ribs on the left side.

"I'm not your sister, either," said Atalin conversationally as she slowly moved around, making me circle to the left, putting a strain on my weakened knee. "I was just made to look like you."

"What?"

"An illegal bodysculpt," she continued. I tried not to pay too much attention to her words, even as my head was swirling, trying to figure out if she was speaking the truth and, if she was, what it meant. This, of course, was her intention. She was trying to distract me for an easier kill.

She continued, still circling, "I was made to look like you before I went to the Academy. House Jerrazis did it."

"Why?" I asked as if I didn't care too much. I knew she was lying, I knew deep inside, and all my real attention was on her eyes and wrist. They would tell me what she was going to do. Not the words.

"Who knows?" said Atalin. "Perhaps you were already seen as being weak and sentimental, Khemri. There's no place for softness in a Prince, or an Emp—"

She lunged at me, full stretch. I tried to dodge, but my knee gave way and the blade went straight through me, into my guts and out the other side. But instead of falling back, I leaned into the blow, slid up the sword, and sank my own weapon into Atalin's chest, just above her left breast.

Atalin let go of her sword and dropped to one knee. I staggered back but somehow managed to stay on my feet.

She slowly raised one hand and gripped the blade of my

sword, just for a moment, in an attempt to pull it out. But she was too weak, the blade too close to her heart. With her augmentation off, blood pumped from the wound, staining the sand at her feet.

"I lied about the bodysculpt," whispered Atalin. "Farewell, brother."

Her hand fell away from the blade, and she slowly crumpled to the ground.

"No," I said urgently. Ignoring the white-hot pain through my middle, I staggered closer to her and knelt by her side.

"Listen! I don't want to be Emperor! I want you to be Emperor, so you can let me go!"

"Go?" asked Atalin, a fleeting smile passing across her face, which was already white. Her once-bright eyes were fading, and there was a blue dullness spreading around her lips. "Go where?"

"Out of the Empire," I said. "Promise you'll get me reborn as I wish!"

"A Prince's promise . . ." muttered Atalin. She was staring at my face, but her eyes saw something else. "Worth no more than sand in the wind."

"Promise me!" I shouted. "Promise me, sister!"

She mouthed something. It might have been "Yes."

Or just as likely "No."

But I couldn't ask her again. She had only minutes, maybe seconds, to live, and I had only that much time to make my plan work. A very risky plan that depended on the Imperial Mind witnessing after all, even though the Emperor had said it wouldn't. I knew from Kharalcha that I couldn't always feel the connection. Surely the Mind wouldn't risk losing the final five candidates in some freak accident?

It had to be witnessing.

Unless there really were more candidates than Morojal had told me. . . .

Exerting all my remaining strength, I somehow managed to stand up. The pain was excruciating, and I almost fell again as it struck me. Sobbing, I wrapped both hands on the blade of Atalin's sword, under the hilt, and steeled myself for what must come next.

I pulled the sword out. It came free with a sickening jolt that sent another blinding wave of pain through me. This time I did fall, onto my knees and elbows. For a moment I almost fell flat on my face, and darkness spread across my eyes, threatening unconsciousness, but I fought back.

I had come so far. I could not falter now.

Atalin still breathed, her pallid face only a handsbreadth away from mine, though surely the end was near.

Up in the box in the stands, a glowing figure rose and began to float through the air toward us. I knew who it must be now. The Emperor, or perhaps a holographic avatar of the current ruler of the Imperal Mind, coming down to welcome Hier successor to the throne.

Which would be me, if I was the last Prince candidate left alive.

Slowly, far slower than I would have liked, I pushed myself up off my elbows. Still kneeling, I reversed Atalin's sword, digging the hilt into the deep sand ahead of me. Then I placed the so very sharp point of the blade at the base of my sternum, leaning on it lightly, just enough to keep it in place.

A triangle of deadly possibility. Me, the sword, and my sister—all together on the sand that was stained with our conjoining blood.

I looked across at Atalin. Her chest rose once, and fell, and didn't rise again. A soft, choking rattle came from her mouth.

In that moment of her death, I let my full weight fall forward upon the point of my sister's sword.

26

THAT WAS MY third death.

Unlike my other deaths, this time I didn't wake in a comfortable bed with the sensation of having been asleep for a long time. Instead, only a moment after I felt the sword run through my heart, I found my consciousness hurtling through space at an incredible velocity, heading straight toward a blue-white ball of incandescent gas while beams of multicolored light sprayed in all directions around me.

Then, all of a sudden, I was inside the Imperial Mind, or it was inside *my* mind. Not just communicating with me but all too present. I felt the incredible pressure of all these other thoughts from a thousand or more former Emperors, so many that I almost lost myself and could not be sure who I was, and beyond the thousand there was an unsortable, unstoppable stream of information flowing from all the millions of Princes out in the Empire who were currently witnessing, all of it swamping into my mind.

I fought them off, refusing to accept the connections, refusing to allow them to draw me into the great mental morass of the Empire.

I will not be Emperor, I told myself. I am Khem, not Khemri. *I will not direct the Mind!*

:But I will. Leave him:

That thought was like a lightning bolt passing through the roiling storm of too much information. It was acted on instantly, the close identities withdrawing from me and the geysers of data from the Princes beyond cut off.

I was alone, a detached intelligence, free of my body, free from the pain of my wounds. I felt detached and light, as in that last waking moment before diving into long-awaited sleep.

But only for a brief moment. The directing thought came again, spearing into me with a jolt that was akin to that sword thrust in the guts. All of a sudden I was connected again, but the minds I had felt before were veiled, the pressure of their thoughts held back by the single presence that spoke to me.

:You were meant to be Emperor, Prince Khemri. Not I:

I felt a tremendous surge of relief, a relief that could not be hidden from this inquiring mind, though I did not articulate it.

My plan had worked. I had died at exactly the same time as Atalin, and I had managed to keep myself separate from the Mind. I was clearly *not* the Emperor.

:We have failed greatly with you, Khemri. You should have wanted to be Emperor more than anything, and claimed it as your right:

:Part of me still does. But it is the lesser part. The greater whole . . . me . . . I . . . I only want to be reborn into my nonaugmented body and be allowed to go where I want:

:To Kharalcha?:

I hesitated before answering, but the Emperor knew anyway, knowing everything about every Prince and priest and connected mind in the Empire—if she cared to look.

:Yes:

:Why should we allow this? No Prince has ever been permitted to leave the Empire in such a way:

:Because you promised, sister:

There was a long silence. I felt the single mind falter and the other intelligences behind it draw closer, like wolves to the kill. All the past Emperors within the Imperial Mind were not going to let me have my heart's desire. They didn't even allow the existence of such a thing, nor recognize any possible familial connection for a Prince.

I thought that I'd gambled and lost, before the lightning thought struck again, splintering the massed, anonymous minds of so many subsumed Emperors.

:I have decided. We shall do as I command:

There was a flash of white light, a single image burned into my mind, and I was gone.

The next thing I knew, I was taking a shuddering breath deep into my lungs. I was born into flesh again, in darkness. Unaugmented flesh, for no systems reported their status and I felt nothing inside me but the slow beat of my own heart, the pulse accelerating in sudden fear. But even as I reached out with trembling arms, I tasted salty water and felt relief as I thought I recognized where I was, something confirmed when I saw a strip of light in the distance.

Climbing slowly and wearily out of the bath, I crawled toward the light. I had made it only a few meters when the door slid open and the familiar silhouette of Elzweko filled the entrance.

"I am not to know who you are," he said, his back toward me. "Do not speak, do not use your Psitek, and put on this suit."

The suit was a current, Imperial-issue Bitek vacuum suit. Elzweko threw the suit backward, touched the panel to bring light to the room, and shut the door again. I crawled to the suit, touched the front, and let it flow over me. The helmet visor was set to be silvered from the outside and had been altered so that it could not be changed.

I lay inside the suit for some time, recovering my strength. As I got up, the Imperial Mind spoke inside my head.

:A capsule has been readied for you. Elzweko will take you to it. He has been told you are an Adjuster on a particularly secret mission. The craft has been directly preprogrammed by me for Kharalcha, which will remain an Imperial protectorate, at least for the next twenty years. Upon your departure from the final Imperial wormhole, your Psitek signature will be marked for immediate pursuit and destruction if you are within the bounds of the Empire. Do not come back, Khemri:

:I won't. But I thank you, Atalin:

There was no reply.

I opened the door and found Elzweko waiting. He did not speak, but as he had done before, what felt like so long ago, he took me through the false wormhole-drive door, past the mekbi troopers there—where I tensed for the final betrayal I still half expected to come—and into the storeroom where once again I was invited to collect all that I might need for my mission ahead.

Sensibly, I took the things I thought that I, or the Kharalchans, might need. It could well be the last chance I had to get my hands on some half-decent tek.

There was another Prince in the dock, a young woman wearing an ancient vac suit rather like my old Ekkie. She glared at me but also did not speak. It was just as well my visor was silvered, for I knew her well. I was only a little surprised to see Tyrtho, though I wondered how her plan to stay on safely at the Academy had been diverted into being recruited by Adjustment.

It was her capsule I was taking, I could see, delaying her test. There was another being readied by mekbi drones, but it would take them hours. I felt a little sad that I could not speak to her, but I knew that doing so would be a death sentence for both of us.

The Empire could never let it be known that a Prince could even want a different life.

Let alone find a way to have one.

Two weeks later, my capsule emerged in the Kharalcha system. There was no report of recent combat this time, but there were ships on patrol near the wormhole. Some I knew as KSF at once, even before the capsule finished analyzing the scan. But there were more ships present, and better ones, and within a few minutes I was being hailed by them, as well as by the KSF.

It was the Confederation fleet, of course, only six months late. But I did not answer their rapid questioning. There was only one ship I wanted to talk to, and more particularly, one person.

"Calling KSF *Firestarter*, KSF *Firestarter*. This is Khem Gryphon. Do you have Raine Gryphon aboard?"

The answer came back after a long, long minute. The voice was familiar, and extraordinarily welcome.

"Khem Gryphon, this is Raine Gryphon, on KSF *Firestarter.* What is your message?"

Raine sounded cool and calm. More than I did, I was sure, particularly as I found that I had been holding my breath. I let it go, and spoke.

"Request permission to be picked up."

"Do you have an atmosphere problem?"

I smiled.

"Negative. Status green on all counts. But I would like to be picked up just as soon as you can."

"Understood, Khem Gryphon. Stand by for retrieval. And . . ."

There was a slight catch in her breath, quickly suppressed.

"Welcome home."

Epilogue

THAT IS THE story of my three deaths. All that I will be able to tell, for there will be no rebirth from a fourth and final death. But I do not regret giving up the long, long life of a Prince of the Empire and all that goes with it. I do not miss the power of life and death over ordinary folk, nor the trinity of teks that lived within me and made me both more and less than human.

For I have gained far more than I have lost, even if not in anything the Empire would care to measure.

Raine and I continue to love each other, something I discover is not an automatic state but must be worked at, like an ever-changing tactical problem, though I would never describe it that way to my beloved.

I am really a trader now, but not a traveling one, and a reserve commodore in the KSF, though I am pleased that apart from my one month a year of active duty, I have been called on only twice in the last decade to actually fight, first against a new pirate force and once against a Deader reconnaissance squadron. That last was tough, for Deaders always fight to the bitter end and self-destruct when they can fight no more, often taking their opponent with them. But thanks to the Confederation, and in some small part to my own knowledge and the old Imperial tek of Prince Xaojhek we found in the gas giant rings, the KSF is about as smart and strong a force as you'll find anywhere in the Fringe.

Raine and I have a child now, too. A little girl who has reached the age of five, who I give thanks every day will never be taken from her parents to be made a Prince.

She calls herself Attie, as does everyone else. It is generally known to be short for Hattie, as it appears in the records: Hattie Anza Gryphon. Only Raine and I know she was named in our hearts for Atalin. That is a name of infamy in Kharalcha, one we could never give a child, but I thought we owed my sister something.

I told Raine everything soon after my return to Kharalcha. That I had been a Prince, that I had been part of the Empire that had killed so many of her people. But she said that was all washed clean by what I had done of my own choice.

Raine said to me then, "The Empire made you into a Prince, Khem. But you have made yourself into a human."

Sometimes I think about that, and I wonder what is happening back in the Empire, though I seldom wonder for very long. Mostly what I ponder is how Atalin might be doing as Emperor, and whether she has been able to make any changes, or has even wanted to try.

I doubt it, but then I remember that single image, that frame of memory that she sent to me, before I was spat out of the Imperial Mind.

It was a toddler's blurry view of two faces staring down with love in their eyes and smiles on their faces. Faces that are familiar and strange at the same time, for they look like me and yet do not.

I wonder how Atalin retained that memory of our parents, and how she managed to bring it to the surface, despite everything the priests did to make us forget all that had gone before our selection. Perhaps she found it during her time as a first-in scout with the Imperial Survey, alone in her ship among the trackless stars, with only her own mind to delve into.

Try as I might, I have never found any such memory within myself. I have only that small vision from my sister, who in the end was far more human than I would ever have suspected.

Perhaps the potential for humanity exists in all Princes.

I can only hope that this is so.

GARTH NIX was born in 1963 in Melbourne, Australia. A full-time writer since 2001, he has worked as a literary agent, marketing consultant, book editor, book publicist, book sales representative, bookseller, and part-time soldier in the Australian Army Reserve. Garth's books include the award-winning fantasy novels *Sabriel*, *Lirael*, and *Abhorsen*; and the cult favorite teen SF novel *Shade's Children*. His fantasy novels for younger readers include *The Ragwitch*; the six books of the Seventh Tower sequence; the Keys to the Kingdom series; and *Troubletwisters*, cowritten with Sean Williams. More than five million copies of his books have been sold around the world; his books have appeared on the bestseller lists of the *New York Times*, *Publishers Weekly*, the *Guardian*, and the *Australian*; and his work has been translated into thirty-nine languages. He lives in Sydney, Australia, with his wife and two children.

GARTH NIX's
New York Times bestselling series
THE ABHORSEN TRILOGY

"Here is a world with the same solidarity and four-dimensional authority as our own, created with invention, clarity, and intelligence. I congratulate Garth Nix. I look forward to reading his next piece of work."

—Philip Pullman